CONTENTS

ADVENTURE TALES 6   **WINTER 2010**

POETRY

ADVENTURE TALES 6

Copyright © 2010 by Wildside Press LLC. All rights reserved.

Authors: We are looking for interesting new or classic works by authors who originally appeared in the pulp magazines of the early 20th century. No other fiction is desired at this time. We welcome proposals for non-fiction articles on subjects related to pulp magazines.

Illustrators: All artwork is either reprinted from classic pulp magazines or commissioned. We are happy to look at samples (please allow us to keep them for our files) and will assign artwork when and if we have an appropriate project.

Letters of comment: Please send us some! Use the address below, or email to wildsidepress@gmail.com. Put "Adventure Tales" in the subject line of emails.

Editor:
John Gregory Betancourt

Assistant Editors:
George H. Scithers
Spencer Koelle

Adventure Tales is published irregularly (but we try for twice per year)
by Wildside Press, LLC.

Postmaster & Others: send change of address and other subscription matters to:

Wildside Press, LLC
Attn: Subscription Dept.
9710 Traville Gateway Dr. #234
Rockville, MD 20850

Single copies: $12.95, postage paid in the U.S.A. Add $5.00 per copy for shipping elsewhere. Subscriptions: 4 issues for $39.95 in the U.S.A. and its possessions, $59.95 elsewhere. All payments must be in U.S. funds and drawn on a U.S. financial institution. If you wish to use PayPal for your subscription, email payment to: wildside@wildsidepress.com.

WELCOME TO THE SIXTH ISsue of Adventure Tales — *late, as usual.*

There are plenty of excuses, more than enough to go around, but I'm going to try even harder to get back on schedule.

At any rate, we have the usual terrific lineup in place for this issue, all hopefully works with which you are unfamiliar. And this is the special issue celebrating the work of H. Bedford-Jones, the self-proclaimed "King of the Pulps."

Although largely forgotten today, the H. Bedford-Jones name on a magazine cover meant something special in the early part of the 20th century: a thrilling tale often in an exotic locale, with whip-tight writing and a breakneck pace. I have tried to include a good sampling of his work. "Mustered Out" is a contemporary story dealing with the question of "what next?" after military service. "The Badman's Brand" is an action-packed western featuring Lefty Sage and Slivers Lawrence.

Rounding out this issue are contributions by more favorite pulp authors: Vincent Starrett (who is still remembered well in the mystery field) returns with a tale of Chicago-based detective Jimmy Lavender, a real puzzler about a walking statue. John D. Swain's "The Miracle" is a brilliant tale set in France, following the aftermath of World War I German occupation. "The Devil's Heirloom," by Anthony M. Rud is a "different" story. We return to the Amazon with real-life explorer Arthur O. Friel, for a tale in his "Pedro and Lourenco" series.

≈

With much sadness, I must report the loss of one of our staff members. George Scithers — founding editor of *Isaac Asimov's Science Fiction Magazine*, former editor of *Amazing Stories* and *Weird Tales* — passed away earlier this year due to complications from a heart attack. He was 80. I had known him since the early 1980s, when I began reading the *Amazing Stories* slushpile while in college. This ultimately led to an assistant editor job, and we continued our association with many later projects, including *Weird Tales*, a literary agency, and more book projects than I can count.

After his retirement, George became a part-time staffer at Wildside Press, contributing much publishing wisdom and sage advice, editing projects such as the "Cat Tales" anthology series, and typesetting many of our pulp-related books, including the *Operator #5* series, the *Phantom Detective* series, and the various Talbot Mundy reprints.

We miss him greatly.

—*John Gregory Betancourt*

MOVING?

Don't forget to take *AT* with you!

Changes of address go to:

Wildside Press LLC
Attn: Adventure Tales
9710 Traville Gateway Dr. #234
Rockville, MD 20850

Not a subscriber yet? Send $39.95 for the next 4
issues in the U.S. ($59.95 elsewhere) to the above
address. Make checks payable to Wildside Press.
Or order online at www.wildsidebooks.com!

THE FUGITIVE STATUE

by Vincent Starrett

Midnight footsteps sounding in a deserted street: what did they portend, of tragedy, mystery, or evil deeds?

I

MR. OAKLEY ASHENHURST removed his pipe from his mouth with his left hand, and with a lift of his chin blew a cloud of smoke at the ceiling of his study. His right hand held open the volume he had been reading spread out upon the table; in the circle of bright light dropped upon the pages by the young man's student lamp the black print seemed doubly black. Ashenhurst yawned luxuriously and lay back in his chair. The corners of his study, which was also his bedroom, sitting-room, library, and, on furtive occasions, his dining-room, were deeply dark with a darkness that lightened by degrees as it approached the spot occupied by the reading table and the funnel of intense light from the lamp. Upon a low mantel ticked a nickel-plated clock, and by a swift movement of the ingenious lamp the student ascertained that it was exactly midnight. At this instant, while he was registering satisfaction and relief, in the street beyond his window Oakley Ashenhurst heard the sound of running feet.

They were steady footsteps, light but sharp, and they slapped the pavement with a staccato quality that was impressive in the silence. They approached, crescendoed before the house, and diminuendoed in the distance, as drumsticks simulate hoofbeats in the theatre. Reclined in his chair, young Ashenhurst heard them come and heard them go, with idle curiosity. Hazy speculations floated through his mind for a few moments; then with an effort he pulled himself together, marked his place in the volume, snapped off the light, and slipped out of his bathrobe and into his bed. In the morning, he thought nothing about the footsteps at all; he had forgotten them.

But the next night, after a harrowing session at the evening medical class in which he was completing his education, as he toiled again over his *Anatomy* in the darkened room, the young man's memory was jogged; he was reminded by the footsteps themselves. As before, they approached with soft distinctness, pattered sharply past the dark dwelling, and melted away in the silence.

Ashenhurst's mind stirred sleepily. Last night—midnight—very curious! He turned the light funnel on the little clock and registered mild surprise. Again it was midnight! An odd coincidence, thought Ashenhurst as he climbed into bed. Somebody in training for a race? The nights were getting cool for track suits, he chuckled. And anyway, why this short, deserted thoroughfare with its straggle of sickly street lamps and its old-fashioned, sober dwellings? Why not the fine stretches of the neighboring boulevard? Or, for that matter, the little park at the corner, with its cinder paths seemingly designed for such an enterprise? He was still speculating when he fell asleep.

As he crossed the park, next morning, on his way to the office, young Mr. Ashenhurst thought again of the footsteps. Decidedly these cinder paths were the proper lanes for training. As a young man on the very brink of becoming a physician, Ashenhurst approved the activities of the midnight sprinter, but as a methodical young man he believed that a sense of fitness should direct the activity; and decidedly these cinder paths were preferable to hard asphalt. He paused for a moment beside the central fountain to admire the graceful figure of the faun from whose upturned pipes, the water burst like iridescent flute notes; he dabbled his fingers in the pool, and tossed crumbs to the stately couple—Mr. and Mrs. Swan he always called them—that sailed its bosom. Then, cheerily whistling, he continued on his way.

"Really," murmured Oakley Ashenhurst, just before he dismissed the matter from his mind, "I must have a look at this midnight runner, if he continues to frequent my block."

So that when, that midnight, again he heard the pattering footsteps in the street, young Mr. Ashenhurst was ready. Assuming that the athlete would operate upon a schedule, and that that schedule would take him past the house at midnight, the prospective Dr. Ashenhurst closed his volume of *Anatomy* at 11:55, snapped out his light, parted his window curtains, raised his window a trifle higher, and seated himself at the aperture. In the darkness, the small nickel-plated clock ticked on toward midnight. A mild breeze blew in from the street and gently stirred the curtains. Immediately opposite the house, on the other side of the street, a street light gleamed through dirty glass; there was no other for some distance, and the surrounding windows were as black as that of Oakley Ashenhurst, whose pipe bubbled contentedly in the darkness.

At the first rumor of the steps, he sat forward and directed his gaze outward and downward. He turned his eyes up the street toward the little park which, however, was invisible. The middle of the street was bare, but something white was coming down the sidewalk on the near side. The slapping footsteps sounded clearly now. Lightly, evenly, with long, running strides, bounding as gracefully as an animal, the racing figure advanced out of semi-darkness into semi-light. Out of semi-light it moved into the rays of the dingy lamp. Then a cry that was a strangled scream burst from the lips of Oakley Ashenhurst, and, rising upright he seized the curtain beside him with such haste and vigor that it tore in his grasp.

His eyes wide with horror, he saw the white figure pass below his window and enter the semi-light beyond. Inexpressibly shocked; he saw it merge from semi-light to semi-darkness, and vanish into darkness. Its pattering footsteps seemed to beat against his stunned and startled brain.

It was the nude stone statue from the fountain in the corner park.

II

AND that was the sensational story I told my friend Lavender, the evening after the occurrence, as we sat in his Portland Street rooms and smoked over our coffee. It was just such a tale, I knew, as Lavender liked, for my friend Lavender, although a consulting detective of wide reputation, boasts as fantastic an imagination as I have encountered in print. He heard me through in silence, but with raised eyebrows that spoke his interest. I admit that I made the most of the incredible tale.

"Extraordinary!" he commented, when I had finished. He added at once, "And, delightful, too! A fine theatrical touch to it. This Ashenhurst, I take it, is a sober young man?"

"Quite," I assured him. "I've known him only a few months, but I like him greatly. He's in one of my classes, and is an excellent student. Not at all given to romancing, I should say. He strikes me as being eminently sane and practical."

"Yet he tells this insane story," said Lavender, "and, if I am to believe you, tells it with entire belief."

"And very convincingly," I added. "He certainly thinks he saw something, and it has upset him."

Lavender laughed shortly. "No wonder," he said. "It would upset anybody. A very ingenious business! What do you think of it, Gilly?"

"Nothing!" I answered promptly. "I think Ashenhurst was dreaming."

"Nothing of the sort."

"You don't mean to say you believe it?" I demanded. "I knew it would please you, but I didn't expect the story to be believed."

"I certainly don't believe he saw the statue, if that's what you mean; but he saw something very curious indeed. Now what did he see? And why did he see it? The second question is the more important of the two, and the hardest to answer."

He smoked in silence for a moment, thinking deeply. When he spoke, the current of his thought had changed.

"You know Ashenhurst's place?" he asked suddenly.

"I've been there once. I know the neighborhood pretty well, and I've seen the statue, so to call it. Of course, it isn't a statue; it's a figure in a fountain."

"A distinction that doesn't help the case," observed Lavender with a dry smile. "Tell me about the street."

"Well, it's called Cambridge Court, and it's only a block in length. It runs from Belden Square—which is the little park—to Crayview Avenue, which is a through street, as you know, popular with motorists. Cambridge Court is an old street, and the houses are old—once toney, but shabby-genteel now. You know the kind; every other family keeps roomers. But it's all very respectable, and the streets surrounding it are highly desirable residence thoroughfares. It's sort of hidden away, as it were, and the people who live in the court have a quiet, subdued air about them—as if the world had forgotten them, and they were glad of it, if you understand what I mean."

"Perfectly," smiled Lavender. "You are a bit of a poet, Gilruth. And the house?"

"Three story and attic, I think. Basement, too, probably. Brick, of course. Porcelain doorknobs. I should think it was a handsome establishment back in 1895. The front windows are bay windows, and Ashenhurst's room looks into the street from the second floor. He rents it from a family named Harden, who live in the back of the house. I think there are other roomers."

"North side of the street? Hm-m! I think I see it. You used your eyes well on your one visit. Well, well! And Belden Square a half-block from, the dwelling. The statue didn't have to run far, did it? It could leave the fountain, run around the block, and be back in no time."

"Oh, easily!" I sarcastically agreed. "Don't you think we ought to watch it tonight, and catch it as it steps out of the fountain?"

Lavender laughed. "Not quite that, perhaps; but there is some watching to be done. I, for one, should like to see the thing. Shouldn't you?"

"I know Ashenhurst would like to have you," I said.

"You've mentioned me to him, eh? Well, you guessed right when you thought I would be interested. I am interested. Something very curious is going on, Gilly, or something tremendously unimportant. I don't know which."

"I don't follow you there."

"I only mean that if your friend saw what he thinks he saw, the matter is most important. If he was deceived—by a resemblance, let us say—then probably the solution is very simple and unimportant. You see, there are a great many possibilities. If Ashenhurst was deceived, then he may actually have

seen only some innocent idiot running off his weight, clad in a track suit or something of the sort. If Ashenhurst had been thinking of the statue, for any reason, and had it in his mind, he might have imagined that he saw it; in which case the solution of the matter is that Ashenhurst needs a doctor and a vacation. Or he may have seen a lunatic running naked; that certainly would heighten the resemblance to our stone friend in the park. In which case the lunatic should be apprehended, although the affair would still be relatively unimportant. But—if Ashenhurst actually saw the statue—that is, of course, somebody made up to look like the statue—the case becomes highly important, for something very significant must be back of such an impersonation; something more than just lunacy, I should say."

"What, for instance?"

He laughed again, and ran his fingers through his thick, dark hair with a familiar gesture that brought into prominence his single plume of white.

"Well, just for instance—to frighten somebody to death! The thing certainly gave Ashenhurst a scare."

"That's quite an idea," I admitted, "but you don't believe it."

"Don't I? You don't know what I believe, Gilly—and I don't know myself yet. How should I? But you're coming with me, of course?"

"Yes," I said promptly. "You may gamble on that."

He looked at his watch. "There's three hours to midnight. I should like to have seen the statue first—out of curiosity, if nothing else—but we must assume that our friend will run again tonight, and I don't want Ashenhurst to be alone!"

Something in the earnestness of his last words arrested me, and I looked a startled inquiry. He slowly nodded.

"Yes," he said, "I don't know why, Gilly, but I've a notion that this may portend evil to your friend. It's just a feeling, too vague to put into logical thought, but—well, for two nights Ashenhurst didn't look out of his window, and last night he did! You see? He saw the thing, whatever it is—and it must have known that he saw it. And so, tonight—? That's all! I can't make it any plainer."

An unpleasant thrill ran through me, for as he spoke I had the feeling, too.

"Come on," I cried; and got quickly to my feet. He followed more leisurely; and as we tramped down the dark stairs I added, "We can cross the park, Jimmie, if you want a look at that thing. It's on our way."

"Well—perhaps," he agreed. "But I should prefer not to be seen evidencing too great an interest in it."

The night was fine, with a good moon and plenty of stars, and when our taxi had set us down not far from Belden Square, Lavender determined to have his look.

"There seems to be plenty of citizens abroad," he argued, "and I'll warrant there are more of them in the park. We may as well chance it."

So, sauntering easily and ostentatiously smoking, we plunged into the little park and began our stroll diagonally across its tapestry of moonlit grass. A number of couples passed us, arm in arm, and as we approached the fountain we saw that at least a dozen persons were patrolling the paths about it. The tinkle of water sounded pleasantly in the night as it rained into the pool, and the moonlight on the stone figure of the piping faun in the midst of the falling water was memorable.

No one paid the slightest attention to us, as we idled for a moment at the stone brink; and after a careless glance or two we turned away.

"A pretty picture," I suggested.

"Very," said Lavender shortly. He added after an instant, "Well, he's still there!"

In five minutes more, still easily strolling, we had entered the little street in which lived and studied my classmate, Ashenhurst.

Cambridge Court interested Lavender deeply, and his glance was everywhere as we proceeded into its dusky canyon.

"Not many lamps," he murmured. "Only three in the block. And the folks retire early. It can't be more than 10:30, yet nearly every house is in darkness. Two lights down there near the corner, across the street, and one here on our left. The nearest, I suppose, is Ashenhurst's?"

I corroborated the supposition, and in a moment we had turned up the steps, to discover at the top, smoking his inevitable pipe, my friend, the student. Ashenhurst's long body uncoiled and rose upright in the darkness.

"Hoped you'd come," he said briefly, but warmly. "This is Mr.—?"

"Yes," interrupted Lavender swiftly. "Happy to know you, I'm sure. Hope the studies are coming along well. Gilly says you're an awful 'dig,' you know."

"Come up," said Ashenhurst abruptly, sensing a mystery, and we trudged after him up the dark stairs and into his room at the front, where he turned a puzzled face to the detective.

"It's all right, old man," smiled Lavender, "but your case is so peculiar that I thought it as well not to shout my name about the neighborhood. One never knows who may be listening. Nothing to add to Gilly's story, I suppose?"

The tall student shrugged, then glanced uneasily at the clock. "Not yet," he answered, with a rueful smile, "Soon, maybe!"

We spoke in low tones for a time, while Ashenhurst and Lavender became acquainted, and then the conversation languished.

"It's getting along," remarked Lavender

at length, "and it's just as well not to talk too much. I've a funny idea at the back of my head. It won't stand talking about, and it involves silence at this time. Literal silence! I may be quite wrong; but I think that from now until midnight we had better sit quite still. I'm sorry I can't be more explicit."

I looked at him curiously in the half-darkness of the room. "The light?" I murmured.

"Yes," he agreed, "let's silence the light, too."

So Ashenhurst, no doubt vastly wondering at this strange conduct on the part of my friend, extinguished his lamp, and in darkness we began our vigil. The moments seemed to crawl as we awaited the zero hour.

From his busy smoking and an occasional restless movement, I knew that Lavender was thinking hard. My own thoughts were bewildered and incoherent, and Ashenhurst's, I fancy, were no better. What Lavender's "funny idea" might be puzzled me profoundly; I had seen and heard all that he had seen and heard, and I was quite at sea. This, however, was the usual way of things, and I knew better than to question his decisions.

In the darkness the ticking of the little nickel-plated clock became intolerable. It seemed that hours had passed before Lavender stirred and came upright.

He moved quietly to the window, and in the poor light from the street lamp opposite, looked at his watch. I noted that he kept out of sight of the street.

"Ten minutes more," he whispered; and again it seemed that the moments crawled.

Ashenhurst moved to my friend's side, and stood behind the curtains. I instantly followed, overpoweringly curious. Lavender drew our heads together and spoke in a sharp whisper against our ears.

"If he does not come tonight, Gilruth and I shall stay here all night. If he comes, as usual, Gilruth shall stay the night alone, and I shall go home."

But he came—whoever he may have been.

Lavender's ears were sharp, but it was the ears of Ashenhurst that first caught the distant patter of feet, as his clutch on our arms betrayed. In a moment we all heard them, swift and terrible in the silence; and convinced as I was that the thing could not be, I felt my scalp stir.

Then the half-darkness opened, and the white figure raced past, as Ashenhurst, with a sharp breath, flung both arms about my shoulders and clung. Lavender's face was a mask set with glittering eyes. And incredible as it might be, it was the stone figure of the white faun that shot by under the window. The lamplight shone on its white clustered curls and shining shoulders, and made a glory of its body in the instant of its passing.

In the stunned silence that followed, Lavender leaped for the electric lamp on the table and snapped on the current, then leaped again for the door.

"Stay here with Ashenhurst, Gilly," he crisply ordered. "If there should be trouble, call me at home in an hour, or any time after that. At any rate, see me in the morning."

A moment later we heard him plunging down the stairs on light feet, heard the street door close behind him, and from the open window saw him run off in the darkness in the direction taken by the fleeing figure.

III

THE rest of the night was uneventful. In effect, we slept upon our arms, vaguely alarmed by Lavender's final remark; but no further sound disturbed the quiet of the little street, and the house itself was silent as a tomb. Not a soul, apparently, had been aroused by Lavender's departure. In the morning, not much refreshed, we both betook ourselves to Lavender's room, for Ashenhurst declared himself much too curious, not to say nervous, to think of work

that day.

We discovered the detective deep in a file of *The Playbill*, borrowed from a neighboring public library reading-room. His feet were on the piano bench on which stood his typewriter, and the room was thick with tobacco fumes. He was shaved but otherwise his appearance was negligée in an extreme degree. He greeted our advent with an appraising grin.

"Had breakfast? So have I! Well, watchmen, what of the night?"

Ashenhurst replied for us both that it had been excessively tame. "Anything," he added, "would have been anti-climax after our adventure."

"Yes," agreed Lavender, "destiny is frequently a bit of an artist. My own adventures ended at the same time."

"He got away, then?" I eagerly inquired.

"Clean as a whistle! I rather expected he would. My start was a trifle late. The best I hoped for was a glimpse, but I was denied even that. The street was blank from end to end when I emerged from the house, and the boulevard was equally deserted. That, of course, is significant, eh?"

"You mean that he didn't run far? That he may have turned in some place?"

"That is one explanation. Another is that an auto was waiting for him at the corner, engine running and all ready for a quick start. That, as a matter of fact, is what I had in mind when I ran out. I thought that at least I might hear it departing. Not a sound! You may be right about his turning in some place; it's the logical assumption, for I wasn't far behind him, surely."

"In heaven's name," broke in Ashenhurst, "what was it? Who was he, if it was a man?"

"I can't say, of course; but I did get an idea during the night, and it has involved all this reading without much result." He indicated the scattered journals and smiled faintly.

"Why *The Playbill*?" I asked.

"Why not?" countered Lavender. "The fellow is no amateur, I fancy. He ran like a professional of some kind—and jumped like a Russian dancer. Consider that, now, in connection with his amazing make-up, and there emerges somebody connected with the stage. Don't you think?"

"Um-m! Maybe!" I was not enthusiastic.

"Oh, it's a long shot, of course. But we must consider probabilities until they are shown to be improbabilities. I base my idea on more than a superficial appearance. I've been trying to guess what lies behind."

"I lay awake guessing half the night," contributed Ashenhurst bitterly.

"And exactly what did you expect to find in *The Playbill*?" I insisted.

"These are old *Playbills*. The file goes back three mouths, and ends with last week's issue. I consider it at least possible that this ingenious fellow had been out of a job for a time. And this valuable weekly carries several columns of cards of professional gentlemen who are 'at liberty.' I'm not looking for any particular person; I'm looking for anybody who fits the description I have imagined. You see, if I am right, this fellow is not the principal in the case. What the case is, we have yet to discover; but I think this man is only a subordinate. He may not even know why he runs as he does!"

"I can't believe that, Lavender," I demurred.

"It's very easy to believe," he assured me. "If for no other reason, I believe him to be a subordinate because he shows himself. If the game is important—and it's too mad not to be—the principal would not show himself so openly. He might be caught. Suppose instead of waiting upstairs in Ashenhurst's room, I had been waiting for him in a passageway. I'd have had him, or seen where he went. I think the principal doesn't care whether this fellow is captured or not. He'd rather the man wouldn't be caught, of course, but it is not of great importance one way or another."

"And this principal?" queried Ashenhurst.

"Is working elsewhere," said Lavender.

"Elsewhere! Then why, for heaven's sake—?"

Lavender shrugged. "Well, well," he said, "I may be wrong. I'm no super-detective, Ashenhurst. It's bad business, I know, to imagine a case and then twist the facts to fit it; but I assure you it's as safe a gamble as any other method. Any way you tackle a case, you're as likely to be wrong as right."

"But, confound it, Jimmie!" I exploded, "why should this fellow show himself at all, in that crazy regalia?"

"Exactly," agreed Lavender. "Why should he? There is only one conceivable reason that holds water: he wants to be seen. If a man paints himself black and parades the city between sandwich-boards, he's bound to attract attention. Obviously then, he does it in order to attract attention. But whose attention does our friend want to attract? Just as obviously, he wants to attract Ashenhurst's attention."

"Good Lord!" exclaimed that young man. "Well, he succeeded!"

"He did, indeed. Oh, I'm sure enough of my ground as far as I have gone. You live in Cambridge Court, and so this fellow runs in Cambridge Court. But other people live in Cambridge Court. You, however, sit up late; your window, at midnight, is the only one in the block that shows a light. There was no other light when I ran out last night, and I am sure there had not been for some time. Further, this fellow ran by four nights in a row—at least four. There may have been other, earlier nights when you didn't hear the footsteps, but on four nights anyway, he ran past your window. The first two nights you did not look out; the third night you did. He heard your exclamation, and felt sure that he had attracted your attention. Last night was the test, as I read it; and last night we all looked out. And last night, he knew he had attracted you."

"The deuce he did!"

"Yes," I said, "how do you know that, Jimmie?"

"Because," said Lavender, "I saw him look up. You fellows were excited, and were concentrating on a running statue. You didn't exactly believe in it, but the statue was in your minds—naturally. So all you saw was a running statue—an impossibility. I knew perfectly well that it was not a statue, and was determined not to be too surprised by the sight. So I watched carefully; and as he fled past he looked up at the window— just a half turn of the head as he leaped, but he looked! I saw him! And your lights were out, and my head was half-visible; I took care that it should be. Ergo, our friend believes he saw you looking out, and today he knows that he has succeeded in attracting your attention."

"Perhaps he saw us all," I remarked.

"I hope not," said Lavender vigorously, "and I think not. I kept you a trifle behind me, in deep shadow. You see, my own plans were laid."

Ashenhurst whistled solemnly for a moment. "And what's the next step?" he asked, at length. "Will he run again, tonight?"

"Oh, yes, I think he will run every night until something happens."

"What?" we demanded in the same breath.

"I don't know," answered Jimmie Lavender.

Ashenhurst whistled again while he thought that over. "You make me nervous," he said finally.

"You have a right to be nervous, perhaps," Lavender nodded. "Although probably you are not in any serious danger. But Gilruth will stay with you every night from now until—well, until the thing happens, whatever it is—and I shall not be far away."

There was a silence for a moment, during which Lavender looked hard at Ashenhurst. Suddenly he spoke.

"I don't want to be impertinent, Ashenhurst, but is there any secret about you? Anything in your life that you wish to conceal? Anything somebody else would like to know?"

"Good Lord, no!" The student's reply was prompt and final.

"You don't conceal a treasure anywhere in your room, by any chance?"

Ashenhurst laughed loudly. "Not by a large majority!"

Lavender's thoughts again revolved. Evidently something puzzled him very much. After a moment he began again.

"Do you ever go out at night?"

"Well, not very often. If you say ever, why, of course, I do, sometimes. But my exams are coming on, and I have to study pretty hard. I suppose I haven't been out after supper for weeks. I'm not much of a social climber, anyway," finished the student with a smile.

"And you are never home during the day?"

"Never except on Sundays. I work pretty hard at the office."

"I'll be hanged if I understand it," declared Lavender, almost indignantly. "My idea is a very pretty one indeed, but I can't make it work. There's something missing; something wrong. Now what the devil can it be?"

"I assure you I'm not concealing a thing," said Ashenhurst, with some dignity.

Lavender laughed good-humoredly. "I know you're not, old man! If you were, it would simplify things, immensely. But how about this family—what's the name?—

Harden! How about the Hardens? What have they to conceal?"

"God knows," replied Ashenhurst, mystified. "They're as harmless an old couple as ever I met."

"And the other roomers?"

"Same thing! Two old maids!"

"And the other floors?"

"Know 'em only by sight; but they seem all right to me. An old man and his daughter downstairs—name of Palmer. Don't know what he does. Not much of anything, I guess. Upstairs, family named Carr. They've got roomers, too—young fellow named Pomeroy, and another young fellow named Peterson. Steady workers, and go to bed early. Oh, the whole house is so respectable it's almost discouraging!"

"It does seem rather hopeless," admitted Lavender. "You don't happen to know who occupies the houses just beside yours? Next door, both ways?"

"Seen 'em, that's all. All respectable!"

"It's a respectable world," said Lavender dryly. "Well, I must get to work, I suppose. I've a long day ahead of me. You fellows can do as you please, but I think you'd better separate during the day. Gilruth can join you after dark—and do it quietly, Gilly! Stay with Ashenhurst all night. I may show up before midnight, and I may not. I'll be there if I think it's necessary. And listen! Don't let our stone friend see you as he gallops past! Keep your light out—and you, Ashenhurst, stare hard out of the window. Gilruth mustn't be seen, but I want you to be seen. And neither of you are to leave the room on any account unless I tell you to."

It sounded rather sinister, and we solemnly pledged ourselves to follow his instructions.

"Can't I go with you, Jimmie?" I asked, somewhat disconsolately.

"Today? It wouldn't be worth your while. Honestly, old man! A lot of tiresome inquiries, that's all. If there were any chance of danger, rest assured I'd want you right beside me."

"I don't see what you can do," said Ashenhurst curiously. "You don't know which way to look, do you?"

"I'm going to look in a number of directions. I expect to talk with detectives, policemen, citizens, and heaven knows whom else. I'll be a busy young man for a time. Also, I want to make some close inquiry about a theatrical family by the name of Jordan."

"Lavender!" I cried reproachfully. "You've been holding out on us! You have found something!"

"Well," he laughed, "just an indication—no more. It's here in The Playbill, and it may not amount to a thing. You may read the notice for yourselves. On my honor, it's all I have up my sleeve."

He selected a paper from the top of the heap and tossed it over to me, then leaned across and placed a finger on a black-face "card," halfway down a column of advertisements. Ashenhurst, greatly excited, bent over my shoulder and we read the notice together.

"Living Statuary," ran the first line; and there followed a brief announcement that the "Famous Jordan Family" was now at liberty and was prepared to accept engagements in vaudeville or circus.

A premonitory thrill ran along my spine, and my old newspaper instinct whispered significantly. Intuitively, I felt that Lavender was on the right track.

"You see," he chuckled, "there are four of them—Tom, Bert, Florence, and Lillian—all of them at liberty."

"By heaven!" said Ashenhurst huskily, "I believe one of them's at *large*!"

IV

THE day that followed was a weary one for me; possibly. for Ashenhurst, also. He solved the difficulty, however, by reporting for work, after all, some hours late, whilst I moped in the bookshops and purchased nothing. At six o'clock I joined Ashenhurst, and we supped recklessly at a favorite restaurant where I had hoped we might encounter Lavender. That ingenious person failed to appear, however, and it was with small hope of catching him at home that I called his number on the telephone. To my delight he was in his rooms; had just entered, in fact, when I rang him.

"You are a clairvoyant, Gilly," he said. "I was just wondering where I could catch you before you started for Ashenhurst's. Where are you now?"

I told him, adding the information that Ashenhurst was with me.

"Good," came the familiar voice, across the wires, "send him home at once. He is to stay there until one or the other of us joins him. You must not be seen with him at this time. Tell him not to leave his room in any circumstances, once he gets in it. You are to meet me as soon as dark has fallen, beside the fountain in the square. Understand?"

I understood perfectly, and said so. Ashenhurst was frankly alarmed.

"He must expect trouble tonight," he said

"All I know is what he told me," said I. "You follow instructions to the letter, Ash, or you may ball up the whole show."

"Oh, I'll behave," he assured me, and he did, admirably.

Dusk was already settling over the city, and I calculated that if I took a street car I should reach the park at about the appointed time. But a wagon-load of cement very nearly ruined the program; it broke down in front of my car, and tied up traffic for an unconscionable period. When I had waited as long as I dared, I alighted and hailed a passing taxi, performing the rest of my journey in comfort. Even so, it was black dark when I entered Belden Square and hastened toward the central fountain.

Lavender, slightly impatient, awaited my coming.

"We can talk here in safety," he remarked. "This is about the last place any of our victims will visit tonight. The fountain, I think, has served its purpose. Tonight its counterfeit will run for the last time."

"Great Scott!" I exclaimed, amazed. "Is it all cleared up?"

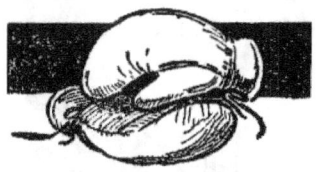

"I know nearly everything I need to know," said Lavender, "except the exact 'why' of it all. That I merely suspect. But the case ends tonight, I feel certain—happily, I hope, for Ashenhurst. But he has a dangerous part to play. He seems pretty husky."

"He's a whale of a boxer," said I. "Do you mean that he's likely to be assaulted?"

"Very likely, I should say. Here's the situation in a nutshell, and you must carry instructions to Ashenhurst. Jordan is the man—Bert Jordan. I'm convinced of that. That is, he's the fugitive statue! With the aid of a theatrical friend of mine, I ran down the 'family'; and the fact is, Bert's missing! I let it be known that I wanted to hire the whole outfit for a street carnival in Aurora, and said I wanted them all to leave town tonight. Couldn't be done; they couldn't locate Bert! Tomorrow night, maybe—they weren't sure. I think they were sore at Bert, for they wanted the engagement; and I think they don't know just what he's up to. I said I'd see them again tomorrow.

"Well, Bert will run tonight, as usual, at midnight; that's a certainty. That's where Ashenhurst comes in. I'll see him before he starts, but you must prepare him. The min-ute he sees Jordan coming, he is to leave the room, run downstairs after him, and follow him down the street. I think Jordan will give battle, and Ashenhurst must be prepared to defend himself. Jordan may be very ugly. Anyway, there'll be a couple of plain-clothes men hidden away nearby, and at the proper moment they'll nab Jordan. If possible, though, I want to know where he goes, for I think he turns in some place in the block, as you once suggested."

"Where will you be all this time?" I pertinently asked, for by now it was obvious that Lavender's role was to be cast elsewhere.

"I'll be in Ashenhurst's rooms, and so will you. You go to Ashenhurst now, with my instructions. Get into the house quietly; it may be watched. We've worked so quickly, though, that I think we have aroused no suspicion. I'll follow you in a little while, and I, too, must get in without being seen. I could tell you all this later, I suppose; but it may be close to midnight before I can risk entering the house."

"One question, Jimmie," I said. "Why is Ashenhurst to run out while we stay behind in the room?"

"Well," smiled Lavender grimly, "I want it to be supposed that when Ashenhurst runs out, his room is empty."

"Oh!" I said, suddenly enlightened. "The principal—"

"Is the man I want. Exactly!"

"I see—I think I do! Then the statue—Jordan—was to attract attention?"

"Quite so, and to draw Ashenhurst from his room. That was the ultimate design. It might never have worked, or it might have worked wrong—as it did, by Jove!—but that was the plan. If it had failed, I suppose some other plan would have been worked out."

"And what is in Ashenhurst's room?"

"Hanged if I know," said Lavender. "Whatever it is, somebody wants it pretty badly, don't you think? And I know, at last, who Mr. Somebody is. I'll introduce you to him in a little while. Now hurry along, and don't be seen entering the house. And not a sound, after you have entered, from either of you!"

Well, the affair was getting warm! And something told me that we were all in for a lively evening.

I left the park in leisurely fashion, and plunged into the inky depths of Cambridge Court. Not a soul was in the block as far as could be seen. The trio of sickly street lamps, long distances apart, blinked sadly in the blackness. I passed the first one hastily; the next was in the center of the block opposite Ashenhurst's room, but on the far side of the street. I approached cautiously, but without ostentatious secrecy, and quietly climbed the stairs of the objective dwelling. The door was unlocked, and I entered without ceremony, climbing stairs again to Ashenhurst's room so softly that when I had closed his door behind me the student had his first knowledge of my approach.

The room, as usual, was in darkness save for the blaze of light from the electric lamp upon the table. This gleamed on one wall, and was faintly reflected on the window; but the corners of the room were black. I motioned Ashenhurst to silence, and whispered his instructions. He nodded understandingly—relieved, I think, that shortly the whole matter would be ended. A glance at the clock showed three hours before midnight, and another intolerable wait was before us.

At ten o'clock, Ashenhurst snapped off his light at the switch, and the remainder of the vigil was kept in darkness. At eleven, the door creaked gently, and through the blackness Jimmie Lavender came to our side.

"All well," he whispered. "Our men are placed, and there ought to be no hitch. You understand your part, Ashenhurst?"

"Every comma," said the long student, in the same tone, "except this damned silence, Mr. Lavender. It gets on my nerves."

"Sorry," Lavender whispered back, "but it can't be helped. The danger is from within the house. I thought you had guessed that. You may smoke if you like."

We felt better when we had all lighted cigars. The room seemed less black, the silence less profound. So another hour passed away and midnight was upon us.

"Ready!" murmured Lavender. "Stand by the window, Ashenhurst; let yourself be seen. When he passes, rush for the door, with some noise, and downstairs after him. Don't upset the neighborhood, but don't be afraid of a little noise. I want it perfectly evident that you are leaving the house."

Ashenhurst followed instructions without an error. The stone faun held no terror for any of us now, and the patter of racing feet in the outside darkness only told us that the moment for action had come. Ashenhurst, leaning far out of the window, cried out once as the white figure shot past, then jumped for the door and pelted down the stairs in the darkness. I moved toward the window, but Lavender's hand restrained me.

"Careful!" he sharply whispered. "The trouble begins now—and I don't know where it will come from!"

Almost as he spoke, there sounded beyond the door a light thudding of feet; then the door creaked and swung inward and a long beam of white light cut a rib-bony path across the carpet. It was followed by the dark figure of a man, holding an electric torch, who, with a swift lithe bound, sprang to a corner of the room and stooped to the boards. It had all happened so quickly that for a moment I was breathless; then as I was about to spring upon the intruder, Lavender's restraining hand again fell upon my arm. There followed a moment of tense and painful silence, then a crackling sound as of splintering wood, and the heavy breathing of the man in the corner. He was working furiously in the patch of light thrown by his torch, and once, as he half-turned, the gleam fell across a hard, seamed face and an eye that glittered like that of a madman. Save for his asthmatic breathing, and the occasional crackling of wood, the room was heavy with silence.

Our time had come. Lavender's hand was taken from my arm. Then his voice, swift and hard, and icy as a mountain stream, cut through the chamber.

"Hands up, Wilcox! Quick!" And to me, "Lights, Gilly!"

But as I sprang for the electric lamp, the intruder, ignoring the command and the leveled revolver which he knew lay back of it, flung himself forward in the darkness in the direction of Lavender's voice. Instantly, I, too, jumped into action, and more by luck than design, blundered at once into the man called Wilcox. In an instant the fight of my life was on.

We met with a shock that was terrific, and clung like tigers. The fellow had a grasp like an animal; against it my own proved powerless. A chair crashed over, and we began to whirl. We whirled until I thought my wits were deserting me. Up and down the room we thrashed, colliding with everything, unmindful of bumps and bruises; and all without a sound from either of us. Inextricably mixed as we were, Lavender could do nothing but encourage me with his voice. My hands tried desperately to work themselves upward to the throat of the man who was crushing me, but I was a child in his grasp. The constant pressure and the wild, whirling waltz had stolen my breath. I felt myself slipping—giving.

At that instant, Lavender, who had dis-covered the lights, out at the switch, flooded the room with light from every bulb; and at the same instant we crashed into the center table. The impact broke my opponent's grasp; he sprang back, then leaped for the door. Two seconds later the fight was over, and the man called Wilcox was helpless on the floor. Lavender, cool and collected, had greeted the fellow's spring with a straight right, shot forward with all the force of the trained back and loins that lay behind it. The blow was terrific, and the man dropped as if he had been pole-axed.

Lavender stooped and studied the hard face for a moment, almost with pity. Then I heard the clink of handcuffs, and with a little shrug my friend rose to his feet.

"Bernard Wilcox," he said laconically. "Paroled convict—used to occupy this room. Planted his loot here and went to jail. Came back for it tonight."

He added with a grin, "R. I. P." Then lighted a cigar and dropped into a chair to await the coming of Ashenhurst.

V

TWENTY minutes later, Mr. Oakley Ashenhurst, wearing a highly decorative black eye and a wide smile, tramped upstairs at the head of an extraordinary procession. After him there entered the room two husky detectives, half-carrying between them what had once been the celebrated Bert Jordan of the "Famous Jordan Family," and behind them stalked a tall, uniformed officer in whom I recognized Captain D'Arcy of the Lincoln Park station. Bringing up the rear was a motley of half-gowned, bathrobed citizens and citizenesses, among whom were the shrinking figures of old Mr. and Mrs. Harden and the two other roomers, elderly women with their hair in curl-papers. It was a sight to move the gods to laughter, and Lavender and I, being essentially human, lay back and laughed. D'Arcy, too, wore a broad grin.

"Got him, I see," said the police captain, with a nod to the prostrate Wilcox. He stooped over the man on the floor. "Yep, it's Wilcox!"

Bernard Wilcox, who had recovered his senses, glowered back with evil eyes.

"And you, I see, have Jordan," said Lavender pleasantly. "The others, I suppose, escaped?"

"Yes," answered D'Arcy with a frown. "Big auto all ready to pick up Jordan, over in the next block. He had to run through a passage to get to it, and they may have seen us nail Jordan in the passage; I don't know. Anyway, all we saw when we got over there was a trail of dust and sound."

"Unimportant," said Lavender, "although you'll probably get them through Jordan. Our statue doesn't seem as lively a cricket as he was a little while ago."

All eyes were turned back to the amazing figure of Bert Jordan of the "Famous Jordan Family." He was an astonishing spectacle. From neck to ankle he was encased in dull white fleshings, above which his white, painted face, like that of a clown, now registered profound depression. His hair, elaborately whitened and held in place by a white net, had been curled in neat horns on his brow and temples, but at the moment it was much disordered. On his feet were white gloves of the sort worn by fashionable bathers in the sands of expensive bathing beaches. But the celebrated Bert Jordan had lost much of his "white" in his tussle with Ashenhurst and the police, and he now presented a very lugubrious appearance. I felt sorry for the fellow, and I think Lavender did, too.

"Want to talk, Jordan?" inquired Lavender. "Might as well, you know."

Jordan grinned sheepishly. "Sure, I'll talk," he said, "What d'ya want to know?"

"What did you soak Mr. Ashenhurst for?"

"Dough!" replied Mr. Jordan promptly. "Plenty of dough!"

"So I should imagine. Mr. Wilcox foot the bill?"

"Whatever his name is," said Jordan.

"He's a liar!" asserted Wilcox, from the floor, with a string of oaths.

"Well, I'll talk," said Lavender. "I'm not a liar. There are some things I want to know. You were out of a job, Jordan, and you met this fellow Wilcox. He offered you a job. Good money in it. You fell for it. But how did you happen to run across Wilcox?"

"Met him in the park up here, one day—near that damn fountain!"

"I see! Of course, that would do it. I ought to have thought of that. Did you know Wilcox before that?"

"He used to be in a circus where I was," said Jordan, "but his name wasn't Wilcox then. It was Brown."

"You're a liar!" declared Wilcox savagely.

"Hm-m!" grunted Lavender, "That pretty nearly tells me all I need to know. The statue, of course, suggested this crazy scheme to get Ashenhurst out of his room some night. Wilcox knew you were in the statue line, as it were, and so was born the great idea. He suggested it, of course?"

"Sure," said Jordan. "He said he wanted to get some guy's goat, and when the guy ran out at me, I was to beat him up, toss him into the auto and take him off somewhere overnight."

"You had no objections, I suppose?"

"Well," hedged the circus performer, "I was pretty broke, and I needed the dough. But I didn't like his dam fool scheme. I told him I'd go up and drag the guy out, if he wanted me to; or throw stones at his window until he chased me. I didn't want to dress up. It seemed kinda foolish to me."

"Quite right," smiled Lavender. "And

what do you think of Wilcox—or Brown—now, Mr. Jordan?"

Jordan looked suddenly significant. He turned his eyes on the recumbent Wilcox, almost stealthily. Then he looked at the police captain, and finally back at Lavender. After these elaborate preparations, he raised his forefinger and touched his temple, where a white curl now hung limply.

"I think he's coo-coo!" he said.

"Excellent," said Lavender. "So do I! I think, Captain, we shall have to make things as easy as possible for Mr. Jordan, who is, after all, only an erring person of temperament. If your men will remove both of these gentlemen now, we'll let these good folks go to bed, and I'll have a chat with you about this case."

When the prisoners had been removed, and the oaths of Bernard Wilcox had died away in the distance, Lavender resumed his tale.

"Jordan is perfectly right, of course," he said. "Wilcox is a bit touched. Nobody but a lunatic would have suggested such a scheme to get a man out of his room. The meeting with Jordan gave him the idea, no doubt; that and the proximity. of the statue."

He turned suddenly to Mrs. Harden, whose attire now had been augmented by a huge shawl,

"Did you recognize this man Wilcox, Mrs. Harden?" he asked.

"Yes, sir, I did! He's the man upstairs they call Pomeroy!"

"Pomeroy, eh? It had to be either Pomeroy or Peterson. I wasn't able to see either of them, and so I couldn't be sure. You see, Gilly, five years ago, before Mrs. Harden had this flat, this Wilcox-or Pomeroy—or Brown—or whatever his real name is-occupied the room now occupied by our friend Ashenhurst. He roomed with a very decent family named Dickson, but he himself was a clever thief. In time, he was caught and sent to Joliet for a stretch. He had planted some of his loot in this room, however; when, not long ago, he was released on parole, he came back here to get it. He couldn't get the same room, but he was lucky enough to get a room upstairs, and there he laid his plans to get down here and recover the stuff he had planted.

"I suppose he did a lot of thinking about it, while he was tucked away down in Joliet, and after a while he became—shall we say, a bit obsessed? Once located upstairs—he had a room at the back, I believe—his problem was to get into Ashenhurst's room some time when Ashenhurst was out. It would seem at first glance to be an easy enough problem, but as it turned out it was a hard one. For one reason and another, he couldn't gain access, and, finally he hit upon this mad scheme to force Ashenhurst out. I saw D'Arcy today, and he was able to give me some information that fitted in with my preconceived idea of things.

"It was obvious from the first that Jordan's amazing performance was to draw attention to himself, and after a bit it became equally obvious that he was trying to lure Ashenhurst from the house. But why? So that he, or somebody else, could get into Ashenhurst's room. I preferred to believe it was somebody else—that Jordan was only a subordinate. This turned, out to be correct, for Jordan now has no idea what Wilcox wanted in this room. It was necessary to find a trace of somebody who for some years had been absent from society, who had occupied this room—at least, this house. D'Arcy remembered a number of men who might answer, among them Wilcox. I looked them all up in the police records, and Wilcox was the man. Under that name he had once been known to live at this address. He had lived here at the time he was sent to Joliet. And when I learned that recently he had been paroled, the whole case was clear. I knew that Bernard Wilcox was somewhere in or near this house, and that Jordan was his agent. I'm hanged if I know whether Wilcox's scheme to draw Ashenhurst out was a stupid one or a very clever one. Its very madness bothered me, and kept me from guessing the motive earlier than I did."

D'Arcy, who had listened with many approving nods, now cleared his throat.

"And exactly what did Wilcox want here?" he asked. "Where is this loot, Lavender?"

Lavender rose to his feet and strode over to the corner of the room in which the convict had been at work.

"It is under this splintered board," he said. "As you represent authority here tonight, suppose you investigate."

The police captain was beside him at a bound. "By jigger!" he exclaimed, and fell furiously to work.

With a resounding crack the board at length came up—and neatly packed beneath it, in the narrow groove, lay little packages of bills and papers, and a bag of jewels, that cleared the mystery of a dozen unsolved robberies.

When the captain, with many eulogies and handclasps, had departed with his treasure, I turned with a broad grin to Jimmie Lavender, and found him grinning at me. The Hardens, who still remained, looked mystified, and Ashenhurst alternately puffed at his cigar and stroked his battered eye.

"There is one question, Jimmie," I began; but he took the words away from me.

"That you don't find an answer to! Neither do I! Gilly, and you, Ashenhurst, and you, too, Mr. and Mrs. Andrew Harden—you have seen me turn over two prisoners and a young fortune to the police. You have seen me do things that no doubt appear very clever. Yes, I am a very clever young man! And from first to last there has been one thing I didn't know, and don't know now. It has bothered me more than any one detail I have ever encountered; and there seems to be no answer. This case is ended—the men are locked up, or will be shortly—and I know that my reasoning throughout has been accurate and justified. But I'm hanged if I'm not still bothered by that one question. Tell them what it is, Gilly!"

"Why didn't Wilcox get in during the day when Ashenhurst was at work? Why did he wait until night when he knew Ashenhurst would be at home?"

"There you have it!" agreed Lavender. "Why—exactly why? It was the obvious thing for him to do, the simplest thing to do, one would think. I have no doubt at all that he tried it and failed—but why? In the morning, no doubt, he would be likely to encounter Mrs. Harden on her cleaning-up expedition; but the afternoons were safe. He had a clear field. From at least one o'clock until five, the house would be practically deserted, and this room would be empty as Mother Hubbard's cupboard. Why didn't he, Ashenhurst?"

A queer clucking noise sounded suddenly from the throat of Mrs. Harden. Her lips were working frantically. It was difficult to say whether she was about to laugh or weep. Lavender gazed upon her with growing suspicion.

"Why, why—" she stammered, "the fact is, Mr. Ashenhurst—I didn't think there would be any harm in it. I'm getting a bit old—and your bed is the best in the house, you know! I was sure you wouldn't mind— The fact is, Mr. Ashenhurst, I always came in here for a bit of a nap in the afternoon— right after dinner—and slept till Mr. Harden came in at half-past five. I'm sure—"

But if she ever finished her embarrassed speech, I did not hear the end, for in the midst of it Lavender, with a joyous roar, flung himself across the bed in question and laughed until he cried.

LINES WRITTEN BY, OR TO, OR FOR, OR MAYBE AGAINST, THAT IGNOBLE OLD VIKING, HARALD HARDASS, KING OF THE CONEY & ORKNEY ISLANDS

by Avram Davidson

Woe is me, and wella-
day, that I set dreaming.
See, the steaming turn-spit
roast the ruptured roebuck.
Mingle men with mead-horns,
horns that hoist the highest,
held in horny hand-grips.

Often, o'er the Walrus-way,
went the wicked Worm-ships.
Scoffing, skim'd past Scilly-land,
smote the smarmy strand-folk.
Leering, lop't their limbs loose.
Debauched their daughters, drooling.

Weary, over white-weave waves,
calmly came to Norse-land.
For the captives, cards we cut.
Glittering gold did glut us,
Limber lads neath larch-leaves.

Pass by me now the potent pot,
Venison roasts vainly.
With rue and grue must guzzle gruel:
Harold has the heart-burn.

—Translated from the original
Old High Middle Autochthonous

THE MIRACLE

by JOHN D. SWAIN

Midnight footsteps sounding in a deserted street: what did they portend of tragedy, mystery, or evil deeds?

I

FOR hours we had ridden across desolate Champagne, our horses picking their way over the pockmarked terrain, littered with the incredible debris of a race of degenerates possessing the strength of men coupled with the wanton destructiveness of children.

The heat of afternoon gave way to the cool breath of evening; the sun set in a fantastic smear of crimson and gold, and the more brilliant stars crept forth from a dome of lapis lazuli. Presently the moon, at the full, rose in almost artificial splendor. Back home they were speaking of it as the "harvest moon." Here the only harvest was that of death, desolation, and despair.

Seen beneath its amber light the picture changed from a landscape in brilliant oils to an etching in monstrous blacks and whites. It was as if we were crossing the ghostly contour of some dead planet. The battle line, stilled by the armistice, was well beyond— the returning tide of scattered inhabitants far to the rear. We were alone in a land at once empty and silent.

Here and there an object caught my eye, and I guided my mount aside to identify it. Once it was the sparkle of moonshine from the staring eyes of a doll. Again, it was a cru-cifix, the wooden figure hacked and defiled. A broken iron pot lay beside a fifteenth-century missal, painfully transcribed and illuminated by some forgotten monk during slow creeping years. A torn placard affixed to a wall announced a boche beer-drinking contest. Beside it was the impaled body of a kitten—a mere scrap of moldering fur.

Oftener there was nothing identifiable: houses had been wrecked and leveled, and then seemingly brayed in giant mortars, that there might remain nothing save dust, to be blown away by the wind and worked up into mud, by the rain—to disappear utterly from the face of the earth and the very memories of men.

We rode in silence for the most part, Lieutenant Paradis and I, depressed by the bleak and artificial desert created by man in one of the garden spots of Europe.

It was then a weird and startling sight which suddenly materialized before our eyes from the fog-wraiths which clung to a winding river—nothing less than a perfectly preserved little town in the midst of all the woeful wreckage.

Not absolutely untouched, of course; looking sharp, one observed where a corner of the church belfry had gone, and here and there a gaping hole where a home had stood, but practically intact, even the stained-glass in the church and most of the humble panes of its shops unbroken.

Here it stood, as if left for a solitary

specimen of the vanished villages of Champagne.

If any such purpose had spared it one could have wished that some other town might have been chosen in its place—for Breaux was unknown to the tourist, it possessed no famous edifice, no supreme example of medieval craftsmanship.

Still, marvelously sweet, it looked sleeping amid its filmy draperies of vapor, beneath the full moon, with its one principal street widening to a civic center where stood the church, the two inns, the town hall, and on whose cobbled pave had for centuries raged no battle fiercer than that of its bareheaded, wooden-shod market women over the prices of fat geese and luscious grapes.

It was silent and deserted as our tired horses clumped through it; I noted especially a little wine-shop, with its sign still in its place over the door, its square bottles still in orderly array upon the shelf behind the copper counter.

That the boches should have spared the church and the tavern answered all queries as to the condition of the other buildings. Breaux had been spared. But why?

We passed abruptly from it to open country, as one does in France, with no tailing off, such as our suburbs reveal. The town ended as if cut off with a giant's knife. A little way beyond I turned in my saddle for a parting glance.

Breaux stood between us and the moon now; and, its nearly horizontal beams striking through the windows and portals, it was as if the entire village was ablaze for some silent and ghostly festival, some voiceless triumph.

Lieutenant Paradis answered the question in my eyes, speaking for the first time in hours.

"It is the town which was saved by miracle," he said. "By the Colonel Eugen Etienne Ste. Marie de Voulx, late of Napoleon's Young Guard, who rose from the dead to preserve the home of his ancestors."

"A miracle?" I responded vaguely. "Ah—yes, like the Angel of Mons and the Christ seen at night upon the battle-fields easing the souls of dying men!"

For some moments Paradis did not speak; and when he did it was not to refer at once and directly to the miracle of Breaux.

"Concerning these things who knows? Not I! I neither believe nor disbelieve. But always, in world crises, these reports are current. It was so when Greeks fought Trojans. And do you recall that when the Turks took Constantinople the wretched people sought refuge in their cathedral, and as the enemy burst in upon them there and began slaughtering young and old, women and children, the priest, who was in the midst of celebrating mass, bore the sacred elements out through a little door in the apse; and the Turks sealed it up, and so it has remained unto this day in the mosque of Ste. Sophia.

"And it is said that on the day when it shall be reconsecrated as a Christian church the little door shall open and the celebrant come forth and resume the canon of the mass, at the point where it was so bloodily interrupted centuries ago."

We crossed the brook by a ford since its bridge had been blown up, and as we clambered up the bank Paradis continued:

"So, in our own war men say that on a certain night when a gap was torn in our lines, a ragged hole open to Calais, and there were no more troops to throw in, there rose silently from the mists strange men in great bearskin shakos, wearing obsolete bandoliers, and carrying clumsy muskets.

"'At their head, upon a gray horse, rode a gray figure, bowed forward in thought, one hand thrust into his breast, a cocked hat upon his head. It was, to be sure, the Little Corporal, risen from the dead to hurl his grizzled Old Guard upon the desecrators of French soil.

"At any rate, the gap was stopped, nobody knows how or by whom. A division rushed up by lorries found no one, friend or foe, when they arrived at dawn—only the waves of dead men as the tide had ebbed and flowed. Myself? I believe that when mankind is in travail, an anguish too great to be borne alone, it flies to Deity as a child to its mother's skirt, or as chicks to the maternal wing.

"It is inconceivable, intolerable, that God should look down a mere spectator upon their agony as from a celestial grandstand. And so there are portents in the sky, and gods fighting with men, and legends passing from one to another the children of hope and fear."

"Merely legends?" I asked.

Lieutenant Paradis shrugged.

"Who can say? Let me repeat what a great philosopher has written: That with so many hundreds of thousands of lusty young souls cut off instantly and in the full sway of the most violent passions, it is inconceivable that they should at once go to their abiding place; rather must the earth be girdled by a stratum of spiritual unrest, reacting upon our minds in many singular and mysterious ways."

Under the waning stars, and to the solemn accompaniment of the slow-coming dawn, Paradis related to me the miracle whereby De Voulx, though long asleep in his coffin, returned to save the village of his forebears from the slime of the green-gray German horde.

Three men sat about a little table in the sacristy of the old parish church of St. Leu in Breaux. It was early fall, the third year of the great war; and save for these three there remained no living inhabitant in the town. All had departed, bearing with them such valuables as could be gathered up before the German onrush.

For days the unfortunates from scores of similar villages to the eastward had streamed through Breaux, pausing long enough to rest for an hour and to whisper of the unspeakable woe that had overtaken their homes.

Breaux was an ancient town, but one never looming large in the pages of history. Its one seignorial family, that of De Voulx, had produced no scions of the first rank. They had been provincial lordlings, stepping high upon the cobbled streets of the town dominated by their rambling château, but seeming ill at ease whenever they, on rare occasions, journeyed to Versailles.

By and large they had dealt wisely and kindly with their tenants and retainers. One of them had saved the town from sack during the Spanish wars. Tradition had it that the very earliest of the name had beaten back the marauding bands of Teutons.

The last of his line, Colonel Eugen, one-time commander of Napoleon's Young Guard, seems to have been a pompous, fussy little man, of no particular ability but unquestioned courage. He was considered to bear some slight resemblance to the great commander himself: a likeness he did nothing to minimize by his dress, carriage, and demeanor.

He died in Breaux upon returning from the siege of Acre; and, in his last delirium, had risen in his bed and remarked in his most characteristic manner that if ever Breaux were in danger of capture they had but to open his sepulchre and he would come forth and save the town, even as the De Voulx overlords had ever preserved it inviolate.

Whereupon he fittingly died without spoiling his utterance by an anticlimax; and he lay in a leaden coffin in the vault of St. Leu, beneath the feet of the three solitary citizens of Breaux, who were, in fact, discussing him in the sacristy lighted by a pair of great altar candles.

The curé, Father Jean, had remained to secure the jeweled ciborium containing the consecrated host and the parish register, together with such portable relics as he could save. Across from him sat M. Pelletier, a heavy, red-faced man with beard cut square like a spade, and who, as mayor, had busied himself securing certain of the town records.

The third was of peasant type, with a face cross-hatched with innumerable lines indicative of honesty, shrewdness, and obstinacy in equal proportions.

It was he, the grandson of the orderly of the late Colonel de Voulx, who was addressing the other two, the big men of his little world, whom he sought to coerce with his dogged persistence, accompanied by many shrugs, outthrustings of palms, elevating of brows, and clicks of his tongue against the roof of his toothless mouth.

"It is I who tell you, *mon père,* and you, *monsieur le maire,* I who had the story from my grandsire (whom the blessed saints have in their keeping!), and after him, from my father, also a pious Christian. It has been kept in our family as a sacred trust. Pardieu! For just such an occasion as this, messieurs! For, as he lay dying, his soul already straining at the halter, if you will permit the saying, mon père—"

The aged priest raised his hand. Both he and Pelletier, and indeed every one in Breaux, down to the gamins who played about its one street, knew the story by heart.

"The minds of dying men wander in blind paths, my son! If I were to consider all the pitiful last words to which I have listened here in our parish during the last half century—"

The old man interrupted him impatiently.

"Of a surety! My own blessed father called for his pipe—and he had not used tobacco for twenty years. But one is to distinguish between the babbling of a simple peasant and the inspired prophecy of a great one like a De Voulx, whose ancestors have preserved this our town since history was written!"

Father Jean smiled faintly.

"Pierre, my son, it is not meet that we should violate the grave of one given sepulture according to the rites of the church, merely to disprove an old wives' tale."

Pierre fairly sputtered with indignation; and ere he could find his tongue again the third man, the Mayor Pelletier, opened his firm lips for the first time.

"You know, begging your pardon, monsieur le curé, for whom I have only love and respect, and you, friend Pierre, that I am an atheist. Religion harms no one—and doubtless consoles old women. As for me, when I die you may serve me as you will. I am dead for all time—as dead as my faithful old dog Bidou, and less worthy of immortality!

"No more than I believe in Father Jean's rites do I credit good Pierre's miracles. We do wrong to waste time here. We are custodians of town property. At any moment the Huns may clatter down our street. I haven't the least superstitious fear against opening our eminent towns-man's leaden casket— but I see no sense in taking time to do so!"

Pierre waved his knotted hands frantically.

"Name of a name of God! You don't see, and you don't believe, and you this and that! How could Colonel de Voulx, with his last breath, bid us commit a sacrilege upon himself, and he a good Christian, shriven by the pious Père Hyacinthe, your predecessor, my father? And you, monsieur, why waste in empty words time enough to open his coffin twice over? See!"

Pierre drew from his blouse a keen adz and brandished it.

"It is made sharp for biting into the lead! If indeed Colonel de Voulx spoke idly; no harm can come of it; do not the thrice accursed boches open every sealed coffin of the blessed dead, seeking for jewels? And think you they will spare this one?"

Father Jean glanced half-humorously, half-sadly into the steady eyes of Pelletier and shrugged helplessly. The latter spoke.

"There are no miracles. There never were! But there are always facts; and one of them is this: the German cavalry will snap us up like trout while we argue here, and with us the records, and that jeweled gewgaw you value so highly, Père Jean!"

Pierre rallied for his final argument. He controlled his excitement with a violent effort.

"Listen, then! It is true that you have heard my story many times. It is true that every breeched lad in Breaux knows it by heart. And I, Pierre, tell you they also believe it And when they shall return, some day, and, fumbling amid the ashes and broken glass, shall seek to trace that place where once burned their hearth fires, think you they shall not say: 'If only Père Jean, and that donkey of a Pelletier, and old doddering Pierre had but summoned forth Colonel de Voulx from his tomb, Breaux would have been saved!'"

He leaned back, the breath whistling between his grinning lips, his shrewd, puckered old eyes, bright and black still, triumphantly seeking theirs.

Abruptly the priest rose, taking one of the candles in his hand.

"Come!" he said. "The thing shall be done, that my poor people may know that our thought was for them and their firesides, even if that thought be impious, which the good God forbid!"

Pelletier said no more, but, accompanied by Pierre hearing his adz, followed the priest through a little door, down a narrow stone stair, into the crypt of the old church beneath the altar.

Here slept the few notables of Breaux: a long line of De Voulxs, the departed incumbents of the parish of St. Leu, a locally famous *avocat,* half a dozen others deemed worthy of internment here. Conspicuous among them, the great casket of Colonel Eugen Etienne Ste. Marie de Voulx, the soft lead deep bitten by a die of the Napoleonic bee, many times repeated, and one terse line beneath his name: "Of the Young Guard."

The place was cool and dry, and the home of many shadows, pursued hither and thither as the great candle held by Père Jean moved in his nervous grasp.

Wasting no time, for there was none to be wasted, old Pierre swung his keen adz surely, and it sank into the lead casing. Matching each succeeding cut with the skill of a forester, he proceeded entirely around the casket, and in a surprisingly short time motioned to the others that he had finished the first part of his task—whereupon they jointly and with difficulty eased the heavy lid to the floor. Underneath was discovered a perfectly sound oak coffin.

From this, too, but without removing it from the outer casing, Pierre pried off the top—and behold! Before them lay the late colonel of the Young Guard in a surprisingly good state of preservation, although his face was swollen and nearly black. Still, one might trace a hint of the likeness to the great Napoleon, so sedulously cultivated by the old soldier.

He was dressed in full uniform: blue, swallow-tailed coat with broad revers and tarnished brass buttons and epaulets, gloved hands crossed over his sheathed sword, cocked hat by his side, long-spurred cavalry boots upon his bandy legs. A row of medals was strung across his breast.

The three men stared at him in breathless silence. The curé and Pierre crossed themselves; Pelletier gravely touched his forehead in respectful salute. Whatever their various ideas, in one particular they felt alike. Here before them, visible to the naked eye, lay one of the officers of a famous and unbeaten regiment of the great military genius of their beloved country.

So absorbed were they, Pierre with his hopes, Father Jean with his apprehensions, the mayor with his respectful interest, that they failed to hear upon the cobbled street above the faint clatter of the advance force of Uhlans, riding cautiously into Breaux; failed to hear them as, having dismounted, they followed the tiny candle gleam down into the crypt, and were shocked into a numb terror only when the captain of Uhlans, in excellent French, addressed them mockingly as he advanced through the stairway door.

"So! It is that Frenchmen rifle the graves of their own dead, that they may afterward cry out upon the German ghouls! The good pastor, too!"

His teeth showing in a wolfish smile, his monocle fixed, one hand at the automatic in his belt, the officer advanced within the circle of light, followed by several of his staff, and, craning forward, gazed upon that which had so riveted the attention of the three Frenchmen.

"You are wrong, my son," Père Jean replied with dignity. "There are no valuables in these, our poor tombs, save the honored dead they hold!"

The Uhlan stared insolently upon him.

"Perhaps you will then explain the trouble to which you put yourself in opening this casket?"

"I will do so," Père Jean responded with quiet nobility of demeanor. "Tradition in our little town has it that this son of the Church and of France, and one-time officer of the great Napoleon, would, if brought from his sepulcher, save Breaux in its day of need from impious hands, even, as his ancestors did in ancient times."

The officer laughed harshly.

"And your theology swallows these children's' fairy tales, worthy pastor?"

The mayor, Pelletier, answered him.

"Neither he nor I, but this descendant of De Voulx's orderly. To humor a good and faithful citizen we assented. That is all."

The German rubbed his hands gleefully.

"Well, well! And why not? Let us see if there be any truth in it. Come forth, my Gallic Lazarus! Save thy ugly hamlet of Breaux! Many prettier towns have gone up in smoke this past week."

Then began a scene such as no other war but this could match. The Uhlan's Teutonic sense of humor rose to the surface. After an orgy of blood and rapine the surfeited beast chose to be good-naturedly facetious for the moment.

Obeying a curt command, two big cavalrymen laid hold upon De Voulx, and twitched him from the wooden bed where he had slept so long. They held him erect, clapped his cocked hat upon his head; then, their captain catching the travesty of the emperor in the bloated features, he bent one arm—the brittle bone cracking sharply —and thrust the hand within his breast. His sword was buckled on; the officer saluted him mockingly, hailed him as *"kamerad!"* and, entering into the spirit of the occasion, the gruesome figure was pushed and pulled about, complimented upon his winning so many medals as colonel of so distinguished a regiment, and then kicked and buffeted for failing to reply to the queries or to return the salutes.

It was to be noted that throughout the incredible buffoonery the little figure of De Voulx seemed to maintain an unshaken dignity which no insult could degrade. Dead this century and more, the deathless panoply of birth and character never for an instant failed to make cheap and bestial his living mockers!

Meanwhile Père Jean had been twitching at the sleeves of his two companions, and step by stealthy step, moving backward toward the little door, they slipped up the crooked stairs, and through the sacristy, and out into the black night, sick at heart, and with the uncouth shouts of the Uhlans sounding fainter and fainter in their horrified ears.

This was the story that Lieutenant Paradis told me as we rode away from Breaux; and at this point we reined up for a final back-flung look at it.

The moon was riding high in the heavens now; and beneath its rays the little town seemed a fragile toy, fabricated of beaten silver.

"Yet you have not told me," I complained, "what really saved Breaux?"

"Colonel Eugen Etienne Ste. Marie de

Voulx saved it!" replied my guide.

"But—but how—"

He turned and looked me in the eye.

"A miracle, so they are already saying. So say I—for of such stuff are dreams and miracles made! De Voulx, as has been learned by painstaking investigation of contemporary records, died of the black death, the germs of which he brought home with him from Asia. His orderly, who had served long in the East, recognized the symptoms, and warned the physician who attended De Voulx and the priest who shrived him.

"He was able to prevent them from contracting the plague, and it was by his advice that the body was hermetically sealed in lead and the secret kept from the village.

"When the casket was opened the germs were still virulent, still lying in wait. None of the three Frenchmen touched the body; but the Uhlans, who did, contracted the black death by contagion; and when the German Medical Staff learned the truth, and had cremated their numerous victims, they drew a circle about Breaux, forbidding, under severest penalties, any crossing of the dead line. And as this order was not countermanded, De Voulx kept his promise, and Breaux stands inviolate today!"

s

WEARINESS OF WAR
translated by Poul Anderson

In 1064 A.D., King Harald Hardrede of Norway and King Svein Ulfsson of Denmark met to see if their long struggle for the Danish crown could be settled. Both brought great armies None knew if the truce would end in peace being made, or in a battle which would resume the destructive war. It was the former which happened. Harald abdicated his claims —perhaps, in part, because of this verse, whose composer is unknown but which was heard in both camps.

Many folk their mouth use at meeting, in each army;
Haughtiness breeds hatred in hosts of Dane and Norseman.
None will wish to nod his neck unto another;
And the kings are angry, egging on the trouble.

Warlike royal wills give warning of ill tidings;
Men who'd act as makepeace measure into scalepans.
Fearlessly and freely folks should say their wishes:
Evil is this hour if enemies go homeward.

— *From the Original Norse*

MUSTERED OUT

by H. Bedford-Jones

I.

SERGEANT ALOYSIUS LARRIGAN inspected the houses ahead—and hesitated. Before he found name and wealth and fame in California film fields, Aloysius Larrigan had been born and raised in New York. Hence, he knew the metropolis. He knew that behind him on Fifth Avenue were the false jewels; and that here ahead of him was the real thing. Here, half a block off Fifth Avenue, was the house of Jim Bleeker, bunky of Sergeant Aloysius Larrigan.

But the sergeant hesitated, gripping the package a little harder in his hand. Then, mustering up courage, he approached the doorway and rang.

The outer door opened, and a stolid butler gazed at him.

"I—I've come to see Mrs. Bleeker," said the sergeant nervously.

"It's quite early, sir," answered the butler, somehow stifling his first instinct of blank rejection. "I hardly think, sir, that Mrs. Bleeker is—"

"Look here!" snapped Larrigan, flushing. "I've just landed from France. My name is Larrigan. Jim Bleeker was my bunky—"

"If you'll step inside, sir," hastened the butler, changing countenance abruptly. "I'm sure that Mrs. Bleeker will wish to see you."

Aloysius Larrigan sat himself down between a mounted piece of fifteenth-century armor and a dull-gleaming Rubens. All this,

he knew, was the real thing. He had guessed that Jim Bleeker was an aristocrat; but—well, all this was a bit crushing. Before he quite realized it, Mrs. Bleeker, in her widow's black, was upon him and holding his hand.

"Jim wrote me so much of you!" she was saying quietly. "I'm very, very glad to know you, Mr. Larrigan. I received your letter from Bordeaux, telling me of the final days—I cannot tell you how I appreciated the sweetness of that letter."

Aloysius Larrigan blushed fearfully. He stammered something and fell silent.

"You must stay for luncheon—but how long shall you have in the city?"

"No time at all, ma'am," returned Aloysius. He displayed his package. "We're going through town to be mustered out, and then I have to hit for California. I've got important business there, you see—a lady I've not seen for a year, and also business. I just got permission to run up here with this."

He thrust forward the package, all his carefully rehearsed speech and actions gone to the winds.

"You see, Mrs. Bleeker, Jim made me promise to bring these things here myself. They are just the little things; well, you'll see. He thought maybe you would like to have them. I have to be back in half an hour."

Mrs. Bleeker took the package, bit her lip very hard, and then threw back her shoulders and looked Aloysius Larrigan in the eye. He realized that hers was a peculiar bravery—the courage of deep things, of rare blood, of a sensitive, inner grief that was tearing her very soul before his eyes.

He felt tongue-tied and extremely uncomfortable, far different from the easy assurance habitual to him.

"Wait just a minute, please," she said, and left him.

He waited, gazing at the velvet hangings, the deep softness of everything around him, feeling himself frightfully out of place. The knowledge that he was an American soldier, and as good as any man alive, did not help him.

Then he smiled grimly at the thought of how little the studio directors knew about the furnishings of an aristocratic home! All the studio men knew about was the flashy emptiness of the newly rich and the professional decorator.

Mrs. Bleeker was before him again.

"I'm more sorry than I can tell you, Mr. Larrigan, that you have to run away so quickly. When you get settled in California, will you please send me your address? One does not know what unforeseen emergencies may arise."

Aloysius promised.

Mrs. Bleeker produced a little morocco case.

"I would like you to have this," she said quietly, very steadily. "I brought it to Jim once; he always wore it. There's no other man I could give it to, Mr. Larrigan—but if you would accept it, you would give me great pleasure."

Larrigan gazed at the scarf-pin, an abalone blister mounted in gold.

It came to him that this was a very precious tribute, a tribute from the woman's heart, meaning more than words could say.

Jim Bleeker had other friends, of course—wealthy friends, college friends, all that a man of his standing would have. But he, Larrigan, had been Bleeker's bunky in France, had watched Jim Bleeker die,

had been more to Jim Bleeker than any man alive.

And this was a tribute, the most precious heart-gift he would ever know.

"I—I'd be very glad," he said, stumbling over the words, cursing himself because he could not express the thing that was in him, the feeling that gripped him in that moment of revelation. " I'll be wearing cits in a couple of days. I—I sure appreciate this very deeply, Mrs. Bleeker."

"There's no other man I could give it to," she said again very softly.

This was all. He was thankful that his face seemed quite unknown to her.

II.

REEVER KEENE was home again—Reever Keene, the great; Reever Keene, the man who had snapped asunder his fabulous contract a year ago in order to enlist as a private; Reever Keene, whose pictures were the greatest drawing-card in every theater of the country!

He had sent no notice of his coming, but the studio knew of it and was ready. As the Overland drew in, sixteen automobiles were waiting, and these automobiles were the cream of motion-picture motordom. All Los Angeles knew that the aluminum car with purple trimmings was Reever Keene's; that his director owned the pea-green Twin Duplex striped with canary; that his leading lady had paid eleven thousand dollars for the screaming blue-and-gold roadster, and so forth.

But a terrible thing happened at the station—a thing which, fortunately, was kept out of the papers by influence. As one of the lesser lights of filmdom grasped the hand of the great Keene he gave a raucous laugh.

"For Heaven's sake, Reever! Where'd you get the abalone sparkler? Wow! Look at it, folks; pipe the—"

Reever Keene's fist smashed him square

in the mouth.

The press-agent wanted to use the story, of course; but Reever Keene took the press-agent by the nape of the neck and kicked him hard. Influence did the rest—advertising influence. The story was killed.

"I can't understand what's got into Keene," said the director, riding back to the studios with the president of the company. "And look at the face of him! We'll have to paint him an inch deep to disguise that brick-red tan and make him come out like the old screen idol! Fortunately his profile is all right still."

The president grunted. He was a wise man, or he would not have been in his present position.

"Keene takes up his contract where he left off," he returned. "That's all I'm worrying about! Let Keene run the whole damned place if he wants. If you'd gone into the army, my son, instead of sitting on your draft-proof job, the Lord knows you'd be a damned sight better director!"

The director looked at his leather puttees and said no more.

"Where's Lola?" asked Reever Keene, driving to the studios in his own car once more, his leading lady and chief supports gathered around him. "Thought she might be around?"

"She'll turn up at the studios," was the response. "Working on a location near Santa Monica to-day. They'll be back for dinner. We're having a real celebration, old boy!"

"Lola's awful proud of that sparkler you gave her," simpered the leading lady. "Heaven knows it was a beaut!"

Reever Keene shivered a little. He was not sure why he shivered; nor was he sure why the warmth and cordiality of his reception at the studio left him cold and hard.

He had not thought it would be this way. He had looked forward to falling right back into the old rut, among the old friends, and he had anticipated swaggering like a good one—all kinds of publicity in it! But, some-

how, he found himself landing with a horrible jar. He was damned glad, he reflected, to be done with the bare simplicity of the soldier's life, with the saluting and uniforms and general prophylaxis; and yet—

Homesickness had glamoured all the old life, but now that he was back in it, the glamour seemed unaccountably like tinsel. The directors, for instance, even his own director and old crony, with their puttees and riding-breeches, general superiority, and bustling business—well, maybe it was the puttees that grated. Keene had saluted leather puttees until he was heartily sick of it; but that was another story altogether.

He wondered inwardly if he had ever been like the men now around him—good fellows, of course, but abominably artificial. These fancy tailored garments, these amber cigarette-holders and sodden cigarettes without a bite, these flashing jewels, and, worst of all, this breezy talk that moved in perpetual high lights—

What the devil was the matter with him, anyhow? Maybe it was because Lola had not come yet.

Well, Lola came, with a stifled shriek and a tiny Peke, and flung herself at him. Good Heaven! Keene had been away from studio paint so long that her appearance frightened him. And had he really picked that engagement ring, that diamond like a walnut? Yes. He remembered hideously the glee with which he had nonchalantly signed that five-thousand-dollar check, and the delight with which he had seen the check pictured in the papers.

"You've been away a hell of a long time, old sport!" and his director clapped him on the back. "But now you're back to the life—the only life, boy!"

"Right you are!" cried Reever Keene, bracing his shoulders. "Let's have a drink!"

III.

THE fact that Reever Keene, home from the army, insisted on working with an abalone blister in his scarf, was an idiosyncrasy good for three-day comment in the press. And the press-agent sighed for the lost opportunities that were closed to him simply by the stubborn deviltry of Keene. Nobody knew what had got into the screen star. He had changed. The abalone pin, for instance, was a sore subject with him.

He never wore any of his former loud attire, and had discarded all his jewelry, which formerly flashed in the cabaret lights of Los. He even wore that abalone pin stuck in the front of his dress shirt, for a society picture; and when the director expostulated, Keene bluntly told him to go to hell—which was no way to treat a famous director.

Then somebody in the scenario department—that is, somebody in the orange-hued flivver class—had an inspiration. He wrote a story about that abalone pin. Keene, according to his contract, had the say about what film stories were to be accepted for his use; and he went into closed session with the scenario department, and there was evolved a scenario which made the director gasp. But the scenario went through; it had to go through, with Keene backing it.

"What's come over him?" said the president to the director. "He used to get stories written by his friends, turn down everything from the department, make us pay five hundred dollars for the stories—and then split with his friends. That's the old stall; what's this new wrinkle?"

"Damned if I know," groaned the director. "It's got society stuff in it, and only last week he said he'd never touch society stuff again. And there ain't any punch, not a bit; it's one o' them bleedin'-heart things, and it ain't got—"

"It's got Reever Keene in it," snapped the president, "and that's enough to put it across anywhere. Do you get me?"

The director departed, weeping.

Worse was to come, however. Reever Keene sold his gorgeous car, and showed up with a plain green-black affair—not even a victoria top to it! Lola refused to ride in the wretched thing, and Keene swore; and the end of this matter was a fine quarrel which the press-agent featured without the least opposition.

And then came the first of the month and the new story.

The story was a society story, right enough. For three days. the company was on location at the Billingkamp residence—you remember, of course, Billingkamp's Canned Soups—and the exteriors were gorgeous affairs.

The trouble was that Reever Keene had been reading some highbrow stuff, and insisted on wearing his silk hat without any of the rakish tilt which is so fetching to the screen folk; and he insisted on throwing out the beautiful white roadster with red upholstery which the director had provided, and used his own sobersides of a car—and other things like that.

In between times the quarrel with Lola was deftly adjusted, the date was set for the wedding, and duly featured by the press-agent.

After that the company came back to the studio, the remainder of the picture being interior sets—and then the trouble really began. Reever Keene had instructed the property-men about the drawing-room set; the director had done likewise. Props, seeing himself between the devil and the deep sea, provided both sets, and left the principals to scrap it out. Which was wise.

Reever Keene took one look at the director's set, and ordered it off the stage. The director was inspecting Reever Keene's set, and Keene met him in the act.

"My Lord!" said the director. "I don't know anything about motion-pictures; I'm just a poor simp who's spent all his life in the game. Look—for the love of Heaven, look!"

"Get down to cases, you," growled

Keene. "Never mind the high-art stuff, now. Just be sensible and tell me what's wrong!

The director swallowed hard and waved his hand at the set. It had been assembled with a good deal of trouble. There was an imitation Rubens; there was a real set of imitation armor that looked from the camera considerably like fifteenth century. The rest was deeply rich velvet and hangings.

"As man to, man," said the director, "I'll put it to you, Keene. How do you think this dark stuff is going to take? All to the bad! It can't be done, man! You've got to have contrast. Now, can't you realize that this picture has got to show a society home? A real swell home. None of your junk, but stuff that spells money. They eat it, the people do!"

"If you knew the money we'd spent on this set," began the property-man plaintively. But Keene interrupted.

"What would you suggest, then?"

"Just what I ordered set up!" returned the director. "Statuary. A nude on the wall. Some o' this here lacquered Chinese furniture—we got Bent's whole store to draw on, and you know the best people ain't buying anything else but lacquered, which shows up like real money. Then that high-colored rug, and so forth. It'll be toned down fine in the film, Keene."

"Maybe so, maybe so," said Reever Keene.

"And then these here costumes. I been reading over your directions." The director tapped the papers in his hand, with growing boldness. "I notice you got white neckties with evening clothes; you know's well as I do they don't make contrast. Then you got the society dames ordered to cut out the low-neck stuff— What the hell gives you such a notion of society, anyhow? Don't you know they run around half naked? And no jewels. My Lord! If I was to run out such a picture the society papers would give me plain hell!"

"If you had ever read them at all," said Keene dryly, "you'd see they do that, any-

how."

A few minutes later the president sent for Reever Keene.

"Take a cigar, Reever," he said genially. "Now, we'll have to cut out this fussing between you and Bob, see? He's a damned good director; I'm not paying him twenty-five thousand dollars for nothing."

"Let him mind his own business, then," said Keene, a little white around the jaw. "I've got a good picture, and he's not to spoil it."

"Sure not," agreed the president affably. "But see here, now. He's contracted to put out your pictures, ain't he? All right. And he's got the say."

"In other words," said Keene slowly, "I'll have to stand for his directing in this picture, eh?"

"Sure. His contract is up in three months. If you want, I'll put you in charge of your own directing after that."

"Then stop work on this picture until he's out of it."

"Can't do it; Reeve—we're a week behind on the next release, and it's got to be rushed. That's why I'm putting it up to. you straight to work in with him now, and we'll work in with you later, see?"

Reever Keene nodded curtly.

"I'll try," he said. " But—I won't promise."

"The hell he won't!" laughed the president later, when he was recounting the conversation to the director. "Like the rest of them—throwing a big bluff so he can strut around the Screen Club and tell how he handed it to me! Well, that's one way of managing these here stars, believe me! This guy's getting more money than the President of these here United States. Is he going to chuck his job?"

"Not him," said the director confidently. "Besides, he's under contract to us, and if he broke the contract—"

"He'd be finished, absolutely!" declared the president. "He's no fool!"

The president was playing both ends against the middle, which is a wise game—sometimes.

IV

REEVER KEENE had been too long in the movie game, and was taking too much money out of it, to have any artistic temperament—that is, when he was on the lot. Movie folk have to keep their temperament out of business.

Still, when Keene saw what his director was doing to the abalone-pin story, and realized that he could not prevent its being done, he boiled with inward and suffocating rage. After three days he was so stifled with fury that he was ready for an outbreak.

He had put Jim Bleeker into that story, and when he saw how the director was handling Jim Bleeker, despite all protests, his fury became white-hot.

On the fourth morning he drove to the studio without opening his private mail. Once in his dressing-room, he glanced over the letters while he was making up; but, for him, that mail resolved itself into just one letter. He propped it in front of him and read it over again:

DEAR MR. LARRIGAN:

Within a few days I am leaving for Europe to take part in reconstruction work. I could not leave without writing you to express anew my very deep appreciation of all your thoughtful kindness to Jim. I know from his letters what your friendship meant to him, and I have learned from other comrades of your great devotion toward the end. Thanks seem but a little thing to offer; yet, believe me, my thanks and appreciation come from the soul.

I know nothing of your financial position or status in civil life, and I do not wish you to think that I am insulting so deep and pure a thing as your friendship with Jim.

However, I am enclosing a card from my attorneys, who are fully instructed to honor it in any way. If you should ever be in need of advice or aid, it will give me great happiness to know that you will make use of this card as though it had been handed you by your friend,

JIM BLEEKER

"Bless her sweet heart," muttered Reever Keene, tearing the card across and tossing it into his waste-basket. He smiled a little, as he thought of his twenty thousand dollars in cash, buried where no one would ever detect it; and of the Kansas oil stock, held by a friend, which brought in itself a comfortable income. Everybody in the business thought that Reever Keene blew all he had, like every one else; but Aloysius Larrigan knew better.

He read the letter again, fingering the blister pearl in his scarf, and forgetting his make-up completely. Once more he was standing in that house, half a block off Fifth Avenue; once more he was living through that moment when Mrs. Bleeker had handed him that scarf-pin, with her quiet, steady voice, and her brave, stricken eyes.

The thought of it made him sit very quiet, staring at the letter. In all his life he had never experienced a moment such as that; no not even when Jim had died, beside him! It had been a moment of the spirit; a moment of absolute integrity, of purity, of unsullied sweetness.

That moment had assoiled many long-soiled years. It had grown upon Larrigan ever since, had grown larger, had grown to mean much more than he had dared admit. Now this letter had come to bring it before him again in all its larger aspects.

He made up mechanically and went out on the lot; for an hour he acted mechanically, obeying the director without protest, without thought. Then, during a change in the set, he went to his dressing-room.

Lola was there, standing at his table,

reading the letter. Something went cold inside Reever Keene, and he stepped forward as if to take it from her. But she turned upon him, a flood of passion in her face.

"Well," she observed with a sneer, "I guess I got your number now, Mr. Larrigan! Lady signs herself Jim Bleeker, does she? Maybe we're goin' to hear a lot of things that happened—"

"You're making a mistake, Lola," said Reever Keene.

"Mistake, am I?" She shook the letter at him with sudden passion. "Maybe I don't know a chicken's writing when I see it, huh? Well, if you think I'm a fool, this ends it! You can go along with your Jim Bleeker all you damn please! When you get ready to talk turkey to me—"

Lola drew off the walnut diamond and laid it, very carefully, on the corner of the dressing-table under Reever Keene's nose. The whole action was very statuesque and very dramatic; at least, was so intended.

An instant later Lola uttered a despairing shriek. Reever Keene had seized the walnut diamond and had hurled it through the open window—hurled it with a swing that sent it glittering through the air to Heaven only knew where!

"Ends it, eh?" snapped Keene. "Then I'm blamed glad of it! So-long!"

Lola fainted as he vanished, and immediately the dressing-corridor was filled with figures answering her final dramatic shriek. Reever Keene went outside and climbed into his plain green-black car and drove down the street to his lodgings.

Once there, he wiped the paint from his face, with a curse, and began to pack up his things. He paid his landlady. He burned Mrs. Bleeker's letter over the oil- stove. Then he threw his stuff together in the rear of the car, and drove down to the bank, where he drew what money he kept deposited there.

This finished, he went to the central gasoline station and turned over his car to be filled with gas and oil, and to be loaded with sundry extra five-gallon cases of the same.

While he was watching these affairs being brought to conclusion he heard a wild hail and saw the president's car stopping at the curb, and the president himself descending, red and perspiring of face.

"Hey, Keene!" demanded the magnate heatedly. " What the devil's struck you? They said you blew out o' the studio like a wild man and quit work! Get on back there—"

"Go to hell!" snapped the star. "I've quit being Keene. I'm Aloysius Larrigan, see? And don't get fresh, you!"

"What! Where you going?"

"I'm going to Kansas, where I got business," retorted Larrigan. "Hurry up with them two cans of oil, over there! And blow up the extry tires while you're about it, partner."

The president seized him by the arm.

"Look here, you!" he exploded violently. "Are you quittin' on the job—quittin'?"

"I am," said Larrigan coldly.

"By Heaven, if you bust this contract I'll see to it that you never get another job in front of any damned camera in the world!" raved the other. "I'll—"

"You," said Larrigan, "and your contract, and your seventeen companies, and your directors, and your money, and your whole damn camera battery, and your entire double-dashed motion-picture industry—go to hell! I'm done! Mustered out!"

He shoved a greenback at the gasoline, dealer, climbed into his car, and went. The president gazed after him with eyes of dulled, glazed despair.

"Bein' in the army—that's what done it for him—ruined the best star in the whole damned works!" he murmured dismally. "Damn the Kaiser!"

❧

THE DEVIL'S HEIRLOOM

by **Anthony M. Rud**

I.

"CUBE" LACEY found Sherrod Guest, his partner and associate in the Search-light Agency, profoundly excited. Guest, a chunky little man with the cheeks and complexion of a cherub, was pacing back and forth the width of the single, partitioned office, brushing away moisture of anxiety from his high forehead — a forehead which did not find its border of tired little blond hairs till it reached the exact center of its owner's crown.

"Thank heavens, you've come!" exploded Guest, wheeling to confront Lacey as the latter strode into the room.

"Landlord been around?" demanded Lacey, grinning wryly as he pried out a thin roll of twenties from his trousers pocket. Along with the bills came an empty sack of tobacco and two pennies, one of which fell to the floor. "A hundred was the best I could charge Lehmann, though it was worth at least an additional fifty. Otherwise he'd have held me up a week or two. This'll give us a ten-spot on which to eat, beside paying the rent. Any clients come in since I left?"

Guest's mouth had opened soundlessly half a dozen times in the attempt to speak. Now he gestured aside the money both of them so sorely needed, granting it only a tolerant nod, and pushed Lacey down into a squeaky swivel.

"Listen to your bright little sunbeam!" he adjured. "Our big client's sent for us, for you, I mean! I didn't know whether you'd get back today or next week, so I tried to sell him myself, but no, that wouldn't do. Kuban Lacey was the only detective he'd have anything to do with. So you beat it down to the sidearm, fill up on beans and excelsior, and hop a cab for — hm, let me see — 3217 —"

"A cab?" interjected Cube incredulously. "Not this starved sleuth! You and I can't afford flourishes of that kind — yet. No, I'll save the extra three simoleons for ham-ends while we're waiting for somebody to kill or kidnap somebody else in a mysterious manner, and demand our services." He opened the tobacco sack, whisked a paper out of its cover, and poured a dusty pinch of yellow flakes, evening it with practised forefinger. "But who is this personage for whom you'd brave the lean and hungry wolf?"

"It's that cranky North Shore millionaire, that hermit chap. If's he's got any kind of a case for us —" stuttered Guest, convincingly. He often had difficulty starting a sentence when sincerely excited, though little else than an epochal event could bring him to this state.

"His name?" interrupted Lacey, an odd, almost belligerent expression appearing in the set of clean, square jaw and narrowing of eyes.

"I didn't say. Name's Noah Lacey — same as yours. He's the old codger who owns that estate up north with all the grounds landscaped in brick. Made his fortune out of manufacturing brick; or, at least, inherited the business and the first instalment of the money from his father. The Laceys have been doing that since about the time Chicago was a frontier post, I guess. Sure he isn't any relative of yours?"

The last was asked in jesting manner, for no one knew better than Sherrod Guest how poverty-stricken both his partner and himself had been since deserting the comfortable reportorial jobs they had held. Oddly, the question brought a wry grimace to Lacey's lips, however.

"I'm afraid you're due for a disappointment here, old man," he answered, watching sympathetically as the glow of buoyancy faded from Guest's expression. "Noah happens to be my uncle — the only other surviving Lacey of our branch in the world. I never have met him. He and my father had a terrific quarrel years and years ago. Think it concerned repairs on a small building they owned jointly, or some such trivial matter. Dad had been disowned, anyway, and perhaps was a little touchy concerning relations with Noah, who was grandfather's favorite. Anyway, Noah and dad never spoke again to each other. Personally I have no hard feelings toward my uncle, but I have not gone near him since coming to Chicago simply because in the past twenty-five years he has become disgustingly rich. He'd be certain that I simply was trying to ingratiate myself. As a matter of fact I don't want his money."

Guest's pacing had slowed. Now he sank dejectedly to the edge of a desk. "Fifty or a hundred bucks of it wouldn't hit us badly just now," he suggested with a feeble

attempt at a smile for this statement which was nothing but the sad truth. After making a considerable name for themselves in crime investigation as reporters — but no money, save their salaries, and one moderate-sized reward which had gone to set them up in business — they had secured only small, unlucrative scraps of work. The first year had been a constant struggle to meet overhead expense and still eat.

"True enough!" agreed Lacey with an exhalation of breath. "I doubt like the mischief that old Noah has any use for a detective or that if he had he would employ us. Still, beggars can't be choosers. I'll call him up and see what he wants." His hand reached for the telephone.

"Not much you won't!" ejaculated Guest, bouncing into action and wrestling the instrument from Lacey's hands. "We may not have the ghost of a chance at any of your esteemed uncle's business, but just the same right now you haven't a thing in the world to do. I have to go to court tomorrow, and I believe Myers has another one of his flea-bite cases for me. Said he'd drop around to talk it over at three o'clock. If you telephoned Uncle Midas you'd be just as apt to tell him to trot around here and hand you his business on a gold plate. Nope! You hustle out, grab a motor bus if you won't take a taxi, and don't waste a minute! Somehow I feel the squirmings of a life-sized poker hunch deep down inside me. I know I'm not much good at five-card whist, but —" He ended his sentence with a comical gesture, half shrug and half peremptory nod.

"Oh, all right," acceded Cube Lacey. He stood up, buttoning overcoat and drawing on his gloves again. He stepped to the door, which had been left one inch ajar. "Hello!" he exclaimed in surprise. The opening door had revealed a person stooping forward, right on the threshold. Lacey saw instantly that the man was a fat, stocky Chinaman, though clad in conventional business garments.

Lacey recoiled involuntarily half a step, while the Oriental glanced up swiftly through slitted eyes, wheeled about and made off with rapid, cat-like tread toward the elevators. Quick conviction came to Lacey that the man had been eavesdropping, though for what imaginable reason only the yellow man himself could say. Lacey, however, had won success in the past by reason of his faculty for grasping and retaining for future use all scraps and odd ends of happenings incapable of instant explanation. Flinging a word of warning over his shoulder to Guest, he made off after the Chinaman. The latter, attempting to crowd his way into an overfilled elevator, was pushed back angrily by the guard. Lacey reached the Chinaman at that moment, and closed insistent fingers upon the stranger's huge but flabby forearm.

"What did you want back there, snooping around my office?"

The yellow stranger's eyelids dropped, but almost instantly he looked up again straight into Lacey's eyes, his glance as innocent and wondering as that of a child. "Me? Oh yes. I lose a dollah. It drop. I t'ink mebbe it loll into office. I see door open —"

"Quite so, and I scared you so badly that you ran away, forgetting all about the dollar, eh?" mused Lacey. The Chinese nodded, wreathing wide mouth in an oily, placating grin. Lacey paid little attention, for he saw the black eyes did not smile. "Better come back and let me help you look for it," he suggested, as Guest joined them, looking wonderingly from one to the other.

The search proved futile, as Lacey had expected. And even the best efforts of the two detectives failed to pry anything from the man. They had to let him go, for try as they might — and did — it was impossible to fathom any sinister reason which would make a Chinaman of intelligence above the average of his coolie kind listen to the purposeless planning of two destitute detectives.

"Now what do you suppose he wanted?"

demanded Guest, when Lacey again was taking his departure.

"Oh, just a mistake I suppose," answered Lacey carelessly. "He probably mistook your handsome face for that of Sherlock Holmes, and thought you were after him for opium smuggling, or something." Nevertheless, Lacey himself was more puzzled by the queer occurrence than his manner indicated. His wonder was in no way abated by the fact that in the corridor below he noticed another Chinaman buying a paper at the newsstand — the identical Chinaman who, five minutes later, sat directly behind Lacey in the motor bus bound northward.

II

IN THE past Cube Lacey had heard of Brick Knob — the unalluring name by which the home of his queer relative was known to newspaper men and the public. Built on a small rise of ground — the highest semblance of a hill within pistol shot of the lake for miles along the shore — it had now, because of high-rise construction, become completely hidden on three sides by a surrounding ring of tall apartment buildings. Only from the front was there access to the small estate, and here a seven-foot wall of brick, surmounted by broken bottles set in the mortar, barred the view of pedestrians.

Cube located a gate in center of this forbidding wall and tried to open it. It was locked. He found a bell at one side, however, and pressed the button. While he waited, he noted the curious fact that this door seemed to be of solid, wrought bronze, as massive as cathedral doors of the Old World. It could have withstood an assault by anything less potent than nitroglycerine.

Five minutes passed. Then a sharp click drew his attention. At the center of the door a panel had been slid aside; in the oblong aperture was framed the stern forbidding face of a man of middle age, lean, clean-shaven, and with grayish skin drawn tightly across protuberant cheek bones. Unmistakable print of a Slavic ancestry lay in both features and expression. Lacey knew instantly that this could not be his father's brother.

"What do you want?" The voice was cold, uncompromising. Lacey guessed irrelevantly that Brick Knob was no favorite resort for hoboes now. Briefly, he explained his errand and tendered business card. One lean claw reached upward to the aperture and seized the pasteboard. A noncommittal grunt was followed by the terse adjuration to wait. Lacey obeyed. As the panel had been left open he took the liberty of watching the figure of this guardian of the gate as he returned toward the house.

Lacey saw a tall, thin man clad in black; a man who stooped slightly as he walked, yet whose figure suggested wiry strength and a resilience of sinew not yet corroded by age. The man probably would prove to be a house servant, though he seemed almost too serious and earnest for such a place. The yard across which he passed was drifted with half an inch of light snow, yet Lacey discerned that the newspapers had told the truth. It was paved entirely with brick. Not a shrub, tree, bench or pergola broke the bare, slanting expanse, which rose like the head of a mushroom to a low summit on which was placed the squat bungalow of brick — that type of architecture which conceals from any casual observer the actual immensity of any building.

The black-clad man moved straight for a flight of stairs giving upward to a broad veranda. Nearing the house Lacey saw him act in a peculiar manner. Suddenly breaking into a run he hastened awkwardly for six or seven steps, and then launched himself in a gigantic stride which covered at least two yards of the brick paving, and which landed him at the foot of the steps. Carried forward by his own impetus he took the latter three at a time, opened a pair of doors, and disappeared, carefully slamming these behind him.

Lacey whistled. Playful skittishness in a stern man of middle age is too unusual a trait not to excite wonder. Also, the rate of speed at which the servant had started to bear his message back to the house had not been suggestive in any manner of haste. The mad caper, and, indeed, the whole layout of house and grounds, were incomprehensible to Lacey, but he foresaw with distinctness that this wealthy relative of his was going to prove to be a curious character indeed.

A matter of what seemed more immediate personal interest drove milder speculation from his mind for the moment, however. Happening to glance across the narrow, motor thoroughfare, he noticed a well-dressed Chinaman sauntering slowly down the sidewalk. Though he could not be certain from that distance, Lacey thought that this was the same man who had followed him from his office building, and on the motor bus. At any rate he was certain that never before had he noticed so many Chinese in Occidental dress upon the streets of Chicago. He followed the casual stroller with his eyes until the latter reached and became lost in a crowd at the corner. Then Lacey swung about in time to see the black-clad man returning. The man now seemed to have lost all his madcap spirit of frolic and hurry. He descended the steps slowly and stalked straight across the intervening space.

"Just a moment, sir," he said, a new hint of deference in his tone. Lacey heard the clank of a chain and the metallic ring of the ponderous lock. Then the massive door swung open three feet — to be closed, locked and chained immediately after Cube had entered. "Mr. Lacey will see you directly, sir."

The two crossed the yard together. Lacey watched for the space where the other's original footprints were spaced by his leap. He noted another curious fact. Three sets of tracks led across the snow, of course. Only one of these showed prints spaced normally. Coming first to answer his ring, and then while returning with the card, the man had leaped across this space! Lacey could be certain because the scuffed spots the man had made in slipping as he landed, were at opposite sides. Twice? Why had the man leaped across the identical spot a second time? It could not be coincidence. Lacey stepped gingerly, falling half a pace behind his guide, who strode across without paying any attention. As Lacey's shoes pressed upon this two-yard interval his hands clenched suddenly in astonishment. Though the sensation was almost imperceptible — something which could not have been noticed unless under close, direct observation — it seemed that the solid brick gave ever so slightly beneath his weight! He was allowed no time for investigation or surmise, though. His guide ushered him into a broad hallway, turning as before to lock the doors with meticulous care.

This hallway appeared to be more of a lounge or den from the luxurious manner in which it was furnished. Sumptuous furniture was placed negligently about, and thick rugs the names of which Lacey could not even guess — realizing only that they were costly importations from the Orient — made footsteps soundless. On a taboret, below open crowded book shelves lining one side of the wall, in a double row, squatted a small bronze Buddha, his mask-like features illumined faintly by a Tiffany-shaded lamp which stood nearby.

On a stand of its own, in a small alcove opposite, reposed a single magnificent vase over two feet in height. In shape it appeared to be designed to hold long-stemmed lilies, though no flowers were in it at that time. Because indirect lights in the walls shed their glow upon it, Lacey saw that it was mottled brown in color, but holding in its glazed surface a curious pearly iridescence reminiscent of the finest work from the Sung period of Chinese art.

In his early days on the paper, Cube had been forced to cram on the subject of pottery and porcelain for the purpose of reporting various exhibits, so he realized that if this vase were genuine — and none of the other furnishings of the hall were of cheap or gaudy nature — it must be of greater value even than the long-napped rugs. One eight-panelled jar of somewhat similar surface, only somewhat larger than a tobacco humidor, Lacey had seen on sale for five thousand dollars. He stepped a pace nearer to indulge pardonable curiosity. . . .

"A remarkable piece of work, don't you think?" asked a quiet voice at his elbow, a woman's voice!

"Yes — eh, I mean, I beg your pardon, miss! I didn't hear you. Certainly a piece of art. Chinese, isn't it?"

Lacey had whirled, for an instant off his guard, but quickly regained composure. He saw that he would need it in this strange house, for not only had this girl appeared in the moment he had spent glancing at the vase, but the servant had vanished! He had heard no doors open or close.

His glance rested upon a slim figure, a woman lacking only a hand's breadth of his own five feet eleven inches of height. A woman in her early twenties, he decided, and one who knew well how to dress to accentuate a most alluring patrician grace. Her face fascinated him, not because of great beauty, hut because all of the features were intended for place in a visage of superlative feminine charm — save only her eyes. These he could not distinguish, as over them lay a distinctly ugly pair of tortoise-shell spectacles, colored spectacles! These lent an odd twist of studiousness to her expression — a quality which a soft curve of chin and lips seemed to laugh at, and which impressed Lacey with a sudden, curious desire to analyze.

She was speaking. Vaguely he realized that she had disclaimed technical knowledge of the vase. Then her next sentence came home to him sharply. "You must pardon uncle if he seems a little grouchy. He has been rather seriously ill the past two or three days. I didn't think him able to see visitors, but he says he called you on the phone and wants very much to see you. You are his nephew, are you not?"

"Yes, Kuban Lacey," he affirmed. Uncle! She had called Noah that. Did it mean that she was his own cousin? He asked.

She shook her head. Lips below those enormous glasses curved upward slightly. "No, not my real uncle," she replied, and he felt rather uncomfortably that the hidden eyes were taking his measure with exactness. "My name is Irene Jeffries. I'm his ward, and he insists upon me calling him Uncle Noah while I'm here. His suite is straight back, at the right as you enter. Go ahead. I'll open the door. Unless it seems necessary, don't stay with him long, please. He seems weak."

He obeyed, draping his overcoat over his arm. She did not accompany him, but stood still, looking after him in an attitude of expectancy. He wondered, with a surge of sardonic humor, if she thought he had come to fawn upon his wealthy relative, perhaps to win a substantial place in the manufacturer's will. But no. This was not that sort of a girl. If only she would grant him a glance at her eyes she might do her worst with Noah Lacey and his millions. Cube had no expectation of being remembered in anyone's will, and had no intention of toadying to secure such recognition.

To his surprise he saw a door opening before him. He glanced back, to see the girl nod at him to enter. The second he did so the tall panel — a door without knob or hinges that he could discern — fell silently and swiftly back into place. An exclamation rose to his lips. No one in sight in the great chamber beyond. No one, seemingly, had opened or closed the door.

"Mr. Lacey?" he questioned, suddenly experiencing a queer chill along his spine. His voice rang emptily in the silence. The chamber, evidently one of a three-room suite, was empty, though the high-posted bed at one side showed evidences of recent occupancy. Framed tapestries on the walls, shelves of priceless porcelain, and a collection of jades on a long table accentuated the Oriental atmosphere, which had been apparent in the entrance corridor. Archaic Sung and T'ang figurines were grouped with three draped, terra-cotta, female figures, the last the only Occidental note in all the chamber. Lacey was not certain, but guessed them to be Tanagras, brought into juxtaposition with the Chinese art objects, perhaps for purposes of comparison.

Lacey, in doubt whether or not to proceed further, was urged onward by premonition that all was not well with the invalid — if Noah now deserved that appellation. Tapestry portières at the doorway to one of the adjoining chambers had been slid aside. Half in trepidation Lacey advanced; finding himself rising to tiptoe, even though rugs would have muffled his footsteps. In the doorway he stopped, momentarily petrified by the sight which met his eyes. At the opposite side of the adjoining room sat Noah Lacey, arms hanging limply over the sides of a deep leather chair, head fallen backward, and sightless eyes — staring wide open from chalky mask of countenance — fastened upon a point on the ceiling at one side.

III

IN A second, professional instinct rose uppermost in Lacey. No longer was he the poor relative, precariously balancing a chip on his shoulder, prepared to resent condescension and accept no favors. He was the skilled crime investigator in pursuit of working data. As he sprang to the side of the unconscious man little doubt was in his mind concerning what he should find. Yet his guess was wrong. Noah Lacey was not dead, though only the faintest flicker of a heart beat testified to continued existence. Beside him stood a small table with a decanter and a few glasses. Cube smelled the liquor hastily and found it to be French brandy. Pouring a tablespoonful into a glass he pressed it to the sick man's mouth. The latter scarcely could swallow, yet a few drops went down. In a moment Noah Lacey's eyes fluttered, he coughed feebly and a quiver ran through his relaxed frame. Cube set to chafing arms and legs. Then a few moments later, he gave the man a little more of the potent liquor.

Noah's revival was quick and complete. Five minutes after the second draft, which he swallowed in its entirety, he straightened and looked at Cube, bewilderment quickly replaced by dawning recognition.

"Reckon — reckon I must have fallen asleep. You are Kuban Lacey?" he asked, voice mounting from initial hoarseness to ordinary quality.

"Yes. Take it easy for a while," advised Cube. "You had a fainting spell. Thought for a moment you were out for good. Shall I send for a doctor?" The question was prompted by the fact that despite the elder man's death-like pallor he seemed to have recovered full command of himself; otherwise Cube would have acted without asking.

"No, it is nothing. I remember now. I just sent word by Kohler Andrews that you were to be admitted. Then I got up to make myself a little more presentable." He waved a hand deprecatingly at his brocaded bathrobe and silk pajamas. "Of a sudden I felt giddy and had to sit down. Wanted to reach for a swig of that brandy but couldn't do it. Always keep it handy because the last two or three days I've had several such spells."

"Then I should think a doctor —" persisted Cube.

"Don't want one!" interjected Noah with unmistakable emphasis. "Don't trust them." He reached for the decanter, poured himself a drink equal in volume to the two Cube had administered, swallowed this, wiped his lips and hunched forward, seemingly ready to take up the business which he had with Cube. The latter shrugged. From harsh lines of arrogance on his uncle's face he guessed that the old man would tolerate no interference with his wishes. Cube decided privately that he would cut short the interview, and on the way out apprise Miss Irene Jeffries that the services of a physician were strongly to be advised. She probably could influence his uncle to a course of greater wisdom. He accepted the chair to which Noah motioned him.

"I want you to give up that tom-fool business you and that other young man are attempting to run at present!" The old man began abruptly. "There's no money either in working for a newspaper or playing Nick Carter. Where did you get the idea, anyway?"

Cube smiled tolerantly. He did not believe the other could get under his skin. Good-naturedly he told of choosing his career because of the two best talents he could boast. His tastes had run to English and higher mathematics. The first had taken him into a newspaper office.

Recognized capability for sustained thinking had encouraged him to desert a sixty-dollar job for the profession of detective. Cube told, with a humor which redeemed his statements of fact that might have sounded immodest, of an uninterrupted string of small successes. Also he was frank concerning the fact that he and Guest had been chronically hard up — and expected a continuance of that unhappy state for weeks or months to come.

"I wasn't going to come out here," he concluded frankly, "but Sherrod seemed to think there was a chance that you might need the services of a pair of investigators. That hunch is absurd, of course?"

A grim smile twitched at Noah's lips. "Let's not tackle that just yet," he cut in. "I'm only fifty-nine years old, but five years of that time would stack up well against two decades of any ordinary life time. I don't go down to office or factory any more. Do most of my necessary work by private wires." He motioned toward a battery of telephones on a table in the corner. "Romantic business, this making of brick. Didn't ever look at it that way, eh? Well, it has its artistic side as well as its humdrum routine. The artistic side is dangerous, too. It takes you all the way from sand-clay-wall brick to — to Ming porcelains. And it gives you plenty chance to fear for your life. But I can explain that better later. What I want to know now is if you'll drop this business of yours and come out here with me. I'll try out that brain of yours and see if there is anything but empty wrinkles in it. Give you something solid to think about — bricks, perhaps. Give Mr. Guest the whole business and office equipment. You'll never miss them — or him."

Cube smiled, but shook his head decidedly. "Sorry, Uncle," he answered, "but I can't do it. I have a sort of superstition about a man who changes his mind too often in regard to what he wants to do in the world. I've changed mine once. Now if I can only make something of a living, I know the future will take care of itself; and I'm satisfied."

NOAH LACEY was obviously nettled; he had not expected opposition to this scheme. Like a good business man, however, he did not lose his temper and thereby precipitate an open break. Instead, he helped himself to more brandy, drew out a cigarette case of hammered copper, and lit a fragrant Egyptian after tendering the case to Cube. "Let's look at the matter in another light then," he continued blandly. "As you probably know, I'm called a rich man. Someone constantly is attempting to defraud or kill me. Note the way in which I've had to protect myself in this house. No one can get in without ringing half a dozen bells. All the inside doors are concealed, and operated by a complicated arrangement of push buttons. No one can enter any room in the house that is occupied without warning the occupant and receiving permission. Provisions and all household deliveries are made through an ingenious arrangement in the wall at the rear. When Irene; Kohler Andrews; or his wife, who is housekeeper, leaves the place she or he must be let out by someone else, or must utilize a secret passage so far known only to Irene and myself.

"Perhaps you can guess now that I could find for you enough work out here to satisfy your detective instinct. Also, in my day I have been an active man. I'd like to have the company in the hands of a youngster who still is able to do things. I might make that youngster a proposition — say of salary as a detective, plus excellent prospects of a substantial legacy later. What do you think of it now?"

Noah Lacey's words lacked any hint

of objectionable quality. It was rather the sophisticated half sneer which lingered always on the elder man's countenance, which antagonized Cube. He saw, or thought he saw, that Noah for some reason had set himself a task of winning Cube Lacey from his chosen life work and ambition. The mention of detective work, of course was mere subterfuge, notwithstanding Noah's evident concern for his own personal safety. Cube felt a queer mingling of pity, contempt and admiration for his scheming relative, yet the whole plan as stated repelled him. If it became a starvation matter between himself and Sherrod Guest, the two could find jobs somewhere out on a paper for a short time. Cube preferred this alternative to the easy way of shiftlessness suggested by Noah. He expressed himself courteously but decisively, arose, and made his way out. His last glance at Noah Lacey showed the old man, after pressing a button controlling the door, helping himself to another glass of brandy.

Miss Jeffries was not in evidence when he emerged. Kohler Andrews, however, whisked into sight from somewhere and conducted him out into the street. Cube ventured to advise medical attention for Noah. "The old duffer has a heart lesion of some sort, I'm afraid," he said. "And that booze is not doing him much good, I'd wager."

No answer was returned to this friendly suggestion. Kohler Andrews maintained the same mask of stern indifference on his accipitrine features with which he had greeted Cube. The young man reached the street outside with something of a feeling of relief. In his mind was absolute certainty that he never would call at Brick Knob again — unless, by chance, at some time he happened to meet Miss Irene Jeffries without her smoked glasses.

But he was wrong. Next morning at eleven o'clock as he sat idly in his office the phone rang. Irene Jeffries was speaking, and unmistakable agitation was apparent in her voice. She dispensed with preliminaries. "Your Uncle, Noah Lacey was murdered last night!" she stated. "Come right out just as quickly as you can!"

To the best of Cube's antecedent knowledge he had been alone in the office. Guest was in court; the flimsy partition door to his half of the office stood open at Cube's left hand. So startled was he by the news he received from Irene Jeffries that out of the tail of his eye he saw only a dark blur as of something descending swiftly. That something landed heavily upon the crown of his head, driving nose forward against the telephone mouthpiece. Cube did not know that minor feature of his injury until later. For him the world had dissolved in a starry swirl of oblivion.

IV

CUBE regained consciousness almost as violently as he had departed that state. Sherrod Guest, bursting in with the epochal news of a seventy-five-dollar fee from a client he had expected to charge only one-third that sum, did not notice for some moments the chaotic disarray of the office. Cube, crouched forward on the desk, looked as if he had fallen asleep. Guest shook him with unrestrained exuberance. Lacey's eyes opened dully and he gazed about at a room which seemed to be swaying like a steamboat cabin in choppy sea.

"Come to! Wake, thou dreamer!" adjured Guest. "A porterhouse steak with plenty of mushrooms looms on the horizon before our hungry eyes! Hey! What's the matter with you? Doped?" At that instant his hand encountered a trickle of dampness on his comrade's scalp. One glance showed him it was blood. From that instant his bombastic manner vanished, and he devoted himself solicitously to bringing back Lacey from his groggy condition.

Thereupon Cube briefly sketched the startling news which had come to him over the wire, and told of his attack by someone who had been concealed in the inner office. Both halves of the place had been wrecked systematically, the files torn open and contents dumped upon the floor, books thrown helter-skelter from their shelves, and the locked drawers of Sherrod's desk pried open with some heavy weapon. Lacey's, because they had been unlocked at the time, escaped with merely having their contents strewn about. For some time Sherrod scarcely mentioned the fact of Noah Lacey's demise. The attack upon Cube and the interior of the office interested him far more.

"What on earth do you suppose they were after? Was it those darn Chinks? There have been half a dozen near me every place I went today!" he exclaimed explosively, ready to launch himself for vengeance in any suggested direction.

Lacey was thoughtful but had no explanation to offer. The wound on his head had transformed itself into a right-angled lump, and it seemed as though the entire roof of his brain had been bruised. Nevertheless he shook himself together and announced an intention of returning immediately to Brick Knob.

"I don't know how you see it Sherrod," he observed, "but it looks to me as though we ought to establish a causal connection between the two ends of this coincidence. Let me sketch it. All in one day, twenty-four hours, we find ourselves beset by Chinese. One followed me all the way up to Brick Knob. Guess I didn't mention that before. These attentions from yellow men are subsequent to a phone call from Noah Lacey. I

go out to his house to find it crammed with objects of Oriental art. He hints to me — though at the moment I confess I thought it nothing but rather clumsy subterfuge to get me out there to live with him — of certain detective work he proposes to me to do. He even admits that his life is in danger, but I only half believe him. I dope him out to be a rank coward, even if he is my uncle. A few hours after I leave, however, he is murdered. Doesn't that appeal to your logical mind as the beginning of a sorites?"

Guest shrugged. "As usual you're several steps ahead of me," he admitted. "Sounds wild, but at the same time reasonable, in a way. What do you want me to do?"

"Stay right here for the time being. I'm not so sure that they won't try to involve me in that mess out at Brick Knob. I'm the only surviving relative. At the present moment I am being cut out for a chance at Noah's fortune by a rank outsider. A girl. Pretty, too, I think. Still, vengeance or some other sordid motive might be ascribed to me. It might have come about that I was the last person to see my uncle alive, though that scarcely appears probable. If you went out with me, they might decide to hold you also as a possible accomplice — or as witness. I'd rather have you on the outside, at least until tomorrow. Then our guesses are apt to hit close to the mark. Get on the trail of these Chinese. If any of them bother you smash after them hammer and tongs!"

IRENE JEFFRIES herself admitted Cube. A uniformed policeman was stationed at the entrance, but Cube noticed that he lacked the officious seriousness usual in striking murder cases. Irene whispered a quick explanation. "Don't mention to anyone just yet that I told you he was murdered," she requested. "They think it was an accident, and I believe it would be best to leave it that way for a time."

Cube stared at her. She had taken off

the atrocious spectacles, and he saw that she had been crying. Gone was the aspect of studiousness, the old-maidish primness suggested by the shell-encircled glasses. She was pretty! Yes, more than that, for in spite of signs of sincere grief a sweet, almost wistful feminine trust shone in her eyes. Though the procedure she suggested was far from regular, in Cube's estimation, he could not question her motive at that moment. He nodded gravely, and took her arm as they descended the steps.

"I — I simply told them that he was dead," she continued rapidly. "They sent down several different officers and Inspector Harris. Dr. Mitchell was here when they arrived. They didn't stay long, because it seemed apparent to them that your uncle died from a fall. He hit his forehead."

"May I see him? You don't need to come, Miss Jeffries," he suggested kindly. "Won't you lie down for a time? When I've made my examination I'd like to have a talk with you."

"No, I'd rather stay with you," she shivered. "This house — well, I know too much about it, and the reasons for its being such a fort. Though you may not believe it, Mr. Lacey had reasons!"

"I am prepared to believe anything," Cube answered, passing back along the corridor to the door by which he had entered previously. This now was propped open. "What time did it — it happen?"

"No one knows exactly. Mr. Lacey ate dinner with me. Then he went down to his workshop in the basement for a few minutes. I tried to keep him upstairs, because I think he was —" she hesitated.

"Drunk?" suggested Cube.

"Well, a little, yes. He insisted on going down, but returned to this floor almost immediately and retired. He was reading, for an open copy of Montaigne lay beside him on the floor. Apparently some time in the night — Dr. Mitchell estimates it at about ten or eleven o'clock — he rose, and started

to walk, perhaps for another drink. One of the spells overcame him, and he toppled forward. His forehead struck heavily against the sharp corner of a chair."

"But I thought you said he was murdered?"

A peculiar expression flitted across her countenance. She started clutching Cube's arm. "It's I, Kohler!" she exclaimed sharply. Cube saw that this was occasioned by the appearance of the servant in the doorway leading to Noah Lacey's private living-room. Andrews held a leveled automatic! He looked as if he had been stopped in the very act of firing, and his pistol had been aimed directly at Cube.

"You may go now, Kohler," Irene continued, a trifle unsteadily. "I'll call you when I leave." The man obeyed, thrusting the automatic somewhere below the left lapel of jacket. He had not spoken, yet as he passed Cube black, beady eyes were fastened suspiciously upon the detective.

"Andrews, hell!" was Cube's silent comment. "He never owned that name honestly. A gunman, too. I'll keep an eye on him!"

Noah Lacey's body was stretched upon a leather couch in the chamber where Cube had seen him on the previous day. Because the coroner had not yet arrived, nothing had been done save the draping of a silk handkerchief over his face. Cube lifted the cloth gingerly. Above Noah's right eye was a broken indentation telling plainly of skull fracture which undoubtedly had caused instant death. The wound immediately attracted Cube's interest for one particular reason. Though the skin was broken open to an extent of more than an inch, little blood was in evidence.

On the handkerchief which had rested against Noah's face appeared only a faint grayish-brown stain. "Who cleaned the wound?" demanded Cube, straightening abruptly.

"No one," she responded. "Dr. Mitchell said that Mr. Lacey must have suffered from a form of pernicious anemia. He had practically no blood. That is strange, too, for until just a few days ago Mr. Lacey possessed a rather florid complexion. He drank a good deal, you know, although the only time I saw him intoxicated in the slightest perceptible degree was after this weakness had come to him."

"When did you first notice the difference in his complexion and strength?"

"Last Wednesday, a week ago tomorrow. Until that morning he had been vigorous for a man of his age. All in one night he seemed to wilt. The color left his face and he began drinking constantly to keep himself up. I tried to get him to consult a physician but he absolutely refused, telling me that no American doctor could help him. But you are more interested now in other things. Here is the chair against which he fell."

She indicated one of three slim mahogany chairs standing before the long telephone table. On the sharp corner of a seat a grayish-brown stain showed above the polished surface. Cube pursed his lips thoughtfully. He could not dispute the girl's statements, for a single glance showed him that the angle of wood fitted exactly the wound which had caused Lacey's death. Oddly enough, however, the stain no more resembled blood than did the clotted moisture gathered upon Lacey's temple. Cube studied it a moment with his hand lens, then taking a pen-knife and sheet of white paper from his pocket he scraped away with extreme care a tiny portion of the stain, placed it on the paper and folded the latter into compact shape.

At this moment the coroner arrived, accompanied by Dr. Mitchell and Inspector Harris. Cube was forced to suspend his own activities while the others retraced his steps. At first, when he made known his identity as nephew of the dead man, the coroner stared suspiciously at him — evidently filing away a mental note to question Cube exhaustively at some later time. After full consideration of apparent factors, though, he expressed

himself satisfied that Noah's death had been a regrettable accident. "I'll have to hold an inquest this afternoon," he said at last, "but it will be nothing much more than a matter of form. Dr. Mitchell states that Mr. Lacey was known to have had fainting spells. Undoubtedly one of these overtook him."

Five minutes after the others had left, Cube turned directly to Irene Jeffries. "Now I am ready to have you tell me why you believe my uncle was murdered," he said.

Without comment she walked to the telephone table, lifted one of the instruments, and handed him a folded sheet of paper which had been concealed there. He opened it and read the following curious statement:

"I am convinced that I have but a few days to live. I am being murdered by members of the T'ao tong. Noah Lacey."

"There have been Chinese about this place ever since I came!" Irene whispered, glancing involuntarily over her shoulder as she spoke.

"Chinese!" echoed Cube, his mind reverting instantly to the tentative theory which he had mentioned to Guest.

"Yes!" she affirmed. "Twice I — I saw them inside this house! Kohler Andrews shot at one but did not hit him. Each time the man escaped, and none of us could discover how he had gained entrance. Mr. Lacey feared them. Somehow he had incurred their enmity. From hints he dropped at one time or another I believe they were trying to get something which he possessed, something he valued more highly even than his life. He never told me anything concerning its nature, but did show me at one time a pink scrap of paper which had been glued against the surface of the hidden door to his suite of rooms. Mr. Lacey took the paper, and I did not get a very good look at the single character upon it. It was a Chinese ideograph, however, one which resembled a turkey track to which were appended several rings and scrolls. I think it must have had something to do with this tong he mentions, for at the time it seemed to disturb him tremendously. He made all of us take revolvers, and come with him while he scoured every nook and corner of the house. We found no signs of intruders. For days thereafter, though, Mr. Lacey seemed to be waiting, waiting for something to happen. He strapped a pistol holster about his waist, and wore it even when he went to bed."

Cube's eyes were enigmatic as he turned toward the telephone table. "Which of these instruments will give me an outside wire?" he asked.

"The one furthest to the left."

Lifting the receiver then Cube Lacey called his own office and spoke long and earnestly to Sherrod Guest. Though he little imagined any such horrible contingency connected with the errand, he was sending his comrade and associate to almost certain doom.

One minute after he replaced the receiver the back basement door of an apartment just outside the wall of Brick Knob opened, and a Chinaman appeared, to glance hurriedly about and then hasten to a point two blocks distant. There at the curb a low-slung roadster awaited.

V

SHERROD GUEST'S initial smile of satisfaction and intensified interest changed into seriousness as he heard the commission given him by Lacey, "Go down into Chinatown and discover all there is to be learned concerning the T'ao tong. Those are the chaps we're after, it seems."

As a reporter Guest once had invaded the queer district centering about Twenty-second and Archer Avenues, in search of material and photographs for an article on Chinese music. Unacquainted with the language and all forms of Oriental belief, he had been forced to confess failure on the assignment. Now he boarded a street car with little expectation of success. For a white man, the job of learning anything pertaining to yellow men's secrets always is made next to impossible. He knew only enough of tongs, their methods and activities, to realize that a westerner would find out just exactly what the Chinese wished him to know, and not a whit more.

He sought first the bland, educated Sam Lee Moy — known as "king of Chinatown," and an oily politician who grafted both from his own countrymen and from the furtive, white-faced individuals who came regularly to pay over their dollars for small tins of a commodity practically unobtainable elsewhere in the city. As usual he was pacing slowly back and forth before the shops and tenements of his small domain, watchful for strangers, though seeming to beam good-nature and fellow-ship toward all who passed. Guest hailed him, and with cynical recognition of Moy's proclivities, pressed a folded two-dollar bill into the yellow palm. Moy glanced at it, and smiled.

"For some it is a symbol of bad luck," he commented unctuously, "but not for me. You are the one who three years ago wished to see some of the instruments for music-making of my countrymen?"

"Yes, you remember me all right," replied Guest, nodding. "I'm not musically inclined today, though. I'd like to have a chat with you in private, Sam. I'm after a little information, and there are more of those little bad luck omens for you if you can tell me what I want to know."

Moy bowed. "I have a room up here," he answered, indicating a narrow doorway behind which greasy stairs led upward into unlighted obscurity. As Guest strode ahead, it was noticeable that Moy lingered the fraction of a second to make a curious sign with his fingers in the direction of a squatting loafer who sat smoking in front of a wholesale grocery several houses distant. The loafer immediately rose to his feet and shuffled away.

Guest ushered himself into the bare, barn-like room overhead, but refused the mat offered him by Moy. "No, it'll only take a minute," he said. "I want to know just a little about these tong societies you fellows have. What is the T'ao tong, and where can I get in touch with one of the head members in Chicago?"

Moy's eyes narrowed slightly, yet the cheerful expression of his features did not alter in perceptible degree. "Tong?" he murmured, as if at a loss for Guest's meaning.

"Yes, the secret societies, I mean. Particularly the T'ao bunch."

Moy seemed to ruminate. "There are many tongs in old China," he admitted, at last. "I know of them, of course, in a general way, for some have branches in San Francisco and elsewhere. You know, however, that I was born in Canada, and never have worn the queue. For that reason I have not become a member of any such order. As a matter of fact I don't believe many of the Chinese in this neighborhood have any affiliations with the big societies."

Guest waved his hand. "Oh, never mind the bunk, Sam," he begged. "I can get all that stuff out of books. You haven't been with these chaps all your life and failed to learn the general stuff I want to know. Just tell me something about the T'ao tong, and we won't waste time with the others. I have some business to transact with them, and I don't find them in the 'phone directory."

Moy's brows wrinkled. "It is strange," he muttered. "I know of the Wah Pu, and the Dragon, and — Really, so far as I know there is no organization by the name you give either here or in China. Gladly would I earn more of your good money, but —"

An idea seemed to occur to him. "It comes to mind," he added, measuring the palm of one hand against that of the other, "that there is one old and very wise man back here who might be able to tell you what you wish to know. Charlie Sing can be approached at any time, for his years rest upon

him too heavily to allow him to walk out upon the streets. Come, I shall show you the way."

Guest acquiesced readily. He knew that among these Chinese any white man seeking information is regarded with deep suspicion. Lengths of red tape have to be unrolled before even the simplest question receives a straightforward answer. Probably Moy wished to divide responsibility, or perhaps this was his indirect method of introducing Guest to the very man whom he was seeking. The latter estimate seemed more probable. Guest took a chance upon it and rewarded Moy with another bill, which was received with profuse thanks — albeit the shadow of a more sinister expression lurked behind the urbane mask of the Oriental.

They did not retrace their steps to the street. Moy led the way backward from the staircase through a musty, unlighted corridor smelling of Chinese onions, and stale smoke of punk. The way elbowed twice, bringing them to a succession of unmarked, dingy doors. Moy opened one of these, turning immediately inside to descend wooden stairs built in a crooked spiral. For the first time a qualm of apprehension attacked Guest, but the cold touch of an automatic in jacket pocket reassured him. He went on, following the shadowy form of his guide. The dank smell of earth mingled now with odors of humanity. Guest knew that they were below street level, in some sort of basement.

At the bottom of the stairs a single candle guttered in drafts from three corridors. Moy stopped. "Follow this hallway to the end!" he directed. "Take the candle, for there are two stairs down which you might stumble. It is better that I do not go with you to Charley Sing, but those you will find in that last chamber will direct you." Presently, with a bow and final smile, in which Guest imagined he detected an odd glint of malignity, Moy was gone. With a shrug for the fears which crowded upon him, Guest took up the candle in his left hand, and grasping the pistol in his pocket with the right, stepped forward into the designated corridor.

No warning came to him, the springing of the trap was accomplished with silent swiftness. All at once a heavy, swathing cloth descended over head and shoulders, extinguishing the candle and enveloping Guest in musty-smelling, suffocating folds. He tried to yank out the pistol, but with practiced dexterity a rope was wound tightly about his arms, pinioning them to his sides. A hand reached up from somewhere and yanked away the automatic, which exploded once, fruitlessly. Another loop tightened about his ankles. Helpless, he toppled into the arms of his captors.

VI

BOTH Irene Jeffries and Cube Lacey were present at the inquest. Kohler Andrews and his wife — the latter a dull, large woman apparently honest enough, but knowing little or nothing save what her husband told her — also were summoned and questioned perfunctorily. It developed that the two had served Noah Lacey for eighteen years, that they regarded him as a generous employer, though one given to many cranky notions. Andrews testified that his master long had left the routine portions of his business in the hands of a business manager, Nathan Hardy by name. Andrews — whose name originally had been Politsky — believed that Hardy had bought out a one-third interest. The fact was corroborated later by Hardy himself.

Noah Lacey never had cared much for the pursuit of money-making. After establishing on a firmer basis his inherited business, he devoted himself, except for eight or ten hours a week, to the artistic side of pottery and ceramics. He had studied abroad, and traveled in the Orient where he had picked up some of the beautiful specimens of fictile art which now decorated his home. He had made much pottery himself, possessing a complete and extensive laboratory in the basement of his house. According to Andrews, however, he had ordered the latter for many years to smash up almost every jar, vase, or completed specimen. "And some of them was worth lots of money, to!" concluded Andrews.

"How do you know?" flashed Cube Lacey, who had been studying the man's iron visage. It had seemed that a momentary flash of apprehension — quite as if Andrews had let slip something he had not intended to mention — had come and gone in the witness's face. Inspector Harris and all the rest turned to regard Cube coldly.

"I fail to see where that question is at all pertinent," rebuked the coroner. "You will kindly not interrupt again, Mr. Lacey."

Cube nodded resignedly. The inquest proceeded, unearthing nothing incompatible with the theory of death by accident, until Cube himself was called. He told of his relationship to the dead man, of his visit on the previous day, and then presented to the coroner the note which Lacey evidently had written only a short time before his death. Cube had considered it his duty to bring forth this piece of evidence, but it received little attention. Noah Lacey was characterized as a man given to delusions. When Cube attempted to mention the fact that Chinese intruders twice had been seen inside the house despite all precautions against their entry, the fact was waved aside.

"Before we place any particular value upon that," replied the coroner, "we must remember that Mr. Lacey continually kept art objects — vases, rugs and other valuable specimens easily transported by thieves — to the value of more than one hundred thousand dollars in the house all the time. I scarcely wonder that he had all these elaborate precautions, or that he was troubled by Chinese thieves. Undoubtedly Chinese not only would appreciate these things most fully, but they would have a ready market, right at hand."

The verdict was predestined. Noah Lacey had died through an accident resulting from a fainting spell brought on by poor health. Of all those present outside of Irene Jeffries and Cube, Inspector Harris was the only one who lingered five minutes after the verdict had been given.

He drew aside Irene and chatted with her a short time, ending by laughing and patting her upon the shoulder in fatherly fashion. Instantly, Cube conceived a dislike for the detective, whose eight years of seniority did not give him any great right to act thus toward a very pretty girl. Cube had considered it his duty to protect Irene, but — well, Harris was different!

One curious fact in respect to the inquest recurred to Cube later. They had not asked Irene Jeffries a single question! Grimly he smiled at this evidence of inefficiency. In a conscientious manner he had endeavored to put forward all the facts in his possession because he did not feel like assuming the whole burden of responsibility. Now, the law had divorced itself definitely from the case, scoffing at the possibility of crime. If Cube and Sherrod Guest could prove that a murder had been committed, and catch the guilty parties, the affair would prove indeed to be the big, spectacular case for which they had hoped!

Harris confirmed this in parting. He stopped a moment at the door. "I've just placed you, Lacey," he observed, smiling condescendingly. "You're the young chap who's running that new detective agency with Sherrod Guest, eh? Well, take a tip from an old timer. Be content with the dough the old bird leaves you. Don't waste time trying to make a mystery out of an open-and-shut case." He nodded affably, and disappeared.

CUBE LACEY was under no delusion regarding a possible share in the wealth left by Noah Lacey. He had been offered such a chance and had declined it. Without doubt Irene Jeffries would inherit; at any rate Cube refused to worry over the matter.

Irene broached the matter of staying longer, as soon as they were alone. "You — won't need me any more now, will you?" she asked, rather timidly.

"Need you?" echoed Cube, mystified. "Oh no, I see what you mean. You won't want to remain in this house over night, naturally. I'll stay on. There are a few things I want to examine this evening — the workshop downstairs, and so on. If you have a place in the city to which you can go, I'll expect you in the morning."

She glanced at him peculiarly. "That wasn't exactly what I meant," she countered. "I — well, since you're here, there really isn't any use my coming back, unless you —"

A light dawned upon Cube. She imagined that he naturally would inherit the house and everything, and that her connection with Noah Lacey was ended! Of course he knew nothing of the circumstances under which she had become his ward, yet Noah Lacey undoubtedly had remembered her handsomely, as he had no other apparent beneficiaries. When his lawyers brought forward his will this would be settled. In the meantime he had no intention of assuming the slightest air of proprietorship.

"Nothing doing, Ir— hm, Miss Jeffries!" he smiled. "Really, as you ought to know, I'm just in this as a matter of business speculation. I am out to make a name for myself, if possible, and bring to justice the men responsible for my uncle's death. But you're the boss, of course."

"Thank you. That's very flattering," she told him gravely, hiding the merry light that had risen to her eyes. "In that case I shall stay on for a time, Mr. Lacey. My own room is safe enough, and I suppose you'll want the Andrews pair to stay on."

"Yes. I'm not through with Kohler Andrews just yet!" he concluded. "But wouldn't it be better if you got someone, even a personal maid, to stay with you?"

"I'm quite capable of taking care of myself, thank you!" she flashed. "Now, about dinner, Mr. Lacey?"

"Call me Cube!" he begged. "I'll be very, very formal in addressing you, Miss Jeffries. Really, I won't presume, but I've been Cube to everyone so long I scarcely know my last name, especially when it's hitched to a Mister. If you'll do that I'll — I'll promise to do my share with the biggest dinner Mrs. Andrews can cook!"

She shook her head. "I couldn't think of it!" she retorted. "How would it sound if I took a liberty you did not reciprocate — Cube?"

"Shake, Irene!" he cried joyfully, thrilling to the sudden knowledge that this girl could be more to him than any of the pretty women he had known previously. She would be a constant gratification to his senses, but beyond that she also possessed the wit and sense of humor so necessary in a real friend and pal.

After dinner, which was one of the most sumptuous meals that Cube had tasted for months, they searched the upstairs rooms for any sign of intruders, or other assurance that Lacey had met a violent end, but in vain. Irene was tired out, so she retired early. Cube tried to get in touch with Guest, but failed. Next morning after breakfast, Irene conducted him to the basement in the automatic elevator — a hidden device reached by springing back a wall panel of Circassian walnut — which gave the only known means of access to Noah's laboratory from the upstairs.

Cube found himself awed by the laboratory. High-ceiled, it formed one huge room corresponding to the entire floor plan of the house. Rows of concrete posts, extending the length of laboratory, supported the weight above. The room, in spite of its size, seemed crammed with apparatus, yet this was not what first caught Cube's attention. The walls were more striking. Formed entirely of fictile material, they were a conglomerate, apparently, of thousands of experiments with brick, tile, and porcelain. Though cemented together cleverly — pieces the size of mosaics lying side by side with building tiles a yard square on their faces — the whole effect was of highly-colored, patchwork draperies hung all about. Here was every shade of the spectrum, every glaze and finish known to ceramics, flung together in an array like the disassorted fragments of a picture puzzle!

"Mr. Lacey experimented for years and years, attempting to reproduce pottery and porcelain the equal of those from old China," Irene explained. "See, here are his earlier bits, near the bottom of the wall. He built it all by hand, as you know. This wall does not support the house. Behind it is another, of ordinary stone and mortar. If you'll notice, there is a line here," she paused to indicate an irregular demarcation approximately four feet from the cork-carpeted floor, "which separates quite distinctly his first work from that which he did during the past ten or eleven years. You can see an abrupt difference. Below, the mosaics and tiles are finished and glazed poorly. Above, they possess delicate shading, luster, iridescence, almost like some of those vases and jugs upstairs. I don't know whether you were told this, or not, but Mr. Lacey made all but five of those vases, and almost every other figure and bit of porcelain in the house! That yellow-brown vase out in the front hall he considered his finest bit. It is an exact reproduction of the Hsien-te nien chih vase by Ch'ai Yao now in the Chinese

Government Museum at Peking."

Lacey gazed at her astounded. "Do you mean to say," he demanded, "that my uncle could duplicate these art objects?"

"Not only that he could duplicate them, hut he could originate vases, urns, and cremation receptacles which the greatest critics pronounced genuine relics of Sung or T'ang periods! Once I remember he was offered three thousand dollars for a tiny piece; offered it by Reynolds Nasmyth, the critic, too! Of course Mr. Lacey didn't accept, but he chuckled over that for weeks afterward. He considered the offer ample recognition of his efforts. I don't think he ever told Mr. Nasmyth, who still thinks he lacked only a few thousand dollars of consummating his happiness by actually owning an antique piece of superlative beauty. Mr. Lacey valued that particular piece simply because of the offer. He never would part with it, but he did send as a present to Mr. Nasmyth a water jug purporting to be of Ming porcelain. That jug made the poor man happier than a ten-year-old boy with a new electric engine!

"Mr. Lacey often told me that if he wanted to hoax the public, he could make more money out of his pottery wheel downstairs than the whole brick business earned. He never did that, however. He was a lover of beauty. I think he planned to make public his processes and secrets. At least he seemed to be writing all of the time he did not spend down here in experimentation."

For a time Cube said not a word. In silence he traced the line of difference between Noah's early work, and that which had formed the culmination of his life of artistic striving. The difference was remarkable.

"What caused the change, Irene?" he asked. "Do you know?"

She hesitated. "I have thought it over many times, but I cannot be sure," she replied. "Perhaps it was the length of time which Mr. Lacey spent in the Orient. It was following that period that he put all these safety devices in and about the house. You see, I have been here only a little over two years. Mr. Lacey was not a man much given to confidences, of course. I only can guess."

"Sounds rational enough," commented Cube. "I have to look it up. Do you think —?"

His sentence was interrupted by a raucous, horrible squall — an inhuman voice which seemed to come from the ceiling directly overhead.

"Cube! Cube!" it cried. "Help! They're tearing me to pieces! Help! Help!"

"My heavens!" cried Cube, yanking out his automatic and running toward the point from which the sound seemed to emanate. "It's — that's Sherrod! Where are you, old man? I'm coming!"

VII

NO ANSWER was returned. For several minutes Cube raced about the laboratory, searching for any sign of Guest, but in vain. Besides Irene and himself the entire basement was empty of human occupant!

Irene shivered. "It's spooky!" she said. "That voice was not human!" She also held a revolver, but Cube did not appear to notice.

Cube shook his head decidedly. "Of course it was," he objected. "He was here somewhere. We must find him, for Sherrod never squeals unless he's badly hurt." Resuming the search, and calling out time and time again, he opened the zinc-lined bins that held clay and plaster, the damp box, and the drying cupboard. He peered behind the "kick wheel," and even opened the doors of the oil kiln and muffle kiln.

Outside of these and benches holding chemical reagents and bacteriological apparatus, a large electric furnace and what seemed to be an aquarium completed the list of sizable apparatus. The supposed aquarium was glass-sided, and covered with heavy plates of the same material. Cube lifted away one of the latter, and peered down into a stagnant, fetid pool of green slime in which sticks of wood and small boulders were placed. No fish or other large organism could live in such water; the odor fairly snatched at human respiration.

"Ugh!" grimaced Cube, drawing back and allowing the heavy plate to slip into place. "He can't be there."

He hallooed again, this time putting all strength of his lungs in an attempt to reach Sherrod's ears. A cackle of raucous, fiendish laughter burst out from a point within a yard of his head! There, clutching the side of one of the concrete pillars near the ceiling, was a common green parrot!

With wings outstretched, the bird glared down, as he snapped his great, curved beak malevolently.

"Don't look down there!" he screamed in a wicked falsetto. "Dash my eyes, I'm right here! They're killing me! Awk!"

Involuntarily Cube dropped back. Irene seized his arm, and he felt the girl tremble as a glint of reflected electricity turned the bird's sinister, knowing eyes into blank circles of red fire. "Wh-where did that thing come from?" he gasped. "Did my uncle —?" Wordless negation was his only answer from Irene. She was staring at the parrot with fascination akin to that of a rabbit transfixed by the glare of a cobra.

"I'm Sherrod Guest!" came the weird, unreal pronouncement again. "Help, help!" With startling suddenness the parrot deserted its precarious perch, swooping with a beating of heavy wings to a shelf of pottery moulds, there to balance and cock his head sidewise at the two.

"We'll have to catch him!" whispered Irene, as the bird started again his strident refrain.

"Wait a minute," cautioned Cube in a low tone. "He's some kind of a messenger, I think. Yesterday, Sherrod Guest went to see what he could discover concerning the mysterious Chinese who have been haunting this household and my office. This parrot must have heard Guest talk. Otherwise he could not imitate the voice. I believe — yes, I'm sure the tong has captured Sherrod."

Slowly then Cube approached the green-plumaged bird, doing his utmost to cajole him into further revelations. His promises of crackers which did not exist, and compliments to the bird's supposed beauty obtained no result, however. Common house parrots might yield to such blandishments, but not Sun Yat, who had dwelt many decades among men whose wisdom he respected much more than that of this foolish American who tried to tempt him with baby talk and empty promises. He squawked his disapproval, and, when pursued from perch to perch by Cube, leaned forward suddenly and pecked a sizable strip of skin from the back of the young man's extended hand.

"Damn!" exploded Lacey, staring down at a spot from which the blood was beginning to stream.

So that was the game! This foolish fellow thought he knew something about swearing, did he? Sun Yat lifted one foot and scratched his head contemptuously. Forthwith from his horny beak there issued a stream of blasphemy and denunciation which would have made a Tien-Tsin desperado blush for shame.

Cube, staunching the blood with his handkerchief, was more wary about approaching the feathered demon, yet he stuck with the job pertinaciously, not suspecting that the bird could elude him. He overlooked one of the narrow, barred windows above the level of the ground, however. One pane of glass had been removed neatly from this. Sun Yat, driven from one place to another, decided finally that he did not care for the basement after all. Hopping to the window he paused to chatter back a final expletive, and then fluttered out into the chill air to spread wings in flight.

Denouncing his carelessness, Cube hastened outside, but the bird was gone. Encircling the house, Cube trod accidentally upon the two-yard strip of brick which gave under his weight. Apparently this strip completely circled the building, and was part of Noah Lacey's intricate burglar-alarm system, for while Cube remained standing on the spot jangling bells sounded within the house. When he stepped off the noise ceased.

Kohler Andrews, sawed-off shotgun in hand, came stealthily from the rear. Cube motioned to him that there was nothing to fear. "This particular bird is probably on his way to Chinatown by now," he explained cryptically.

IT TOOK only a short session with the telephone to prove that Sherrod Guest had not been near his office. The client, Myers, was angry. He had kicked his heels outside a locked door for twenty minutes after the time of his appointment; now he expressed coarsely but adequately his opinion of ham detectives who didn't have sense enough to perform a job satisfactorily when they got it.

Cube did his best to assuage the man's temper, but in truth Cube himself was too disturbed to bother about a matter like possible evidence for Myers's possible divorce. He phoned the rooming house in which Guest lived. The landlady informed him that Sherrod had not put in an appearance the previous night, and had left no word concerning present whereabouts. Sickening certainty began to descend upon Cube. Guest had gone after information and had been trapped by members of the suspected tong. Cube himself knew little of such organizations, yet in newspaper offices he had heard gruesome tales of Oriental torture and punishment. He shuddered. For the time being he would have to abandon this end of the investigation, for duty to a living friend superseded duty to a dead man. Irene agreed with him. She promised to be watchful and careful in his absence, and said that if no word from him arrived by evening she would repair to a hotel for the night.

Cogitating whether or not to place this new development in the hands of the police, Cube went downtown. He decided finally not to mention the fact until he discovered that it held a more direct bearing upon one or the other horn of the dilemma. Inspector Harris and the rest would not listen to a wild tale of clues furnished by a talkative parrot. They would scoff, and Cube realized that the problem long since had ceased to be a laughing matter.

On the way to the office Cube remembered the scraping which he had taken from the telephone chair. An analytical laboratory lay on his way, so he dropped in, searching out Lester Krahn, a young scientist who, combining extensive knowledge of physiological chemistry and bacteriology, had been depended on by newspaper writers for years. Krahn took the specimen, listened to a brief sketch of the circumstances and Cube's desire, and promised to have a report ready in the course of three hours.

Cube thereupon visited his office which, naturally, was empty. Steam heat had been left turned on, and excessive temperature inside denied that anyone had visited the place that day. Cube did not waste much time here, but started a systematic search for his associate throughout the Loop. When this proved fruitless he sought the telephone and located a professor of Oriental languages at the University of Chicago. Making an engagement with the latter, he taxied out immediately. Albert Benson, Ph. D., had little that was reassuring to offer, though.

"Your case is exceedingly interesting," he answered, after listening to a résumé of the story, "but I scarcely see wherein I can help. Now that tong of which you were speaking; few white men really know anything concerning Chinese secret societies. No white man, or even half-caste Chinaman, ever became a tong member, however. I believe that even Chinese born in the Western Hemisphere are excluded."

The good man would have gone on interminably expounding these views which did not seem to Cube to be especially pertinent. The detective, though, managed to precipitate more concrete information. He asked point-blank if the professor ever had learned anything concerning the T'ao tong.

"I never before have heard the name," was the answer. "It does not occur in the list of forty-three known societies of that kind. This does not mean that such a tong is not in existence. Practically all of the Chinese in this country come from the single province of Shensi. Natives of other provinces might have a hundred more tongs for all I know. Probably they have. The word Tao appeals to me as decidedly interesting in light of what you have told me. I suppose you know that it means pottery and ceramics — embracing all of the fictile arts, in fact."

Cube's eyes narrowed. This was information indeed! "No, I didn't know that," he answered. "Thank you, doctor, I guess that narrows the sphere of my investigation considerably!"

ANOTHER and still greater surprise awaited Cube when he returned to the laboratory, however. Lester Krahn approached him with a puzzled frown on his countenance. "See here, Lacey," he began quizzically, "are you trying to spoof me, or what? This stuff never flowed in the veins of a human being, or if it did I'd certainly like to see the person!"

Wonderingly, Cube assured him that there had been no practical joke intended, and asked the reason for Krahn's surprising statement. Silently the scientist beckoned him to a stand near the window where a microscope was focused upon a freshly prepared slide. "Take a look!" bade Krahn succinctly.

Cube glanced into the low-powered lens. After a moment of careful focusing through the depths of a murky spatter lying beneath the cover glass, he could see a picture which brought an involuntary exclamation of puzzled surprise to his lips. It seemed that he was looking upon a vast field of gigantic poppies! The flowers seemed to be growing in a profuse tangle. A time or two he had glanced at human blood under the microscope, but the picture before him now held no hint of the same character which appealed to his unpracticed eye. "Why, it looks like a flower garden!" he muttered.

"Exactly!" confirmed Krahn. "Tonight I'm going to take that slide over to McKenzie the botanist. Perhaps he'll be able to tell me something more about it. First though, was the surface of the chair from which you got the scraping moist or moulded at all?"

"No, it was highly polished mahogany. Not even dusty."

Krahn nodded grimly. "I know you're not lying," he commented, "and so I'll tell you a funny thing about that specimen — a fact which may go far to help solve the mystery of your uncle's death. In that slide appear scraps of fibrin, platelets — the substances in blood which cause it to clot, you know — a terrific number of white blood corpuscles, which are the buzzards of the circulating stream, but almost no red blood corpuscles at all! Something seems to have attacked them — that something being the mysterious 'poppy field' you see. I'm not going to say what I suspect those growths to be until I see McKenzie, but you can bet your boots I wouldn't want them rioting around in my blood!"

VIII

BY NATURE something of a fatalist himself, Sherrod Guest did not struggle longer against either the smothering cloth or the ropes which trussed his arms and legs. Upon loss of the automatic he realized resistance to be useless. Trusting himself to the tender mercies of Sam Lee Moy — particularly, when engaged upon a deliberate quest of the men who had wrecked his office — had been the ultimate in folly. Regrets were of no avail now, however. He felt himself borne on swiftly along a corridor which seemed ever to descend and turn to the left. Judging that he had been below street level at the moment he had been overpowered, Guest's imagination ran away within him. Though actual descent was only in the neighborhood of fifteen feet, he would have sworn that he was being taken to the very bowels of the limestone stratum underlying Chicago.

The padding of slippered feet on earthen floor came to an abrupt end. Guest was then thrown down like a sack of potatoes. Strong hands fastened upon his feet, dragged him forward until he felt himself suspended over vacancy — with only shoulders and heels touching upon solid ground. His feet were fastened to stakes in a fashion which allowed him freedom of movement only through six or eight inches. Then the rope binding his ankles was removed. His wrists were retied, being fastened down rigidly across his waist. Then the smothering cloth was removed.

Guest found himself blinking in the smoky radiance of seven large lamps with floating wicks. The oil being consumed possessed a strange, sickly sweet aroma; it furnished a yellowish-green glare of light most unpleasant to Occidental eyes. The chamber itself was perhaps twenty feet by twelve in size, with ceiling reinforced by rough beams, supported by thin wooden shafts of rickety, insecure appearance.

Squatting on mats in a semi-circle before him sat seven Chinese, all of them smoking long-stemmed pipes and betraying not by the flicker of a muscle the fact that they were aware of his presence.

Four more Chinese, heavy-set, unintelligent-appearing specimens of the coolie class, completed arrangements in regard to Guest. One placed a black lacquered box, of approximately a bushel capacity, on the prisoner's middle, lashing it into place by a rope attached to two handles on the sides. Another drew down a curious spout or pipe of wood, until its ends swung one foot above the box. A third Chinaman pulled on a heavy gauntlet of leather which reached up above his elbow. Then, kneeling, he plunged his arm down into the black void beneath Guest, who had been straining his muscles to keep from slumping into this hole.

The Chinaman came up with a wriggling serpent the length of his arm clutched in the gauntlet. The snake, grasped firmly just behind the head, writhed earnestly in an attempt to escape, but in vain. The Chinaman, maintaining the same grim silence, held it up before Guest, who realized with a shudder, that it was a copperhead, the deadliest snake of North America. Then the coolie tossed back the serpent into its hole in the ground. Sherrod Guest, though his joints were beginning to ache, found new incentive to keep himself from slipping head first into that pit.

He smiled grimly. "Well," he remarked, his voice echoing strangely in the inclosed chamber, "the party seems to be ready to proceed. May I inquire why I am the recipient of such elaborate attention?"

Not a word came from any of the Chinamen. They continued smoking imperturbably. The four coolies, their tasks completed, turned and left the chamber by the single entrance. At that moment Guest, squirming in discomfort from his strained position, observed something which brought a gasp of dismay to his lips. The wooden spout which had been pulled into position above the box on his waist, led upward to a large container, raised to the ceiling by means of wooden stilts. From the mouth of the spout now a whitish, powdery trickle began. It fell directly into the box, a tiny stream of sand scarcely as thick as a shoe lace, and seemingly innocent of all ability for harm. Quietly, implacably it continued, however, while the seven Chinese sat and smoked. If they saw Guest or the sinister trickle of sand at all they gave no sign.

COLD perspiration broke out on the captive's forehead. There was no need to tell him the diabolical plan. Already his body sagged merely from its own weight. Continually, as he remembered that hideous wriggling death beneath him in the pit, his muscles tensed and strained. Even without the sand it would be only the space of an hour or two at most before he would be able no longer to hold himself stiffly in this position. The weight of sand, though scarcely a matter of ounces yet, would increase steadily, surely until it crushed him down. In spite of natural bravery and fortitude a cry of horror was wrung from his lips.

As if this had been the signal awaited, one of these seven smokers arose and waddled to his side, gazing down at Guest in impassive silence. The latter decided not to give the watchers the comfort of hearing him voice his terror; but at length he knew that the Oriental would stand there immobile for hours if necessary. Guest shuddered. "Oh, what is it you want? Why have you brought me here?" he cried.

"You and your honored companion, Mr. Kuban Lacey, have received the accumulated wisdom of Cho Keng Lu and Chingte Chien T'ao Lu. This is our property and for it we have searched twelve years. Only because of greed of a white man who was treacherous to his master did we come upon any trace of it. Already it has cost the life of the guilty man, he who robbed our tong. His purpose was known. You and his kinsman, Lacey, were given charge of the trea-

sure. Because we know that you are not sufficiently skilled to betray any of the secrets, without the manuals by which to proceed, we offer to you, to Kuban Lacey, and to the woman known as Irene Jeffries freedom and life in exchange for complete restitution of that which we seek. Otherwise —" He motioned significantly at the trickling sand.

The offer was almost as intelligible to Sherrod Guest as if it had been couched in Sanskrit. He realized that this was indeed an assemblage of the T'ao tong, and that the quiet yellow men before him were not of the type that wastes either words or actions. Even the spokesman, who used academic English with not even a trace of sing-song accent, impressed Guest as being in deadly earnest. The weight of sand, now becoming appreciable against his chest and stomach, backed up the threat with unmistakable vigor. Guest was certain that if he could not appease these men he had only a matter of minutes to live, yet the most desperate striving of imagination could not encompass the nature of treasure supposed to have been given into his keeping. Noah Lacey might have passed something to Cube, but if so the latter had not mentioned the fact.

Controlling his voice as best he could, Guest professed entire ignorance of what was desired from him. He possessed no treasure of any kind. He was no coward, however, and did not pretend bravado or bluster. In this subterranean chamber, cut off by his own folly from any chance of communication or help, he simply could disappear — after whatever tortures these silent, serious men deemed necessary. Nevertheless he pleaded to be told more concerning the mysterious treasure, explaining in brief sentences that he had sought out members of the T'ao tong for the reason of investigating the wrecking of his own offices. Had these Celestials expected to find the treasure there? The last words came from him with difficulty. Muscles of back, legs and chest ached fiercely now, and each breath was torture in itself.

The tong man who had delivered the ultimatum, however, folded his arms and stared down at the victim in impassive silence.

Apparently he considered further words a waste of time. he would wait, wait, until the desired confession burst from the prisoner's lips, or paralyzed muscles gave way beneath the mounting weight of sand.

In vain Sherrod argued and pleaded for a chance to ask his partner concerning the treasure, and denied utterly any knowledge of it. The Chinaman remained unmoved and silent, and the sand trickled down. Not a sound came from any of the other six. At last Guest understood. He was doomed. From that moment he lapsed into dogged silence. Labored breathing came in gusts between set teeth. He hung on valiantly, blindly, but without a vestige of hope. Fifteen minutes passed. Twenty. The end came suddenly. Overwrought nature surrendered. Guest fainted.

THROUGH dim beginnings of regained consciousness he was aware mainly of a sensation of surprise that he still lived. Sand was in his eyes, nostrils and all over his body. The contents of the box had overturned upon him when he fell. What had become of the snake?

He simply had underestimated his foes. They had carried out their threat to the dénouement they had expected, but had saved him from death — for further torture. The serpent evidently had been removed from below.

He was in a different position now, held to the wall of the chamber by a shackle attached to one ankle, and another which fitted closely about his neck in the form of a brass collar. A chain, attached to the latter, looped loosely upward to disappear through an interstice in the wall.

The Chinamen had disappeared. The only other living thing in the chamber beside himself was a wise, nonchalant-appearing parrot who perched himself across on the end of the sand spout, which now was shut off. "Well, Polly," began Sherrod ruefully, "what are they doing to you?

The bird turned and eyed him sidewise. "Murder! Tear him to pieces; Awk!" remarked the parrot with grave indifference, biting off his lurid words with impassive gusto.

In spite of his predicament Guest chuckled. The mirth was short-lived, however. Of a sudden he felt himself jerked upward to his toes. The slack in the chain attached to his collar had been taken up! He was stretched to extreme height along the wall, with chin uptilted by the collar of brass.

Five seconds, ten seconds, he stood thus, wondering what would come next. Then behind him in the wall sounded a dull click, as of a pawl slipping one notch over ratchet wheel. The chain attached to the brass collar tightened the length of a single link!

How long he stood there he never knew. It seemed a nightmare of hours, but probably only minutes passed before the same Chinaman who had presided over the previous torture, appeared. The latter bowed gravely to the prisoner.

"It is a maxim of law in your country," he began suavely, halting before Guest, "that a man cannot be executed or punished twice for the same offense. There is no such custom in my country. There a man may die a hundred deaths —" he paused significantly, gesturing at the shackles.

"But I swear to you that I know nothing of what you want!" cried Guest, his voice cracking under the strain of the collar on his throat. At that moment a second click and tightening of the chain informed him that the diabolical device would continue to strain at his frame until ligaments were torn from joints, or his neck broken.

"That is our misfortune, and the misfortune of several of your people," countered the Oriental gravely. "Right now through the corridors near here your friend Mr.

Lacey is searching for you. He has several policemen with him, but they will be unsuccessful in their search. The chambers are sound-proof, so you may call to him as you will." He bowed again and departed.

Until the chain had tightened two more links Sherrod Guest shut his lips against the cry of useless warning and appeal for help he craved to utter, but then it was torn from his lips. He could have guessed — if time for cold examination of the statement had been given to him — that Cube Lacey was not in this section of the city. Time had not been given for tracing the movements of Sherrod Guest, but the latter was too disturbed for careful thinking. He cried out warnings and appeals for help at the top of his lungs. The parrot, still perched upon the sand spout, squawked out his agonized cries in ghastly imitation.

IX

CUBE LACEY was so interested in the possibilities held forth by the half-promise given him by Krahn, the scientist, that he prevailed upon the latter to phone immediately to the botanist McKenzie. "Never get him at this time of day," cried Krahn. "He's too busy."

Perhaps it was the timbre of excitement in the chemist's voice which decided McKenzie. Perhaps it was the fact that time is always of the essence where examination of a fresh specimen is concerned. At any rate the jovial, canny Scot agreed to run out to the laboratory and glance at the curious puzzle awaiting him under the microscope. An hour later he arrived, greeted Lacey and Krahn with offhanded courtesy, and demanded immediately to be shown this mysterious vegetable interloper they had found in a specimen of human blood.

Drawing up a chair he seated himself before the microscope, removed his heavy eye-glasses, and adjusted the height of the microscope cylinder to his own myopic vision. An inarticulate exclamation left his lips. The two watchers saw him hunch up closer as if in excitement. His finger fumbled in jacket pocket, coming up with a small leather covered notebook and stub of drawing pencil.

"Very — ah — unusual!" he muttered. "Strange, yes, very strange!" He focused and refocused, searching out each detail of the picture unfolded beneath his eye. Then with many hasty glances down into the microscope, he sketched a picture in the notebook of an oval cell from which sprouted a curious organism — the one which Lacey and Krahn had likened to a poppy. Where the roots of the plants burled themselves in the oval cell the wall of the latter was broken down. Part of the contents seemed to have been sucked out by the tendrils of root.

A full hour McKenzie pored over his diagram, changing details gradually until he had a completed picture. Then he snapped the notebook shut and placed it carefully in an inside pocket, as though it suddenly had become valuable.

"A new species!" he said with emphasis, getting up from the chair. "Tell me all about it, where you found it, and everything concerning its relation to this mystery of which you were speaking, Krahn."

The younger scientist, with the help of many elaborations from Cube, did as requested. Strangely enough, McKenzie's interest seemed to center upon the change of complexion in Noah Lacey immediately prior to his death, and the fetid vats of green slime which Cube had discovered in the laboratory.

"Take me right out to that place!" McKenzie demanded seriously, every trace of joviality gone from his manner. "I think that you two have made a very striking discovery, one hitherto unknown either in botany or physiology. A fungus! One that grows in the blood stream of human beings just like its relatives live in sea water!"

"All right," acceded Cube thoughtfully. "You are welcome to the discovery, Mr. McKenzie. Personally, I don't know a fungus from a cabbage. What I have to learn, however, is the relation, if any, which this has to the death of Noah Lacey. Do you think —?"

"Guessing has no place in scientific investigation!" rebuked McKenzie gruffly. "After about twenty minutes out there, provided everything is as you say, I shall be able to tell you pretty well how your relative died!"

A STRANGE sense of emptiness assaulted Cube as soon as he and the others had entered the portals of Brick Knob. The front gate stood unlocked, which was unusual enough. No one came to meet them as they crossed the yard, ascended the steps and entered the front hallway. Cube called aloud to Irene, and then rang for Kohler Andrews. No one appeared. Vastly perturbed, Cube nevertheless led the two scientists to the basement laboratory, after pointing out to them the telephone chair against which Noah Lacey had fallen. In the basement both McKenzie and Krahn gave immediate absorption to the glass-lined vats of greenish slime. Krahn had brought with him his microscope and a set of slides. The two busied themselves in the examination of specimens taken from the vats.

Cube excused himself and went upstairs, starting a search through each of the rooms of the house from front to back. He found no one. Worried by an apprehension he could not voice, he called up the hotel to which Irene had promised to go for the night. It was scarcely dusk as yet, but she might have become frightened and left early. No one by name of Jeffries had registered!

Thoroughly aroused now, Cube hastened through another, more thorough search of the house. As he reached the front hall for a second time, a sound of voices out in the court attracted! his attention. Glancing out of the window he saw two men, carrying a stretcher upon which lay a blanketed figure, crossing the yard. Accompanying these were two stalwart policemen in uniform.

Chill apprehension gripped Lacey, and he cried aloud from dreadful certainty that the figure on the stretcher would prove to be Irene Jeffries. For an instant it seemed as though the solid floor beneath him had given way. The girl who, a moment before, had been recognized only as delightful companion and comrade now seemed inexpressibly dear to him. Throwing open the doors he advanced to meet the sombre cortege. One of the two stretcher bearers was known to him. He greeted the men and then, as the officers bustled up, took the liberty of throwing back the covering which veiled the face of the quiet figure on the stretcher. With a gasp, first of horror, and then of relief as he recognized the face, he saw feminine clothing. The woman was Mrs. Andrews.

"D'you know her?" demanded the first of the officers. "She come running out and fell right into me arms! She was shot, I guess. Anyway, Doc Stone says she's dead now. How did it happen, anyway?"

He and the other bluecoat crowded close to Lacey, exhibiting a disposition to run the latter in without further clamor. A glance at Lacey's shield was necessary before they consented to view the matter with open minds for the time being.

Lacey ushered them into the house,

saw to it Mrs. Andrews was placed upon her own bed, and left the officers poking around the unfamiliar house while he descended in the elevator to apprise Krahn and McKenzie of the latest development.

He found the two scientists far from the microscope which had formed the center of attraction for them earlier. Krahn, clasping a large plaster mold, crouched beside one wall of the basement. McKenzie, holding a heavy green jug of earthenware over his shoulder, waited on the opposite side. Both seemed about to spring upon a square of empty floor!

"Sh-h!" cautioned McKenzie, pointing cryptically at the ceiling between them. "He'll be coming down now, I'm thinking."

Involuntarily Cube glanced upward. It seemed to him that the tiles above moved imperceptibly. He started back, yanking out a pistol. A section of the laboratory ceiling perhaps twelve by thirteen feet in dimension, swung down slowly by one end. Cube saw that the upper side was runged in form of a ladder, The lower end reached the laboratory floor, and almost immediately a stocky individual began to descend. He came down backward, not vouchsafing a glance to the room below. Smiling grimly, Cube replaced the automatic in his pocket and crouched for a leap. In spite of American clothes, he saw the man to be Chinese. Silently he motioned the two scientists not to interfere.

Before the newcomer could swing about Cube hit him. It was a clean football tackle, catching the Chinaman just above the knees and bearing him heavily sidewise to the floor. The weighted stairs swung slowly upward, ending in its original position flush with the ceiling.

Cube did not give his quarry a chance to struggle. Versed to some degree in the arts of wrestling and ju-jutsu, he quickly overpowered the surprised Oriental. The man was heavy, but flabby of physique, and put up a desperate though useless struggle.

In twenty seconds Cube was astride his chest, and holding out the doughy arm flat to the floor. In the meantime Krahn had discovered a spool of copper wire on one of the tables. With this crude but efficient agent they bound the wrists and ankles of the captive.

"Now you have a lot to explain," commented Cube savagely, addressing his prisoner. "Where is Sherrod Guest? Where is Irene Jeffries? And Kohler Andrews? How did you kill Noah Lacey?"

The Chinaman, evidently recognizing the hopelessness of his predicament, gazed about stolidly at first. Lester Krahn pushed forward. "McKenzie can answer that last question for you, I believe," he stated. "You're probably more interested in the rest right now however. If there is any way in which we can help —"

Cube scowled menacingly. "I'll get the truth out of him!" he muttered. "Don't worry about that." His hand dropped suggestively to the butt of his automatic.

"Violence will not be necessary!" broke in the Chinese unexpectedly. "For me the end has come. I it was who killed your esteemed uncle. My associates now hold the detective whom you are seeking. There is only one way in which you ever will see him alive. Deliver to us the manuals stolen from the T'ao tong by your uncle!"

"Manuals? What do you mean?" demanded Cube blankly.

The tong agent's face wreathed in a cynical, disbelieving smile. "Explanations are unnecessary!" he snapped, and then as if suddenly invoking the spirits of his ancestors, the man broke into guttural Chinese.

While the three Americans gazed at him in perplexity, he leaned forward suddenly, gnawing at something on the breast of his blouse. Too late Cube guessed the reason. Half of a black button had been chewed away. The Oriental quickly swallowed this, a convulsive shudder almost immediately attacking his frame. In a few seconds he fell back limply, stone dead.

Krahn leaned forward, gingerly holding the chewed button to his nostrils. "Potassium cyanide!" he commented wryly. "Looks like he half expected to be caught at something. Prepared to cash in his own checks rather than take a chance with execution — or torture."

X

"HOW did you come upon him?" demanded Cube, somewhat ashamed and angry with himself for allowing the Oriental's suicide. The man might have been made to divulge all of the secrets now tormenting Lacey; but the method of carrying a load of poison disguised as a common button had been novel to the detective.

"He came upon us, rather," responded McKenzie. "We weren't looking for visitors at all, but a squeak like a rusty hinge sounded behind. We turned, and saw a whole piece of the wall swinging open over there." He gestured at a blank stretch upon which Cube could discern no hint of door. "Knowing it couldn't be you, Krahn and I dodged behind two of these pillars. A Chinaman came in, but only glanced about casually. Probably he didn't know we were in the house at all. He turned and did something in the wall, pressed a button or something, I suppose, and those stairs swung down. He climbed up the stairs and out of sight. Where do they lead?"

Lacey considered the ceiling. "To my uncle's rooms, I believe," he answered. "But this door of which you spoke, let's find it, and discover where it leads. Miss Jeffries knows of the passage, but she is not here at present. I'd rather not have a helpless girl along, anyway, if there proves to be trouble. We might locate a dozen more Chinese."

McKenzie grimaced, glancing down at the dead Celestial. It was plain he had little relish for active adventure of so serious a type. Cube caught the expression. It fitted in with his plans exactly. "If you'll do something, Mr. McKenzie," he added quickly, "I believe Krahn and I can handle affairs down here. Will you go up and inform the officers of what has happened. Tell them that inspector Harris ought to be notified. We're likely to need help before this is over."

The botanist obeyed with alacrity, slamming the door of the elevator hastily when he glimpsed Cube hand one of his automatics to Krahn. "Know how to use it?" asked Lacey.

"Never fired one in my life, but I'm glad to get hold of it!" replied the chemist pluckily. "This little dew-dad is the safety catch, isn't it? Do you have to pull the trigger for every shot, or does merely keeping it down make the darned thing work?"

Cube explained and demonstrated, and then the two approached the section of wall in which the door to the secret passage was located. Lacey realized that perhaps his greatest danger now would come from the weapon in his companion's hands, yet between himself and Krahn lay an unexpressed kinship of liking for unusual adventure which possesses an etiquette of silence all its own. Men will risk serious injury or even death itself for it, rather than take the obvious and commonsense course of obviating risk to which they have committed themselves.

Without fore-knowledge of the fact that a door actually existed, neither of the men could have discovered it. Even Krahn, long-trained in impressing photographic detail upon sensitive negative of brain, could not trace with any surety the irregular line. He indicated a one-foot space, however, in which he swore the door edge existed, and though Cube, after hasty examination looked at his companion doubtfully, Krahn found it himself. The aperture had been fitted so closely that only the breadth of a thin penknife could be inserted. Prying open was obviously impossible, but Cube accidentally solved the new riddle. Knocking each tile beside the length of the door, with his knuckles, he discovered a small mosaic which rattled in its place. Quick experimentation with this showed that it slid forward and back; pulling forward released a catch, allowing the door to swing open the distance of three inches. Cube caught it and flung it wide, propping it open with a heavy mould. "Might want to come back in a hurry," he explained succinctly.

One glance had shown the men that instead of the narrow passage both of them expected, the door opened upon a chamber extending at right angles to the line of house wall. Outside of faint illumination from laboratory lights it was pitch black, but Cube, after exposing himself in the doorway for a fraction of a second, boldly flashed his hand torch. He saw that the chamber stretched outward from the house wall a distance of twenty-five or thirty feet, and that on the far side a black opening indicated a continuation of the passage. This was not surprising, in view of the fact that electrical connections for the six-foot zone with burglar-alarm connections in the dooryard necessarily must have some means by which electrical contacts could be installed or repaired. The chamber lay directly below the strip.

This feature was not what caused Lacey to stop as if petrified. On the floor fifteen feet distant, and strutting about like a drum major leading dress parade, was the parrot!

"Hold up!" cried Lacey, thrusting back his eager companion. "I want to catch him!"

Krahn, not understanding, obeyed nev-

ertheless. Lacey walked cautiously forward, groping for a notion of what the parrot likely would do in this low-ceiled room. "Pretty Polly!" he exclaimed cajolingly.

The bird lifted one leg and scratched his head. "Well, I'll be switched!" he squawked.

In that second the detective dove, crushing the green plumage in his arms just as Sun Yat decided that the vicinity of floor he had chosen had become dangerous. "Got you now!" Lacey gasped, the breath knocked from his lungs by his sudden header to the brick floor, He clasped the bird's head expertly between two fingers, seeing to it that the fiendish beak got no chance at his flesh.

"Aw hell!" remarked Sun Yat disgustedly. "We got a lady now. A lady! Haw!"

"A lady?" cried Cube, horrified that the bird might be repeating real information he had heard somewhere. Then he tried in vain to get it to repeat his message — if such it was — but nothing was forthcoming save a stream of invective. Taking the parrot back into the laboratory, Cube imprisoned him under an inverted bushel basket, wedged beneath a bench in such manner that the bird's struggles would be as ineffectual as his language. Then Cube and Krahn returned to the underground chamber.

Luckily, the corridor beyond proved to be empty. It ran straight for a distance of sixty feet, then angled to the right to end in another door of masonry. The latter was equipped with a heavy iron handle on the inside, which manipulated the lock. Turning this cautiously, Cube discovered that the door opened inward. Peering through, he saw the reason. Boxes and barrels were piled against it, making a climb necessary.

The two men listened intently, but only dull noises from some distance overhead reached their ears. They were in the basement of an apartment building, not far from the huge boiler of the steam plant, for the air was hot and sultry. Cautiously they emerged, but no one was in sight. The way lay open to the street outside via a tunnel-like passage between two wings of the building.

Here Cube, searching carefully as he proceeded, descried something white and rumpled lying on the cement. He picked it up, and a cry of dread apprehension and certainty was wrung from his lips. The bit of cloth and lace was a woman's handkerchief; daintily embroidered in one corner was the monogram I.J. The parrot had been coached in the truth!

XI

INSPECTOR HARRIS was inclined to scoff at first when Lacey's message reached headquarters. The sight of the dead Chinaman sobered him, however, and when Cube insisted that Irene Jeffries, Sherrod Guest, and Kohler Andrews doubtless all were in the hands of the tong he had little to say. After viewing the parrot, however, he let slip one surprising item of information.

"Those Chinks are apt to discover that they've got hold of a pair of Tartars!" he commented grimly. "That is, if your friend Guest is as much of a detective as Irene."

"A — a what?"

"Sure, didn't you know she was an operative? Well, she is. With Pinkertons. Old Lacey employed her right along, getting her to stay here at the house and pretend she was a ward of his. But let's get busy. Maybe that Chink has something in his clothes which will give us a steer."

Search of the corpse revealed nothing of the sort, but from an inside pocket Harris drew forth a small rubber bellows. He was in the act of squeezing this when Krahn caught his hands.

"Don't," cried the chemist sharply. "Here, drop that thing a minute. It's deadly! Take a look at it, McKenzie. Don't you think —?"

The botanist nodded slowly, staring down at the bellows in fascination. "Probably so!" he agreed. "Mr. Lacey, did your uncle snore?"

Cube looked blank. "Heavens, I don't know," he answered.

"Sa-ay!" broke in Harris, frowning in exasperation. "What are you three trying to do; kid me? This is a blamed serious matter."

"Quite true," agreed Krahn acidly. "It would have been still more serious if you had blown the stuff which is in that bellows around this room where we could breathe it. Tell him, Macs!"

The latter was nothing loath. He launched into a technical description of the lower forms of plant life — bacteria and fungi. Harris, still suspicious, listened impatiently. "What all this has got to do with murder I don't see," he interrupted.

"Well, in so many words," answered McKenzie, "our tests of blood from Mr. Noah Lacey reveal the fact that his circulatory system was crammed with fungi! These had been feeding parasitically on his red blood corpuscles. Though he actually died from the blow on his forehead, these fungi caused the fainting spell. They'd have killed him in another day or two, anyway. The fungi, I believe, are a species new to scientists here. That green slime over there in the tank is almost a pure culture of the organisms. The dampness keeps them from being much of a menace, however. The murderer of Mr. Lacey took a quantity of the fungi, dried it out, and then blew some of the spores from this bellows — probably over Lacey's bed while the victim lay asleep. The reason why I asked concerning the snoring was that, if these had been drawn through the nostrils, many of them never would have reached the lungs and the blood stream. Of course only a few spores actually had to be inhaled."

"Good night!" exclaimed Harris. "And this was the bird that turned the trick, then!"

"Yes, he confessed it. Until I saw the bellows, though, I had been trying to imagine the means employed to get the spores into the air. They'd be mighty dangerous to handle in the dry state."

Harris shivered. "If it's all right with you," he said, "I'd like to wrap up that thing and let you carry it. I don't fancy getting a load of green slime in my blood."

HARRIS employed ordinary police methods. The inspector was not brilliant, but he went forward in ordinary routine, bulldog manner, and had at his back all the necessary resources of his department. He began by questioning everyone, by calling in Chinese residents of different portions of the city in the attempt to identify the dead man — a possibility which did not materialize immediately in admitted recognition, though behind masks of disinterest worn by two merchants of Chinatown, Cube fancied he detected curious flickers of alarm. Harris was confident enough that sooner or later he would succeed in naming the suicide, for it was plain the man had been a member of the ranking classes, educated and well-to-do.

Harris began an examination of all Noah Lacey's papers, emptying two bank lockboxes. In all this mass of material, however, was not one word dealing directly with tong, or indeed, with any part of the past which seemed to have bearing upon the fact of his murder. An old will was uncovered, by the provisions of which all his wealth was bestowed upon an organized charity which had gone out of existence six years before. His lawyers, Barnes & Tegardine, came forward with a recent codicil, however, by which bequests of five thousand dollars each were named for Kohler and Mrs. Andrews, twenty-five thousand dollars for Irene Jeffries, and three or four other small

amounts given to various organizations in which Noah Lacey had been interested. The residue of the estate — estimated conservatively at something over four million dollars — was willed to "my contrary-minded, but admirable nephew, Kuban Lacey!"

The young man, however, was in no mood to realize or rejoice in his good fortune. The great fact that Irene Jeffries and Sherrod Guest were in the hands of the tong drove him frantic. He divorced himself as quickly as possible from Harris's humdrum procedure, and wracked his brain to imagine a shortcut. Krahn stayed with him, deserting his laboratory for a day; the scientist set himself the job of supplementing Cube's experimental logic. He seemed to believe that in the mysterious manuals spoken of by the dead Chinaman would lie a direct clue.

"From what you've told me," he said to Cube, glancing questioningly about the tiled walls of the laboratory, "I think your esteemed uncle must have had some sort of a repository here in this house. Certainly nothing like manuals of any description have been uncovered in his safety deposit boxes. Don't you suppose really that those manuals had something to do with the art of ceramics?"

Cube flashed a look of interest. "That's exactly what I've been thinking," he agreed. "Irene told me that he had learned how to reproduce ancient pieces of pottery and porcelain."

"Worth a great deal of money?"

"Ye-es — although he never sold the reproductions."

Krahn waved this aside as unimportant. "Then," he deduced with a hint of triumph, "if this tong's name means the fictile arts; if they have committed murder and abduction to regain certain manuals stolen by your uncle; if after his visit to China he suddenly learned how to manufacture art objects which previously had lain beyond his skill, it appears to me that the stolen manuals must have made the difference — and that they must have been concealed down here in the laboratory where he could get at them constantly!"

Cube nodded slowly, hope firing his eyes for the first time in hours. "I know a little about the way vases are made," he said. "Do just what I say for a second, Krahn. You're almost exactly my uncle's height."

Obediently the chemist stood before the "kick wheel" — that device for "throwing" pottery shapes by centrifugal force — raised his right arm toward the wall and watched while Cube marked out a circle of normal reach. Inside the circle, all the tile, brick and mosaic were too small to house a single receptacle, and anchored firmly by mortar. Cube, however, was not dismayed in the least. He had not expected to find anything here really, as manuals suggested a table or bench upon which they might be spread for consultation.

Next in order came the bench upon which were placed the plaster slabs for mixing and working the pastes and clay. After marking out as before the entire space circled by the radius of Krahn's reach, Cube went over it quickly with a small hammer, sounding each tile. Midway in the length of wall he stopped, uttering an excited exclamation. A large tile before him sounded more than ordinarily hollow, and shook in its socket of mosaics under impact! Quickly, fiercely, Cube battered at it, not waiting to attempt discovery of possible secret button.

The tile cracked. A fragment came away. Ten seconds more and Cube thrust a hand through the aperture.

"It's here!" he cried exultantly, bringing forth two encased rolls, the covers of which seemed to be of waterproofed, silken fiber. Beside these — one of which Krahn immediately slit open — a single envelope lay back in the tile repository.

"These are all in Chinese!" exclaimed Krahn in a disappointed tone, unwinding part of a beautiful fabric of watered silk upon which six columns of "running writing" were done in black and lavender. "Still, they're the manuals, I'll wager. Couldn't really expect them to be translated for us. But what is that you have?"

For a second Cube did not answer. He had broken open the letter, and was reading. "This is what we were looking for!" he said huskily. "Listen!" He read the terse paragraphs, which were addressed to himself. The date on the latter was recent — the identical day upon which Noah Lacey had met his death:

My dear pig-headed nephew —

Because of that old quarrel with your father, I never bothered you until today — when I realized that death was standing at my elbow. I am weak, and growing steadily weaker. Even whisky isn't worth much. My precautions have been useless. the tong has done me in — how, I can't say. That's up to you. I had intended to tell you all I knew, and keep you with me till the last, but you were too all-fired independent. Frankly enough, you made me angry for a few moments, but a dying man can't afford to cherish animosity long. I've followed your attempts at making a living, and while I don't care much for your election of profession, still I presume you have as much right to choice as I had.

If you're any good at all you'll realize the fact that I have been murdered — if not at first, at least when the tong gets after you. Run them down, if you can. If you can't, you won't live long to enjoy the wealth I am leaving to you. Any time you see a Chinaman or a parrot, dodge — and watch your step thereafter! The tong has a method of imparting unpleasant information by a wise old parrot. I imagine he must have been one of the pets of Confucius.

The trouble all has arisen because of the two manuals you find herewith. They are written by Cho Keng Lu and Chingte Chien T'ao Lu — the latter the founder of the T'ao tong. The manuals reveal secrets regarding the making of fine pottery and porcelain — secrets which have been unknown both to white men and to all save certain art guilds in China, for centuries. In a word, the secret of fine luster and glaze has lain in the use of certain fungi, mixed with cultural media and left to work in the glaze before it is applied. You will find a tank full of the fungi down here. The guilds, always selling fine vases and other "genuine" relics of past ages, were very jealous of the secrets. I suppose they are worth millions, really. Anyway, the tong let me give them the slip, and I can't imagine how they ever got track of me again, as I never sold any vases — and gave only one away.

My intention was to translate the two, and then return the originals to the owners when my books were published. In fact I really did finish one translation, but it was stolen. Luckily they did not find the originals.

What you wish to do with the manuals is strictly up to you. The tong is after them, and will keep after them until either the manuals are secured, they are published in translation and therefore worthless except as relics, or all the tong members are dead. I believe in all there are only some two hundred members, most of whom probably will keep after you while you have the manuals.

That's all. In case you go ahead and have them translated and published, you may consider my legacy a fee for a lifetime — probably mighty short — of excitement and trouble.

NOAH LACEY.

P. S. When you reach an age of discretion you night do much worse than marry Miss Jeffries. She's a corker. If I'd been ten years younger I'd have proposed to her, myself.

N.L.

Krahn exhaled sharply. "If I were in your place, Lacey," he advised, "I'd get rid of those confounded things just as fast as I could!"

Cube nodded. "Yes, they're stolen goods," he said. "We have no right to them. The first feature is to find Irene and Sherrod, however, and I believe a glimmering of an idea of how to accomplish it is creeping into my head!"

"How?" demanded Krahn.

"Ask the parrot!" responded Cube, smiling grimly, and immediately hastening up to Harris to demand a loan of the loquacious bird.

XII

CUBE'S plan, which came to him while reading the letter, like an inspiration of Providence, was regarded by Harris with much more tolerance than the man would have exhibited a day earlier. Harris, be it known, though he was sufficient of a sport in his own estimation to admit himself wrong and Lacey right at the start, gnawed his lip in rage when the best work he could put upon the case yielded no tangible result. In his way he admired Irene Jeffries, both as a member of his own profession and as a very pretty woman, and the thought of her in the hands of members of the tong nearly drove him into black fury. He suspected that she and Guest both had been killed, yet he held his tongue and acquiesced with good grace in Cube's plan for instant action.

Obedient to his hurried orders, six of the best operatives in the city were summoned and disguised in the garb and complexion of Orientals as well as men owning the names of McManus, Casey, Goelitz, Marge, Liebacher, and Krych could be disguised. Behind the car in which they rode came two loads of bluecoats — their machine just keeping in sight of the car ahead. Two blocks ahead of them limped a clumsily disguised Chinaman carrying a wooden cage in which squalled the ill-tempered Sun Yat. Cube Lacey had been careful to see that while costume and facial coloration might pass muster with Americans, the dullest observer among the Chinese would guess his probable nationality in a second. On this lay the greater part of his hope.

All cars were left some blocks from the intersection of Twenty-Second Street and Archer Avenue. Loitering along singly, the six "Chinese" followed Cube at a respectful distance. The police, whose job was to scatter through the district back in the alleys — always keeping the next member in sight and one at least, watching the pseudo-Orientals — did not appear on either of the two main streets. Cube was far from certain that this was the district in which the tong held forth, yet he relied upon the light of fear he thought he had surprised in the eyes of the two wholesale merchants questioned by Harris. The shops of these two fronted upon Archer.

Cube stopped to gaze in one of the drab, unornamented windows. At that moment a squatting beggar near at hand, who had watched the queer visitor for several minutes through close-slitted, curious eyes, rose energetically and shuffled away. It was noticeable that soon afterward the watchful Sam Lee Moy appeared, strolling casually along this street of his domain. He appeared to examine the parrot with interest.

Came a mellifluous question in the Shensi dialect of China, which Cube, of course, could not understand. He shrugged, motioned to his ears and then to his tongue, as if pretending to be deaf and dumb. Sam Lee Moy grinned satirically to himself, and

began muttering something in English about liking the looks of the parrot, and would his countryman sell?

Cube, pretending not to understand — merely to follow his original idea — employed signs, indicating that he could be persuaded to part with the bird for ten dollars. Sam Lee Moy appeared to hesitate. Then after a swift glance up and down the street he beckoned to the owner of this famous parrot, and led him to a doorway. As he entered, Cube contrived to spill to the sidewalk a lump of ordinary anthracite coal, but to this lump was attached a length of black silk thread, the spool of which lay in Cube's pocket. Until one door closed upon the thread the detective was careful to pay it out generously, for fear of causing inexplicable gyrations of the innocent lump of coal.

For some reason, when his own quarters were reached, Moy appeared to grudge the payment of ten dollars for the bird. He remonstrated, speaking sometimes in English and sometimes in Chinese. The burden of his remarks was that he had hoped to buy Sun Yat at a cheap price, because a certain parrot fancier lived nearby. Moy would have liked to sell the bird to this other unnamed individual, himself, but since the stranger was so high-priced and obdurate, he could complete the sale himself. Moy would show him the way, if he cared to go?

Cube Lacey cared. He had taken his hint from Moy's words and manner, and realized that even if he had made the price of the bird ten cents instead of the really ridiculous price of ten dollars, Moy still would have found excuse to consult this collector of parrots. That way lay death, perhaps, yet Cube was in no mood to measure personal risk. On the slender thread which led backward to the street lay his hopes of escape, and of rescue of the others — if this proved indeed to be the place to which Irene and his comrade had been taken — but he fell in with Moy's suggestion as if greedy to meet the man who would pay ten dollars for his parrot.

The automatic in his pocket, at least, would account for some of the conspirators if worst came to worst. His only fear came from the actions of Sun Yat himself. The parrot refused to be silent. He either squawked out Chinese oaths, or repeated parts of the monologues which he had overheard. He recognized the smells and darkness of the corridor, and knew he was approaching home. If Cube only had guessed the fact, the parrot's noise was the detective's real salvation: it made Moy hurry on and down, not stopping to notice that his supposed victim was paying out length after length of the black silk thread. Some of the Chinese living in the cave-like rooms opening off this corridor were law-abiding, and not in sympathy with the T'ao tong. Moy was succeeding too well to be panic-stricken, yet he threw back over his shoulder several sharp commands in Chinese to the parrot — commands which Sun Yat contemptuously ignored. He cared nothing for Sam Lee Moy, or the foolish white man who carried his cage. When he got out he would nip both of them till they squealed! He, the honored member of a household which had furnished China with a dynasty of emperors!

At the end of the last corridor — the one which Sherrod Guest had traversed three days earlier — Sam Lee Moy began to chatter loudly. The reason was plain to Cube's ears. Behind the doorway ahead came mingled groans and execrations, tones which even the staccato shrilling of Moy could not drown. Cube's only comfort lay in the fact that he could not distinguish a woman's voice — yet Irene might be dead by now. One day and two nights she had been in the hands of the tong. Cube gripped his automatic, but his lips smiled.

Moy shifted something between his hands as he came to the last doorway. Cube, from the tail of his eye, saw that it was a loop of silk cord. Moy, bowing, stood aside as if to usher in his guest. As Cube reached Moy's side he brought up the silk loop. It never reached its mark. Dropping the parrot cage, Cube shot through his jacket pocket. Moy dropped with a grunt. The detective charged into the tong chamber.

A half-dozen Chinese ran to meet him. Cube got only a flash of Sherrod Guest, spread-eagled on the earthen floor beyond, and then he was shooting.

Two heavy-set Chinese went down before his bullets. A third staggered away screaming, as a bullet tore away part of his lower jaw. Then weight of numbers overcame Cube, who fell backward to the floor, albeit fighting with tooth and nail.

His automatic exploded once more before it was torn from his fingers, but the bullet impinged harmlessly upon the wall. His fingers, clawing, clutching, found the throat of another antagonist, and clung there, through the latter — as a last resort — went after a knife in his belt. When the conflict was quieted, only two unwounded Chinese remained, and one whose jaw wound threatened to kill him. Four husky coolies ran in, however, and were directed by one of the remaining tong members, who had helped to overcome the detective.

"This is one more, and the last one," observed the Chinaman calmly. "I know him. He is named Lacey, and he is the one to whom the manuals probably were given."

This was in English, for Cube's benefit. Followed sharp commands in Chinese, and Cube was shackled to the wall in the identical position once occupied by his comrade, Guest. Cube, overcome by loss of blood from a knife wound in his shoulder and upper arm, stared goggle-eyed across the chamber to a sinister armchair, in which he saw the pale, horrified face of Irene Jeffries. The girl was bound and helpless, yet Lacey breathed in momentary relief at the mere fact that she still was alive.

"Drink this!"

The fat, imperturbable Chinaman who had guessed his identity, held a small cup to

Lacey's lips. The latter, on the borderland of unconsciousness, obeyed without question. If they wished to kill him they could accomplish the deed without troubling to employ poison. He found the drink to be fiery, distilled liquor — probably saki. In the space of two minutes it brought back life to his brain and body. He was able to remember that close on his footsteps would come the detectives and police. He grinned weakly at his captor.

"You've got us," he said, sparring for time, "but it cost you a fair price, the way I see it."

"Price in lives or money is no object," returned the Chinaman in perfect English, and without betraying the slightest animosity. "For many years we have searched for our stolen property. Now we will have it. Mr. Noah Lacey gave it to you, of course?"

Cube essayed a laugh. "What would you say if I told you that your whole bunch has been barking up the wrong tree?" he asked. "If none of us ever had seen the manuals of which you speak?"

"I should say that you were lying."

"Well, think so if you want to. I don't know what I can do about that. As a matter of fact my uncle did not give the manuals to any one of us. Just today we found a clue. Oh yes, we had heard about them, well enough, but never had we seen them. I think perhaps I know where they are. Will you exchange the lives of us whom you hold captive for possession of the manuals?"

The Oriental was silent half a minute. "There is no need," he answered then, deliberately. "We cannot afford to release you. We can obtain the manuals, since you acknowledge that you know where they are. Then we shall kill you all — mercifully. You may choose your own deaths. Perhaps opium, gold leaf for the throat, or the strangler's cord? Otherwise, torture awaits all four of you. The three others have had some taste of our abilities already. Suppose you speak with them?"

"Well, perhaps that would be a good idea," responded Cube, on edge for the first sign of the detectives, who seemed to be taking an incomprehensibly long time. Had the silk thread been discovered? Or broken?

"If we can't win freedom I'd prefer, of course, a nice, clean sort of death rather than the torture I suppose you employ. Let me free an instant and I'll talk with Miss Jeffries and Mr. Guest."

The Oriental did not grant his wish. Smiling ironically, he bade two of the coolies release Cube from his bonds. A slip noose was placed over his neck, however, and his arms still remained shackled. A coolie walked behind, holding the other end of the noose, which could be tightened in the split part of a second, and which actually was sufficient of a bond to cut off part of his breath, even as adjusted.

He approached Irene. "This may be the end," he said, breathing with difficulty. "Before they do me in I want to tell you one thing. I love you!" He stopped. The answering light of wonderment and questioning in her eyes was his sufficient reward. She did not speak.

"This is the old choice," he continued, speaking louder for the benefit of the Chinese. "I know where the manuals are located. I found them today. In exchange for my knowledge they offer the three of us — I reckon Kohler Andrews must be here somewhere — a chance to die by a knife, bullet, opium, or in any other way we name. it's not life, but it really is better than the alternative, I suppose. They probably could torture us."

"Oh Cube!" she cried. "If it has to be, then let us tell them what they wish to know! I — I did not know. They have already —"

She got no further. In that second the door burst inward, and two husky Irishmen sprawled forward on the floor. Behind them came a multitude of others, however, men who shot first and waited until afterward to ask questions. The two first-comers rose, and added their streams of bullets. In eight seconds after the door went down not a Chinaman remained standing. Beside the two who still wriggled a detective sat with ready revolver.

The policemen, coming too late to enter the conflict, were dispatched to sentinel posts in the corridors. Krahn, his right hand covered with blood, found keys and unlocked the shackles of all four victims, cutting such bonds as he could not unlock.

"Poor Andrews is about done in," he said while freeing Cube. "I don't think he can live."

Cube scarcely paid attention. He was at the side first of Sherrod Guest. In the light this individual exhibited a terribly altered appearance, His sparse hair was dead white, and deep lines on his cherubic countenance testified to the suffering he had undergone.

"I've heard all about those damned manuals," Guest said huskily. "You want to get rid of them, of course. Weil, I'm through with detective work. Give me those manuals and I'll see that they are translated and published! The tong did not own them. They have been stolen many times. Give me that much revenge, will you Cube? I'm a broken man, I tell you!"

The detective regarded him solemnly. "As God is my judge I cannot fathom the rights of this," he said then. "I think I'm going to bank on you, however, Sherrod. I'll give you the manuals — providing only that you notify the T'ao tong of your intentions. And I'll give you money enough to carry through your purpose! It seems to me that this knowledge ought to be given to the world."

XIII

SHERROD GUEST never told the story of his tortures. Such as Irene had witnessed had been carried through more for the purpose of dragging a confession out of her than because of any further hope on the part of the tong that the secret of the manuals could be pried out of the man.

Finally they had given her up, also, convinced that neither of the two was in possession of the silken rolls. From that time on the Chinese treated both well enough, but held on to them as a bait for Kuban Lacey — who must have the manuals. What might have occurred in that grisly subterranean chamber, had Cube come alone, is better unimagined. None of the prisoners believed that, given a free hand after obtaining what they sought, the Chinese would have failed to exact vengeance in full for the trouble to which they had been put by the search.

Kohler Andrews paid the price of treachery, though the actuating reason for his torture was the fact that on many occasions his armed vigilance had frustrated plans of the tong. Once, also, a bullet from his revolver seriously wounded the chief of the conspirators, who thereafter thirsted for revenge. Before he died Andrews confessed to having sold three of Noah Lacey's vases which should have been destroyed. These, the tong — watchful for a number of years for sign of someone using the secret — traced back easily enough to Noah Lacey and the latter's laboratory.

The fact that Lacey, in the meantime — well realizing how insecure his life was bound to become at some time — had ensconced himself in the fortress-like Brick Knob, did not balk the tong delegation. Taking their time to search, they located various men who had been employed in building Brick Knob, and learned every feature of the dwelling, including all electrical devices, the tunnel opening for the laboratory into the basement of an apartment building owned by Noah Lacey, and the secret stairs leading downward from the owner's rooms to his laboratory.

Then they set spies upon Lacey. Many times these men remained inside the house for hours without being discovered. Once, when Noah Lacey brought up his finished script of the first roll meaning to revise it at his leisure, they found and stole the English version. All of their cunning failed, however, to locate the tile cache.

Despairing eventually of finding the manuals before Lacey somehow managed to translate them and send them out for publication, they decided to kill him, banking on the probability that in ensuing confusion the manuals would be brought to light, and that for a time, at least, none of Lacey's heirs would imagine them valuable enough to guard with care.

Except for the accidental intrusion of Irene and Cube, the murder never could have been suspected. The method of employing Noah Lacey's own fungi as the agent of his destruction — even if guessed by American doctors — must have made the death seem an accident.

Cube wasted no time in seeing to it that the fungus tanks were emptied. Also, while a certain investigation of his own was proceeding, he spirited the manuals out to the university, and gave them into the keeping of Doctor Benson, the professor of Oriental languages who had helped him earlier. Because new spies from the T'ao tong could not reach Chicago for some time, this seemed safe.

Though the Chinatown rooms occupied by agents of the tong were only temporary accommodations — commandeered from the sleek Moy for the use to which they were put — certain records unearthed there by Harris proved beyond a shadow of a doubt that the two manuals never had belonged by right to the T'ao tong, but had been stolen by them centuries ago from an historical museum. Noah Lacey simply had

employed the tong's own methods.

As soon as he knew this, Cube gave qualified permission to his comrade to go ahead with the translation of the rolls, making only the stipulation that when the English volumes were completed that the ideographed rolls be returned to the Chinese Government. Guest readily consented to this, and accepted a loan of twenty thousand dollars — money which once had belonged to Noah Lacey — to enable him to pursue the task. When he visited Benson he found that professor wildly excited, and clamoring for a chance to do the actual work of translation. The danger did not frighten him in the least. Guest, glad of such an accomplished ally, made an arrangement by which the two set up a laboratory in a place known not even to Cube.

While Benson translated, Guest worked out the processes practically, learning the ceramic art from the top down, as it were. The two men have been at work part of a year, at the present time. Occasionally an enthusiastic letter — enclosed in a plain envelope and post-marked New York City, which is not the place of their endeavor — comes to Cube, telling of great progress. Each one Cube burns carefully after reading it aloud to Irene.

He takes no chances, in spite of the fact that one of the wounded Chinese sent back a message — carefully translated by Benson — to the effect that neither Cube nor Irene Jeffries ever would have the manuals again. What the tong would make of the message was problematical.

Irene spent four days in the hospital recovering from her ordeal. Three young men — two of whom stared at each other inimically, and in speculative fashion at the third — delivered roses each day.

Krahn knew he was not in the running, and laughed at himself ruefully — yet persisted until the day when both he and Harris, admitted together as visitors, found Cube seated on the edge of Irene's bed, and that young woman wearing two full-blown roses in her cheeks that certainly had been given her personally by Lacey.

Harris scowled, but his heavy shoulders came up in a shrug of resignation as Krahn, spying the solitaire on her third finger, thrust out a hand in generous congratulation of his successful rival.

"Never was born lucky!" growled Harris. "But maybe this is the break. With Irene to look after, Lacey, you'll never have time to butt into my cases any more."

"Don't be too sure about that, Mr. Harris!" countered Irene, smiling as her arm replaced itself about the shoulders of her fiance. "Don't you think we'd make a good team? Cube says we'll just take the cases that you think are open-and-shut."

The police inspector's reply was unintelligible, though vehement.

AFTERWARDS
By Clark Ashton Smith

> *There is a silence in the world*
> *Since we have said farewell;*
> *And beauty with an alien speech*
> *An alien tale would tell.*
> *There is a silence in the world,*
> *Which is not peace nor quiet:*
> *Ever I seek to flee therefrom,*
> *And walk the ways of riot.*
> *But when I hear the music moan*
> *In rooms of thronging laughter,*
> *A tongueless demon drives me forth,*
> *And silence follows after.*

THE TAPIR

by **Arthur O. Friel**

I.

THAT IS A QUEER thing, *senhores*. You say that the tapir, so common here in South America, is found in no other continent except Asia, and there only in a section which you call Malaysia; and that place is thousands of miles from our Brazil and across a vast ocean. How could our tapir have gotten there? He never could swim so far!

Oh, I see. Pardon my foolish question. Long ago there were tapirs all over the world, but now they have died out almost everywhere? Yes, I can believe that, for the tapir has no defense except his thick hide and his habit of jumping into water when attacked; and both animals and men must be able to defend themselves, or they will be wiped out by others which are more fierce and better armed. So perhaps the odd part of it is not that there are so few tapirs on earth now, but rather that there are any at all.

He is a shy fellow, the tapir. He needs to be, for he is hunted both by beasts and by men. Among the wild Indians of our jungle, as you perhaps know, the greatest hunter is he who can find and kill that big, thick-skinned animal with funny nose. The prowling jaguar, too, is always eager to make a meal from him. Possibly you two North Americans also, during your explorations here at the Amazon headwaters, have slain a tapir or two for the sake of fresh meat. Yes? Then I need not tell you any more about that animal, for you probably know as much about him as I.

Still, I can tell you a tale of a tapir tonight, while this steamer slides along down the Amazon, which probably will amuse you. You have seen the tapir, observed his ways and tasted his flesh. But did you ever find one up in a tree, moaning and weeping from love?

Yes, it sounds ridiculous. But let me tell you, *senhores*, if ever I meet another lovesick tapir I shall go straight away and leave him, unless I am willing to get myself into trouble. And this is why:

ONE DAY in the flood season I was paddling down a swollen little river among wild hills in the Javary region — whether it was in Brazil or in Peru I do not know, for I had been on a long rambling trip into unknown country and neither knew nor cared where the boundary might be. With me was a fearless young comrade named Pedro, who, like myself, was a rubber-worker on the great *seringal* of the Coronel Nunes. The floods having stopped our work in the swampy lowlands, we had taken a canoe and gone out to seek adventures — and had found them. And now, having used up nearly all our cartridges in a battle with headhunting savages, we were on our way back to the headquarters of the *coronel*, paddling with our regular, long-distance stroke and expecting nothing at all to happen. But suddenly from the jungle near us came a mournful sound.

We held our paddles and looked. Only a few feet away was the hilly western shore of the stream, thick with bush. The sound had come from there, seeming to be a little distance away from the water and quite high up in the trees. We could not see anything in the tangle overhead, nor hear anything moving there. So after a minute I said softly to Pedro —

"Only a sick monkey grunting to himself."

He nodded slowly, as if in doubt, and continued squinting upward. I stroked again with my paddle, intending to go on. But before I put any power into the push the noise came again. I halted my arms.

"O-ho-o-o!" wailed a voice. "Oho-oo! Boo-hoo-hoo!"

We looked and listened. There was no sign of any man being in this place, but the voice was that of a man crying. It was a heavy voice, which ought to belong to a strong man; yet it was snuffling and sobbing there in the bush like that of a woman. To me, and I think also to Pedro, that sound was more dreadful than a cry of pain or a scream of fear; for it seemed that the man must be in a terrible condition to break down in that way. We turned the canoe, which had been drifting down the current, and silently paddled back.

Pedro, in the bow, jerked his head toward the shore. Looking closely, I saw what I had not noticed before — a quiet creek almost hidden by big drooping palm-leaves. We slipped the canoe through these leaves and stopped short. A few feet ahead of us was another canoe.

Then the voice came again. It was up over our heads.

"Oho-oo! What shall I do? I cannot live!" it sobbed.

More than twenty feet above the ground we spied a sort of house built in the branches of a big tree — a hut made from split palm logs and palm leaves. Up the trunk of the tree ran a stout notched pole making a ladder, such as we rubber-workers use in high tapping.

"The man must be dying alone up there, poor fellow," said Pedro.

I nodded. We stepped out on shore and went to the pole.

"What is the matter, friend?" Pedro called.

No answer came. There was a dead silence. Then we heard a slight movement up there, and out from a doorway at the top of the ladder came a head. We saw a dark face, with black hair and eyes. It peered down at us, and we started back. Then, without replying, the man swung himself out of the hut and came down the pole.

"Por Deus!" muttered Pedro. "He is not dying, nor even sick. He is as big and healthy as — as a tapir."

It was so. The fellow was so broad and heavy that it seemed as if the pole, stout though it was, ought to snap under him. Yet he was not clumsy; he came down so easily that we knew his muscles were strong and worked smoothly. I began to believe that there must be some one else up in that house, for it did not seem likely that this big man would have been moaning and blubbering so. But when he stood on the ground I saw that his eyes were wet and his face streaked, and the corners of his mouth turned down as if he were ready to start crying again.

As I looked at him I could not help grinning — partly because I was relieved, partly because his doleful face looked funny to me, and partly because Pedro's chance remark about a tapir was so near the truth. Above his heavy body and thick neck was the face of a tapir: for it was much narrower at the jaws than above the eyes, and the nose was so long and curving that it seemed to be not a nose but a snout. And, as I have said, the face was very dark, as the face of a tapir would be. He was a caboclo, with some white blood in him. Still, he looked like a good-natured young fellow, and he was not enough of an Indian to keep from showing his grief.

"What is the matter with you?" Pedro repeated. "We thought you were dying."

The other's mouth worked, and he sniffled.

"Maybe I am," he said in a choked tone. "I think I shall die. Oh, my poor little Bellie! Ah-hoo-wow!" He began to bawl.

"Your poor little belly?" demanded Pedro. "What ails your belly? It looks very healthy to me. Have you swallowed a live turtle?"

I snickered, and the tapir-man himself laughed. In the middle of a wail he changed his noise to a snort, and that in turn became heavy laughter. But then his mouth turned down again.

"You do not understand," he said. "I have lost my so-beautiful Bellie. It is a great misfortune, and not a thing to laugh about."

"Lost your appetite, do you mean?" asked my comrade. "That is nothing to make so much noise over. And I do not think your belly is so beautiful. It sticks out too much."

"No, no, you have it wrong!" the Tapir protested. "It is true I have no appetite — I have eaten nothing today, except some *chibeh* and a few handfuls of *pirarucu*-fish and some monkey-meat and a few other things. But that is because they have shut up my little Bellie for so long and will not let me have her. Even when they let her out I cannot have her — ah-hoo!"

"Stop that noise!" I ordered. "And stop your weeping also — it is wet enough here from the rains. Now tell us, what is this Bellie that gives you so much trouble? The matter must be serious if, as you say, you cannot eat more than two men need."

He nodded as quickly as his thick neck would let him, and told us:

"Indeed it is serious. My Bellie is a girl who has come to womanhood and should be given in marriage, but her father has not made ready for the feast, and so she is shut up. And the father does not favor me, but will give her to Gastoa. So you see it is a terrible misfortune."

"So I see," I said, "although I do not yet know just what you are talking about. Why is your girl shut up, and what has the feast to do with it? Tell us all about this matter. We are Pedro and Lourenço, *seringueiros* of Coronel Nunes. Perhaps we can help you."

He looked at us as if a little doubtful.

"I do not think you can help me," he said.

"What I, Deodoro Maia, cannot do for myself is something no strangers can do for me. And perhaps even if we could free my Bellie I still should lose her. She likes men who are tall and handsome."

He looked at Pedro as he spoke. Pedro made a very low bow.

"Thank you, friend Deodoro," he laughed. "But have no fear. Girls do not interest me much. And if they did, I think perhaps I could get one without stealing her from another man."

Deodoro thought this over and nodded again.

"I think that is true," he admitted. After looking at both of us a while longer, he said: "Yes, I will tell you all about it. Will you come up into my house? I have some *cachassa*, but no tobacco."

"And we have tobacco but no *cachassa*," I replied. "It is a fair exchange — a smoke for a drink."

So I climbed the ladder and entered his house. He and Pedro followed.

IT WAS DARK inside the place, for it had only one small window-hole, its doorway was hardly big enough to let the tapir-man in, and the daylight outside was dull. Yet the hut was comfortable enough, and it was dry. When we were all inside Deodoro lifted a jug from a dim corner and passed it to us. After a good pull at the *cachassa* which it contained we sat down on the floor, with our backs to the wall, and tossed him the makings of a smoke. He could hardly wait to roll the cigarette before he lit it.

"Ah, that is good!" he grunted, sucking a huge drag of smoke down into his lungs and blowing it slowly out. "I have not had a smoke for days."

"That may be one reason why you have felt so badly," I told him. "It is a mistake to be without tobacco when you are in trouble. A drink and a smoke will go far toward easing any kind of pain."

"That is so," he agreed. "But I have been

so miserable that I did not think of it. Besides, there is only one place where I can get tobacco — that is at the town; and Gastoa and his brothers and Bernardo, the father of my Bellie, drive me away from there."

We said nothing, but waited. Sitting in his big hammock, he puffed at the cigarette until it burned his fingers. The tobacco soothed him, as we knew it would; and with the smoke, another drink, and somebody to talk to, he became quite cheerful. Then he told us of his trouble.

He, Deodoro Maia, was a native of a small caboclo village some miles to the west, on another little river. The people of this town were jealous of their women and watched them closely. The young girls, who were only children, had nearly as much freedom as the boys; but from the time when a girl reached womanhood until she was married she was watched continually — and after marriage too, for that matter. And it was the custom among these people, when a girl was old enough to take a man, for her parents to make a feast, and a celebration was held and everyone was told that the girl now could marry.

Now this custom, like many others, had both a good and a bad side. Whenever a girl grew up the whole village could have a merry time at the celebration. But the rule of having a feast at that time was so strong that unless the girls' parents were able to give that feast she could not be declared marriageable. In that case she was in a bad position; for she was no longer a child, with the child's freedom, nor yet a woman in the eyes of her people — she was nothing at all. Because of this, and also to keep her always guarded, her father would shut her up until he could give the usual feast.

This did not mean that she only had to stay in the house. A cage would be built — a tight, strong cage of woven cane inside the house — and she would be put into that cage and kept there like a beast. She might have to stay in that thing for many days;

there was no escape for her until the feast was ready. Deodoro told us that sometimes a girl would be shut up so long that when she came out her copper-colored skin had faded almost to white.

Now Bernardo, father of the girl whom Deodoro wanted, was lazy and drunken, and meant to use his pretty daughter for his own benefit. So he intended to give her to a fellow named Gastoa, who was considered rich in his own village and had brothers who might help support the old drunkard in idleness; at least that was the father's plan. The man Gastoa was known to be cruel, and the girl feared and hated him; but that made no difference to old Bernardo, who thought only of an easy life for himself. He was so worthless, though, that when his girl-child turned into a woman he had nothing with which he could give the feast. Worse yet, he would not do enough hunting to get the monkey-meat usually dried and kept for the celebration. He only shut the girl into a cage and kept on drinking and sleeping.

SO THE MOONS came and went, and poor Bella — or Bellie, as the Tapir called her — was still a caged woman with no prospect of release.

The girl's mother did all she could for her. She worked hard to grow enough green foods for the feasting, and she tried to get Gastoa and his brothers to kill monkeys and salt away fish. But Gastoa was so sure he would have Bella in the end that he could not see any use in doing so much work for her, and so he and his family only laughed and sneered and did nothing.

And then a misfortune came to the crops. A herd of peccaries got into them and tore up almost everything, so that Bella's family had hardly enough left to live on, and all hope of the celebration was destroyed until new crops could grow.

When this happened Bernardo flew into a drunken rage. As might be expected, he vented his spleen on those who were not to blame. He beat his wife, and then he dragged his daughter out of her cage and beat her too because she was causing so much trouble to him. While he was still ugly Deodoro came in. A fight followed.

Deodoro, hoping to win the girl for himself, had done the thing which both Bernardo and Gastoa refused to do — he had hunted monkeys, birds, and fish, and dried or salted their meat. He had been very quiet about this, doing his work here at this house which he had built up in the tree, where nobody would be likely to find him. Now, with some of the best pieces of meat, he had gone back to the village to tell Bernardo he would give all he had toward the feast if he could have Bella for his own. But he came at a bad time, for, as I have said, Bernardo was ugly.

When he heard the young man's proposition he called him a vile name and kicked the meat into the dirt, where some dogs snatched it and ran off with it. Then he ordered Deodoro out; and when Deodoro hesitated he struck him. This was too much for even the slow, good-humored tapir-man to stand. He hit back and then started in to give the old fool the best thrashing of his life.

If he had been let alone he might have beaten some sense into Bernardo. But Bernardo, getting the worst of it, yelled for Gastoa to help him. Gastoa came, and his brothers with him, and jumped on Deodoro. They gave him such a beating that he was lucky to escape alive. Then they threw him out of the village, warning him not to come back.

In spite of this, Deodoro went back — though he took care not to go openly. Several times he went by moonlight, late at night when he knew the village was asleep. He even succeeded in talking a little with the girl through the thin cane wall of the house, and offered to cut a hole there and take her away with him. But, though she hated to be shut up so, still she wanted to be made a woman with the usual ceremony, and she would not consent to running off to some unknown place where she could not see the people whom she had always known. Besides, she did not think very seriously of Deodoro. Nobody did, he said.

When we asked him why this was, he said it was partly because of his white blood. He was neither a full-blooded caboclo nor a white man. His mother's father, he said, had been a white Brazilian trader who stayed for a time on that river while buying sarsaparilla for the market. Before his mother was born this man sailed away, and he never came back. So the girl was laughed at by the others because she had no father, and when she grew up she was sneered at because she was half white. In the same way her son Deodoro was laughed at in his turn, though his own father was a caboclo. The only one who did not jeer at him, he said, was the girl Bella, who sympathized with him when the rest mocked him.

THIS STORY made us sorry and angry — sorry for the young fellow and angry at those who had treated him so. We saw that he was not by nature a fighter, and that, with the whole town against him and the girl unwilling, he felt that there was nothing he could do but stay in his tree and be miserable. He was much in need of help.

"The big question is, does the girl care for you?" said Pedro. "Does she want you more than another?"

Deodoro stared out of the door awhile before he answered.

"I do not know just what she wants," he said then. "I do not think she knows either. She has not seemed to think much about men. I know she likes me as well as any one, and much better than she likes Gastoa. She does not like him at all."

"She likes you but she does not admire you," said Pedro. "Then you have two things to do — to free her and to make her respect you. Women admire men who are strong and bold. Be strong and bold, friend, and she will realize that you are a man. Now she thinks of you as a boy. Am I right?"

The Tapir thought again and agreed.

"You have it right," he said. "But what can I do? I can not go into the town and shoot everybody that tries to stop me from taking her away. My bullets are all gone."

We laughed.

"Of course you can not," said Pedro. "That would be a blundering way. Even if you shot down the whole town you would not win what you want most — the girl herself. She would then fear you more than she fears Gastoa. "You want her to admire you, not to be afraid of you. Now let us try to make a plan."

So we talked about different ideas that came to us, but none of them got us anywhere. At length I said:

"We are wasting time. You and I, Pedro, have never been at this place where Deodoro lived, and all we know about it is what he tells us. We might sit here and talk for a week, and then go there and have our great idea smashed by some little thing none of us had thought of. The one thing we are sure about is that first the girl must be gotten out of her cage. The best way to get that done is to go ahead and do it."

Deodoro nodded seriously, as if I had said a very wise thing. Pedro laughed, but he agreed.

"That is the best plan of all," he said. "Let us go with God and trust to luck."

We arose and turned toward the door. But Deodoro halted us.

"Wait," he said. "I am feeling much better, and I think I can eat something before we start. I have all the meat I saved for the feast — except the few pieces I lost at Bernardo's house — and now I shall not give any of it to those who have not treated me well, but will keep it for myself and Bellie and my friends Pedro and Lourenço. I think we had better have some of it now."

"You have spoken most wisely, friend," Pedro answered with a grin. "My comrade and I have not been eating much for the last few days. We have been on a long trip and our supplies are nearly gone. So we shall not throw your meat to the dogs as Bernardo did. But where do you keep it?"

"Since you are my friends, I will show you," he replied with a sly look.

Lifting a couple of the split palms that made his floor, he brought out meat.

"See, my floor is double," he explained. "The big branches of this tree hold up my house, and between the branches I have made boxes, and then covered branches and all with my floor. It is a good way to hide things."

"Deodoro, you are one of the cleverest fellows I ever met," said Pedro. "Few men would have thought of such a thing."

Deodoro's face beamed. Probably it was the first time anybody had ever praised him; and somehow he seemed to grow bigger as he thought about it. Pedro gave me a slight wink, and I saw what he was trying to do — to make this shy, downcast fellow think well of himself. And indeed, *senhores*, that is a thing that has much power to help or harm a man; for if he does not feel himself to be the equal of other men, who else will believe him to be so? Seeing Pedro's thought and realizing its value, I changed my own manner toward the young tapir-man and no longer treated him as a boy.

We went down the pole, built a little fire and ate. Pedro and I were hungry, and we did not spare the meat; but I do not believe that both of us together ate as much as Deodoro put away alone. When the food was gone he was still hungry, and he climbed the ladder and brought down more. This time he brought down his jug also. We found that it held more *cachassa* than we had thought, but we emptied it. Then, feeling quite merry, we got into our canoes and pushed out into the river.

WITH OUR NEW comrade leading, we paddled downstream until he swerved to the left. Up another quiet creek we followed him. The stream widened into a long swampy lake which seemed to have no end, for it wound along among the low hills so that whenever we thought we had reached the end we found that there was more of it. At length, when we had about concluded that it was no lake but a flooded arm of the river ahead, Deodoro led us into another narrow stream. Down this we went, and soon we came out into another river.

"It is not far now," said Deodoro in a low tone. "It is only a short paddle upstream."

"Very good," Pedro replied. "But why do you speak so quietly? You are not afraid if the whole world hears you."

Again Deodoro seemed to swell.

"No!" he agreed, and his heavy voice boomed like a gun. "I do not fear any man!"

He began paddling again with a bold stroke.

As he said, it was not far to the town. We heard it before we saw it. Shouts and laughter came to us, and then some one began to beat a drum in Indian time. Deodoro suddenly stopped paddling.

"There is a celebration," he said. "I wonder — it can not be — it is not possible that Bernardo has made the feast!"

"If there is a feast, so much the better," I said. "Everyone will get drunk. Is it not so?"

He nodded.

"Then it will be easier for us to do what we come for," I explained. "When all are drunk, who shall stop us?"

He made no answer. We saw that he was worried, thinking the noise might mean that his girl was given to the man Gastoa.

"Come, comrade," said Pedro. "We are slopping here as if we were afraid."

The hint was enough. Deodoro's head came up, and he swung into his stroke as if he owned the river. Pedro let out a yell, and we joined in. Shouting and paddling hard, we surged up to the town like men sure of a welcome.

LIKE ALL TOWNS in that region, it was on a hill above the reach of any floods. In the dry time it probably was some distance from the stream, but now the high water made it easy for boatmen to land beside it. As we stepped out on shore the drum-beating stopped. Several men came to meet us, and some barking dogs rushed at us.

Pedro knocked the dogs aside with his rifle. I had no gun, for I had broken mine and lost it in that fight with the headhunters of which I have told you. But I had two good feet in heavy boots, and I used them. One of the dogs, an ugly brute, snarled as if about to spring at me, but I kicked him again so hard that he yelped and retreated. At this, one of the men scowled at me in evil fashion.

"Kick my dog again and you will get yourself into trouble," he growled.

"I am used to trouble," I retorted. "And I kick an ugly dog wherever I meet him — whether he stands on four legs or on two."

He glared and took a step toward me. Then he halted as if not quite sure of himself. After glowering at me for a minute he shifted his gaze to Deodoro.

"You Deodoro!" he snarled. "Did I not tell you not to come back here?"

"You did, Gastoa," answered the tapir-man. "But you see I am back. I think I shall stay, too." His voice was strong and steady.

Three other men scowled when they heard this. I judged that they were the brothers of Gastoa, who had helped to beat Deodoro and drive him out. More *caboclos* had gathered around us now, and among them I noticed a short, piggish-looking man of middle age who seemed quite drunk. Pointing at Deodoro, this man yelled:

"Throw that one into the river! Throw the others in! Drown them all! What business have they here?"

Gastoa and his brothers growled again, but they did not quite dare to rush us. We stood shoulder to shoulder, and they could easily see that we did not intend to be driven away without a fight. Before they could decide just what to do Pedro spoke.

"Is your name Bernardo?" he asked.

The drunken man blinked at him.

"Yes, I am Bernardo."

"I thought so," said Pedro. "I had heard that in this town lived a man named Bernardo who was a know-nothing and a drunkard. I knew you must be the one, because nobody but a drunken fool would try to drown strangers who came to trade and make his town rich."

Bernardo became furious. He screeched that Pedro lied. But the other men looked at us with a new expression in their faces. Then one of them roughly told Bernardo to be quiet; and when he kept on yelling two others shoved him away. By this time everyone in the place was there at the shore. They all stood staring, and I saw some whispering to one another.

"Is that the truth?" demanded Gastoa. "Have you come to trade?"

"You do not think we came to look at your handsome face, do you?" sneered Pedro. "Who is the head man here? I will do my business with him."

The crowd opened, and out stepped a man who was rather old but looked strong and shrewd.

"I am chief," he said. "I, Araujo."

His sharp eyes went to our canoe, which now held only the few supplies that remained after our long trip.

"If you come to trade, where are your trade goods?" he asked.

"Greetings to you, *compadre*," said Pedro, as if the head man were no better than the rest. "Surely you do not think we would bring our goods in that little canoe. It will take a big *batelao* to carry the things we have for you — that is, if we decide to trade with you. This is not a small matter of wax and salt fish."

HIS INSOLENT manner made Araujo frown, but I could see that he and all the rest were impressed by it and by his big talk. I had no idea of what tale Pedro intended to tell, but I saw he had made a good beginning; so I tried to look like an important trader, instead of what I was — a bush-tramp with hardly enough food and cartridges to get home on. The thought came to me that Deodoro might show surprise and betray us. But a glance at him showed me he had more sense than that. His face was like wood, and he was looking straight ahead.

"What do you want for this *batelao* full of riches?" asked the head man.

"We will talk alone with you about that," Pedro told him. "We do not do our business on the riverbank. And before we do any business at all we want food for ourselves and this guide of ours, Deodoro."

Araujo looked as all over again, staring hard at Deodoro, who stared back at him. Then he nodded and turned away. We followed him, and I noticed that the crowd now was looking in friendly fashion at our Tapir companion and sourly at Gastoa. The reason was easy to see; they believed Deodoro had brought us there to make them rich, and that Gastoa had angered us and might have lost them their chance to trade. I had hard work to keep from grinning.

"You have come in time to eat at the feast," said Araujo. "This is a feast-day here. A girl has come to womanhood."

"What girl?" asked the Tapir.

"Not the one you are thinking of," the old man answered. "It is the youngest daughter of Fontoura."

"Oho! So you have a girl here, Deodoro!" teased Pedro, as if he had not heard of it. "You sly fellow, why did you not tell us?"

Deodoro looked queerly at him, but made no answer. The head man chuckled.

"There are several men between him and his girl," he explained. "And the girl has not yet been made a woman. So I would not say that he has any."

We had gotten away from the crowd by this time, and he stopped.

"Now you can tell me your business," he said,

"*Amanha* — tomorrow," Pedro answered, "I never do business on a feast-day; and since we have been lucky enough to come at a time of merry-making, we will join you in it. Tomorrow, when I have rested, we can talk of this matter."

Araujo scowled again. So Pedro added —

"Today it is enough to ask you whether you can get sarsaparilla roots, and perhaps Peruvian bark, for us from the forest near here."

The face of the chief brightened.

"Yes, yes! There is much in the hills above here."

"Then our guide has not lied to us," said Pedro, as if well pleased. "Perhaps you have heard of the big new company of Englishmen who now are working out of Tabatinga and preparing to buy these medical things for the markets in Europe?"

Araujo had not. Neither had I, and neither had Pedro. But the chief now thought he understood.

"And you are the scouts of this company," he guessed. "You are very welcome. We can make much trade for you. What do you give for those roots?"

But Pedro shook his head.

"*Amanha*," he said again.

So, seeing that he would talk no more of business that day, Araujo told us the town was ours.

The drum started up again, and others joined in. Men came to us with liquor and meat, and we ate and drank well — for we had paddled several miles since eating at Deodoro's tree-hut, and our appetites again were strong. Everyone made us welcome — that is, all but Bernardo and Gastoa and his gang. They stayed by themselves, talking angrily and drinking much.

I was glad to see that they drank, for I felt that they were the ones whom we needed to watch most, and hoped that in the end they would make themselves senseless. If we waited until night, I thought, it should be quite easy to get the girl out of her prison and escape with her. But Deodoro spoiled that plan.

BEFORE LONG the *caboclos* formed for a dance around the drummers. It was not much of a dance. They only trotted around and around, yelling and laughing, and dropping out one by one for a drink now and then. Araujo, the chief, trotted with the rest, tooting solemnly on a little tin whistle he had gotten somewhere. Some of the men shouted to us to join in, and I saw several young women making eyes at Pedro; but we said we were tired and squatted by ourselves, smoking and watching. Then Pedro said to Deodoro:

"Now is a good time for you, comrade, to slip away and talk to your girl. She must feel very badly at hearing all this merriment, knowing that it is for another girl, while she remains cooped up. She ought to be ready to run away with you now. If she is, tell her that at the right time we will take her where she can be happy."

The young fellow started to rise. Pedro grabbed him and pulled him down.

"Not like that!" he cautioned. "Do not get up and walk away in plain sight. Creep around behind us and then crawl behind this house at our backs. After that you can walk."

The big fellow grunted and obeyed. Like the tapir he resembled, he was not very good at creeping. He made some noise as he went. But nobody seemed to notice his going. Between the liquor and the dancing, the *caboclos* now were getting quite drunk and thinking of nothing but their own fun. So our companion got away without being seen.

We sat for a while longer watching the circling crowd. Then Pedro said:

"They are a worthless lot, Lourenço. Even if we were the traders they think us to be I doubt if I should want to do business with them. They look lazy, mean, and treacherous. They have no welcome to a stranger unless they hope to make something from him, and their laughter now is only the kind born of drink and drums. I shall be glad when we are out of this place. This is the first time I ever took a hand in a woman-stealing."

"That is the way I feel too," I agreed. "I am not afraid of them, but I dislike them all. And unless Deodoro's girl is better than the women I have seen here she is hardly worth our time and trouble."

"He thinks she is," he laughed. "And every man must be his own judge in such matters. But I wish he would come back. I want to get up and walk around — those drums make me restless. If we do that, though, the *caboclos* will notice that he is gone."

It did seem that Deodoro had been gone for some time, and as the throbbing of the drums went on I too wished I could move around. A few minutes later I was moving around more than I had expected to.

A yell broke out. The dancers stopped. We hopped up. Then, before a house near the water, we saw men fighting and a girl running toward the stream.

"The fool!" snorted Pedro. "He has let her out too soon!"

WE RAN toward the struggle. So did everyone else. One of the fighting men broke away and dashed after the girl. Another fell backward and lay still. But there were four of them left, and three of them were attacking Deodoro. They were Gastoa and two of his brothers. The man on the ground was the third brother.

As we reached them, Gastoa himself went down. The Tapir was fighting only with his hands, but those hands were terrible enough.

He got a clumsy swing into Gastoa's face, and it cracked like flat wood hitting water. Gastoa fell like a dead man. After he was down I caught a glimpse of his face. It looked as if a real tapir had jumped on it — mashed flat.

Pedro and I knocked down the other two men and yelled to Deodoro to run. All three of us jumped for our canoes. We ran into the girl and the man who had seized her. She was screaming and trying to escape. The man was her father, and he was striking her brutally in the face and body.

Pedro, the quickest of us three, reached them first. He jolted Bernardo in the head with his rifle-butt, and the drunkard fell sprawling. Without a pause Pedro snatched the girl off the ground and kept on running. But the crowd was almost on us, and as we slowed at the water's edge they caught us.

"Go!" I grunted to Pedro. Then I yanked his gun from his fist, whirled and struck around me. Men fell, but others swarmed in. I heard grunts and blows beside me and knew somebody was helping me to fight, but I had no time to see who it was. I thought it must be Pedro. Later I was surprised to find that it was Deodoro.

Pedro had hastily pushed the girl into our canoe and then turned back. But Deodoro, thinking only of getting the girl away, shoved Pedro backward so that he tumbled into the canoe, and then he heaved the boat out into the river. In falling, Pedro hit his head hard against the bottom of the canoe, and the blow stunned him so that he lay there a few minutes while he and the girl drifted away downstream. Then the fighting Tapir wheeled back to help me hold off the furious crowd.

Between us we did some rough work. But we were outnumbered; and to tell truth, *senhores*, I never got such a beating in my life. I have fought hard before and since that time, and have had far more serious wounds than I received then; but those *caboclos* knew how to hit where it would hurt. If they had had their weapons they would have cut me to pieces. But none of them had stopped to pick up a knife, and now they could fight only with hands, feet, and teeth. But those were enough.

Somehow I did not think of shooting. I

could not have shot well if I had tried, for they were too close. They wrenched at the gun while they beat me, and how I kept it I do not know. But I did keep it, and slugged around me with muzzle and butt. Finally, though, they knocked my legs out from under me. I fell hard, and they jumped all over me.

I kicked and squirmed and bit, but they had me. Then suddenly I felt a tremendous tug at one foot. I went sliding and bumping down the bank with two men hanging to me. Blows sounded and the men fell away. Somebody tumbled me head first into a canoe. The canoe slid outward.

A raging yell sounded behind me. Sitting up, I found myself afloat. With me was the Tapir. His face was battered and his big snout was gushing red, but he was as strong as ever. He had grabbed a paddle and was shoving the boat downstream with strokes so powerful that the dugout seemed to leap from the water. As I looked at him he grinned through split lips.

"I had to pull hard to get you out of that tangle," he said. "You seemed stuck to the ground."

I tried to answer, but all I could do was to make a wheezing sound. The wind was beaten out of me. So I sat still while my breath came back and my head grew clear. I saw that the *caboclos* were jumping into boats and coming after us. Then we caught up with my own canoe, where the girl was crouching and Pedro was getting up and reaching for a paddle. Pedro had a surprised look, as if wondering how he had come there, but he wasted no time in talk. Scooping up a handful of water, he threw it on his head and then began to paddle hard.

I looked for a paddle too, but there was none. Deodoro was using the only one in this canoe. I still had the rifle, though; and, seeing that the maddened men behind were gaining on us, I began shooting. I did not shoot to kill, for I do not like to kill men if it can be avoided. At the same time, I shot

close enough to make them think I meant death.

Aiming carefully, I sent several bullets thumping along the sides of their dugouts. They slowed up at once. Some yelled to stop, others shouted to go on, and they paddled both ways at once — some trying to keep after us and others backing water. While this was going on we drew away fast.

THE TAPIR swerved into the bank and up the same stream we had traveled before. Pedro followed. For some time we kept on at the same rate of speed, and then we came out into the long crooked lake. There we stopped, listened — and heard nothing.

"They have given up," panted Pedro.

The Tapir shook his head.

"They have gone back for guns, and they follow," he said. "But we can dodge them. There is more than one way out of this lake."

Looking around as if to get his bearings, he pushed on again. Down around a bushy point we went, and there turned sharp to the right. A short arm of water ran that way, and we traveled down this until we seemed about to bump the shore. Then he swung to the left, and we were in a quiet, winding stream. There we stopped.

I got up with grunts and groans, for I had been sitting still and my bruised muscles had stiffened so that each one had a pain of its own. Deodoro grinned again. The grin annoyed me.

"Now," I demanded, "tell me why you got us into all this trouble. Why did you not come back to us and wait until we were ready?"

"You said yourself that the first thing to do was to free Bellie, and that the quickest way to free her was to go ahead and do it," he answered. "So I went and did it. And your comrade Pedro told me to be strong and bold. Have I not been strong and bold?"

His face and voice were so serious that Pedro and I laughed.

"More bold than we wanted you to be," I told him.

"I am sorry you got hurt," he said. "But I went and talked to Bellie and found her mad to get out at once. So I thought I had better take her before she changed her mind, and I cut a hole and pulled her through. If Gastoa and his brothers had not sneaked up just then we should have gotten away without trouble. And nobody would have thought you two traders had anything to do with it, because you were sitting in plain sight all the time."

"I see," I said. "And now that we are all here I think you had better take your girl and let me get into my own canoe."

We had been holding to bushes while we talked, and now Pedro drew our canoe up beside me. For the first time I had a good look at the girl, and after that look I did not blame Deodoro for wanting her. She was very pretty. True, she looked thin and weak, and her skin seemed pale; but I remembered that she had been caged for a long time, and knew that a healthy life outdoors and plenty to eat would quickly make her plump and strong. Her eyes and mouth were beautiful, and she looked no more like the other women we had seen than a butterfly looks like a mud-worm. Remembering the evil face of Gastoa and the brutality of her father, I was glad I had gone to help her, even though I now was full of aches and pains.

Then I noticed something that was not so pleasing. She did not want to leave Pedro and come to Deodoro. She looked long at Pedro, then glanced at the tapir-man and wrinkled her nose. I too looked at both the men, and saw what a difference there was. Pedro was a graceful fellow, with merry brown eyes and curly hair; and he had not been hit during the fight, so his face was not marked at all. Deodoro, with his clumsy-looking body and lank hair and big nose, was not a beauty at any time; and now his eyes were swollen so that they peered through slits, and his whole face was bruised and bloody.

It came to me, too, that though Deodoro had given the girl her chance to escape from the house, it was Pedro who had attacked Bernardo when she was being beaten and had run with her in his arms to the water; so that she might easily feel that it was the handsome stranger who had saved her. Besides, she had not seen Deodoro's one fight at the house, because then she was running for the river. And she probably did not know much about his battle on the bank, for then she was floating away and we were all tangled up in a lighting knot. Poor Deodoro! Everything seemed to be against him.

WHETHER he saw all this I did not know, but I hoped not. When the girl made no move to change canoes I spoke gruffly to her, telling her to make room for me. She rose then though slowly, and took my place without a word.

As I settled down and picked up my paddle I heard voices out on the lake. We slipped the canoes silently downstream and looked. The Tapir was right — two boatloads of armed *caboclos* were passing, the men working hard and looking ahead. Others came behind them. We kept very quiet until they were gone.

"They will go down the lake to the end hunting us," said the Tapir. "Then they will work back and search all the coves. We shall be at my house long before they have finished here. Are you not glad to be free, Bellie?"

The girl made no answer. Her eyes came again to Pedro's face, and then she looked down into the water. Deodoro looked long at her, then at Pedro, then at me. His face grew sad. With a deep sigh he pushed his canoe against the slow current, and we passed silently up the creek.

After a time we came into a network of winding water courses without any current that I could see. Deodoro hesitated several times, but seemed always to pick the right one. At length we found ourselves again in flowing water, and now we went downstream instead of up. At length we entered the river on which Pedro and I had been traveling that morning.

There our leader turned downward, and we saw that he had brought us out above his house. Keeping near the left shore and watching sharply for *caboclos*, we soon reached the little inlet masked by the palms.

"Now you are safe, Bellie," I said when we stepped out on shore. "See the fine house Deodoro has built for you up here in the tree, where you can always be dry and comfortable. It is much better than any house in your town, and you will never have to live in a cage again. He has much meat too, and you and he will have plenty to eat. You will be very happy here."

"Do you two stay here also?" she asked.

"No," I said. "This is Deodoro's place. We must go on, for we live far from here."

She glanced once more at the house in the tree. Then she cried:

"I do not want to stay here, I will not stay here! Take me away!"

We all stood silent, staring at her. I wanted to scold her, but knew that would do no good. So I said the first thing that seemed best.

"We cannot take you away today, Bellie — it will soon be night. And we two are not going until tomorrow. We shall rest and eat here. Tomorrow we shall see what is best to be done. Now go up and see what a fine house that is."

She stood still, stubbornly, until Pedro also told her to mount the ladder. Then she obeyed, climbing as if afraid she would fall, but going upward until she got into the hut.

"*Nossa Senhora!*" muttered Pedro. "Now this is a pretty mess! After all our trouble she wants to go back home."

Slowly the Tapir shook his head. His face was full of pain.

"No, it is not that," he said. "It is as I told you before we went. She likes tall handsome men, and I am not tall nor handsome."

He swallowed hard, as if trying to keep from crying. And then, through his teeth, he added:

"She wants to — to go with you, Pedro. If she will — be happier with you, comrade, then — then you had better take her with you."

He choked and turned away.

For an instant Pedro stared. Then he sprang and caught him by the shoulder.

"*Por Deus*, you are a man!" he said. "Why, comrade, I do not want your girl! I do not want any girl at all. And you are wrong — she does not want me either. She may be interested in me because I am a new man whom she has not seen before, but after I am gone she will quickly forget me."

But Deodoro shook his head again, and so did I. I had seen women fall swiftly in love with Pedro before this — women who knew more about men than this little girl-woman knew; and I felt that Bellie would not forget him so quickly as he said, and that neither she nor Deodoro would be happy because of this. When Pedro asked me if I did not agree with him, I said no.

"There is some truth in what Deodoro says," I told him, "If she had not seen you she might have been happy with him. I think our work is only half-done. We have freed her, but how are we to make her satisfied?"

He scowled and stood thinking. Then his eyes began to twinkle, and he threw up his head and laughed.

"Deodoro, let me talk to you," he said. "Lourenço, climb up and talk with her so that she will not overhear us. Ask her if she would like to go away with me — but try to show her that she would be foolish to do such a thing."

I did as he said. Up the pole I went, and in the hammock I found the girl, looking very small and sad and dissatisfied. When I came in she brightened up and glanced beyond me as if expecting someone else. Seeing that nobody followed, she seemed disappointed.

"The others will be up soon," I informed

her.

Then I sat down against the wall, grunting from the pain of my stiff muscles.

"I am very lame," I went on. "Still, I am glad I am alive to feel lame. If it had not been for the splendid fighting of Deodoro I should probably be dead — and you would be back in your cage, to be beaten by your father and given to Gastoa."

She turned more pale at that thought, but looked surprised too. And she asked what Deodoro had done that was so brave. So I saw that I was right — she did not realize what a fight he had made. Taking care not to praise him over-much, I told her how he had fought off the gang of Gastoa and then battled beside me so that she could get away, and how he had pulled me out when I was down. Her big dark eyes grew larger as I talked.

THEN, when her mind was full of this new fighting Deodoro, I suddenly asked her whether she would like to go away with us.

"My friend Pedro likes you," I said, "and if you want to go with him we can fool Deodoro in some way. You might not be happy with Pedro, but —"

"Why not?" she cut in.

"Well, of course he is a handsome man," I pointed out, "and other girls like him very well, and you could not expect him to give all his time to you. He would not stay with you as this simple Deodoro would do. And he likes his fun with men too, and so he would drink and gamble with them. And he is restless and will not stay long in one place — and you know he would not want you trailing after him everywhere. If you expected him to be as faithful to you as Deodoro would be, you might not be happy. But if you are willing to be reasonable about those things we can take you away when we go. He is keeping Deodoro down below while I ask you about this."

Senhores, that gave her a good deal to think about. At first she looked as if she wanted to cry, and I felt sorry for her — but I did not let her see that. Then, she asked the question I expected.

"If he wants me, why does he not talk to me himself instead of sending you?"

I laughed as if that were a foolish question.

"Because Deodoro would probably fight to keep you, and Pedro knows how hard he would fight. Pedro probably would get his handsome face hurt. And besides, what is the sense of fighting over a woman? Deodoro thinks you are the only pretty woman in the world, but Pedro and I know you are not."

She looked at me then as if beginning to dislike me. Before we could talk more we heard Pedro's voice down below, and it was loud and ugly,

"Then if you have more *cachassa*, why did you not say so?" he demanded. "I want a drink and I want it now! After we have gone to that dirty town of yours and brought back that female for you, I call it shabby treatment to try to hide your liquor!"

"You can have a drink if you want it," came the voice of the Tapir. "But do not speak so of my girl. She is not the kind of girl that a man like you ought to talk about."

"Bah! The world is full of girls, and not one of them is worth anything. I want that drink!"

"Then come up and you shall have it."

I stuck my head out of the door beside me and looked down. Deodoro, I noticed, had washed his face and looked much better. As he came upward and saw me he grinned. Pedro, behind him, winked at me. But when they came into the house their expressions had changed. Deodoro looked very serious, and Pedro scowled.

The Tapir lifted part of his floor again, and this time he pulled up a jar which he handed Pedro. My partner seemed to take a huge drink. When he passed the jar to me, however, I found that very little of the liquor was gone. I took as much as I wanted, and then held it out toward Deodoro. But Pedro snatched it and appeared to swallow about half of what was left, making a guzzling noise and letting some of the *cachassa* drip off his chin. The girl watched all this, and a look of disgust crept across her face. The thought came to me that my comrade's actions must remind her of her drunken, worthless father.

Then Pedro slumped down beside me and rolled a cigarette. Usually he was very deft at making a smoke, but now his fingers seemed clumsy. He spilled most of his tobacco, and then he snarled. He tried again, and made a worse mess than before. Finally he ordered me to make his cigarette for him. I did so, but I took my time about it. Then he abused me because I was so slow, and growled once more at Deodoro because he had not been more free with his liquor. After the cigarette was lit and going well, though, he quieted somewhat.

NONE OF US spoke while he smoked, Deodoro watched us solemnly, and I saw the girl studying him and Pedro in turn. Pedro's face grew more heavy, as if the *cachassa* were working on him. Presently he began to leer at Bellie,

"Think I will take you downriver with me, girl," he said roughly. "You do not want to stay here and you do not want to go back to your cage. You have to go somewhere, so come with me."

She looked him straight in the eyes. Then she said —

"I do not think I want to go with you."

"What!" snapped Pedro. "Do not be a little fool!" He looked at Deodoro and grinned in a nasty way, as if the liquor had given him courage which he had lacked before. "You, Deodoro, you can stay here with your *cachassa*. I am going away with this woman of yours. I am going now!"

He lurched up and staggered toward the girl.

Then the Tapir moved. He swooped at the rifle Pedro had left leaning against the wall. He jammed the muzzle into my comrade's stomach, and I heard the hammer click back.

"Stop where you are!" he ordered. "You shall not take her away. She is too good for you."

Pedro stood very still, staring down at the gun as if stricken with fear. I got up as quickly as I could, drawing my machete, for I did not like the sound of that hammer going back. But before I could get within arm's length of Deodoro the girl jumped at me.

She came so suddenly and swiftly that before I realized it she had knocked my bush-knife from my hands. With another lightning move she threw it out of the door, and I heard it thump on the ground below. Then, her face full of fury, she warned me —

"Keep back or I will tear your eyes out!"

I kept back. Her nails were very long, and I had seen how quick she was. Her sudden action had taken us all by surprise, and we stood staring at her. Then Deodoro spoke again to Pedro.

"If she wished to go with you and if you would be kind to her I would let her go. But I know you have other women. You boasted about it when you first came here and drank my *cachassa*. You said you only played with women, and that when you tired of one you left her and got another. You will not do so with Bellie."

Pedro made no answer. He looked at Bellie. She looked back, at him as if now she hated him. To Deodoro she said:

"You are the only honest man I know, Deodoro. I will stay with you and be your good girl. Drive these two into the river! This one is no better than the other." She pointed at me. "He wanted me to fool you and run away with them. Drive them out!"

"Get down the pole!" grunted the Tapir savagely. "Bellie, stay here!"

Pedro glanced at me and jerked his head toward the door. We went down the pole, Deodoro still covering us.

"Do not touch that machete!" he warned, as I stepped toward my knife. "Go to your canoe."

"Come, Lourenço," whispered Pedro. "He will follow."

So we got into our canoe. Deodoro came down, picked up my weapon and. stepped into his own boat.

"Out into the river!" he commanded.

Pedro, looking much afraid, splashed his paddle quickly into the water and we moved outward. Behind us came the Tapir.

As we went downstream I felt the canoe shaking. I could not understand this until I looked at Pedro.

The drunken look was gone from his face, and, though he made no sound, he was laughing so hard that he could scarcely use his paddle.

"Over to the right, where you see that massaranduba tree," came the voice of the Tapir.

We turned to the place. Below the tree we found a little cove which twisted around like a hook. At its end, where it could not be seen from the river, was a small hut.

There we got out. Pedro leaned on his paddle and laughed again. The Tapir, grinning, handed us our weapons.

"You can sleep dry here, comrades," he said. "I built this place while I was hunting monkey-meat, I do not think the men from the town will come to this river until tomorrow — the darkness is coming. If they should come, they will not find you here."

"Be careful that they do not find you either, friend," Pedro answered.

"They will not find us. If they do they will be sorry,"

He spoke with a calm strength that made me think what a difference a few hours had made in him. That morning he had been a blubbering boy. Now, with the knowledge that Bellie was his own and that he could thrash any two of those *caboclos* who had made his life and hers so wretched, he was a man. Rather slow of thought, perhaps, but able to take care of himself from this time on — that was the new Deodoro who now talked so surely and called us "comrades." His eye was steady and his head was up, and he feared no man.

"I am sorry that I had to drive you out in such a way," he went on. "You are the first men who ever did anything for me, and you have done the greatest thing any man could do for me. So I do not like to seem ungrateful, even though you understand and know that I am not. If ever I can do anything for you, Pedro and Lourenço, call on me and I will do it, not matter what it is."

He grinned again.

"That was a very wise plan of yours, Pedro — you know women better than I do. But Bellie nearly spoiled it all when she jumped at Lourenço. I almost forgot everything you had told me to say and do."

"So did I," admitted my partner, "After she did that it was not really necessary to talk about the women I had abandoned — ha ha ha! I nearly laughed in your face. But she is all yours now, friend. Treat her well — but be strong and bold, strong and bold!"

"I will," the Tapir promised earnestly. "*Adios*!"

He stepped back into his canoe and left us. Pedro took cartridges from a pocket and reloaded his rifle.

THUBWAY THAM'S DOG

by **Johnson McCulley**

Descending the rickety, narrow stairs in the lodging house conducted by Mr. "Nosey" Moore, where he had a furnished room that he called home, Thubway Tham reached the level of the street and discovered that it was a splendid day.

For a moment he remained standing before the open doorway, looking up and down the busy street, for Thubway Tham had not left his bed until a late hour, and the city already was at work, the streets filled with vehicles, the walks thronged with human beings in much of a hurry.

"It ith a fine day," Thubway Tham remarked to himself. "And I feel that it ith a lucky day!"

Thubway Tham grinned broadly as he said that. Now and then Tham was sure to experience that subtle and unexplainable thing most men call "a hunch," and whenever he experienced one he was certain to act upon it. He had found that it paid.

Breakfast was in his mind, and he left the entrance of the lodging house and started along the street toward the little restaurant he patronized. He glanced down and found a dog before him.

Thubway Tham, be it known, did not possess a great deal of knowledge about dogs. To him a dog was a dog, possibly a small dog and perhaps a big dog; but when it came to breeds and pedigrees and such things Tham was as a stranger in a strange land.

It would have taken a corps of experts to explain the dog that stood before Tham now. He was a dog, and that was all, with a body that was Airedale and ears that were spaniel. There was a trace of hound about him, a hint of setter, and not a little terrier. He was yellow in spots and brown in spots. His eyes seemed to gleam; he appeared to

be laughing, and his stump of a tail wagged in furious rhythm.

"What theemth to be the matter, dog?" Thubway Tham asked.

Evidently nothing very serious was the matter. The dog sprang back joyously a few feet and gave a sharp bark. Then he frisked to one side, sprang into the street, dodged between two taxicabs, and darted back to Thubway Tham's side as though he had been demonstrating what a sure-footed dog he was.

"My goodnethth!" Tham said with a gasp. "You'll be gettin' run over one of thet-he fine dayth."

The dog barked again, stood upon its hind legs and waltzed a measure or two, and then crept forward once more. Thubway Tham bent over and patted the canine on the head, thinking that would settle it — and it did. Knowing nothing of dogs, Tham was of the opinion that now this animal would scamper away. Instead, the dog glued to Thubway Tham. He had adopted a new master. Tham did not notice it as he walked briskly along the street toward the restaurant, for his mind was upon breakfast and nothing else. He passed into the eating shop, and was hailed by the snappy head waitress.

"Mr. Tham, you can't bring that dog in here. You know very well that it's against the rules!"

Thubway Tham turned in surprise to find the dog at his heels. His face grew red.

"It ith not my dog," he explained. "He jutht followed me down the thtreet. Dog, get out of here!" He motioned toward the street. The dog barked once, then darted away. Tham went on to his table.

Having partaken of his usual breakfast, Thubway Tham paid the amount of the check and stepped out upon the busy street once more, his intention being to walk up to Madison Square, rest there on a bench, and watch the crowds for a time, and then, when the rush hour arrived, descend into the subway and make an effort to "lift a leather."

"Thith ought to be a good-luck day," Tham mused.

A subdued bark caused him to look down. There was the dog. It flashed through Thubway Tham's mind that the canine had waited in front of the restaurant like a faithful animal, and now was ready to proceed.

"Dog, don't follow me," Thubway Tham said commandingly. "I don't crave it. You couldn't follow me into the thubway, tho you might ath well thtop now."

The dog retreated a short distance, but he followed Thubway Tham through the streets, across busy corners, and to the square. Tham found his favorite bench unoccupied, and sat upon it. He watched the throng crossing the square — clerks, snappy stenographers, young attorneys — and he listened to the wild talk of loafing men who desired to reform the world more to their individual likings. It was all old stuff to Thubway Tham, but he never tired of it. Madison Square is a liberal education for a man who keeps his eyes and ears open.

Crouching at the end of the bench beside Thubway Tham's feet, the dog seemed fully content to rest there with his nose on his paws and his eyes rolling up every few seconds toward the face of his new master.

A man stopped beside the bench. Thubway Tham glanced up lazily to find that it was Detective Craddock. Between him and Tham there had been warfare for some time. The former had taken an oath to catch the little dip "with the goods" and have him sent "up the river" for a long term. The latter had sworn to himself that such a thing never would occur. Each respected the other as a foe worthy of steel.

"Tho!" Tham said. "Tho I thee your ugly fathe again, do I? I wath jutht thayin' to mythelf that it wath a lovely day, and now you come along and thpoil it."

"Indeed, Tham?" Craddock said. "I regret it exceedingly. But my duty, you know, compels me to wander hither and yon, as the saying is."

"Uh-huh!" said Tham with a grunt. "Hither and yon ith right. But it theemth to me that hither and yon alwayth meanth where I happen to be at."

"Tham, your grammar is shocking this morning."

"You," said Tham, "would thhock anybody."

"I see that you have picked up a little stranger."

"Meaning —?" Tham questioned.

"That nameless and not-to-be-analyzed specimen of canine that reposes at your feet."

"Oh!" Tham exclaimed. "He ith a cop hound."

"Yes?"

"Yeth! He can thmell a cop a mile away. He barkth twithe when a plain-clotheth man cometh along."

"But he did not bark when I approached."

"I mean a regular plain-clotheth man," Tham said. "He knowth the real thing from an imitation every time."

Craddock's face flushed, but he controlled his temper. "However, Tham, I am glad to see a dog with you," he said. "When a dog takes up with a man, it is a sure sign that the man has at least some good in him."

"Oh, my goodnethth!" Tham exclaimed.

"I remember a particularly atrocious murderer years ago who had a dog that grieved when we jailed the master. We couldn't understand it at first, and then we found that even the atrocious murderer had his good side. He never killed anybody on holidays."

"Uh-huh!" said Tham, grunting. "That dog ith one that jutht happened to tag along behind me thith mornin'. I don't even know hith name, Craddock."

"Perhaps he is better nameless," Detective Craddock suggested cruelly.

"Craddock, what do you want to knock that dog for?" Tham demanded. "Maybe he ith a good dog. He thhowed thome thenthe pickin' out me inthtead of you."

"Huh!" Craddock exclaimed. "I fail to see, Tham, how you expect to use him in your business. He'll be a pest in the subway, and you don't work anywhere else."

"Craddock, if you mean to inthinuate —"

"Cut the comedy!" Craddock suggested. "We understand each other, old boy. Were you thinking seriously of taking a ride in our beloved subway today?"

"Poththibly."

"Maybe I'd better tag along with you, then, and look to the interests of such of our estimable citizens who happen to possess those things termed wallets."

"Thuit yourthelf," Tham responded. "The day ith yourth, I thuppothe, to do ath you like with it."

"I'm truly sorry, Tham, but I can't be your little playmate today," Craddock replied. "I happen to be out looking for a regular crook — a burglar."

"Well, my goodnethth!" Thubway Tham exclaimed. "Whoever told you that a burglar wath a regular crook? A burglar ith nothin' more than a high-clathth thneakthief!"

"This professional jealousy is a terrible thing," Detective Craddock observed. "I must toddle along, Tham, but we'll meet some other day. You said that pup was a cop hound. Are you quite sure, old-timer, that he isn't working with the cops instead of against them?"

"He lookth like a dethent dog," Tham answered. "At that, he probably hath more thenthe than motht copth."

"Yes?"

"Yeth!" said Tham. "Don't let me detain you, Craddock, if you are in a hurry."

"I am in a hurry," Craddock admitted. "But one of these days, boy —"

"I know," Tham interrupted. "One of thethe dayth you are going to catch me with the goodth. That will be when I am blind and deaf and dumb, Craddock — ethpethially dumb!"

Detective Craddock grinned and then continued his way through the square, looking searchingly at those he passed; and Thubway Tham glared after him, and then glared down at the innocent pup, who promptly thumped his stump of tail rapidly against the surface of the cement walk.

An hour passed. The big clock in the tower chimed. Thubway Tham came from a reverie, got up, and walked briskly across to Broadway and toward Times Square, where, he had decided, he would descend into the subway and catch an express for downtown.

As he reached the subway entrance he discovered the pup at his heels. Thubway Tham made an angry gesture. "Go back!" he commanded. "You can't come into the thubway, pup. Get out! My goodnethth, what do you want to follow me around for?"

The pup retreated for a moment, a playful gleam in his eyes, but when Tham started to descend the steps the dog darted forward once more. Again Tham threatened with words and gestures. The pup seemed to be of the opinion that it was a game, prancing and barking at Tham and attracting a great deal of attention, including that of a policeman in uniform.

Thubway Tham growled low down in his throat and walked on along the street. How could he go into the subway with a policeman watching him? He said mean things to the pup in undertones, but the pup seemed to think that they were nice things and continued to dodge other pedestrians, clinging closely to the heels of Thubway Tham.

Near a corner Tham found a bit of stick that some playing child had dropped. He picked it up and hurled it angrily at the pup, who barked his joy, scampered after the stick, and returned it to Thubway Tham promptly, his eyes bright and his tail wagging. Tham almost cursed.

Coming to another subway entrance, Tham had an inspiration. He hurled the stick as far as possible from him, and then darted down the steps. But before he could reach the bottom the pup was at his side, carrying the stick.

Tham went back to the street again and walked briskly and angrily along. He had believed that this was going to be a fortunate day, and here was a playful yellow pup spoiling it. And so he came, after a time, to the Fourteenth Street subway station, and there he had another brilliant idea.

"You thtay here!" he told the pup. "Lie down there, and thtay there!" There was something commanding in Tham's voice. The pup stretched himself on the walk.

"Thtay right there until I come back!" Tham commanded.

The pup seemed to understand that. He put his nose on his paws and watched Thubway Tham closely. Tham went down the steps, now and then glancing back and motioning. The dog obeyed, remaining stretched on the walk above.

Tham boarded a downtown express and glanced about with an eye to business. His lips curled in disgust. There was nobody in the car who looked as though he possessed a wallet.

Leaving the train far downtown, Tham caught another express and doubled back. His disgust deepened. Station after station was passed, and no prospective victim got into the car.

"It ith that blamed dog," Thubway Tham told himself. "He ith a jinx. Everything wath nithe until he came along!" He left the train at Times Square, went to the street and walked around for a time, and finally entered the subway again. The platform happened to be thronged, and Tham was gratified to see a number of prosperous-looking gentlemen waiting for the train.

Tham followed them aboard. One man in particular appealed to him. He was large, prosperous-looking to a high degree, and the tails of his coat swung free of his hips. As he brushed against another man, Thubway Tham noticed the top of a wallet in a hip pocket.

That one glance told Tham that it was a large wallet, a well-worn wallet, just the sort that should contain a goodly amount of currency. He edged closer to the man he picked, but in such a manner that none noticed it. All he needed now was an opportunity, the moment when the train thundered into a station and the doors were opened, when the throng fought to get out of the cars and into them.

The moment came. Thubway Tham brushed forward, and his clever fingers did their work. Tham attempted to go past the others and hurry to the street, but his victim kept in front of him. He, too, seemed to be in a hurry, and, reaching the street two steps in front of Thubway Tham, greeted two men who seemed to be waiting for him and stepped forward.

At that moment Tham had a feeling of disaster. The victim reached toward his hip pocket.

"My wallet!" he exclaimed, making a quick stop. "My wallet's gone!"

Thubway Tham was within a few feet of him, just at the level of the walk. He saw a policeman a few feet away whom he did not know personally, but it did not follow that the officer did not know him. Thubway Tham felt cornered. There was but one thing to do — get rid of the "leather" quickly.

His hand darted into his pocket as the man ahead stopped. Taking the wallet out, he tossed it aside as he walked on straight toward his victim, with the intention of passing him and hurrying up the street. Tham gave a sigh of relief. He had lost the wallet, but they could fasten no crime upon him now. If it was found then and there, the big man would think that he had dropped it as he came up the steps.

Just then Thubway Tham, glancing back innocently, gave a gasp of terror. That confounded yellow pup was tearing along the walk after him. Tham had forgotten that he had told the dog to stay there until his return. He had done his "trick" and left the subway at Fourteenth Street, where he had left the pup waiting some time earlier. But the worst of it was that the pup had in his mouth the wallet which Tham had tossed away and the pup had retrieved.

The bird-dog part of him was being uppermost for the moment — he was playing a game with his master again.

"My wallet! The dog's got it!"

Thubway Tham stood as though turned to stone. His feet seemed unable to move, though his mind told him to run. The pup stopped before him and wagged his tail, holding up the wallet as high as he could and prancing around on his hind legs.

"That your dog?"

Tham gulped, but he could not answer.

But the big man gave him no chance.

"That's my wallet," he explained. "I must have dropped it as I left the subway. These men will vouch for me."

"Aw — all right," Tham said, gasping.

"My name's Chester Jonebin. You'll find the name in the wallet, cards, et cetera. Kindly look."

Tham took the wallet from the dog and verified the name.

"No money in it," said the big man. "But those papers — if they had been lost it would have caused no end of inconvenience. I feel that I must reward you, my man, for having such a sensible dog. Allow me!"

The big man reached into a pocket of his waistcoat, extracted some currency, and handed Thubway Tham a fifty-dollar bill.

"It's worth it!" he said. "Serves me right for being careless. Legal papers, you understand. Depositions and such. No thanks — it's coming to you!"

And before Thubway Tham could speak, the big man and his friends were hurrying along the street. Tham looked at the bill; then down at the yellow pup.

"Dog," said Thubway Tham, "you come along with me. I know where they thell meat! And if Nothey Moore won't let you thleep in hith kitchen, then we'll get uth another roomin' houthe. Come with me, dog!"

The dog wagged his stump of tail and followed. It was a lucky day, after all, especially for the dog.

THE BADMAN'S BRAND
by H. Bedford-Jones

I.

TWO horses stood under a dreary live oak, on the upland of Mesa Verde, rifles in saddle boots. Two men stood at the edge of the low-hanging boughs, taking turns looking through a pair of fieldglasses and sampling the contents of a flask. Both men wore the stars of deputy sheriffs.

"Sure?" said one, wiping his mustache. "Gime a look. Take a drink, Pete."

"Sartin," returned Pete, swapping glasses for flask. "Calico hoss. Can't see his face."

The other looked long and earnestly. In the rarefied air of New Mexico, where distance means nothing, the distant rider on the up trail was clear-cut; the focused glasses brought out his face in sharp relief as he turned to look over his back trail. The face was young, but bearded.

"It's him, by gosh!" cried the gazing deputy sharply. "And he's headin' for town, Pete! By gosh, it's him! I seen his face plain! What's the program?"

"Ain't no program." Pete flung away the empty flask and turned. "Lead them hosses back to the other tree out o' sight from the road. You stay this side. I'll stay the other. When he comes to that there sage-brush clump, plug him — both of us. Don't give him a chance."

"I don't aim to," was the reply. "Not with that feller, by gosh!"

The lone rider slowly approached the crest of Mesa Verde and wound his way along the yellow road. He was young, bronzed, quick of eye; his clothes were faded and patched, his leather chaps badly worn, his Stetson told of several years of sun and rain. At either hip hung belted gun but he carried no rifle.

He neared a large patch of sage, now fresh and green from the recent rains, and his eye rested on it with appreciation as though he liked the sight of it. The clump grew just beside the road. Other clumps were all round, but this one was particularly large and handsome, if sage is ever handsome. Here and there were other splotches of color — red and yellow cactus blossoms, and an ominous, purplish patch of loco weed.

The rider was jogging along negligently when, as he looked at the sagebrush clump, his eye was caught by something in motion just beyond, back of another clump. Only an Indian-trained eye would have caught the motion where there was nothing in sight, where there was not even a breath of wind to account for it.

Like a flash, the rider acted. He bent over as though to pat his horse, then reined the animal sharply sidewise and with the same movement slipped out of his saddle. One spur caught, and as he hit the ground he went down and rolled over.

To the right of the road a rifle cracked, followed by a second splitting report to the left. The calico horse plunged at the sound, started to run, then stopped. The fallen man, dust spurted into his eyes by the bullets, relaxed and lay quiet.

"Hooray!" came a hoarse shout from the left of the road. "Got 'im, Pete!"

The two deputies, rifle in hand, rose and started for the road. The calico horse stood and gazed at them. The huddled shape lay motionless in the white sunlight.

"Get that hoss," ordered Pete. "No mistake about it, anyhow. Sure was his face, all right — durned lucky thing he didn't know that tourist female took a photygraft of him when he held up the Socorro stage,

"Huh? Well, here's where we collect the reward — my good gosh — look out!"

Too late.

The huddled shape in the road seemed to give a convulsive twist. Then a revolver shattered the noontide silence. The heavy report was repeated. Two shots.

To the left of the road, one deputy plunged forward and lay quiet. To the right, Deputy Pete staggered, turned around, and his knees buckled under him. In the road itself, the huddled shape of the hunted man arose: unhurt, bare headed, hawk eyed.

"You durned fools!" he said in soft, drawling contempt.

He went to his horse, which had not budged, and mounted. Then he started out over the mesa road, and sniffed.

"Thought I smelled liquor," he commented. "So somebody got a picture of me, huh? That kills the whole game, blast it! Now they're after me. Now . . ."

He frowned, looked again toward the distant town of Bear Falls, and shook his head as though telling himself the game was not worth the candle. He turned the calico horse about and rode back whence he had come, and was presently out of sight.

Among the rocks, Deputy Pete rose, held a hand to his head, wiped blood out of his eyes, and cursed in a heartfelt manner. He staggered across the road, took one look at his companion, and then sought his horses. So ended the drama of Mesa Verde, which was destined to have far-reaching consequences.

THAT same afternoon the Santa Fe stage lumbered into Bear Falls, much to the relief of Slivers Lawrence, who had a deal on with some Navajos who were living off the reservation. Slivers ranched up in the White Mountains when he felt like it, and at other times did some odd trading with the Indians, and was the last man in the Southwest to know the taste of beaver-tail and wild turkey.

Slivers was law abiding, as a settled and respected citizen of forty should be, but he had a blood-feud or two on his hands none the less. Just now, he had some trading to do, and was most impatient for a trunk load of stuff he had ordered. So he was in town to meet the stage and his trunk, when the unexpected happened.

The stage drew in, unloaded a general assortment of drummers and other impedimenta, one or two punchers, and a sad-eyed young woman. Slivers thought to himself that she looked like a stray lamb in a flock of wolves, then forgot her at a hail from the stage line agent.

"Your trunk's in, Slivers! Haul her away if you want her quick."

Slivers decided there had been a mistake from the size of the trunk, but none the less he got a loafing gentleman of fortune to catch hold of the other end, and carted it into the hotel, where he had a room for the night. When he had it safely stowed in his room, he looked it over carefully. He had ordered a trunk with his name on it in bright red letters, and certainly had got that much — it would tickle Piegan Shortyup pink, this trunk would. But what about the contents?

Not to mention the keys. There were no keys in sight, but Slivers had a bunch in his pocket and fell to work. In ten minutes he had the trunk open. Then he blinked, took another look, and gasped for air as he stared goggle-eyed at the assortment of feminine garments, corsets, and lace goods that met his eye.

"My good gosh!" he exclaimed. "This ain't my trunk!"

Mr. Lawrence buckled on his gun and went to the lobby of the Aragon House, intending to settle matters with the stage line. As he left the stairway, the clerk behind the desk called to him.

"Hey, Slivers! Come over here!"

Slivers turned, and saw before the desk the same sad-eyed young woman who had descended from the stage — only just now she was mad eyed. The clerk spoke up quickly.

"Been some mistake about trunks, Slivers," he said. "Mr. Lawrence, meet Miss Bessie Lawrence — Eastern female just struck town. Looks like one name between two folks had mixed things. Miss Lawrence claims she ain't got the right trunk, and you look sort o' put out. . . ."

"Pleased to meet you, ma'am," said Slivers. "I reckon we can straighten things out in no time. Gosh, I'm glad you got mine! I sure ain't got the right one."

In no time at all, Slivers was sitting in a chair and telling Miss Lawrence that she could command him in any way, shape or manner. Not that she was pretty, for she was not, nor that Slivers was given to being commanded by the gentler sex, for he certainly was not; but he decided that she needed help. She looked it.

"It's mighty good of you, Mr. Lawrence," she replied, that same lost and distressed look coming back into her eyes. "I'd thank you from the bottom of my heart if you could help me find my brother. You see, I came from the East to meet him here, but he doesn't seem to be here and nobody knows anything about him. I can't understand it at all. I don't seem to know . . ."

Slivers scratched his brown chin and told himself that she didn't know the half of it. Bear Falls was no lovers' lane, and was no place for unescorted ladies from the East. There was trouble all over the hills with the Mexicans, there was a county seat war on with Silverton, and the ruby silver strike over at Yellow Gulch had attracted rough gentlemen, not to mention a dance hall and two new saloons. Bear Falls, in fact, was loaded for trouble.

So Slivers, having effected the exchange of trunks, promised to give Miss Lawrence some news of her brother after supper, and went forth to seek said news. He found none. Nobody had ever heard of Ed Lawrence. Slivers met the lady after supper and reported failure.

She looked more rested now, and not half so sad; her simple dress bespoke neatness rather than luxury, but she had character, and Slivers liked her. She told him she had been a school teacher in the East, and had come West when her brother sent her money and an invitation to join him. Also, she had done some inquiring herself.

"They tell me you're a desperate character, Mr. Lawrence," she said, smiling a little. "That you're always shooting up Mexicans and so forth."

Slivers reddened. He knew well enough that nobody had blackened his reputation, but had not thought she would hear about the greaser business.

"I got into trouble with some greasers, all right," he admitted reluctantly. "Ain't nothing to brag of, ma'am — but they're a rough bunch out here. A lot o' bad ones have come up from over the line. Well, now about this here brother who ain't showed up . . ."

He was stumped, for if the brother had not kept his engagement, it was probably because six feet of ground held him occupied. Slivers knew the Bear Falls country like his own ranch, and the only Lawrence west of Jornado was a gray-headed old crook who operated a trading agency on and off the Navajo reservation territory.

"Would a picture help?" asked Miss Lawrence. Slivers turned and brightened perceptibly.

"It sure would, ma'am! Good — this is something like!"

"I just got this out of my trunk this afternoon," she said.

He looked at the photograph, expecting to behold a total stranger; and he was not disappointed. He had never before laid eyes on the alert, reckless-looking young devil who looked up at him.

"Well," he suggested, "s'pose you let me tote this around some to-night. I'll take right good care of it, you bet. Might be I'd run into somebody who'd know of your brother by sight, but hadn't learned the name."

"It's good of you to take so much trouble, Mr. . . . ."

"Nope, just plain Slivers," said Mr. Lawrence, and his bronzed features were good to look upon when he smiled. "I may be a desperate character, but nothing makes me more so than to be called 'Mister.' So, if you don't mind . . ."

"All right, Slivers — and thank you," she said, smiling, and Mr. Lawrence wondered that he had ever thought her homely and sad eyed.

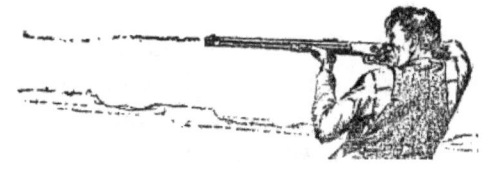

II

BEAR FALLS had plenty of gossip that night, for Pete the Deputy had come in with a bullet scrape across his head and a dead companion across another saddle. Slivers Lawrence heard about it soon enough — the pair of them had nearly trapped Lefty Sage, and Deputy Pete did not yet know how the trap had failed. The badman and road agent had slipped away again, leaving a new victim in his wake.

"And," wailed Pete over the bar of the Blue Front, to a circle of sympathizers, "That gosh-dinged sheriff don't give a durn, I tell you! He says we hadn't ought to have tried to plug anybody with rifles — that we deserved all we got! Them was his very words, by gosh!"

"If I was you," said somebody, "I wouldn't go to disputing with old Simpson none whatever, feller. If you laid out and tried to plug a gent as he came by, and he got you instead, I reckon my money lays on him every time!"

Overhearing this, Slivers drifted down the street to the sheriff's house. He had known Jim Simpson for ten years, a man of wide acquaintance and a square-shooter, an old-timer in the hills. If anybody knew of this Ed Lawrence, Simpson would do so.

The sheriff welcomed him cordially, took him into the parlor, and they lighted up together after a suitable libation.

"This here ain't no official call," explained Mr. Lawrence. "I s'pose you're all het up over what happened to Pete?"

"Nope," said grizzled old Simpson, grinning. "Served him right. I don't go to lay under cover and put a bullet into no man. What's on your mind? You look durned troubled."

"I am," said Slivers. "Right now, you're Jim Simpson and not a sheriff, savvy? If that goes with you, I'll let loose what's eating me. Otherwise, we'll stick to politics."

"Durn politics," said Simpson promptly. "Shoot! How you like these here new teeth, huh?"

He proudly displayed his handsome new store teeth, and Mr. Lawrence duly admired them. The original set had recently been ruined in the Apache Gulch fracas — but that enters not into this relation. The history of Jim Simpson's life would cover most of the historic battles of the old Southwest.

Mr. Lawrence told about the young lady, the missing brother, and then hauled out the photograph. Sheriff Simpson regarded it, stroked his rainbow mustache, and shook his head.

"Nope," he said with decision. "You're the only Lawrence I ever heard of around here, old-timer; and this ain't you by a good deal. Never laid eyes on this here jasper, and it's sure he ain't wanted. I been running over the wanted notices, hopin' to corral some o' these fellers comin' through in the Yeller Gulch strike rush. I'm right certain. Sorry I can't help you none. Reckon you ain't seen my Lefty Sage picture?"

"Picture?" asked Slivers, pocketing his photograph. "Of Lefty Sage? Didn't know you had one, Jim. Nor anybody else."

"Got it recent," said the sheriff, "and had some copies made. Remember when he held up the Socorro stage and drilled a feller? They was a woman aboard with one of them cameras, and she snapped him without him knowing it, when his handkerchief slipped off his mug for a minute. They all said he was bearded, but nobody could describe him any two alike, and it was sure an accident she got his picture. Hold on a second — I got a copy of it upstairs."

Slivers Lawrence knew about Lefty Sage, of course — everyone in the Southwest did. He had started in the gunman business on the other side of the Rio Grande; he always shot with his left hand, when he was not shooting with both hands, and he left his trade mark on every Mexican he sent into eternity — a small sprig of sagebrush left on the corpse.

Then Lefty, as he was known, came up north and went to work for a sheep outfit beyond Socorro. He might have gone straight, but his reputation followed him, and a Mexican went after him; the gentleman was full of marihuana and was out for blood, and Lefty had to shoot him four times before stopping him. Nobody would have objected to this, but a white herder went after Lefty soon afterward, and passed out by the same route.

Lefty started to leave the Socorro neighborhood, but when he was buying supplies, a trader wanted to square accounts for the dead herder — and there was one trader the less. This brought the law into it, and the next heard from Lefty Sage, he was holding up stages with some regularity and with several killings to his credit. To a certain extent he had been a victim of circumstances, but he had himself pushed the circumstances farther, and now he was being very actively sought in various quarters, for large rewards.

Sheriff Simpson returned, handed Mr. Lawrence a picture and resumed his pipe.

"This here will help us a lot — only Pete got too durned anxious to-day, when he seen the gent," he observed. "Nobody ever give us a good clear description of this here hombre before, but now we got something to go on, better'n a weejee board and messages from the spirit world could give. Come a couple days, I'll have more copies o' this picture, and then we start out systematic to round up the hills. We'll sure get him — unless the greasers get him first."

"Mexicans?" said Slivers, lifting his bushy eyebrows. This interested him. "Why them?"

Simpson blew a cloud of smoke. "This here feud that has trailed Lefty from down below, savvy? I done heard a gang o' killers had come up north to lift his scalp. Well, no differ to me! If he kills off the greasers, I ain't mourning none; and if they knife him, Sanburne County will be saved the expense of chasin' him."

"Huh!" said Mr. Lawrence, very thoughtfully. "If you was riding down the road and come into the middle of a fight betwixt Lefty Sage and a gang o' greasers, which side would you take?"

"Ask me something easy," and Mr. Simpson guffawed. "Me, I'd prob'ly fly straight to heaven or somewheres. I hear you sort of got a greaser war on your own hands, Slivers — huh?"

"I ain't right certain," confessed Mr. Lawrence. "I know danged well that I don't leave town without toting a rifle, that's sure."

It was late when Mr. Lawrence came back to the hotel, to be informed that Miss Lawrence had gone to bed, so far as was known. He did not pursue his inquiries, but settled down in a chair, took out a pencil and made some light strokes on the photograph of her brother. Then he erased the strokes, rolled a cigarette, and pocketed the picture with a frown.

"Dang it" he observed to himself, having confirmed his worst fears. "The beard makes a heap o' difference, for a fact — dad blame it! This sure is a fine can o' sardines I've opened! If she finds out about it, what's she going to do, huh? My gosh, if it ain't up to me hard!"

Mr. Lawrence was not easily taken aback, but this time he was positively appalled. There was no doubt whatever that Lefty Sage was merely Ed Lawrence with a beard.

And what was he to do about it? If he told everything to the sister, he was going to cause a lot of woe, no doubt about it. He had taken upon himself the position of protector, and now he was paying for it. His first thought was to get out his buckboard, load his trunk and shove for the high places; but Slivers Lawrence was hardly the sort to run from trouble.

Now he understood things plainly — things the sheriff certainly did not know. Lefty had been coming to town to meet his sister when the deputies sighted him and his horse, of which they had a description. Probably he had sent for her when he was working as a herder and hoping to live down his record below the border. And now Lefty would certainly do his best to get into touch with her — badman as he was, he would not leave his sister in Bear Falls without a word.

Mr. Lawrence was decidedly worried, and he did not sleep his usual snoring slumber that night. He dreaded the morning, dreaded facing this little woman with the sad eyes, dreaded breaking the news to her — for he could see no way out of it. At the same time, he wished for luck.

When he went down to breakfast in the hotel dining room, he found her at a table and joined her. She greeted him cheerfully, and there was a dancing eagerness in her face that was explained when she handed a note across to him.

"Good news — read that!" she exclaimed. "I won't need to trouble you any further, Mr. Slivers. You've been most kind — well, everything's right here."

Slivers eyed the note, which was scrawled in pencil:

Dear Sis:

Important business prevented me meeting you — please forgive me. Meet me at Golden's ranch, three miles north of Ragged Ridge. A team from the livery will fetch you out. I'll be watching and waiting. With love.

Ed.

Lawrence looked up, relief in his weather-seamed features.

"Good news is right!" he said, with a smile. "Me, I couldn't get no track of him."

"How can I get out there — a team, he said?" Her voice was eager. "Is it far from here?"

"Yep, middlin' far," said Lawrence reflectively, giving no indication of his rapid thought. "Let's see, now . . ."

A dozen things occurred to him. Golden's deserted and ruined ranch was located in a God-forsaken region; he knew that Miss Lawrence was a stranger to the country and its ways. He thought of the turbid ford, about the slatternly hangers-on at the livery, about who would have the job of driving her out, about the ever-present menace to Lefty Sage, about this woman herself — and he knew what he must do.

"Listen here," he said. "I got my buckboard here, and my road goes right out past Ragged Ridge. No sense in your hiring a team at the livery, if you'll travel with me. I can hitch your trunk on alongside mine, if you say the word. Maybe you'd better leave your trunk here for a spell," he added, "until you arrange things with your brother. Take a grip with you."

"Fine!" she exclaimed, her eyes alight. "Are you sure it won't take you out of your way?"

"Not a mite," lied Mr. Lawrence. He did not say that from choice he would not have ventured into the Ragged Ridge district without a troop of cavalry and a few machine guns. "Not a mite! But I got a little trading to do first. If you'll be ready in about half an hour, I reckon I'll have the buckboard up in front all set to go."

His trading was a highly important item, since he had neglected bringing any rifle to town — and if he were heading for Ragged Ridge, he meant to take no chances. A number of gentlemen with swarthy skins and Spanish names were very much on the alert, to catch Slivers Lawrence off by himself; for Lefty Sage and his outlaw friends were not the only badmen up from the border with killing in mind.

Thus it happened that, half an hour later, Mr. Lawrence was seen, amid the intense astonishment of all Bear Falls, to hitch a lady's grip alongside his lashed trunk, load the lady herself into the seat beside him and drive off for parts unknown.

III

THE TIPSY trail struggled toward the hills whose tops glistened whitely against a perfect sky. It was not a good trail, once they left the highway, and this helped Miss Lawrence and Mr. Lawrence to get better acquainted.

"How long?" she demanded.

"Anywhere from two to four hours," said he, missing a jagged boulder by inches. "Depends on Jack and Jill here — temperamental on the upgrade, like all females. We climb all the way."

"And all females are temperamental on the upgrade?" she asked, a laugh in her eyes.

"All," he affirmed gravely. "Only some don't show it so much."

Mr. Lawrence was not in any talkative mood this morning, for the farther he got the more he regretted coming. Lefty Sage must realize his sister would not come alone — and a third party might get her into hot water. And how was the girl herself to receive the news that her brother was an outlaw? Evidently she regarded this brother as a little god, expected him to provide a nice home on a verdant hillside.

"My gosh!" and Slivers groaned to himself at her air of happy expectancy. "We'll have to postpone the agony if we can — it's a rotten shame to think of it all!"

With the bright idea of preparing her mind for the shock, he switched the talk from cliff-dwellings and petrified forests to the need for weapons, their use, and the badness of greasers, but Miss Lawrence was more interested in the White Mountains and the ranch there.

"Beaver and wild turkeys — in New Mexico!" she exclaimed, when Slivers mentioned the fact. "Who would believe that, now, if they read it in a story? Or are you joking?"

"Well, you come up to my place and you'll get a mighty nice beaver coat for a visiting present," said Mr. Lawrence hopefully, and then pointed. "See that ridge? Looks right next door, but it ain't — two miles south o' that is Golden's ranch. We'll come into a branch trail right quick that'll lead us there."

He pulled in the team suddenly, as they swung about a bend and came upon a horseman in the middle of the road — a dark-skinned, insolent young man astride a tired-looking cayuse, rolling a cigarette and gazing languidly at the buckboard.

"If you got no serious objections," said Mr. Lawrence, "and if you ain't too tired to mosey over a bit, we'll go ahead."

The Mexican lighted his cigarette nonchalantly. Lawrence saw by a dozen small indications of gear and clothes that the man was Mexican and not a native, but as the man had no rifle, he left his own gun at his feet, untouched.

"No entiendo," said the other languidly. "¿A donde vais, señor?"

Mr. Lawrence smiled to himself and started to descend, unhurried. He need not cramp his vocabulary on account of the lady from the East — he could speak out his heart, freely and openly. The Mexican's form of address had been a deliberate insult, of course.

So, walking up to the rider, Lawrence smiled sweetly at him.

"You think you're addressing another son of several things like yourself, do you?" he said, while the other puffed smoke and grinned. It was the grin of an amused wolf, showing pointed yellow teeth. "When you say 'vais' to me, Señor Caballero, you're not speaking to another peon, and if I hadn't this señorita along, you'd learn it quick. Now, my personal opinion of you is thus and so, Señor, . . ." and he delivered his opinion without heat, but fluently.

The Mexican laughed. "This road is closed, Señor," he responded. "It has been closed by me, Pancho Valquez. You may go back unharmed."

Lawrence was staggered. He was also encouraged to be himself, because this was not one of the gentry with whom he was at feud. He had heard of Valquez, and since the man was here, others were apt to be well away.

"Why, you several kinds of a mesquite worm, do you know which side of the Rio Grande you're on?" he demanded. "Greasers like you ain't quite so important as coyotes, sabe? When it comes to closing roads — "

Señor Valquez made a sharp and unexpected move, and Mr. Lawrence found the violent end of a revolver looking into his face.

"And to Pancho Valquez, gringoes are less important than greasers," said the man from below, with a glint in his eye that meant business. "You speak our language well, señor, so perhaps you may be interested in learning my opinion of you and your señorita over there! She is quite able to amuse me, and I shall be glad to entertain, her. You may return home and tell your friends what has become of her. As for my opinion of you . . ."

Señor Valquez delivered his opinion without heat, and Mr. Lawrence said nothing. He noted the peculiar hue and expression of Valquez, however, and wished he had not left his rifle on the floor of the buckboard. He knew a marihuana fiend when he met one, and the only good thing about it was that Valquez was not full of the drug now, or he would be out for blood of man or beast.

"None of your big talk," he rejoined sharply. "That señorita doesn't stay here — "

"No, she goes with me," said Valquez. "And you'll stay here if you object — "

"¡Los manos arriba!" cut in a pleasant, but decided voice. "¡Pronto!"

Valquez looked up, spat an oath, and dropped his revolver as he reached for the sky. Slivers Lawrence jerked around, and his jaw dropped.

"My good gosh, ma'am!" he exclaimed, reddening. "I never supposed you talked Mex — my gosh!"

Bessie Lawrence, keeping the new rifle leveled at Valquez, laughed a little. There was a lively color in her cheeks, but whether from excitement or from the choice below-the-border phrases which filled the air, it were hard to say.

"If you don't mind, Slivers, take his gun and send him on his way," she said.

Mr. Lawrence did not mind — in fact, it gave him exquisite pleasure to do as much. Valquez took the matter with a scowl, and eyed Slivers.

"Perhaps I may have your name, Señor — if you are not afraid to give it to me?" he said silkily.

"Hardly," and Lawrence looked into the murky eyes. "A few of your friends have had reason to know me pretty well, Señor — Slivers Lawrence, at your service."

"Oh!" said Valquez, and grinned. "I know you now! Hasta luego Señores!"

With this parting shot — "until soon" —

he wheeled his cayuse and went his way with a dig of his big spurs.

"Gosh, Miss Bessie!" said Mr. Lawrence, solemnly removing his hat and bowing. "I got to take it off to you — and beg your pardon. I never dreamed you savvied Mex. What's the matter?"

For she had turned pale, and her mouth was quivering.

"Nothing — it's all right," she said, and her eyes were brave. "I just had to act without thinking about the consequences. . . ."

"I hate to think what you'd do when you stopped to think of 'em, then!" said Lawrence admiringly. "Well, ma'am," he added, climbing up beside her and putting the captured revolver into her lap, "this sure belongs to you. Good thing that greaser wasn't full of marihuana — he's a fiend, or I'm mistaken!"

"Marihuana?" she questioned.

"A form of hemp-weed," said Lawrence, glad to divert her. "They eat it or smoke it, and it makes 'em want blood and want it quick. I've known a greaser get in a corral o' cattle and go to slashing — but where did you learn Mex?"

"I taught Spanish in school," she returned, laughing a little. "Enough for him to understand, eh?"

"You bet," agreed Lawrence fervently.

"I hope there aren't many around here like that man Valquez?"

Lawrence blinked at the horizon, and his heart flopped. The road closed — and Valquez an outlaw whose name was known! This could mean but one thing. The Mexicans from down below were hot on the trail of Lefty Sage — he might even now be cornered at Golden's ranch!

His apprehension was contagious, or his sunburned features must have betrayed his thoughts, for the woman beside him touched his arm.

"Is anything wrong, Slivers?"

"Well," he returned slowly, picking his words, "I just been thinking — the sheriff said a bunch of greasers had cut loose and were running wild. They might be after your brother."

"After him? Why?"

Mr. Lawrence cursed himself for the slip. "Oh, because he's white and they ain't," he said. "Likely he's got the water hole and they've tried to drive him off — that's why he couldn't meet you at Bear Falls. Y' see, water's plenty scarce around here. Golden's has the only water — "

"Then get along," she said, to his surprise, "and we'll give him a hand if he needs it!"

"Better go back to town and get the sheriff," said Lawrence gloomily.

"Nonsense!" Her eyes were glowing now. "Don't waste time — why, we're nearly there now! Get there and take him away with us — talk to those horses of yours, Slivers!"

Mr. Lawrence gulped hard, and obeyed.

IV.

IN the mind of Slivers Lawrence, the little woman's illusion was a sacred thing. He had not lied when he spoke of the danger to her brother, but the reasons behind it — well, he could not bring himself to make the inevitable revelation until all known varieties of lies had failed. He must hope for luck, that was all.

The more he thought of it, the more certain he was that Lefty Sage had been run down by his enemies. With a vendetta on their minds, and marihuana to keep it in good running order, the greasers would make short work of the job once Lefty was in the trap — and he might be in it this min-

ute. Golden's was deserted, had been unused for years.

So, giving all his attention to outrunning Valquez, Mr. Lawrence talked to his horses and talked hard. He would not have worried a particle about the situation had he alone been concerned, for he did not love Mexicans and might even have relished a little action — and he lelt a certain sympathy for Lefty Sage. But the presence of Bessie Lawrence complicated the affair, and he dreaded the moment when she must be disillusioned about her brother.

The branch trail, which cut off a mile or more to Golden's, was rough and to spare, but there was no sign of anyone in the vicinity. Presently they sighted the place — a shack that stood on a rise of ground in a valley, partly hidden by the piñons that clumped about the shack. In the background, the hills rose sharply, with play of sunlight on silver aspens, to the background of Ragged Ridge.

"Is that it?" exclaimed Miss Lawrence suddenly. "Oh! There he is now."

A figure had come out of the shack, walking to the edge of the trees. He stood there gazing at them, lifted his hand, waved to them. And Mr. Lawrence, his eyes bulging, was speechless. For this was not the bearded ruffian in the picture shown him by the sheriff — not a bit of it! This was the reckless young god in the girl's photograph, with perhaps a healthier and more alert expression. A razor had wrought the transformation, but had not been able to color chin and cheeks, as the New Mexico sun had colored forehead and nostrils.

The evil moment had come, and Slivers Lawrence knew that he had to do some fast work. He stopped the team, and his passenger leaped out and was clasped in her brother's arms, talking rapidly. Lefty Sage held her tight, and looked over her head at the rapidly acting Lawrence, who used his hands with all the grace of an Indian hard at work.

Peace sign repeated — then finger to

lips, then a solemn wink — this was enough. Lefty Sage grinned amiably and returned the wink.

"This is Mr. Lawrence — Slivers Lawrence," exclaimed the girl, turning. "He's been kindness personified, Ed — I don't know what I'd have done if he hadn't helped me."

"Heard of you, Slivers," and Lefty Sage held out a hand which Mr. Lawrence gripped heartily. "Glad to meet you, and thanks a heap for helping Sis out. Sis, you can wash up at the house, if you want — Slivers and I can chin for a bit. I want to ask about a few things."

She nodded, and with a bright smile was gone among the trees. Lefty Sage produced the makings, rolled a cigarette, and flung Lawrence a quick look, as he handed over the tobacco.

"Well, partner? You can wigwag all right."

"She's not on to you, savvy? Sheriff's got a picture of you, but it shows a beard. She thinks the greasers are after you on general principles."

"Huh?" Lefty started. "Greasers? You ain't seen any?"

"Yep — Pancho Valquez." Lawrence described the meeting in the road, and was not slow to catch the alarm in the eyes of Lefty Sage. "Looks to me," he concluded, "like we're going to be in hot water if we don't get out of here on the jump. I reckon they want you bad."

"They're not the only ones," said Lefty Sage, with a direct look.

"Shucks," said Mr. Lawrence guilelessly, "I don't know what you mean, feller. In fact, I don't know nothing — I'm the most ignorant cuss you ever seen! Sheriff showed me a picture of Lefty Sage, like I said, but I don't know nothing about that neither. I'm plumb ignorant."

"I get you," the outlaw grinned. "And thanks, Slivers. I've heard of you as the squarest man north of the Line. I reckon

we'd better light out."

"Yep, we sure had. You alone?"

"Got my hoss, but plumb tuckered out. Rode to town and back last night, and lamed the poor critter. Valquez — he's plumb bad, Slivers. We'd better light a shuck and talk later."

"Hop in the buckboard, then — get your stuff, if you got any," said Lawrence. "I reckon it's the best we can do."

The outlaw hesitated, his eyes clouded. "You hop in with her and beat it," he said slowly. "I'll fix up a lie to cover it, Slivers. They ain't after you — I'll set here in plain sight."

"You go to hell," said Mr. Lawrence flatly. "Anyhow, they sure won't come in on us until dark, and we ain't going to linger that long. We'll get a bite to eat — I got a basket of lunch here — and you can figure up some sort o' lie that includes you in the party. Your hoss done up?"

"Might last for a mile or two," said Lefty Sage, as they turned together and headed for the shack among the trees. "Strained a tendon, I reckon — might as well leave him here. Then the program's to load in and go?"

"You and her in back, covered with sacks," said Lawrence. "Fix you up a good lie."

Lefty Sage did just this, and did it very well, over the basket of food. Lawrence saw with half an eye that he was not the only one who hated to spoil the girl's illusions — he realized that Lefty Sage was shrinking from the inevitable moment, also.

The story ran plausibly enough in regard to outlaws and horse thieves, and Lefty went on to say that he had sent the note to town yesterday and had also sent to the sheriff, but had not yet heard from the latter. The Mexicans had cut him off on his way to town and he had taken shelter here — his own ranch, he explained, was miles back in the hills.

"We'll head for there now," he said, in conclusion. "With my horse lame, I couldn't get on, but I can go in the buckboard. You and I can lie down and cover up, Sis, and probably the greasers won't trouble Lawrence. He'll jerk us out of this, and take us to the Ragged Ridge trail, and we'll get a posse out after these fellows and clean things up."

Slivers nodded assent. Privately, he concluded that Lefty Sage had some friend back in the hills — probably had some hiding-out place there.

"It's really dangerous here, then?" asked the girl anxiously.

"It is," said her brother. "I reckon you're going to see bullets fly, Sis — but we'll do our best to pull you through, so buck up and face the music. Slivers, let's go out and get things in shape."

The horses had been led into the lean-to behind the shack, without being unhitched. Lawrence had looked at the bronc belonging to Lefty Sage, and judged the latter's diagnosis correct; the animal might cover some ground, but how much was a dubious matter.

"I reckon we're ready," said Lawrence, after leading out the team and backing in the buckboard under shelter. "Think you and she can hang on?"

"I reckon," said Lefty. "Here's a pile of sacks and rubbish. Oh, Sis! Come on."

Fairly well covered from observation by the trees about the house, brother and sister took their places, and Lawrence covered them with sacking.

"I'm going to hit hell for leather," said he, as he climbed to his seat. "If you folks feel like you're going to fall out, holler! Otherwise, we hit the high spots. Gidap!"

He laid on the whip, and headed his team out at a sharp trot for the road.

As he came clear of the trees, he scanned the landscape but could see no sign of danger. His rifle was under his feet, ready. Any of the boulders that strewed the valley might hold concealed enemies, however — the only chance was to get through while they thought him alone and before they noticed

the back end of his outfit.

He lifted his whip — but it never came down.

The off horse reared straight up, screamed, came down in a heap. The other simply dropped and sprawled out. Two rifles cracked, and not far away either.

Before the buckboard went over, Lawrence had his rifle in hand and saw whence those two shots came. He struck the ground, rolled clear of the tangle, came to his feet with his rifle up. He shot rapidly, fast as he could pump the bolt and aim. To this third shot a man rose from a clump of rocks to the right and pitched forward.

"Get back, you fool!" came the sharp voice of Lefty Sage.

Lawrence glanced around. He saw the girl, unhurt, running for the trees. Lefty was just throwing up his gun; the sharp reports of the forty-five came rapidly. Into the background scurried the figure of a running man, dodging from cover to cover.

"Two of 'em," said Lefty calmly. "One got away."

"Well, get in out o' the rain," said Lawrence, and they turned for shelter.

Distant rifles gave voice, and dust spurted, but the enemy were too far off to effect any hits. The hills and valley looked innocent as before; only the twisted, smashed buckboard and the two dead horses there in the sunlight told of what had happened.

The three gathered in the ranch shack. Lefty Sage was bruised, but the girl was unhurt. The situation was clear enough to all of them. Lefty rolled a smoke calmly.

"Well, they got us penned up," he said. "There's still that hoss o' mine; but he ain't up to takin' the three of us aboard and going into a race for it."

"What do you think will happen?" asked his sister quietly. The eyes of the two men met, and then Lawrence shrugged.

"Might as well tell her the truth — she can stand it," he said. "Why, what'll happen is that they'll work around here to-night and clean up. That's certain. They'll prob'ly burn out this place, once they reach the trees."

"Couldn't I take your horse," and the girl turned to her brother eagerly, "and go to town for help? I'm not as heavy as a man, and might make it."

"Nothing doing," said Lawrence quickly. "It'd be your only chance at a pinch — but that gang would murder a woman quick as not. They'd never let you by."

"I could go right now, while they're still away off," she exclaimed. "There were only two of them close up."

"No," said Lefty Sage. "Nothing doing; Sis! That hoss of mine could outrun anything on four legs if he was sound, and I'd let you chance it in a minute; but he might not go a mile like he is now."

"What else is there to do?"

"Trust to us." Lawrence squinted at the sun. "Afternoon ain't more'n half gone. Feller, let's you and me go lay out in the warm sun and sort of scratch up the ground and see if we can pick off anyone, We might keep 'em from closing in, anyhow. They're all up around back of here, I reckon."

"Good idea," Lefty nodded. "My rifle's in the lean-to. I'll take the east edge of the trees, you cover the other side. So long, Sis — be a good girl, and don't be scared. We'll pull out of this all right."

As he kissed her, she clung to him a long moment. Lawrence took his rifle and went out. Long before he was in position, he heard the crack of Lefty's rifle. Then, after a time, rifles spoke from the hillsides and to his amazement he made out Lefty Sage working down to the spot where the team lay dead. His rifle covered the advance, however, and presently he saw Lefty dash to his feet and leap forward, stoop over the body of the dead Mexican and then drop from sight as bullets spurted. Lawrence could not figure it out at all, as Lefty almost at once worked back again, but gave his attention to the enemy.

These, who had tried closing in, found themselves nipped by the two rifles. Lawrence calculated there were a dozen or more of them; Valquez, then, had brought along his entire band of border bandits. With night they would easily work in — perhaps; but night had not yet come, and now they suffered. Lawrence was certain that he downed two of them, perhaps a third — hard to be sure.

At all events, they moved back, almost out of range, and seemed to be grouping for a consultation, leaving out only two or three marksmen. It was at this juncture that Lawrence caught a sudden wild, wrathful, jubilant yell from Lefty Sage and twisted about.

From the trees was coming Lefty's cayuse, and in the saddle was Bessie Lawrence.

The first thought of Slivers was that she had come with her brother's consent, but Lefty's shouted yells to come back disabused him of this notion. The girl sighted him, waved her hand, and then leaned over and put her bronc at full speed. She could ride — no doubt of that! And for the moment, she was going like a whirlwind.

Lawrence jerked up, scanned the hillsides sharply. Men were running — Lefty Sage was firing at them as they ran. But Slivers looked for something else, and presently saw it; a mounted man, urging his horse downward, heading for the road to cut off the girl. He settled down, elevated his sights, began firing slowly, steadily. Barely within range, if he could make it. . . . At the fourth shot, the rider went down. The horse had been hit.

Bessie Lawrence was gone, a little spume of dust settling in the road in her wake. No other Mexicans tried to follow; whether there were other guards out, like Valquez, was impossible to say. She did not know the way to town, she was unlikely to meet anyone on the trails — well, Mr. Lawrence snorted to himself and headed back for a confab with Lefty.

"A fool trick," commented Lefty Sage,

with profane emphasis. "Anyhow, she's out of this mess, and that's something."

"It's a whole lot," agreed Mr. Lawrence complacently. "And if the hoss don't bog down — "

"Don't you think I know my own hoss?" snapped Lefty. "That hoss won't go two mile. If a miracle happens and she does get through 'em, she won't reach town until midnight or after. And that ain't going to do us much good."

"Well, I'm satisfied to take the deal as she lays," said Lawrence. "Let's go eat what's left of the grub and have a drink or two, and then go and kill some more greasers."

"You're on," and Lefty Sage grinned.

V

"WHAT were you doing down by that dead greaser?" demanded Slivers. The two men were polishing up what was left of the luncheon. Sunset was at hand, the swift sunset of the Southwest.

"Branding him," and Lefty Sage grinned. Lawrence stared.

"Branding him?"

"Bit o' sagebrush."

"Oh!" Lawrence grunted. "Your dog-goned fool advertisement, huh? Lefty Sage, sure. Say, is Valquez heading this bunch?"

The outlaw shrugged. "Search me. He's only one. I got a private war on with quite a few — Tio Hernandez is one of 'em."

Slivers Lawrence grunted again, this time with understanding.

"Well, that explains how come they fired on me with the team," he said, and grinned. "I got a war o' my own on with Tio Hernandez — done killed his brother. I expect he

recognized me, huh? That's why he opened up. Valquez done told him my name."

"That makes me feel better about draggin' you into it," and Lefty Sage chuckled. "Well, old-timer, think we can hold 'em off until dawn? I expect they'll try rushing us sure."

"You hold your side and I'll hold mine," said Slivers, as they exchanged a smile of perfect comprehension. They knew well enough there would be no holding when the time came. "Say," he added, "be honest about — her. Think she's got a chance?"

"Not a chance in the world," said Lefty Sage, his eyes narrowed and ominous. "They'd follow her sure as hell — and that means they'd pick her up. I saw a pair of 'em cut over the hill but couldn't drop their hosses. All we can do is make 'em pay for her."

"All right," said Slivers curtly.

Make them pay — that was all they could hope to do! Sunrise would tell the story, right enough. If by some miracle Bessie Lawrence got away and reached town, morning would bring a rescue party; whether it found the two men dead or alive, depended wholly upon them.

"If they get up guts enough to rush," thought Slivers Lawrence, as he worked out on one side of the trees and got position among the boulders, "then they sure will get us. If they don't, we got a chance."

SO THE night began.

It was a clear, starry night, without a moon, and the attackers had advantage enough but not too much. Lefty Sage did a little shooting, but Slivers lay silent and hidden, refusing to give away his position. He could not see distinctly, but he could hear excellently, and slight sounds carried far on such a night.

An hour passed, and, another. Slivers knew almost to a T where the Mexicans were converging on his side — at times he could even see their figures flitting among rocks or sage. There was nothing green on the hillside except the piñon trees and clumps of sagebrush. Slivers gradually got the foremost men located, and bided his time. He judged that three of them were working in carefully to close quarters, hoping to reach the shelter of the trees and so cover the rush of the others.

He got his three located — well within fifty yards of his position. When he heard a guttural word exchanged among them and knew they were about to make a dash, he chuckled to himself and put his rifle to his shoulder. Thinking themselves safe enough on this unguarded side, the three came to their feet and started forward at a run.

Mr. Lawrence made two out of a possible three, missed the third man with two more bullets, and then rolled aside as rifles spoke from above the bullets pinged off the rocks around. He gained another shelter and lay low. The attack was spoiled, for this time!

Perhaps half an hour later, he heard a sudden outbreak of voices — wild, jubilant yells that swept up fiercely and then died. There was no more shooting, except an occasional shot from a man posted near the dead team, evidently to serve as a sentry, and prevent the two men escaping. At a call from Lefty, Slivers presently came back to the trees.

"Hear 'em yelling?" said the outlaw, his voice anxious. "Looks bad, Slivers."

"Yeah," agreed Slivers, with a muttered oath. "I was afraid so my own self. I done got two of 'em — they ain't tried any more tricks."

"If they don't," said Lefty Sage, "then, by gosh, she's done for."

And, as the hours passed, they did not. No explanations were needed. The two riders Lefty had seen putting off had overhauled or located the girl on her crippled horse, and had brought her back; this was why the jubilant yells had gone up. Slivers

grew hot and cold at the thought of it. Only this, too, would explain why there was no more attack, no further rush. Valquez was waiting for morning now — a crafty, venomous, Indian-blooded half-breed who desired vengeance to the utmost and preferred it by daylight for fuller enjoyment.

The hours crept past. A little before dawn, Slivers drew his cramped body into shelter of the trees, went to the shack and met Lefty Sage. They enjoyed a cautious cigarette in silence, then Lefty spoke wearily:

"Better keep watch, I reckon."

A drink, and they went back together to the edge of the trees.

Still nothing happened. Red and gray streaked the sky, deepened into yellow, and just before the sun broke the horizon, Slivers spoke.

"See him?"

"Yeah."

A man was coming down the farther slopes and crossing to the rise — Valquez himself, bearing a white cloth tied to a stick.

In the fresh morning light, the Mexican swaggered along with insolent ease, lighting a cigarette as he came. The two men rose up and came to join him. Obviously, it was no trap — he would not take any chances on his own yellow hide. He greeted them with a graceful wave of the hand.

"Ah, Señores! A fine morning," he said mockingly.

"Well, what you want?" demanded Lefty Sage.

"You, caballero," said the Mexican. He put a hand to his pocket and produced a bit of blue cloth. "Perhaps you know this?"

Lefty grunted, frowningly, but Slivers Lawrence took the little handkerchief, sniffed it and compressed his lips.

"Hers, I reckon — same perfume," he muttered, and looked at Valquez. "Well?"

"The señorita met with misfortune last night," said the Mexican easily. "She is in our camp now; but do not be alarmed, Señores. She has not been hurt, for we are caballeros. Perhaps you would like to be sure I am not lying to you?"

He turned, and lifted his voice.

"Ho, there, Gomez! A little scream from the señorita — touch her with your knife — "

"Stop it, you devil!" cried out Lefty Sage. Valquez flashed them a smile, then from the background came response.

"She has fainted, señor — shall I wake her?"

"Leave her alone," said Lefty Sage, hoarsely. Valquez waved his hand.

"Do not wake her," he called, and turned back to the two with a smile that showed his pointed teeth.

"What you want?" snapped Lawrence. Valquez grinned at him.

"Your friend Tio Hernandez was killed last night, Señor, and you are of no interest to me. You may go freely, and take the señorita with you — provided Señor Lefty here gives up his gun and comes with me."

Lefty Sage was white, but he looked at Slivers and nodded.

"There's no argument, I reckon," he said quietly. "Not with Sis in their hands."

"My gosh!" exclaimed Lawrence. "But — "

"No buts neither," and the outlaw shrugged. "They got the whip hand, Slivers. All right, Valquez, you win. Send her down and. I'll go."

Valquez smiled a little.

"No, Señor — I do not trust anyone. You can trust me, for I have no time to waste on women, and when I've tied you to a horse, we head for the Rio Grande. Come with me."

Lefty Sage nodded, took out his gun, and gave it to Lawrence.

"Here y'are — shake! You'll see Sis safe to town?"

"Sure," said Slivers. A lump was in his throat, and words came hard. There was nothing he could say — Lefty was doing the only possible thing, the thing he himself must have done had their positions been reversed.

"All ready, Valquez," said Lefty Sage quietly, leaving his rifle where it lay. "So long."

"So long," said Slivers huskily, and that was all.

The two walked off together.

They had gone perhaps a hundred feet, when from the farther hillside came a sudden short, sharp yelp. Lawrence stared, wondered what it meant. He saw Valquez swing around and jerk out his gun, and instinctively reached for his own rifle. Then his eye caught a moving streak of dust down the valley.

Like a flash, it all came to him — they had missed the girl after all! Yet, unwilling to risk a battle, the wily Mexican had worked a ruse — probably Bessie had lost her handkerchief when the wagon went down, and the sentinel there had found it.

"Lefty! Look out — cover up!" yelled Lawrence frantically.

Too late.

Valquez, warned, had seen the dust streak also, knew riders were coming there, and coming fast. He whirled and deliberately shot Lefty Sage — shot him twice. Lefty took a step, staggered and went down in a heap.

His killer leaped for the nearest rocks, while rifles blazed lead at Slivers Lawrence. But Mr. Lawrence cared nothing for bullets. He stood, aiming carefully, firing slowly. He put a bullet through the leg of Valquez, who went down and began to crawl. Unhurried, Slivers took good aim and smashed the other leg. Valquez yelled to his men, waved his hand.

Lawrence grinned cruelly, took to cover, waited — and then fired again. This time, Valquez fell forward and lay quietly beside the man he had murdered.

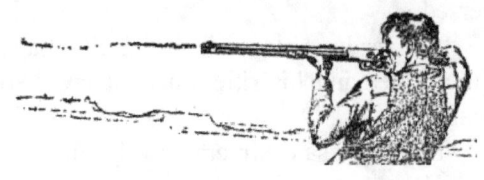

VI

SHERIFF SIMPSON and two other men stayed on. As the sheriff said, his posse was able and willing to run down greasers without his help.

"Yep, she done insisted on comin' with us," he said uneasily to Slivers Lawrence, as they watched the grave being dug among the trees. Bessie Lawrence was in the shack, with the body of her brother. "Hell of a note we didn't get here before, Slivers! Done the best we could. Say, there's quite a reward on this here Valquez — he done held up a bank or two down below and so forth."

"T'ell with the reward," said Mr. Lawrence curtly.

"You'll change your mind," and the sheriff caressed his false teeth. "Say, Slivers — I been thinking about this here female and her brother. I never seen this jasper before, and you're the only Lawrence around here. I got a slant at his face when we lifted him into the shack, and I've got more'n a notion that with a beard — "

Lawrence looked the sheriff in the eye.

"Listen here, old-timer," he said slowly, "you've done heard how he passed out, huh? And you know what that girl thinks of him. Now, I might have notions my own self; but what she thinks of her dead brother is worth a great deal more to me by far."

"Huh!" said the sheriff. "Dang it all! I get you, Slivers. Yeah, I get you all right, and I reckon it's so, too. She done talked a lot about her brother on the way out here. Huh! Yeah, you're right. Say, I done noticed a dead greaser layin' down near that team of yours, and he had a tuft o' sage layin' on him."

"Uh-huh," said Mr. Lawrence. "Mean anything to you?"

"No, you danged lousy coyote, it don't," said the sheriff.

When they were ready to put Lefty Sage into his last home, they found the girl gone, and called. She came, stumbling through the trees, tears on her cheeks, a little heap of green twigs in her arms.

"They — they were all I could find," she sobbed, as she knelt and laid them upon the still breast of her brother.

The eyes of Sheriff Simpson and Slivers Lawrence met across the grave, and the sheriff swallowed hard and turned away. For the sprigs of green that the girl laid upon the body of her brother were fresh green shoots of sagebrush — the badman's brand.

And there is one secret that Slivers Lawrence has never told his wife.

&

LANCELOT BIGGS
COOKS A PIRATE

by Nelson S. Bond

THE whole trouble started with Slops. Slops wasn't a *bad* cook, you understand. He just wasn't a cook at all, rightly speaking. He had what you might call a "tapioca complex." It was tapioca for breakfast, tapioca for lunch, tapioca for dinner. Every day. Boiled tapioca, stewed tapioca, even fricasseed tapioca —

Ugh! When you hop gravs twice a month on a lugger shuttling between Earth and Venus, you can't get by forever on a diet of ta — that stuff!

Anyhow, it finally got to be too much for even an iron-bellied old spacedog like Cap Hanson. So when we pulled into the Sun City airport, Cap said firmly, "You're through, Slops. And I do mean through!" And he kicked our (alleged) chef off the Saturn, along with his clothing, his back pay, his harmonica and his ta — you know what.

Which left us way out on the end of a limb, for it turned out that there wasn't a single spaceriding cook dry-docked in Sun City. While the Saturn was taking on its cargo for Earth, pepsin and medical supplies, mostly, with one or two holds full of *mekel* and *clab,* the Skipper did his doggonedest to scare up a grub- wrangler. But no soap.

An hour before we were scheduled to blast off, he ambled up to my control turret. He plumped himself into my easy chair and scratched his gray pate nervously.

"Damn it, Sparks," he complained, "I thought I was doin' the right thing when I fired Slops, but —"

"You were," I told him. "By chucking that grease-ball off the ship you saved fourteen lives. The crew. They were planning on either mutiny or murder, they didn't care which, if they had to eat one more dish of that goo."

"But," he continued worriedly, "in another hour we throw lugs for Earth. And we don't have no cook. What the blue space are we goin' to do?"

Our First Mate, Lancelot Biggs, had entered as the skipper was talking. Now he offered, helpfully, "I'll ask Slops to come back if you want me to, Captain. I saw him at the Palace Bar —"

"No!" said the Cap and I in the same breath.

Biggs looked hurt. His wobbly Adam's-apple bobbed in his throat like an unswallowed orange. And he defended, "Well, after all, tapioca's good for you! It contains valuable food elements that —"

"Shut up!" howled Cap Hanson. He wasn't in a mood to take advice from anybody, and especially Lancelot Biggs. Perhaps that was because our recent "transmuting trip," in the course of which we had attempted to turn lead jars to platinum by exposure to cosmic radiation, had failed. The Corporation had carpeted Cap for that, and Cap was sore at Biggs because the whole thing had been Biggs' idea in the beginning. "I'll murder the guy who even mentions that — that stuff!"

Mr. Biggs said aggrievedly, "I was only trying to be helpful."

"You're as much help," the skipper told him caustically, "as fins on a dicky-bird's chest. Now, git out of here! G'wan! Git!"

Our lanky first mate turned and started to leave the turret. And then, suddenly —

"Wait a minute!" yelped Cap Hanson. "Where do you think you're goin', Mr. Biggs?"

Biggs gulped, "Why — why you told me to —"

"Never mind what I said! Do what I say! I think I've got the solution. Mr. Biggs, that cranium of yours appears to be stuffed with miscellaneous lore. Do you by any chance happen to know anything, about the art of cooking?"

"Who?" said Biggs. "Me? Why, no, Captain. But I don't imagine it would be very difficult. After all, it is based on elementary chemical processes. By exposing certain organic substances to the action of hydrogen dioxide, under suitable thermostatic conditions —"

Cap Hanson's jaw dropped open. He goggled me. "Wh-what's he sayin', Sparks?"

"He means," I translated, "that cooking is easy. All you need is water, heat and victuals."

The skipper grinned ghoulishly. "In that case, our problem's solved. Mr. Riggs, you've just earned a new private office an' a new unyform. You'll find both of 'em below decks, third door on your right."

It was Biggs' turn to look shocked. His protuberant larynx performed a reverse Immelmann. "H-huh? But I'm not a cook, Captain. I'm your First Mate!

"You *was* my First Mate," corrected the Old Man coolly, "until just now. The IPS codebook says, 'It is the captain's privilege to draft any member of crew or command for any duty in times of emergency.' This is an emergency. An' besides, you just got done sayin' that cookin' is simply a matter of exposin' certain hoochamacallits to the action of thingamajigs. So — " He brushed his hairy paws with a gesture of finality, "That's that! To the galley, Mr. Slops!"

AND he was right. That was that. But the funny part of it was that, forced to a showdown, Lancelot Biggs came through!

The first meal out, which was lunch served at noon Earthtime, I went down to the dining hall thinking anything might happen and expecting the worst. I got the shock of my life, and shocks are a not inconsiderable part of the life of a spacelugger radioman.

Mr. Lancelot Slops had pulled a banquet out of the hat! We had fried chicken with cream gravy, hot biscuits, candied yams, a side dish of stewed *clab,* Creole style, raisin pie, and the best damn coffee ever served on the wallowing old *Saturn.*

What the other men of the crew thought, I have no idea. They didn't say. Every manjack of 'em was so busy shoveling grub into his puss that the conversation was dead as a Martian herring. But after I'd bulged my belt to the last notch with fried pullet, I waddled into the galley and confronted Mr. Biggs.

"Biggs," I said accusingly, "you've been holding out on us! Why didn't you tell us before you could cook a meal like that?"

He shuffled his feet sheepishly. He said, "Was it all right, Sparks?"

"All right? It was terrific! I haven't had such a feed since I was a kid."

He looked relieved. "I'm glad. Because, you see, that was the first meal I ever cooked."

"It was the first — *what!*"

"Mmm-hmm! But there were lots of cook books here in the galley. And I figured so long as I had to do it, I might as well do it right — " He grinned at me shyly. Once in a while I wondered, briefly, whether any, of us understood this strange, lanky genius, Lancelot Biggs. This was one of the times. "I — I found it rather interesting, Sparks, to tell you the truth. It is, just as I told Cap Hanson, just a matter of elementary chemistry. The pots and pans are the test-tubes; the stove is a huge Bunsen burner."

I said admiringly, "I'll hand you one thing, Mr. Biggs. You believe in sticking to theories, don't you?"

"But of course. 'Get the theory first';

that's the big secret of success in any undertaking." He looked pleased and a little excited, too. "We're going to have a good trip home, Sparks. There's plenty of food here to experiment with. And in the holds —"

It was just then that I caught my number being buzzed on the intercommunicating audio. I cut through and yelled, "Sparks speaking. What's up?"

"Sparks?" It was my relief man calling from the radio room. "You'd better come up here on the double. A message from Sun City, and I think it's bad news."

"Right with you," I hollered. I snapped a brief "See you later!" to Biggs and raced up the Jacob's ladder to the turret. My relief man was there, also Cap Hanson and the second-in-command, Lt. Todd. All three of them looked a bit grim and a bit glum, and quite a bit apprehensive. My relief shoved a wire flimsy into my hand. It was a cipher message from Sun City spaceport. I knew the code as well as I know English and Universal, so I read it aloud.

"HANSON COMMANDER IPS SATURN EN ROUTE VENUS-EARTH. TURN BACK IMMEDIATELY FOR CONVOY. PIRATE HAKE REPORTED ON COORDINATES THREE FIFTEEN PLUS NINE OH NINE YOUR TRAJECTORY." It was signed, "Allonby, Comm. S.S.C.B."

I stared at Cap Hanson, wondering if my face were as queasy as my tummy felt. I said, "Hake! Runt Hake!"

Hanson said, "Yes, but that's not the worst of it, Sparks. Tell him, Mr. Todd."

Todd wet his lips and faltered, "We — we're in a serious spot, Sparks. We accelerated to max twenty minutes ago and cut motors for the free run. And since we had — or thought we had — almost nine days of idleness, I told Chief Engineer Garrity he could take down that number Three hypatomic that's been missing."

That still didn't make sense. I said, "So he took it down? So what? He can put it together again, can't he?"

"No. He found the casing worn, melted it down for a recast. We — we can't recast it for at least two days!"

FOR the sake of you Earthlubbers who don't get the lingo, let me say it in words of one syllable. We were in a hell of a jam! The hypatomics are the motors that operate spacecraft. In this case, one of them had shown signs of weakness. With the ship "free wheeling," so to speak, in space, the engineers had taken down the faulty motor, discovered it needed remoulding, and had melted down the casing. As Todd had said, it would take at least two days — probably more — to recast the moulding, put the hyp together again, so we could blast.

But the worst of it was–Hake! Runt Hake. There are pirates and pirates in the wide transverses between the planets. Some of them are good guys, that is, if an outlaw can ever be considered a "good guy." Like Lark O'Day, for instance, that gay, smiling bandit who always gave lugger captains a signed receipt for the cargoes he stole, and who had once let a tramp freighter go through untouched because the Captain acknowledged his life savings were wrapped up in the cargo. Who had once stopped a passenger superliner for the express purpose of stealing a single kiss from its charming passenger, the newly crowned "Miss Universe."

But others were skunks and dogs and — well, think of the nastiest things you can think of. Then multiply by ten, add infinity, and you have Runt Hake,

Runt Hake was a killer. A throwback to the rotten old days when men's first thoughts were of death and war and violence. He was a pirate not so much because of the value of the cargoes he lifted as because he liked to do battle. And he had a sadistic strain in him somewhere. His idea of good clean fun was to board a freighter — like the *Saturn* — unload the cargo at his convenience, then blast a slow leak through the outer hull.

After — I might mention — having first removed all lifeskiffs and bulgers from the ill-fated victim. Once, in the asteroid Sargossa, I saw a ship that had been scuttled by Runt Hake's cutthroat crew. Its crew still remained with the ship. But not as recognizable human beings. As raw and frozen clots of pressured flesh.

Oh, a swell guy, this Runt Hake. And now we, disabled and helpless, were drifting right into the trajectory where he awaited us.

Cap Hanson said grimly, "There's nothin' much that we can do about it, of course. We've got one six millimeter rotor-gun for'rd. We'll give him that."

"And get ourselves blown to atoms," interjected Todd, "with his pierce-guns. No, Skipper, that's no good. But how about the Ampie? If we set out our Ampie, maybe —"

An "Ampie" is that strange, energy-devouring beast from Venus whose inordinate appetite for electrical power forms a shield for spaceships penetrating the Heaviside layers of the various planets. It wasn't altogether a bad idea. But Hanson shook his head.

"No. It wouldn't work. An Ampie couldn't take a heat ray. There's only one thing to do. Send word for the convoy to come on the double-quick — and hope it reaches us before we run into Hake."

That was my cue. I shoved the relief man to hell off the bench and got the wobble-bug going. And, mister, I filled the ether with SOS's — and added a couple of PDQ's for good measure. I picked up an acknowledgment from Sun City, and threw them a hasty explanation. They wired back that the convoy cruiser would make all haste, and to not be frightened.

Ha! Can I help it if my knees chatter?

THERE was one thing you could absolutely depend on Lancelot Biggs to do. And that was — stick his nose in at the wrong minute. For as we three were giving the sob-towel the good old go-over, the door popped open and who' gangled in but Mr. Slops, First-Mate-and-Bottle-Washer! His face, in contrast to ours, was radiant with joy and delight. He had a grin on his phizz that stretched from here to there and back again. He chortled, "Hey, Cap —"

"Go 'way!" mourned Cap Hanson. "I'm thinking."

"But, look!" Biggs, opened one hamlike paw. And there was a wee, gray ship-mouse. He placed it on the floor before him. "Look what I found in the No. 4 Bin. It acts so darned funny —"

"Go 'way!" repeated the skipper, still gloomily. "If you make me lose my temper —"

Biggs said, "But he *does* act funny — " And to tell you the truth, the little mouse did. Usually, you know, a mouse is the scaredyest thing alive. Put him down in a place like this, surrounded by giant humans, and he'll run like mad to the darkest corner.

But this little twerp didn't run. Matter of fact, he deliberately moved to the man nearest him, Todd, that was, and began to nuzzle himself against Todd's shoe! Just as if the Lieutenant were an old and loved acquaintance! Mr. Biggs chuckled again.

"See that? Do you know what makes him act that way, Skipper? I'll tell you. It's the prol —"

"Mister Biggs!" The Old Man's face was fiery red with rage. "This is no time for nonsense. Within hours, or perhaps minutes, we may all be dead! Now, for the last time, get out of here!"

Biggs, sort of stunned, said, "Y-yes, sir!" He retrieved his curiously-acting little pet from where it rubbed its soft muzzle against Todd's shoelaces, put it in his pocket, and backed out the doorway. As he went he tossed me a beseeching wigwag. I nodded; then when no one was paying me any neverminds, joined him in the runway outside.

"What's wrong, Sparks?" he demanded.

I gave it to him, both barrels. He had

a right to know. Every man has a right to know when it's bye-bye time. "But don't tell the crew." I warned. "The Old Man'll do that if he thinks best."

Biggs' eyes were huge and round. "Runt Hake! Gee, no wonder the Skipper was cross." He plunged into one of his characteristic silences. Then, suddenly, "Hey!"

"Hey, what?"

"They say Hake is a show-off. Likes to crack the whip on captured ships, ordering up big meals and so on before he scuttles it —"

"Well?" I said. "You think you're going to poison him, maybe? Don't be a dope. He'll make you swallow a pussfull of everything you serve him."

"Never mind. I'm not sure my idea is any good--yet! But have you got a book on physiochemistry?"

"In my office."

"Swell. Get it for me, will you? I'll explain later."

Well, I got him the book and he jammed it into his pocket and disappeared toward the galley, jogging along like a stork on stilts. But I had no time, now, to laugh at Biggs' physical or mental peculiarities.

Because my ears had just caught a sound they did not want to catch. The sound of metal grating on metal near the off-port. The banging of a mailed fist on *permalloy,* the asthmatic wheeze of the airlock, a sailor's shout ending in a choked gurgle —

I charged back into the radioroom. "Cap," I yelled, "at the airlock! Somebody. It must be —"

It was. Runt Hake and his pirates.

YOU wouldn't think, to look at Runt Hake, that he was a killer. True, he held a hand pierce gun on us as he approached, moving smoothly, lightly, up the runway. A half dozen men behind him also held their side arms poised, ready for action, while another half dozen deployed down the side corridors toward the engine rooms and control turrets. But as Hake came nearer he tossed back the quartzite headpiece of his bulger, and I saw that his hair was wheat-gold, his lips curved into something like a tender smile, his cheeks smooth, soft, boyish.

His voice was gentle, too. He said, "You offer no resistance, Captain? That is wise."

Cap Hanson said, "Hake, I surrender my ship to you freely. But do not harm my men. That is all I ask. My men do not deserve —"

"But, Captain!" The slender little pirate's eyebrows lifted archly. "Surely you are a little premature in your pleas? We have just arrived. There are so many, many things to be done before we — ah--enjoy our little pleasures."

And then, as he said that, I saw why men cursed the name of Runt Hake. It was not in his face. His golden hair, his pink cheeks, his soft mouth — all these were but gilding for the rottenness within him. The real Hake was in his eyes. Those dancing, glinting, gloating eyes that leaped into swift, flaming delight as he hinted at that which was to come.

He was a devil. A pint-sized devil, perhaps, but a devil nonetheless. I knew, now, that the stories were all true; that we could expect no mercy of this man. He would amuse himself with us for a while, toying with us in feline fashion. Then he would leave. And we would stay. Like the broken things Iliad seen in the Sargossa.

He was speaking again. Softly, melodiously, as if he were a warrant officer at some cargo port on Earth rather than a midspace pirate appraising his "take".

"The cargo, of course, Captain, is mine. Even now my men will be transferring it to my ship beside yours. But there are a few other things we will do while aboard. It is lonely, being in space for months on end. And we do not dine luxuriously. You have, I suppose, a well-stocked larder? With fine foods; wines, perhaps, to tempt the palate?"

Hanson tried again.

"We have, Hake. And they are all yours if you'll promise me the men will be unharmed." He hesitated. "Take me along as hostage, if you want to. That'll be all right. But —"

"But, no, Captain! That would never do. I think you had best remain — with your men." Again there was that tiny, dancing light in Hake's eyes. "You see, many know my name, Captain, and I understand I have a small reputation. But none have ever seen my face — and lived. It would be unfortunate if I were to be identified, would it not?"

He turned to his followers.

"Disarm them," he designated us negligently. "And. when the cargo has been transferred, have our men come in to dine. We will dine aboard the Saturn."

* * * *

YOU Earthlubbers will think this part strange, maybe? That we showed no more resistance than this to Hake's invasion? Well, I don't blame you. I've read *Martian Tales* and *Spaceways Weekly,* too. The writers for those mags would like you to believe that every freighter captain is a horny-fisted John Paul Jones. But think it over! The *Saturn* was a lumbering old cow compared to Hake's streamliner. Hanson had adopted the only sane policy. To placate the pirate, be nice to him, hope we could stall off his scuttling plans until the S.S.C.B. cruiser reached us.

So for more than two hours, unarmed and disconsolate, we of the *Saturn* sat around and diddled our fingers while Hake's men, using our engine crew, the wipers and blasters, for porters, transferred the more valuable parts of our cargo to their ship. They didn't take the bulk stuff. Just small necessities that could be fenced from a hideout on one of the rogue asteroids.

Meanwhile, Runt Hake had made at least one special trip. Down to the galley. He took Todd and Cap and me along so he could keep an eye on us. Down there we found Lancelot Biggs, quietly reading.

Hake said in that soft purr of his, "You — you're the cook on this ship?"

Biggs answered, "Mmm-hmm."

"You will address me," suggested the little outlaw, "as 'Sir.' Very well, Slops. I want you to prepare a meal for us. A good meal. Fresh meats and vegetables. You have no idea — " He drawled this last to Hanson. "How one wearies of canned concentrates."

Hanson just glowered. But Biggs looked confused. He said, "I — I'll have to get produce from the storage bins if you want a big meal. This galley's small — " He looked about him helplessly.

Hake nodded. "That is granted. But, mind you, attempt no medieval — ah — toxicological exploits. I remember the chef of the *Spica* tried something of the sort. Poor lad! He screamed horribly . . . I shall never forget it."

I bet he wouldn't! The louse. But I hoped, now, that Biggs would understand I had been right. He couldn't pull any funny business on Runt and get away, with it.

He seemed to understand, all right. He said, goggling, "I'll do the best I can — sir. It will take a little time, of course."

"We have time and to spare," agreed Hake. "A good meal, that is what we want. And now, gentlemen — ?"

He motioned, us toward the turret room. We started to leave the galley. I was the last to pass through the door. As I did so, I felt a fumbling at my side. Mr. Biggs was shoving something into my pocket. He whispered in my ear, "Sparks — give each of our men a piece. Tell them to chew it!"

FOR a moment my hopes flamed high. I didn't know what Biggs had up his sleeve, but I dared dream that he had devised some way of overcoming the pirate menace. But when I managed to get away, unobserved, a few minutes later to see what he had thrust in my jacket, my hopes died as suddenly as they had been born.

The stuff was nothing but pepsin. Plain, ordinary pepsin; a by-product from the out-spread Venusian ranches.

I was half minded to chuck the damn stuff away. I thought maybe worry, desperation, had made Biggs slips his gravs. Then I thought better of it. After all, he may have had some reason. And in a spot like this, any gamble was worth taking . . .

So, slowly, I started getting the stuff distributed around. I managed to slip half the package to Doug Enderby, the steward, with instructions to get it to the black gang. I met Chief Garrity 'tween decks, and gave him some for his engine room crew. Todd took a piece, wondering, reluctant, but put it in his mouth when I signalled him to do so. Me? Sure, I had some, too. After all, it tasted good. And a man might as well check out with a clean taste in his mouth.

The only man I couldn't slip a piece to at any time was Cap Hanson. Runt Hake had the old eagle eye on the Skipper. Matter of fact, Hake had the eagle eye on all of us. He didn't miss a trick, that murderous little squirt. Just before dinner was served he made my heart miss a beat when he asked, "What are you chewing on, Sparks? Gum?"

He gave me the fright and the out at the same time. I nodded. "Yeah," I said. Then, fearful not to ask, "You want a piece?"

He shuddered delicately. "Barbarian custom. I do not want a piece."

Boy, was that a break for our side!

SO, like I said, Biggs donged out the dinner call, and we all went into the mess hall. Talk about irony! Here we were, a score of honest, hard-working spacemen and an equal number of pirates, sitting down to the same table, eating the same meal.

Screwy? Sure — but that was Hake for you. As Mr. Biggs had said, he was a showoff. But don't think he took any chances. We were unarmed, his men were walking hardware stores. As for the conviviality of that banquet, that was strictly on the stinko! To outward appearances, we were all pal-sy-walsy at the banquet table; actually we of the *Saturn* were being fattened for the slaughter to follow.

Still — well, you know the old gag. "The condemned man ate a hearty meal." That's what I did, and that's what most of the other fellows did, too. Because Mr. Lancelot Slops had come up with another Q.E.D. that cooking is, after all, nothing but applied chemistry.

We had, just to make you drool a little, chilled consommé with a light sherry. Then a tempting wisp of baked whiting, served with Moselle Erdener Treppchen, and was the Old Man fuming! (He'd been saving that for his golden anniversary). Then a chicken sauté Florentine.

They were the preludes. The main drag-'em-out was a saddle of lamb accompanied by peas in mint, potatoes Parisienne, and served along with Pommard, 1974. The salad was a Salad Alma; the dessert was something which Biggs told me later was Plombière a l'Havane Friandises (pineapples, bananas, frozen custard, and not a damn bit of tapioca in it!)

This came along with the Piper Heidsieck, '65. A demi-tasse was next, then liqueurs —

It was here that Runt Hake called a halt. "We'll transfer the beverages," he said, "to our own ship. We want no drunkenness aboard while we — ah — do that which is now necessary. Captain Hanson?"

He nodded significantly toward the turret room. I rose, so did Todd. Surprisingly, Biggs joined our group as we moved up deck. Hake said, with a malevolent regretfulness I shall never forget, "We have enjoyed our banquet exceedingly, Captain. But you understand I can allow nothing to stand in the way of my next — ah — duty. So —"

Hanson said stonily, "You will give us a lifeskiff before scuttling the *Saturn,* Hake?"

Hake lied, "Captain, I had planned to do that very thing. But a most unfortunate accident . . . it seems that some of my men were so careless as to blast holes in each of the skiffs. Of course if you'd still like to take your chances in the damaged craft — ?"

Oh, he was a whipper, that Hake! I looked at Todd and saw the same thought mirrored in his eyes that I was thinking. This was our last chance. If we didn't get Hake now, it would be too late. I tensed myself. If we could grab the pirate chieftain, maybe his men would not dare do anything for fear of hurting him. And Hake, quick as he was on the trigger, might not get us both before

Then once again Lancelot Biggs intervened. To me he barked, "No! No, Sparks!"

And to Hake, quietly, almost tenderly, "Why, Mr. Hake — it's all a big mistake, isn't it? These rough, nasty old men think you want to hurt them! And you don't at all. Aren't they the old meanies?"

AND then — hold your hats, folks! — and then Runt Hake's soft mouth began to twitch! Yes, twitch! It pursed up like the mouth of a kid, his eyes wrinkled, and he began to blubber!

"Hurt them?" he complained. "Me hurt them? Why, I wouldn't do a thing like that! I love them! They're my pals." And he tossed his pierce gun away, reached out and patted Biggs' cheek!

Beside me I heard Lt. Todd whisper hoarsely, "Good gods of Greece, what is this?" I myself was stunned for a moment. But I had sense enough to stoop down and get Runt Hake's gun before this crazy interlude had passed. "He's blown his fuses!" I squalled. "Grab him, Todd! Mr. Biggs, come with me! You and I will round up his crew —"

But Biggs said quietly, "Take your time, Sparks. There's no hurry. See?"

He stepped to the wall; flicked on the visiplate that showed the interior of the mess hall. And there, where a moment before, a grim-faced score of space pirates had maintained watch over our crew, now our crew were standing staring with blank, uncomprehending faces at twenty men who looked and acted for all the world like affectionate puppies!

They were hugging each other, patting each other's arms and faces, murmuring soft words of endearment. It was stupefying. More than that — it was embarrassing! Off in one corner a bearded, one-eyed outlaw dandled a companion on his knee. Another burly bruiser, big enough to tear a man in half with his bare hands, was playing piggyback with a buddy!

I gulped and stared and gulped again. I choked, "But, what — what —"

Biggs said suddenly, "Sparks! You didn't give the Skipper a piece of that pepsin!"

"I didn't get a chance. But how —"

Then I saw. The Skipper and Runt Hake were sitting in the same chair, murmuring soft words of tenderness at each other, stroking each other's hair fondly. Just as I looked, the Old Man leaned forward and gave the pirate a big, juicy kiss on the forehead!

And just then there came a welcome interruption. The audio throbbed to electric life; a brusque voice rasped, "Calling the *Saturn! Saturn,* ahoy! S.S.C.B. Cruiser *Iris* calling. Stand by! We'll come alongside you in twenty minutes . . ."

AFTERWARD, when Runt Hake and his pirates, still babbling incoherent protestations of endearment, had been removed to the patrol ship and taken back toward the Venusian prison that had long awaited them, we held a confab in my radio room. Todd was there, and Chief Garrity, and Lancelot Biggs and myself. Also a very foggy-eyed, befuddled Captain Hanson who seemed to be having a hard time keeping from saying we were all "dear, sweet boys" — as he had told us quite a few times in the past hour or so.

I couldn't make head or tail of it. So I asked Biggs bluntly, "But what was it, Mr. Biggs? We all-know it was something you put in the food. Something from which the pepsin saved us. But what? Surely no drug would make a man act like that."

Biggs grinned, his Adam's-apple jerking amiably. "No, not a drug. But a chemical. Prolactin, to be exact. If you'll remember, I started to tell you we were carrying a load of it to earth."

"Prolactin?" said Todd. "What's that?"

"An extract of the pituitary gland; the hormone that governs human affections. Prolactin is the hormone that is responsible for all acts of parental love. It causes roosters to brood and set on eggs, tomcats to give milk and milk-deficient females to become normal. It is commonly known as the 'mother-love' crystal."

"And we," I. said, "were carrying a load of it. I still don't understand, though, why we had to chew the pepsin. And why it failed to turn all of us into bunny-huggers like —"

I glanced at the Old Man, then glanced away again. He looked at me fondly.

"Well, you see," explained Biggs, "prolactin happens to be a pure protein. And pure proteins are insoluble in most things, alcohol, water, anything you might normally take in your diet.

"I cooked Hake's banquet, and his goose, with liberal sprinklings of prolactin. But, as you had previously pointed out, I had to find some way of keeping *our* men from being affected by the hormone that disrupted their morale. Pepsin was the answer. Pepsin breaks down pure proteids into soluble peptones. That is why it is commonly used as a digestive agent."

"Drwstbynlvy — " mumbled the Skipper soothingly.

"Eh?" I demanded, "What's that?"

Biggs looked embarrassed. "I'm not sure," he said, "but I think he's saying, 'You're a dear sweet baby and I love you very much!' Er — Sparks — I think maybe we'd better put him to bed until it wears off . . ."

So that was that. And maybe I shouldn't have told you all this; I don't know. Because the Skipper, recovered now from his spell of "maternal affection" is rather sensitive on the subject. And I'm still clicking the bug on the *Saturn*.

Anyhow, now you know. But if you ever tell Cap Hanson I told you, it's going to be just too bad for I may have to catch the next express for Pluto and points west. Me and Biggs both. There's not much "mother love" in Cap Hanson's right cross!

THE GRAY MOUSER: 1

by Fritz Leiber

The city lifts black roof-shields toward the stars
And shuts the jungle out with mortised stones
And seals the scent of flowers in glass jars
And locks the Earth's secrets up in brass-clasped tomes.
No satyr may live there, no faun survive
The stench and clangor of each crowded street.
The white-fanged beasts of night cannot contrive
To gnaw an entrace through its black concrete.

Yet 'mongst the gargoyles on the slated roofs
One gray-masked face peers down with living grin
That mocks the scurry of the city's floor.
Two gray-gloved hands tease ope' the library's door
And break the ponderous books and scribble in
Footnotes that give the lie to all proud proofs.

A SURPRISE IN SULPHUR

by H. Bedford-Jones

It wasn't the jolt so much as the way Uncle Dudly handed it to me. Whenever he made up his mind where a man ought to get off he rigged a thank-you-ma'am and bounced him in a way that left a profound impression.

After hanging on to the ragged edge in Denver for two weeks, trying to promote a played-out sulphur mine to the tune of $50,000, I picked up a copy of the Meteor and casually hit upon this:

> Attention, Ladies (single) — How would you like a dower interest in $75,000? Just one condition; a man goes with it. Don't all flock down here in a bunch; write first to Old Man Blue (not the party), Hot Sulphur, Arizona, via Happenchance.

Old Man Blue, otherwise my respected Uncle Dudly, had put a one-way ticket to Denver and six dollars in my pocket and told me to go promoting for a month and bring back fifty thousand. While I conned his personal, wondering what in Sam Hill had struck said Old Man Blue, this reached me by wire:

> GEORGE AUGUSTUS BINGS, DENVER:
> COME HOME. YOU COULDN'T PROMOTE A CASE OF MEASLES IN A PEST-HOUSE. BRING WHAT'S LEFT OF EXPENSE MONEY.
> D. BLUE.

Was there a Piute buck anywhere on the reserve who would have played it that low down on a paleface? And he asked me to bring what I had left, when I'd been sleeping in an alley to save room-rent and pulling up my belt a notch every twenty-four hours because my meal-ticket was full of holes!

I went back on the trucks as far as Happenchance. There I switched into a two-seated buckboard, putting up my German silver Waterbury for the twenty-mile ride to Hot Sulphur. Chuck Anthony, the driver, was piling mail-bags all over the buckboard; when he got through we looked like a toy wagon toting canvas for a three-ringed show.

"Somebody moving his household goods by parcel post?" I asked, sitting on two bags and looking at Chuck over a third which he had deposited in my lap.

"Several-kinds-of-a-thing mail for that petered-out several-kinds-of-a-thing town of Hot Sulphur," growled Chuck, with a degree of emphasis hard to describe.

"Our usual mail used to be two letters, a postal, and four papers twice a week," I said. "Maybe the mail-clerk was keyed up and dropped off the bags for Utah, Oregon, and California by mistake."

Chuck's language continued to be piratical. "Every ounce of stuff is for your Uncle Dudly," he averred between remarks more or less irrelevant.

"Then it'll take him five years to open it and the rest of his natural life to read it. He slips around anything with more than two syllables."

"Huh! How many folks yuh got left in Hot Sulphur?"

"Fourteen, now I'm back."

Beyond a disgusted snort Chuck addressed no more remarks to me. About every twenty minutes he had to get down and gather in a mail-bag that leaked over. As a consequence we pulled up in front of Alfalfa Smith's Bazaar, which was the general store and post-office, three hours late.

Hot Sulphur had just two diversions. One was watching for the water to bubble back into the pool and the other was watching the stage roll in. The whole town was on the platform that day.

Foremost among it was Uncle Dudly — big, broad, and mighty crochety. With him were Pete Jewell and Monty Richards, proprietors of the Palace. Ollie Ferguson, who clerked in the Bazaar until the spring went dry, Dutch Charley, of the Delmonico short-order joint; Wun Choo, Charley's cook; Pegleg Pringle, Stumpy Smith, Welcome Perkins, and Grouchy Smiley. In the background hovered Mr. Golightly in his wheel-chair, the invaluable Wilson at the push-handle.

"Moses to Moses and all hands round!" sang out Alfalfa. "What you got in them bags, Chuck?"

"Mail," roared Chuck. " Mail for Old Man Blue!"

Uncle Dudly went up in the air with a yell. "Who says it don't pay to advertise?" he whooped. "Seen anything of George Augustus, Chuck?"

"Here," I says, disturbing the mail-bags slightly.

There was a rush and Chuck tipped me out of the bags into the arms of the citizens. They played football with me until I had to sit down on the platform and shoo them off with Chuck's forty-four; my arrival, it seemed, had broken the hoodoo of thirteen men on a dead town's chest.

While the citizenship gave its attention to the mail Uncle Dudly grabbed me by the collar and pulled me around back of the Bazaar.

"What's the trouble?" I asked.

"Trouble?" he snorted. "George Augustus, you don't know the brand when you see it. You knew my hot spring in its prime; you knew it could cure anything from mumps to meninjeetus; you know that when the blamed earthquake ripped along and dried up the spring everybody not interested in real estate pulled out. You know all that, don't you?"

I was painfully aware of it. Hadn't I been imported from Nogales to clerk the Hot Sulphur House, which Golightly's money was helping to build when the spring went dry? The sulphur water was gone, Golightly's money was gone, and every one and thing else was gone that had the price to go, while the hotel was an abandoned skeleton of two-by-fours.

"George Augustus" — and Uncle Dudly buttoned the frayed Prince Albert over his ample chest — "a month has passed. You've been two weeks in Denver, trying to sandbag the money market — but you don't know the first rudiments of the game. Stacking the cards or shifting the cut is a gift you didn't inherit and can't acquire. But, George, something has happened during that two weeks!"

"Water come back?"

"Nix. My superior intelligence has laid in a few licks and found a bonanza."

"Quartz or placerings?" I emitted huskily.

"Neither. The thing's off your sky-line, so don't try to look till I ring up the curtain. The railroad is coming south from Happenchance: whether it hits Hot Sulphur or strikes fifteen miles east through Ace High depends on our raising a fifty thousand bonus."

"Uh-huh," I said wearily. "You called a mass meeting and the citizens attended fourteen strong. You passed a subscription paper and got pledges to the amount of eighteen dollars and thirty-five cents, digging up enough for a one-way ticket to Denver and my six dollars expense money. Say no more."

"Let it pass," and Uncle Dudly waved an airy hand. "We who are interested in Hot Sulphur real estate must raise fifty thousand. If the railroad comes this camp will be the base of supplies for the mining and cattle country. Ace High will pick up its slap-shanties and move over. Property will go rocketing, and we, the fourteen faithful stand-patters, will lay back in luxury. Our only hope was the spring, but we've got a better."

"The bonanza?" I inquired sarcastically.

"Which is Ferguson — that drooping, sandy-haired, wall-eyed false alarm of a genus homo? He's sprung into prominence like a wart on a sore thumb. Fergy had a rich uncle; lawyers wrote him from Chicago that he had been left one hundred and twenty-five thousand dollars by his uncle — on conditions."

"They usually do," I ventured caustically. "I had a rich uncle —"

"Shut up! This scheme is gilt-edged. No one ever caught me standing on a housetop howling for the common herd to look and admire, yet for all that my faculties can pan out more color in an eight-hour day than you could show in a year. That's me — George Augustus — dedicated to the interests of —"

"Get to the point," I broke in brutally. "I'm hungry."

"Well, Fergy must be married on or before his twenty-eighth birthday, or this rich, ripe plum drops into the lap of a Home for Superannuated Bachelors. Well, sir, Fergy rounds up nerve enough to come to me in the emergency. Being bashful and retiring as he is, how was he to fulfil his part of the contract? Would I help him? Would I? Would a Ute squaw reach out for a string of glass beads?

"What did I do? Why, I called a mass meeting, suggested that we elect three citizens to comprise a Matrimonial Bureau, and then corral Fergy's inheritance. I'm one of the bureau, you're another, and Grouchy Smiley is the third. Our work is to get a help-meet for Fergy, with fifty thousand commission. I put an ad in —"

"I saw it. Shove ahead."

"And you rode out with the first lot of answers. You follow me?"

"It's a little uphill," I admitted, but I can keep in sight."

"That's all I expect of you. Who's the clear quill in this town, George A.?"

"Old Man Blue," I replied.

"Your head's level on that, anyhow. Run along and sit in at Dutch Charley's for your afternoon provender, then come back to Alfalfa's and help the rest of the bureau look through the mail."

I hurried, you can lay on that. When I got back to Alfalfa's I found Grouchy and Uncle Dudly in the rear room, helplessly adrift on a sea of correspondence. Fergy, hovering, around a partly opened door, was nervously asking for photographs.

"Scatter!" yelled Uncle Dudly to the inefficient bonanza. "This part of the job is ours. Come in, George."

"Hadn't Fergy better be here to pass an opinion?" I ventured.

"He can pass the spuds or the ants any time of day, but he's not qualified to pass an opinion. When we locate the party, the ceremony follows Fergy's introduction. The bureau will trail along in the rear of the honeymoon to Chicago and collect; the bureau will then cut loose, return via Happenchance, and lay fifty thousand in the hands of a grasping corporation. We'll have Ace High too dead to skin."

"What's the ante?" and Grouchy lit his corn-cob. "I'm tired. There's a ton o' this stuff and we ain't got past more'n a peck."

"That's the point which commands my attention," returned Uncle Dudley. "Fergy's past twenty-seven now, and he'll be past a hundred before we wade through this. Then, I reckon, there's more to come."

"How long's the ad. in for?"

"One issue. The coin I gave George wound me up. We're going on what Stumpy can borrow at the ranch. George Augustus, admit Fergy and blindfold him."

Fergy tottered in and I hoodwinked him with a bandanna. Then, under Uncle Dudly's direction, he floundered among the letters and pulled out a square envelope.

"Good-by, Fergy," said Uncle Dudly. "Get on the other side of the door now, and remember that you picked the lady yourself."

The bonanza faded with a look of helplessness. Uncle Dudly passed over the letter to me; it was scented with cologne.

"If it reads like it smells," sniffed Smiley, "I reckon we got the goods sure."

Here's the letter:

Old Man Blue, Etc.
Kind Sir & Friend:

I am a lady in stratened circumstance in whom your advertisement hits a responsive cord. If this party is halter-broke and warranted kind I've a trustful heart that will appeal. Besides, I need the money. Can come by first train.
Confidingly,

Cactus-Blossom,
P.O. Box 1509, Phoenix.

"That got the proper sound," said Uncle Dudly. "Spelling O.K., George?"

"Fair enough."

"I's dotted and t's crossed?"

"They are."

"Stops, semistops, and other dewdabs dropped in proper?"

"Absolutely."

"Whoop! Any woman who can spell and hold her breath long enough for an occasional period must be a whole team in domestic economy. Let's size up the writing."

I handed over the letter.

"Graceful, that's a cinch. Gents, we couldn't find anything to beat this. 'Cactus-Blossom,' eh? A strong hand and the poetic instinct ought to do Fergy a world of good. Write her *muy pronto,* George — say we'll be here to meet her. Hey, Fergy! You're a lucky dog!"

"I wisht I knew!" gulped the bonanza, listening at the door.

"We know, which is plenty. Build a bonfire with the rest of these, George — hold! Build the bonfire to welcome the lady when she comes. And, now, Grouchy, on to the palace! We'll take a couple to the future Mrs. Fergy!"

So I wrote the letter. The town drew a long breath and held it for three days; then came the answer, and everybody was happy with the exception of Fergy. Cactus-Blossom would come. We could expect her on the Thursday stage. And would the "party in question" please wear a red rose in his buttonhole so he might be at once apprehended?

Naturally, there wasn't a red rose within a thousand miles of us; but Dutch Charley jumped into the breach. With a piece of wire and some red tissue-paper from a festoon in the palace he fashioned a scarlet wad that looked enough like a rose not to be mistaken for much of anything else.

A hiatus of harrowing hours chinked in between the second letter and Thursday. Hot Sulphur went back and forth and in and out, staggering under a load of suspense, while the bureau packed up for Chicago.

There was a J. P. at Ace High, and it was quite fitting, said Uncle Dudly, that the knot,

equivalent to a hangman's knot for Ace High, should there be tied; so Stumpy Smith was to be on hand with a team to take the happy couple and the bureau over the hills.

By Thursday morning the groom had wilted perceptibly; when he moved he tottered, and when he looked at you it was with a hunted and apprehensive glare in his faded eyes. Pegleg and Charley were appointed best men in order to make sure the groom stayed in town.

The stage was due at 2 P.M. All the bunting in town had been flung to the breeze. Pinochle Pete's artistic taste had run riot all over the front of the Palace in new red paint.

Alfalfa Smith had erected a triumphal arch of greasewood at the edge of the platform, with the bride's name worked on top in calico letters. Uncle Dudly had dug up some old sticks of dynamite and sunk them in the empty sulphur hole back a piece from the Bazaar, with a long fuse attached.

"Best bib and tucker" was the order, and save for Wun Choo every citizen's hair was parted in the middle. For a stranded outfit we did pretty well, too. You'd have known Fergy for the bridegroom a mile off, between the bunch of red paper in his coat and the best men's forty-fives handy.

Golightly looked better than for weeks past. Originally he had come to the spring to help his rheumatism; and a few immersions did him so much good that Uncle Dudly got his funds for the hotel. The receding waters had left Golightly neither physical nor financial ability to join the exodus, and Wilson, his attendant, had also stayed, mostly on faith.

Hot Sulphur meandered over a flat in Hatch-a-kew Gulch. A mile to the north the Happenchance trail struck the rim of the gulch and from there lumped right down into the flat. Uncle Dudly kept his binoculars trained north along the rim and sighted a sail at two sharp.

"There she blows! Chuck's in sight!"

A wild cheer went up. Stumpy drove his wagon around and backed up to the platform; he had trimmed up the old ore-carrier real fancy with greasewood and calico. The binoculars passed from hand to hand.

Chuck and the buckboard were only half a mile off when Pinochle Pete and Wun Choo got a look. They took a long one, then Pete said he felt thirsty and excused himself. Wun Choo merely faded into the scenery, puzzled like.

We were too interested to notice them, and Uncle Dudly kept the glasses himself the rest of the time. As the buckboard got nearer I saw the best men slowly abandon Fergy and head south. Fergy roused himself with an effort, hovered ineffectually around, then bolted. Wilson was snaking Golightly out of sight when I jumped for the spring-house.

I plumb forgot that Uncle Dudly had just lit the fuse to the dynamite, and the last I saw of the reception party was he standing there completely absorbed in watching the fluttering skirts on the rear seat of the buckboard.

Alfalfa had skipped into the Bazaar, and Stumpy was rolling along toward the ranch, the others crowded into his wagon. I laid low in the spring-house, watching.

Chuck Anthony pulled up, a grin on his salmon colored visage. Uncle Dudly looked like a man in a dream. I saw him start, stare about, and call my name; but somehow I failed to hear. Meanwhile, Cactus-Blossom had alit and was comfortably filling the triumphal arch.

Cactus-Blossom was right. An airy creature of some two hundred pounds left the arch and tripped in Uncle Dudly's direction, the arch rocking like a ship in a storm at each step.

She was armed with a cotton umbrella and carried a grip of the vintage of 1860; her skirts swept her boot-tops, and as for her face — well, a casual glance through the glass at half a mile had been enough for me. Closer inspection left nothing to be desired.

Uncle Dudly had retreated to the edge of the platform, where he stood looking as if he was going under for the third time with no straws in sight. All of a sudden I remembered that fuse and the dynamite. I started for the open, then I ducked back; being between the devil and the deep sea, I took the deep sea and slid under one of the cast-iron seats with my coat over my head. I judged the paradise ferry would be along directly.

"Well, here I am!" rumbled a voice. Uncle Dudly cleared his throat. "Togged up a consid'able, didn't you? Say, are you the condition that trails along in the wake of that seventy-five thousand dollars?"

I went hot and cold, thinking of that dynamite.

"Er — ahem, ma'm — I'm Old Man Blue —"

"Oh, you are! What d'you mean saying you ain't the party in the ad., then showing up with my rose?"

I peeked out. Dutch's American Beauty was hanging off Uncle Dudly's coat — bravo, Fergy! I could have patted the bonanza on the back if I been several miles away.

"What you toting the label for? Trifling with me, you off-colored specimen —"

I heard something that sounded like an umbrella slapping a Prince Albert, but just then things happened to the dynamite. I shot square through the side of the spring-house and took most of it with me at that.

The dynamite giving me a flying start, so to speak, I kept on down the gulch when I found my legs weren't busted off, and two mile farther on met Golightly, blue in the face and walking north.

I asked him about Wilson and the chair, and he said Wilson couldn't get into his third speed and he'd forgotten about rheumatism. We stood and conferred a bit until Grouchy showed up from the bushes.

Then we sort of skirmished back to see what had become of Uncle Dudly. On the way Alfalfa came to meet us — he came on the run, too, with half his shirt gone, and

sort of discouraged us by telling how Cactus-Blossom had gone through the Bazaar.

After an hour we went forward in light order. When we got in sight of home the buckboard was just streaking along the rim of the gulch, a fluttering of skirts in the back seat.

To our surprise — and his own, too, I reckon — Uncle Dudly seemed safe and unharmed and was standing near the remnants of the spring-house. A black eye didn't improve his looks, and he began capering around as if he was touched by the sun. I felt him out a bit.

"Take it easy, uncle," I says. "We'll see that nothing hurts —"

"Take it easy!" and he looked at me wild-eyed. "George Augustus, we're it! Let me take your hand!"

"I judge I won't!" and I backed off a piece looking him over pretty careful. "What's on your brain, anyhow?"

"Water!" he yelled. "Sulphur water! The blast brought it back, boys! Hot Sulphur is made — three cheers for Old Man Blue!"

The bunch came up with a yell, and we found Uncle Dudly had given it to us straight. That blast had filled up the empty spring-hole as nice and neat as it ever was in its best days!

It was hard for us to realize at first, until we explored the ruins of the spring-house and actually drank some of the bubbling stuff ourselves. Then Alfalfa had an inspiration.

"Say, boys," he yelled, "three cheers for Cactus-Blossom!"

The next minute he was looking into a pair of blued barrels.

"Drop it," says Uncle Dudly real slow and careful. "The first man that says Cactus-Blossom to me will gather roses on t'other side the divide. Maybe they won't be regulation roses, but it's a cinch they won't be made out of red paper!"

Which is mainly the reason why Hot Sulphur retained its name.

PAYABLE TO BEARER

by Talbot Mundy

CHAPTER 1
Ikey and His Trade.

IF you bring a woman into a story you spoil the story, and in all probability libel the woman; everybody knows that. But there are two women in this story, so get ready; they always have crept in, and they always will — and we have to make the best of it. In this instance, though, the first person to creep in was Ikey Hole.

The police in particular, but almost everybody who knew him at all intimately, called him Keyhole Ikey, so that by the time that he crept into the story he was laboring under an extra syllable as well as a kit of scientifically constructed tools distributed about his person. It was a second story that he crept into — through a bedroom window.

Ikey started in business at the early age of sixteen as a porch-climber, and by the time he was twenty he had become a past grand-master of his profession; but since by that time porches had grown a little out of fashion in New York, he began to make a specialty of fire-escapes, and from that time on he throve amazingly, as everybody does who is sufficiently far-sighted to move with the times.

He was a very careful man, was Ikey. He considered every little detail, just like the big interests do; but, unlike them, he was contriving to salt away quite a snug little fortune without running the risk of being muckraked.

He agreed with the big interests in detesting publicity, but he differed from them again, in having nothing whatever to do with gentlemen's agreements. Ikey had no pals; he always worked alone.

He closed the window carefully behind him, leaving just sufficient space open at the bottom to enable him to insert his fingers should he have need to open it again in a hurry; then he pulled down the blind.

That left him in pitch-darkness, but not for long, for he produced an electric torch from his sleeve and pressed the button; that gave him just sufficient light to examine the door by.

The door proved to be unlocked, and the key was on the outside; so he opened it very gently, removed the key, and locked it on the inside.

Now, economy was one of Ikey's strong points, and burning that electric torch of his cost him good money; so he extinguished it and replaced it up his sleeve.

Then he switched on the electric light that was hanging in the middle of the room; it was a sixteen candlepower tungsten lamp, and, besides being a whole lot better to work by, the use of it cost him nothing.

The sudden flood of light revealed his figure full length in the pier-glass that stood facing him in one corner of the room, and he nearly jumped out of his skin with fright.

"Gee," he muttered with a low chuckle; "I'm gettin' nervous! Have to cut out coffee and cigarettes for a while!"

Coffee and cigarettes were Ikey's chief solace in his hours of ease; but there was the making of a hero in Ikey, and he decided to give them both up on the instant, and with as little compunction as he would have felt in refusing an offer of employment; he knew what suited him, did Ikey, and he never broke his word to himself, either, whatever he might do to other people.

"Woman," he muttered to himself, looking sharply round the room and twiggling his nose. His nose had escaped being prehensile by very little; it was big, curled over at the end, and he used it to talk to himself with, just like a mouse does that is peeping out of a hole; you could almost read his thoughts by watching that nose of his twist and wrinkle and squirm, and he had a pair of little beady, black eyes above it that were not at all unlike a mouse's.

In addition to all that, he had rather large ears that stood out on either side of his head and were pointed at the top. So he was really very like a mouse, was Ikey.

As he stood surveying the room, buttoning the top button of one of his black kid gloves that had come unfastened, you would never have mistaken Ikey for a big-hearted man; you would have probably mentally assessed him as a "piker," and it would never have entered your head that he might possibly possess both characteristics.

"Woman," he muttered, "lemme see — under the mattress? no; under the rug? no; nice little dinky tin box under the bed? like as not; no, nothing there. Um-m-m! Tucked in the folds of a nighty in the middle of a bureau drawer? No, not there, either." He pulled out handful after handful of lingerie, tossing the garments into a heap on the floor. "All pretty cheap stuff this — midsummer sale sort of stuff; heaps of it, though — guess she spent all her money at the sales. Dashed robbers, those department-stores — guess there's nothing doing here. Hello! Ah, here's a drawer locked! There may be somethin' inside worth lookin' at."

He tugged at the top right-hand drawer of the bureau, and his nose wriggled, and his little black mustache stood straight on end on either side of it as his lips straightened into a grin, and his little black eyes glittered like jewels in a setting of crow's feet when the drawer refused to come open.

"Love-letters, like as not!" he muttered. "Too much fluffy white stuff here. I reckon somebody's goin' to git married. I'll bet a nickel that's what's the matter. Better have a look though."

Ikey always traveled prepared for every possible contingency, except fighting; he never fought, and he never murdered people; but, like Dan Cupid, he laughed at locksmiths.

He produced a short, stiff, crooked piece of wire, which he worked about with his thin, restless fingers for about half a minute; then he inserted it gingerly in the keyhole, jerked it, drew it back a little, jerked it again, and *click!* went the lock, and Ikey opened the drawer.

"Gee!" he exclaimed, out loud this time, wriggling his whole body and twisting one leg round the other in excitement. "Gee — *whiz!* Gee — *Rusalem!* By the blue beak on the map of a traffic-bull in winter, if here ain't all the money in the world!"

He pulled out a bundle of bills from beneath a pile of lace-handkerchiefs and began to count.

"Fifteen, sixteen, seventeen! Mother of me, what a haul! Twenty-five, twenty-six! I wonder if I'm drunk? Thirty-three, thirty-four, thirty-five — this is like findin' money! Forty-six, forty-seven! By the red face of a thirsty bull on pay-day, if here ain't fifty centuries! Fifty one-hundred-dollar bills! Fif-*tee* little yeller plasters o' one hundred plunks apiece, payable to bearer on demand, and me the bearer! *Me!*"

He slipped the whole bundle into an inside pocket, hardly able to contain himself with glee; but he would not have been Keyhole Ikey if he were not still careful; he unlocked the door again and replaced the key on the outside before going, with the laudable intention of causing suspicion to fall on someone in the house.

Then he switched the light out and slipped noiselessly through the window, closing it behind him; he even took the trouble to fasten the window-catch again from the outside.

"I do hope the lady came by the mazuma honest!" he remarked to himself, as he started to climb down the fire-escape. "I surely would hate to handle any o' this money if it was tainted."

Then he dropped ten feet or so into the yard below, making about half as much noise as a cat would have done in performing the same feat, and vanished into the darkness, still chuckling.

CHAPTER II
Which Introduces Woman Number One

IT was at least two hours after Ikey Hole left through the window that the owner of the bedroom entered through the door. She is woman number one, who helps to spoil the story, so perhaps her name is relevant; besides, a name is one of the few things in this world that don't cost anything, and even school-teachers have them; her name was Lizzie Wingfield. Describe her for yourself.

Imagine the prettiest girl you can — not too tall and not too short — fair or dark as your fancy dictates and multiply the resulting loveliness by two; after that you've only got yourself to blame if you don't like her, and the story will get along famously.

I've told you she was a schoolteacher; she was dressed in a low-cut evening gown, for description of which see any one of the current fashion magazines; and she didn't look like a school-teacher in the least — at least not like your idea of one. The point is that she was a school-teacher, and that she had been to a dance. Remember, I said *was*.

Her mind was still centered on the gaiety and the garish lights and the lingering airs of waltz music; as she entered the room she was still humming the air of the last tune she had waltzed to. As she walked across the room she stumbled over the pile of lingerie that Ikey had heaped so carelessly on the floor, and the humming ceased. Then she turned on the light.

No. She didn't swear. Ladies don't do that. At all events, her sort don't.

But she sat down on the bed and stared at the confusion, and wished that it were proper for her to swear, and you will admit that that is a bird of quite another feather.

She still had a certain amount of equanimity left, for the knowledge that she had so much frilly stuff to scatter about was, so to speak, forced on her notice; no woman in the world can repress a quite pardonable feeling of pride when she realized the extent of her possessions of that kind, and especially when the garments in question are all new and clean, and were bought at absolutely bargain prices.

But then she noticed that the right-hand top drawer of the bureau was not quite closed; and she had left it locked. Her heart began to flutter now in real earnest. She was afraid even to open the drawer and look, she was so frightened.

She sat on the edge of the bed and stared at the bureau, and felt herself going goose-fleshy all over, and for two whole minutes she could not screw up sufficient nerve to investigate.

Then she seized the knob and jerked the drawer open, as though to get the worst over quickly, and her face grew as white as the pile of petticoats on the floor as she discovered what the reader knows already — that the fifty beautiful, new, crinkly, yellow hundred-dollar hills were missing.

No. She didn't scream. And she didn't wring her hands, or the bell, or the neck of the answering chambermaid; and if that doesn't make you like her, nothing will. She just stood still and turned over the handkerchiefs and all the other things in the drawer one by one to make sure, and then — guess! She looked under the bed for burglars!

Not a hurried peep, either; she took a good, hard look, and made absolutely certain that there weren't any. Then she knelt down on the floor and laid her arms on the bed, and laid her head on her arms and sobbed and sobbed and sobbed.

Poor little woman! She had a right to sob. She had resigned her position as school-teacher that very day with a view to getting married the following month, and that five thousand dollars was all, absolutely every cent, that she and her intended had got to marry on. And the worst of it was that he was nowhere near to comfort her; he was all the way across the continent in San Francisco.

She couldn't rush downstairs, and down the street a couple of blocks, and round the corner, and ring the bell of his flat, and weep on his big, broad bosom; she had to weep alone, and that is an unsatisfactory business. She realized it before long, and left off weeping.

Although *he* was not near to comfort her, his letters were — two or three hundred of them; the burglar hadn't taken those. She took a bundle of them from the back of the drawer and untied the piece of blue ribbon, and removed the top letter and opened it; but she extracted very little comfort from it.

It was the very last letter he had written her, and the five thousand dollars had been enclosed in the same registered envelope. No. We won't look over her shoulder.

A man's love-letters make disgusting reading, and for that reason they ought to be sacred, if for no other. But part of that letter has a bearing on the story, and, as he was a very business-like young fellow for a lover when he was writing about business, and as he put all the poetry and kisses in the first six and the last ten pages, we can give part of the middle page without making anybody's gorge rise or offending anybody's sense of propriety. It was something like this:

> I have only saved five thousand dollars in all these years. *[NOTE — He had on been saving for five years and five months. Pretty steady sort of young fellow that, eh?]* It makes me feel like a beast when I think that I have only that much with which to begin life with you; if I had on met you earlier I would have saved more, for I would have had something to work for. I am sending you the money enclosed in this envelope; take it round to any good bank in your immediate neighborhood and open an account in your own name. The money will surely be safer in your hands than in mine, and as long as you've got it I sha'n't be able to embark on any speculative undertaking without your consent. One of my chief faults is a desire to speculate and get rich quickly. A man came to me yesterday with a proposition that absolutely glittered, and I have seldom felt more tempted in my life; what made it still more tempting was the fact that I had the money; it was out on mortgage and I had called it in; the mortgagor, who happens to be a friend of mine, paid me yesterday. So in order to put myself out of the reach of further temptation of that kind, I am mailing the whole of the five thousand dollars to you, where I know it will be safe.

She read no further than that. She couldn't. The bitter irony of it was too much for her, and she knelt down again beside the bed with the letter all crumpled up in her fingers, and dropped great big salt tears all over it, and sobbed as though her heart would break.

It wasn't all her fault, but what difference did that make? The money was gone. And *he* had trusted her. The registered letter had arrived after banking hours, and she had thought that the money would be safe in that drawer for one night, especially as nobody in the house knew she had it.

Of course, she ought to have given it to somebody else — her landlady, for instance — to keep for her, but she hadn't thought of that; she had been too busy thinking how proud she was to be trusted like that, and how good Walter was — yes, his name was Walter — and what a fine, honest, straightforward, manly fellow he was, and how she loved him! And then she had gone to the dance! That was the cruelest part of it; if only she had kept her trust and stayed at home to watch the money, she could have fought for it, and died over it if need was; but the money had disappeared while she was out enjoying herself. And Walter had worked for five long years to save it!

It would be kinder to leave her there to sob herself to sleep, but we can't do it; the requirements of a short story are as inexorable as fate itself, and she had more mortification in store for her yet.

There was still a chance to recover the money, although it was a slim one.

She summoned her landlady first; and when that elderly and excitable person had finished telling her what she knew already — that she was a ninny and a donkey and a rash, foolish, thoughtless female for leaving all that money loose in a bureau drawer — the two of them ran out just as they were, without either hats or cloaks on, to look for a policeman. And, of course, they couldn't find one.

So they came back again and did what they should have done in the first instance — telephoned to headquarters; they overlooked that idea at first in the distress and excitement of the overwhelming disaster. After an almost interminable delay two policemen came — one in uniform and one in a blue serge suit. They both had muddy boots.

They examined everything in the room, the window especially. They looked extremely wise at first, until they realized that Ikey had left no tracks at all; then they looked scornful and began to take notes.

They trampled mud over everything, including some of the lingerie that was still lying on the floor; and they asked Lizzie Wingfield her age. and how long she'd lived there; and the landlady her age, and how long she'd lived there; and one of them sat on the bed; and the both of them kept their hats on, and when she didn't know the numbers of the bills they looked openly incred-

ulous, and even the sight of the registered envelope in which the bills came failed to convince them.

They said that they would make a report, and that the matter would be fully investigated, and went; but they left the impression behind them that they believed the whole thing to be a frame-up, and that young women who lived in rooms away from their parents, even when they were school-teachers and hadn't any parents, were people of no account, to put it mildly.

And Lizzie Wingfield turned the light out and threw herself down on the bed without undressing and sobbed herself to sleep. And there for the present we will leave her.

CHAPTER III
Ha, Ha! Woman Number Two! The Plot Thickens!

KEYHOLE IKEY sat in the front parlor of his seven-room flat in Eighty-First Street, and crooned the burglar's lullaby to his eldest-born. It is a sweetly sentimental song, and gets the youngsters off to sleep better than anything. Try it. This is the first verse:

Sleep, my grafterling! None o' your lip!
You'll be a "baron," though daddy's a
*   "dip"!*
Daddy is watching for "buzzards" and
*   "screws,"*
Cops cannot catch you; it's slumber for
*   youse!*
The son of a "gun" should know better
*   than weep,*
For "suckers" are born for him while he's
*   asleep!*
Sleep, my grafterling! Cover your glims!
Dreams of the "boodle" are better than
*   hymns,*
So dream of the "boodle" and dream of the
*   "dough,"*
Dream of the dodges a "grafter" should
*   know!*
Hurry to dreamland before it gets light!
Daddy must go on the "rustle" tonight!

There are six more verses, and Ikey sang them all; while his eldest and only son lay face upward on his lap and knocked pieces off the welkin in celebration of the arrival of his first tooth. But Ikey was a proud and devoted father, and amazingly patient, so he sang the song all over again from the beginning.

"Hush, sonny!" he exclaimed when he had finished. "You're fitter to be a bull than a gun if you make so much noise! You gotter learn to keep quiet!" But sonny wouldn't hush — not even when Mrs. Ikey came in and cuddled him.

She is the second woman, so take due note of her. Petite, svelte, good-looking, copper-haired, tailor-made, neat, not in the least degree flashy. She was wearing just that amount of jewelry that the "countess" in the home notes column of the *Married Woman's Weekly* says one should wear in the park of an afternoon, and not one sparkler more.

The diamonds were good ones, even if they did rightly belong to other people, but they were none of them very large or noticeable.

She was quite an unusual woman was Mrs. Ikey, in more ways than one. She labored under no delusions as to Ikey's method of earning his living; she never had done, for that matter. She had married him with her eyes open after careful consideration of all the points involved.

She had come to the conclusion that physical comfort, and nice dresses, and plenty to eat, together with the company of a crook who loved her, were preferable to the long days of toil and tribulation in a department-store, where she worked when Ikey met her. She herself was intensely respectable, and never even used slang.

She went to church, and called on her friends, who were quite the "best" people in her immediate neighborhood; and she was charitable and agreeable, and not in the least stuck-up; in fact, as I said before, she was quite an unusual woman.

She never came into contact with the tools of Ikey's trade, because Ikey did not keep them at the flat.

Ikey had a little office several blocks away, with an electric meter in it that occasionally registered enormous quantities of current; but as Ikey always paid his bills promptly, it was nobody's business to make inquiries about that, and the sort of electric furnace that Ikey used takes up so little room that it is quite easily concealed.

Mrs. Ikey handled the investment end of the business. She took the pecuniary proceeds, after Ikey had settled with the "fence," and invested them in real estate bonds in her own name, so that even if Ikey should happen to be "unfortunate," and get "rapped," and "soaked the limit," she would be well provided for, anyhow.

And Ikey had drilled her carefully in all the devious by-routes of the criminal law, so that if he should happen to get "lagged" she would know exactly what to do and when to do it.

She smiled at him bewitchingly as she relieved him of the squalling infant, and Ikey looked the very picture of contentment. Why shouldn't he? He had never for a single instant had cause to regret his marriage, and the pleased air of proprietorship with which he surveyed her would have made any woman proud; so she smiled at him again, and Ikey's world was all rose-pink and beautiful.

"I'll take him in the park a while. Ikey," she said; "perhaps the fresh air will send him off to sleep."

"Nothin' else will," said Ikey. "I've tried all the other stunts; sometimes the last shot sinks the ship, though; you go ahead and have a try. Say, but you're the swell guy this afternoon! They'll be thinkin' your husband's one o' these society dudes! Go on; you cut along into the park afore I fall in love with you all over again!"

So Mrs. Ikey, smiling sweetly at her lord and master, put the baby into a brand new hundred dollar perambulator and wheeled him off to Central Park, while Ikey stayed at home to cogitate.

As a matter of fact, Ikey never did go about much in the afternoons; quite naturally he slept rather late, and ate his breakfast when other people were eating their luncheons; and after that he liked to sit about and read the paper. But this afternoon he was more than usually anxious to stay indoors and think.

He had five thousand dollars in his coat-pocket, and he was undecided what to do with it. Added to what Mrs. Ikey had salted down already, it was still not quite enough money to retire on; doubled it would just do. And Ikey was by birth, and upbringing, and instinct, and inclination, first and last, a born gambler. Mrs. Ikey had weaned him of the habit at the time she married him; but the desire still remained; and here was a gorgeous opportunity for one big, final plunge without consulting Mrs. Ikey.

If he lost the money she would know nothing about it, for he had said nothing to her yet about his haul of the night before; and if he doubled it, or trebled it — Gee! It was almost too good to think about. He was still undecided when Mrs. Ikey came back two hours later with the child.

He noticed that his wife seemed to be singularly disturbed about something on her return, but he asked her no questions; Ikey had ideas of his own about the management of women, and having found them successful in practise, he acted up to them.

It was a part of his fixed policy never to meet trouble half-way, and to wait until his wife chose to make a disturbance before attempting to find out the reason for it or to quell it. So he sat back in his armchair, and held his tongue, and waited. But he had not to wait for long.

She put the infant to bed in another room, and in less than ten minutes' time she was back again into the parlor to talk to him; and Ikey, irritated into a condition of ex-treme sensitiveness by his abstention from coffee and cigarettes, knew at once, even before she put her arms round his neck, that something big was coming.

"Where were you last night, Ikey?" she asked him.

"Business, as usual," said Ikey, who hated talking "shop" when he saw no necessity for it.

"I'll tell you why I want to know. When I was going into the park just now, Ikey, I passed one of the prettiest, sweetest-looking girls I ever saw. She was sitting on one of the seats crying. I sat down on the seat beside her; I simply couldn't go past her, Ikey, she looked so sad and miserable; and after a while I got into conversation with her. One couldn't sit there and say nothing; it was simply heart-breaking; so I spoke to her after a while, and asked her if I couldn't do anything for her, or help her in any way."

"And she touched you for a five-spot, I suppose?" said Ikey.

"Oh, no! She wasn't that kind at all. She said no, and got up and wanted to go away; she was evidently an awfully nice girl, and didn't like talking to strangers. But I held her back, and after a minute or two I convinced her that I really wanted to hear her story and see whether I couldn't help her. She said she was sure I couldn't help her, but she told me the story."

"Some 'con' game, I'll bet!" remarked Ikey in an undertone.

"It seems she is engaged to be married. The man she is going to marry, or was going to — she can't marry him now — lives in San Francisco, and he sent her five thousand dollars, all the money he had in the world, to keep for him until he came to New York."

"What a rummy!" murmured Ikey.

"She put the money in a bureau drawer and went out to a dance; and while she was away somebody came into the room and forced the drawer open and took it. Was it you, Ikey?"

Ikey said nothing.

"Because if it was you, Ikey, I'd like you to give it back to her. She's a nice girl — you'd never believe how nice until you'd seen her — and taking her money is the cruelest shame I ever heard of; I wouldn't stand for it a minute; Ikey, I wouldn't, really! Was it you, Ikey?"

Ikey said nothing.

"Of course, Ikey, if you had taken it I should quite understand that you did it not knowing the circumstances; you couldn't possibly have known. And I'm ever so sure you wouldn't do a mean thing like that with your eyes open, would you, Ikey? And now that you do know, and supposing you did take the money, you'll give it back, won't you, Ikey?"

Ikey still said nothing, and she laid one hand on each of his shoulders and looked him straight in the eyes. And Ikey hung his head. He still said nothing.

"Now, Ikey, you know when we married we both of us promised we'd never tell each other any lies, whatever we might agree to tell other people — didn't we? You're not going back on that promise now, Ikey, are you? Was it you that took that five thousand dollars, Ikey?"

"Yep," groaned Ikey, "I took it."

"Where is it?"

"I got it here."

"Well, then, give it back."

"You bet your life I'll give it back!" said Ikey, turning at last, as any worm will turn, and throwing her hands off his shoulders. Then he grasped her shoulders in turn and shook her almost savagely.

"See here, my gal! I love you good and plenty, and we've got on good together. I've told you no lies, and you haven't told me any, an' that was part o' the bargain. But there was another part to that bargain, and you seem to be forgettin' it. How about your promisin' not to chip in until I gave the word? Now didn't you promise?"

"Yes, Ikey," she answered, "I promised. But this isn't exactly chipping in. This is different. That girl has got to have her money back! I'd hate to think I was spending so much as a penny of it — it would make me wretched. Think how happy we've been, Ikey! You wouldn't like to take away that girl's chance of being happy too, would you, Ikey? She's a good girl, and a nice girl; she never harmed anybody in her life. You couldn't do it, Ikey! I know you couldn't! You're not mean enough!"

Ikey swore. Never mind what he said; this is a moral story; it is sufficient to say that Ikey felt his determination slipping away from under him, and that he swore.

"How d'you know it's the right girl?" he asked. "How d'you know it ain't one o' these here wise molls pulling off a 'con' game? Did she give you her address by any chance?

"Yes. I asked her for it. Her name's Lizzie Wingfield, and she lives in that big apartment house four blocks away from here on the north side of the street — the Harlemia it's called — and she rents a back bedroom in one of the flats on the second floor. Now, Ikey, does that tally? Wasn't that the one?"

Ikey nodded.

"And you'll give it back?"

I'll see!" said Ikey, getting up and reaching for his hat. "Lemme think it over; I'll see!"

"Very well, Ikey; think it over! But if you want me to go on loving you, think twice, Ikey, and let it be yes both times!"

"NOW isn't that just like a woman?" mumbled Ikey as he started down the stairs.

When Ikey reached the bottom of the stairs he paused for a moment in the hallway. He was thinking of that gambling notion of his again, and the thought of it was singularly sweet. Horses were his pet fancy.

He knew nothing about horses themselves, but he knew all about their form on paper, and there had been a time, not so very long ago, when Ikey was known personally to every book-maker on the turf.

"I've got it!" he exclaimed suddenly, laying his long index-finger to the side of his extraordinary nose. "That's a swell idea! A1. Couldn't beat it! If I win I'll do what the missus says, give the gal back her money, suit myself and the missus and everybody else, and be five or ten thousand in. And if I lose I'll be no worse off, anyhow! It's a bet! I'll do it!"

He walked about eight blocks to let the idea soak in, and on the way it occurred to him that there might be some difficulty about placing a big bet on the course unless he made arrangements for it.

So he turned into a hotel where there were writing-tables provided in the foyer, and wrote the following letter:

> DEAR ABE:
>
> You've not seen me for quite a while, but I ain't dead yet not by a darn sight. I've only been a bit broke, that's all, and you know I always bet big, and never bet at all unless I've got the cash. I'm coming down to the course on Saturday next, and if you're there I'm going to have a try for some of your money; I'm bringing down about five thousand of the real thing with me, and I'm going to make a real big splurge with it. I've got some inside dope about a certain horse that'll act on your bank-roll like a Turkish bath; It'll thin her out considerable. So bring along plenty of mazuma with you, and get ready to leave it behind you with a good grace, for I shall surely clean you out. Hoping this finds you as it leaves me, A1, believe me,
>
> Yours till the last bell rings,
> IKEY HOLE.

He sealed the letter and addressed it to Mr. Abraham Maxstein, turf accountant, and he posted it with a grin that savored of pleasant recollections.

That done, he strolled, home again leisurely, and told his wife that he would take an early opportunity of returning the money. When she pressed him for information as to the exact date on which he would do it, he answered "within a week," and not another word could she get out of him.

When she finally left off nagging him about it, he settled down in his shirt-sleeves to the careful study of a Turf Guide, and he got so much interest out of it that he had to he summoned twice to dinner for the first time in history.

CHAPTER IV
Enter the Hero! The Plot Gets Thicker Still

NOW we must see what Lizzie Wingfield is doing all this time. A young lady who has just lost five thousand dollars, to say nothing of her hopes of an early wedding, at one swift, sudden swoop cannot fail to be interesting, even if she is too unhappy to be amusing.

As we have seen, a strange lady met her in the park and talked to her, and was very sympathetic, and found out her address; but that hadn't helped her in the least so far as she could see; she was still hopeless, and from time to time she still wept.

She had written to San Francisco — a long, tearful letter, in which she told Walter Bavin all about it — how the money had disappeared, and how she had informed the police, and how rude the police had been, and how she would never forgive herself even if he forgave her, which she had no right to expect he would do, and oh! reams and reams of that kind of thing; the extra postage on the letter had cost her thirty cents. And all she had to do then was sit down and wait for the answer.

She could hardly be expected to be happy. Letters take several days to get to San Francisco, and answers take several other days to come back again; she figured it out closely, and saw no prospect whatever of getting an answer before Saturday, and waiting for it was just like sitting in an electric chair and waiting for the warden's assistant to turn on the current.

Why shouldn't she weep? The suspense was partly broken on the Wednesday, for she received a telegram from Walter — Walter Bavin — that evening; but it was so short, and the contents of it were so unexpected and so altogether irrelevant that she extracted very little encouragement from it; in fact the only consolation she drew from it at all was the fact that he had apparently forgotten to cancel his engagement. It ran:

> Your letter received. Say nothing. Inform nobody. Await my letter.
> WALTER BAVIN.

Now what the dickens could that mean? What sort of consolation could a poor girl drag out of that? She puzzled over it, and worried about it, and lay awake at night trying to read all sorts of possible and impossible meanings in between the two brief lines, until she became very nearly ill.

But there was nothing else for it but to wait for the promised letter, and obey orders in the meantime by holding her tongue; and no woman, young or old, likes to do that.

She would very likely have gone mad, and spoiled the story in that way, if she hadn't been a school-teacher; but school-teachers are so used to putting up with diabolically ingenious torment at the hands of other people that the ordinary slings and arrows of outrageous fortune don't break them down as they would ordinary people. She kept a sort of half-Nelson on her sanity, and wept and waited.

Then came the letter. It was shorter than usual. There were two whole pages less of love-stuff; she knew that because she read them first. The beginning of the middle part amazed her, because Walter Bavin appeared to care much less about the loss of the five thousand dollars than he did about its loss becoming known.

There were two whole pages of reiterated commands to her to hold her tongue, though he only used that coarse expression once; all the other times he expressed it quite courteously but firmly none the less.

By the time that she had skimmed through the first seven pages of the letter she was almost ready to scream for she had been brought up to always know the reason why of things, and her every instinct tended in that direction, and here was a long-drawn-out pen-and-ink mystery that cut off her woman's one prerogative of talking without a word of explanation. But she read on. And presently she did scream.

Her whole world, or all that the vanished five thousand dollars had left of it, her faith in humanity, her hopes for the future, and, worst of all, her belief in her lover seemed to be sliding away from under her feet.

The room rocked and swayed; the electric light above her head seemed to be going round and round and round; and the letter swam before her eyes until she couldn't read it; and then big tears began to fall on it; and the storm broke. Never mind what she did then.

It is neither decent nor amusing to intrude on the privacy of a young woman at the moment when the crisis of her life arrives, and she stands stripped suddenly of faith and hope and charity to face the world alone, This is part of what she read:

> Those fifty one-hundred-dollar bills were stolen from the trust company of which I am cashier, although they were not stolen from my department, and as yet the directors do not suspect me. They will, though, if you advertise the loss of them, and then it will be all up.

So — he had lied to her! He had said they were his savings, and all the time he knew they were stolen money. He had — But let us draw the curtain, and leave her alone. We can't help her, or at least not yet, and the agony of a fellow creature, especially of a lonely fellow creature, is not a pleasing spectacle.

CHAPTER V
In Which Ikey Makes a Killing, and Enjoys Himself

WATCH Ikey now. He is off to Aqueduct races in a chess-board suit of gray with a red stripe in it; he is wearing a purple tie fastened with his lucky topaz stick-pin, and a broad-brimmed derby hat with a low crown, and purple socks that just show over the edge of his shiny brown shoes.

He doesn't look a bit like the same Ikey. His furtive look is gone completely, and he strides along with quite a jaunty air, smoking a twenty-five-cent cigar with a big red and gold band round it. Cigars were not included in his oath of abstinence.

He has eaten fish for breakfast, because he always has good luck on the days when he eats fish; and he has given half a dollar to a blind man, and has patted a spotty dog; and when he got out of bed he carefully put his left slipper on his right foot; and he has bought a new pack of cards at the nearest stationer's and cut the ace of diamonds at the first try; in fact he has left no stone unturned and no deed undone that could help to make the day auspicious. And to crown it all, as he walked toward the railway station, he saw a skew-bald horse between the shafts of a grocer's cart and two milk-white horses immediately afterward.

"Gee!" said Ikey to himself. "This is my lucky day! I know it!"

He wasn't known as Keyhole Ikey on the race-course. Not a bit of it. There they all greeted him as "Old King Cole," and were uncommonly glad to see him. As Old King Cole, and "Coley" for short, he had accumulated in days gone by a reputation as a "fall guy" and a "good spender" and a "sucker" — just the sort of man they like to see at a race meeting.

Naturally it was the bookies who liked him the best, and they greeted him most effusively; but on this occasion Ikey had very little to say to any of them. He kept his own counsel, and worked his way gradually to where Abe Maxstein, a Hebrew gentleman of plethoric paunch and purple countenance, was bellowing out the odds on the first race.

"Hullo!" shouted Abe. "Why, dash my Sam if here ain't Old King Cole again! Lookin' like a winner, too! How goes it, Coley?"

"Fine!" answered Ikey. "How's yourself? Get my letter?"

"Sure thing. What's your fancy in the first race?"

"Nix!" said Ikey. "Ain't bettin' on the first race."

"Never! You standin' out while there's anythin' on four legs runnin'. I don't believe it! What's come over you all of a sudden?"

"Goin' to have a plunge on the third," answered Ikey, his face screwed up knowingly, and that remarkable nose of his twitching thirteen to the dozen; "a feller I know pretty well slipped me the dope."

"All right, Coley, name your gee! You can get all you want here. I'll lay you the odds against any horse you like in the third race — here's the list — now, then, what's your fancy?"

"Guess I'll wait till the numbers go up," answered Ikey.

"No, you don't! Come on now! I'll lay you a fair price and give you a run for your money. If the horse don't run you get your money back. Now then, which is it?"

"Tiddliwinks," said Ikey.

"Ho, ho! So that's the lay of the land, is it?"

"Evens so."

"Tiddliwinks! I'll lay you even money. That horse'll start two to one on or I'm a liar! How much d'you want at evens?"

"Five thousand," said Ikey quietly, handing up the fifty hundred dollar bills all fastened neatly together with a rubber hand.

Abe Maxstein's face froze like an iceberg. But Abe had offered Ikey all he wanted, and the crowd had heard him, so Abe had to make good his boast. He examined the bills very closely, and counted them very carefully, but he did not slip off the rubber band, and he tossed the whole bundle into his bag just as Ikey had given it to him.

"Ten thousand dollars Old King Cole on Tiddliwinks in the third race!" he said to his clerk, and the clerk wrote it down.

"You been robbin' a bank, or what?" he asked Ikey.

"I'm goin' to rob you, same as I warned you in my letter," Ikey answered. "It's a cinch — almost a shame to take the money!"

"I seen some o' your cinches before!" said Abe scornfully, and Ikey sauntered away to the grandstand to watch the running.

Abe Maxstein's clerk had been busy chalking up the runners and prices for the third race on a big blackboard, seeing that people seemed already anxious to bet on that race; and against the name of Tiddliwinks he wrote "evens." Abe Maxstein turned and looked at it; and then he looked at Ikey, fast disappearing in the crowd.

"I wonder what that guy knows!" he muttered. Then he wetted his fat thumb and rubbed out the word "evens," and wrote instead the cryptic figures ½; he had laid all he cared to against that horse.

Every other bookie on the course followed suit promptly, and Ikey had the satisfaction of changing the quotation of a horse by his own unaided effort for the first time in his life.

Ikey took not the slightest interest in the first two races, for he had no money on. He watched them, but his face wore a cynical smile, and as the first two horses in the second race fought it out neck and neck near the winning-post, he actually turned his head to light a fresh cigar. But the third race

was quite another matter.

He began to grow excited the moment the saddling-bell rang, and he craned his neck so eagerly to see the horses come filing out one by one onto the course that the man standing next to him turned and cursed him soundly for crowding.

Ikey did not even look at the horses, but he studied the jockeys' jackets and the numbers intently, and from the moment that his eyes rested on the red and yellow jacket with green stripes that Tiddliwinks's jockey wore they never left it again for an instant. He hardly even blinked.

It was a short race — six furlongs — a mere scamper between two poles; but there were sixteen runners, and more than a little depended on luck at the start.

Ikey watched the kicking, plunging, fidgeting field that lined up to the barrier with eyes that were almost starting out of his head, and he made a sound that was half squeal and half grunt as the barrier went up, and the horses shot away, with Tiddliwinks well in the lead.

Down the course they came — a thundering, flogging, panting stampede of men and horses — and Ikey twisted and squirmed and swore, and rubbed his nose, and tugged at his little black mustache, and bit his new cigar in two in an ecstasy of torture.

Neck and neck went Tiddliwinks with three other horses, all four of them straining every muscle and every nerve that was in them, and not one of them so highly strained as Ikey; his heart was in his mouth and in his shoes alternately as first Tiddliwinks and then some other horse took the lead for half a second.

The thing was over like a flash. All four horses streaked past the winning-post in a bunch, with the other twelve trailing out at intervals, behind them. The thing was so close that nobody on the grandstand could tell which of them was the winner; it looked like a dead heat of four horses.

"Tiddliwinks!" roared somebody; "Jonas," shouted ten other men; "Galahad," yelled a crowd of people; opinions were pretty evenly divided. Ikey watched the number-board. And Ikey groaned. And Ikey's fingers were clenched so tightly that they hurt his palms.

Ikey's face was as pallid as a sheet, and his knees trembled, and his breath came through his quivering nostrils in short, sharp gasps, as he held it till the last possible second, and released it suddenly, and filled his lungs again th a jerk. And then up went the numbers, and Ikey sighed; 7, 13, 5 in that order.

Seven was — Tiddliwinks!

Tiddliwinks had won. And Ikey had enjoyed himself.

Ikey was the calmest man on the course now. Unless you had watched him while the race was on you would never have believed that he had had a cent on the result. He left the grandstand quite leisurely, and strolled toward Abe Maxstein's stand with his hands in his pockets and an air of almost boredom.

"Hello, Coley!" shouted Abe. "You made a killing that time, and no mistake! What are you goin' to bet on in the next?"

"Nix!" said Ikey. "I'm through! This is where I draw your money, same as I promised!"

"What? Not goin' to have another bet!"

"Not today! Come on, shovel out! It's about your turn!"

"All right, Coley, all right. Suit yourself! I'll have it all back again one o' these days. You watch! Here y'are — here's your five thousand back — same bundle you gave me. Looks like good money to me, all right, but you never can tell. Anyhow, you've got it back again, whether it's good or bad; and here's the rest. That's a thousand-dollar bill, in case you never seen one before; an' there's two o' five hundred, an' here y'are two more fives, an' five, ten, fifteen, twenty centuries. There! Are ye satisfied?"

"Right y'are!" said Ikey. "Always did get a square deal from you, Abe! S'long!

Oh, hi, Abe! Half a minute! Got change for this thou?"

"Nope. You stick to what you've got, and thank your lucky stars you've got it! No time to make change! Now, then — runners in the fourth race." And he started calling out the names. And Ikey pouched his money, and turned his face homeward with a bulging pocket and a feeling of absolute contentment permeating his whole anatomy.

CHAPTER VI
In Which Ikey's Streak of Luck Begins to Hold Out Symptoms of Getting Thin.

THESE rapid changes of scene are growing just a trifle bewildering, aren't they? But there is worse to come. We're back again now with Lizzie Wingfield. She hasn't gone to bed yet. She hasn't even undressed. She is sitting in the rocker by the window, crying a little from time to time, and much too miserable to notice anything, or care about anything, or even think about anything except the hollowness and mockery and rottenness of all the wide, wide world.

Very nice people who have very nice ideas always tumble down into the depths of despair when their exquisitely fine-drawn notions fail for once to pan out. It is only crooks and people like ourselves who can view things dispassionately.

If you had told Lizzie Wingfield at that minute that there was any common honesty or kindness or sense of fair play to be found in the universe, she wouldn't have believed you. She would have been quite polite, but unconvinced.

There was a little noise that came from just behind her — ever such a tiny little noise — the sort of noise that a mouse might make. And she didn't notice it. The noise was repeated two or three times.

It came from underneath the blind that hid the window behind her chair *scratch! scratch! tick! tick!* — and then, all at once — *snack!* quite loud and sudden. But still she didn't notice it. Then the window began to rise, slowly, gently, ever so gently, inch by inch, Silently, until the bottom half of it was up almost as far as it would go.

She felt the draft then, for the wind blew the blind out into the room until it nearly hit the back of her chair; and she got up to change her position.

She started to pull her chair over into another corner of the room, and in doing so she faced the window; and as she faced it the blind went up suddenly with a *whir-r-r* and a *clack!* and the black, dark, rainy night outside became visible, with something almost as dark that crouched and moved on the window-sill between her and the murkiness beyond. And she didn't scream. Like her now, eh?

"Hush!" said a voice. "Hush, missie! Not a word! I won't hurt yer! I'm comin' in, but I won't do a thing to yer! Not a word, now! Quiet!"

She didn't care. What if all the burglars in the world came in! They could take her wedding trousseau if they cared to. Goodness knew she didn't want it, and there was nothing else to take! And if they killed her? Bah! What did she care for that, either! She would be really and truly glad to die.

She drew the chair back to make room for the burglar, or whatever he might be, and Keyhole Ikey stepped down into the room — Keyhole Ikey, dressed in his professional costume of almost black serge suit, black gloves and very dark gray cap.

"Hush!" said Ikey again, turning to close the window after him, and holding one warning finger up to his wicked-looking nose. He closed the window carefully and then pulled down the blind.

"Darned clumsy of me!" he remarked. "I oughter ha' got used to them roller-shades by now. Fancy me springin' that one like a new beginner! Now, missie, is the door locked?"

"You can see for yourself!" she answered. "Why do you ask? Have you come to kill me?"

"Kill you! Lord love you, no! The very idee! Look alive, missie, an' lock that door — that's a good gal; I gotter be kinder quick. Go on, now; it's up' to you. You're runnin' this apartment — not me!"

She walked over to the door and locked it, amazed at her own meekness in obeying him so promptly. Then she leaned her back against the door.

"Now, what is it?" she demanded.

Ikey fumbled in his inside pocket. In one pocket he had the fifty hundred-dollar bills that he had stolen, and in the other was the bundle of odd amounts that the bookmaker had paid him.

Both amounted to the same sum; but whereas it could make no possible difference to the lady which roll she received so long as she got her five thousand dollars back, it might make a lot of difference to him. A hundred-dollar bill is easily negotiable anywhere, and a thousand-dollar bill is not. He found the right pocket at last, and laid the bookie's money on the dressing-table.

"There y'are, missie! There's your money back! I'm the guy what took it! A little bird told me as how you needed it bad, so I brought it back to yer. It ain't the same identical money; but it ain't green goods, I give yer *my* word, an' it comes to the same amount. Go on count it! I'm in a hurry!"

He pushed the bundle of bills a bit farther along the dressing-table and drew back toward the corner, so as not to frighten her.

Imagine her sensations! Here was the utterly unheard-of happening under her very eyes — apparently the key to half her troubles thrust into her hand by an absolute stranger in her own room at half past eleven at night, a self-confessed burglar handing back the money he had stolen, and without a hint of compulsion!

It was not a bolt from the blue; it was a bomb from the black. Of course, she didn't believe it. She stood staring at him, with her eyes wide open, round and wondering. And Ikey laughed, and his laughter broke the spell to some extent.

"It's quite true, missie! I ain't kiddin' yer! Come on — count your money an' let me git!"

She walked over to the dressing-table and counted the bills like a woman in a trance, and still refusing to believe her senses. But there was no blinking the fact that on the table lay five thousand dollars. She counted it twice to make sure.

"That right, missie?"

She nodded.

"But I don't understand. I — "

"I know you don't! O' course you don't — don't try to! Lord love yer! Why, what's the matter with the woman? I took your money, an' there it is back again; there y'are! There it is, an' that's all about it! All you've got to do now is hold your tongue an' look wise — savvy? Put me down as a white guy that didn't want to harm yer, an' there you've got it. Now, good night, missie! Take my tip an' go to bed — hit the hay an' play you've been dreamin'! You'll find the money all there in the mornin', so kid yerself you never lost it! An' shove it in the bank first time you get the chance, missie , so's folks like me don't get another chance at it. So-long, missie. Good luck!"

And Keyhole Ikey opened the window again softly and disappeared by the way he had come. When he had gone, Lizzie Wingfield stood and stared first at the closed window, and then at the money in her hand, and stared, and stared, and pinched herself to see if she were dreaming, or dead, or what; but the bills were there, and they were tough and soft and crinkly; and the pinch hurt her, and made a little red mark come on her white arm, and no, she didn't believe it. It was altogether too impossible, and too absolutely good to be true.

Once again Ikey climbed quietly down the fire-escape and dropped ten feet or so into the yard beneath him. Then he crouched in the shadow of the wall for two whole minutes and listened. There was nothing moving that Ikey could hear, so he sneaked out of the yard, following the passage that led to the street in front.

At the end of the passage was a gate; it was an iron gate that squeaked on its hinges when people opened it; so Ikey placed one hand on the top of it and vaulted. And as he sprang an ominous blue form stepped out from the darkness, and a voice said gruffly: "What ha' you been doing in there?"

Ikey ran. Goodness, how he ran! And he could sprint, could Ikey. He ran like the wind, dodging all the time into the shadows, thinking as he ran, and picking his way where it might be hard to follow him. But Patrolman Baines was on his track; and Patrolman Baines had done a quarter once in fifty-two. He was new to his job; and keen as mustard, fit as the proverbial fiddle, and game as a wagon-load of tigers.

Ikey panted, and swore beneath his breath. Patrolman Baines panted, and put on a spurt and grabbed him. Ikey ducked. The patrolman stumbled, and Ikey tripped him.

But Baines was an athlete as well as a sprinter; he grabbed Ikey more firmly as he fell, and the two went down together, and in less than a second Ikey lay face upward on the pavement in the grip of a hammerlock hold that nearly wrenched his bones apart.

"Now," said Patrolman Baines, "you'll come along o' me an' give an account o' yourself. Are you comin' quiet?"

"Yep," said Ikey. "Go ahead; I know the way." The patrolman held him by the sleeve, too confident in his own strength to trouble about putting on the handcuffs.

"What were you doin' in there? he asked. But Ikey, with the wisdom of the wise, said nothing.

They welcomed Ikey at the station-house — gave him a ringing welcome, for they all knew him.

"Aw! Can all that chin stuff!" said Ikey. "What am I charged with?"

"With being a suspected person," said the lieutenant, writing in the book before him. "Put him in the cooler and search him." So Ikey was led below.

It took them just ten seconds to find the five thousand dollars in Ikey's pocket, and thirty seconds more to tell the news to the lieutenant, who wrote down the numbers of the notes carefully and then rang up police headquarters on the phone. After about five minutes' conversation over the wire, during which he referred repeatedly to the notes in front of him, he hung up the receiver with a jerk and ordered:

"Fetch that guy up here again. We may as well alter the charge now as later." So Ikey was once again stood up before the lieutenant's desk.

"You're charged now," said the lieutenant, "with being in possession of stolen goods, to wit, book-notes the property of the San Francisco, Los Angeles, and Sacramento Trust Company, as well as with being a suspected person and being found in possession of burglar's tools."

"Aw!" said Ikey. "That all? Can't yer think o' somethin' else? Ain't the city hall missin', or somethin'?"

"Put him back in the cooler!" ordered the lieutenant; and back Ikey went.

CHAPTER VII
Across the Continent

THERE is no means of helping Ikey just for the moment; the police have got him, and it takes a bigger pull than we have got to unclutch their fingers. So we must leave him in confinement, and leave Mrs. Ikey — tailormade and tearful — rushing round New York arranging bail bonds.

She ought to be able to manage that all right, seeing what careful drilling Ikey has given her with a view to just such an unfortunate occurrence. This story has got to move, and we must move with it; so we are in San Francisco now.

The offices of the San Francisco, Los Angeles, and Sacramento Trust Company stand at the corner of one of the many streets leading down to the harbor, and the president's suite is in 4, the front of the building, two flights up. We are in the president's private office now.

We have finished gaping in silent and respectful wonder at the richness of the furnishings and the splendor of the ten-pile turkey carpet, and we are watching the president himself — a middle-aged man with a red neck and a parting that reaches from ear to ear. He looks angry, and he is. He has reason to be.

"Come here, Brown!" says the president in a voice that sounds like a garbage-can being dumped into an ash-cart. And a long-nosed, pale-faced man named Brown comes running from the next room.

"Sit down!" orders the president; and Brown sits down opposite to him.

"I can't make head or tail of this business," says the president; "and what's more, I've got to start for New York on tonight's train; so I've no time to look into it. You'll have to do it. If only young Walter Bavin were here! But just when I want him most the young idiot throws up his job and goes to New York to marry some infernal woman!"

"I didn't know he'd gone." Brown, be it noted, is a superior sort of person who affects to ignore anyone below the rank of manager.

"Well, then, take it from me that he has! That'll save time! He left the day before yesterday, and I'm sorry he's gone. Now, then, you remember that five thousand dollars that was missing from the receiving-teller's department a short time ago? Well, all I did about it was to notify the police and give them the numbers of the missing notes; we'd had them straight from the United States Treasury; so that was easy. I didn't offer a reward, and, in fact, I thought very little more about it; the sum wasn't big enough to make a fuss over. But see here what's happened. Look at this — and this — and this!"

He tossed three envelopes onto the table, and in each of the envelopes was five thousand dollars in bills. In the first envelope, which bore the San Francisco postmark, was a piece of white paper, on which was written in a disguised hand, "Returned with thanks by the man who took it."

In the second envelope, which bore the Los Angeles postmark, was another and smaller envelope, on the outside of which were written the words, "Herewith the missing five thousand dollars."

And in the third envelope, which had the New York postmark on it, was a telegram-blank on which somebody had printed, in capitals, "This money was recently stolen from you; please take it back and forgive the thief."

None of the three communications bore any signature, and, beyond the postmark, not one of them gave any clue to its sender's identity.

"And now, look here!" said the president. "Not one of the bills contained in either of those envelopes bears a number corresponding to any of the stolen ones; and here's a telegram I've just received from the chief of police in New York, stating that they've captured a man there with every one of our missing notes in his possession. Now, what d'you make of it?"

"Did all those letters come today?"

"No, they didn't. You've only got to look at the postmarks to tell that! The point is, they're here. We lost five thousand, and, counting what the police in New York have captured, we get twenty thousand back. That won't do, of course; all this money here belongs to somebody else; our money seems to be in New York; and as I'm going there on tonight's train, I will attend to that end of it myself. You must see to this end."

"But what do you want me to do?"

"Your suggestions are very helpful to-day, aren't they? In the first place, all those letters were registered; that ought to afford some clue."

"I'm afraid not. The post-office people aren't allowed to give any information."

"I know that. But aren't there ways and means?"

"Not that I know of."

"Well, get hold of Newman, then; he's the receiving-teller that is responsible for the missing bills. Find out what he knows about it. I've suspected that man ever since the money was first missing, but there was no proof to go on; so I said nothing. But get him up here again and give him a regular grilling, and find out what he knows; I haven't time to see to it myself. I've several other more important things to attend to, and after that I've got to go home and settle up some business there before I catch the train; so I must hurry. Now, have you got that? Is there anything else I can tell you? Very well, then. Wire me in New York if anything turns up, and I'll wire you if I get any news from that end. Between the two of us, we ought to be able to throw some light on the mystery."

CHAPTER VIII
Which Enlightens Lizzie Wingfield and Certain Others.

LIZZIE WINGFIELD might be mournful and hopeless, but she had to have some exercise. Even beautiful maidens whose last left belief is in the scoundrelly depravity of all humanity are apt to study their complexions; she studied hers in the mirror, and then concluded to go out for a walk. Besides, she wanted to meet the tailor-made lady again with the perambulator and tell her all about the burglar who had brought the money back.

So she arrayed herself in the "going away" dress that formed part of her marriage trousseau and in the dream of a hat that she had bought for the wedding and might just as well take into use now that the wedding was "off," and started down the stairs.

And at the top of the front steps she stood still for a second to feel whether or not her hat was on straight; then she glanced once up the street to the left, and once down the street to the right, and nearly fainted. She would have surely fallen down the steps and broken her neck or twisted her ankle or something if Walter hadn't caught her.

Yes, there was Walter, just that minute arrived from San Francisco — big, strong, broad-chested, gray-eyed — handsome as any man has a right to be, and neat as a bridegroom. He caught her in his big, strong arms, and so saved the situation and the story. He didn't kiss her, though. It wouldn't have been proper to do it out there in the street, and, besides, he wasn't quite sure yet how he stood. He kept his arm round her, though, in case she should happen to fall again.

"Oh, Walter!" she exclaimed. "How could you! You a thief? And to think that I loved you and trusted you! Go away! I never want to see you again! I sent you a telegram saying that everything was over between us!"

"Yes," said Walter grimly; "that's why I came! I can't see any reason for calling the engagement off just because the money was stolen. I'm just as fond of you, and I don't see how you could have helped it. Besides, why call me a thief? I didn't steal the money!"

"Oh, but Walter, you did! You said so in your letter!"

"Did I? I'd like to see the letter! I must have been dr — I mean I think you must have read it wrong!"

"Oh!" Her eyes lit up like jewels, lighted from behind by the joy that was new-born in her. "You mean that, Walter? You mean — "

"I mean exactly what I say, and you're a little goose! Come, let's go sit somewhere where it's quiet, and I'll tell you all about it and we can compare notes. But tell me first, is the engagement still off?"

Her answer was inaudible, but its purport must have been absolutely clear to him, for he took her in his arms and kissed her right there and then in the street, to the awful disgust of two elderly ladies who were passing and the horrid envy of a patrolman. But patrolmen don't count, anyhow. Then they walked into the park, having nowhere else to go, and sat down on one of the benches.

"Of course," said Walter, "it'll be awfully awkward now that we haven't got that money; but I must ask for my job back again, and you'll have to come with me to Frisco and try to make both ends meet on my pay. Say, though! I'd give something to lay my hands on that burglar!"

"The burglar wasn't a bad man at all — he brought me the money back again!"

"Wha-a-a-at?"

"It's a fact, Walter!"

"Then you've got it after all?"

"No, indeed I haven't. You see, Walter, I thought — I thought you'd stolen it; so when the burglar gave it back to me I put it in an envelope and posted it straight to the president of the trust company, with a little note inside asking him to forgive the thief."

"Well, I'm —" Walter Bavin didn't finish the sentence. He just stretched his legs out in front of him and threw his head back, and laughed for about five minutes without stopping.

"Look here, little woman," he said when he had got his breath back again, "listen, and I'll tell you all about it. That money of mine was out on mortgage. I'd lent it to a fellow named Newman on the security of his house. Newman is receiving teller, and I was paying teller in the same office. Newman had to repay me the loan by a certain date, but he hadn't arranged for a new mortgage to replace the old one, and he hadn't the cash; so he stole it from the safe, meaning, of course, to pay the whole lot back before anybody found it out. I didn't know about it at the time naturally; but I discovered it almost directly after I'd sent you the money, and as luck would have it the general manager missed the money from the safe on the same day.

"Now, Newman's a life-long friend of mine, and I wouldn't give him away for worlds; but in common honesty, if I didn't give him away, and especially seeing that I had had the money, I'd got to take the loss on my own shoulders — I mean it was up to me to repay the bank or else expose Newman. Then I got your letter saying that the money was stolen, so I couldn't get it back from you. But I'd got to do something pretty quickly, so I went to my uncle in Los Angeles and told him I needed five thousand dollars at once. I wouldn't tell him why, but I suppose he knew I wouldn't have come to him unless I'd simply got to have it; at all events, he gave me five thousand dollars in bills, and I put them in a registered envelope and arranged for another fellow to post them to the bank from Los Angeles. I did it, of course, to save Newman; but it seems the bank's been paid back twice over."

"Did you tell that horrid man Newman what you'd done?"

"Why, no. I didn't get the chance. When I returned from Los Angeles he was away from the office on some business or other; and before he came back I got your telegram saying that it was all over between us, so I caught the next train to find out why."

"Well, what can you do about it, Walter?"

"Dunno, I'm sure. I've got a few hundred dollars with me — enough for a week's hotel bill and our two fares to Frisco. I vote we get married first and talk about ways and means afterward."

AND they did, too, that very day, and went and stayed at the Kickerbocker Hotel, and she wore the hat and dress at her wedding after all! What do you know about that?

She tried to persuade him to stay somewhere that was a little bit less expensive, but Walter wouldn't hear of it. Walter was wise.

He thought he would be more likely to meet people there who were worth meeting, and so he did. He met the president of the San Francisco, Los Angeles, and Sacramento Trust Company.

The president walked in one fine morning and began opening letters and telegrams in the foyer, and Walter, who was loafing in the foyer, walked straight up to him.

"Glad to see you, sir!" said Walter.

"Are you?" said the president.

"I want my job back."

"Oh. Well, I'll talk to you about that in half a minute. Wait while I open this telegram."

The president tore it open with his thumb and scowled over it.

"Thought so!" he muttered. "That accounts for one of them! Read that!" he ordered, handing the telegram to Bavin, "and tell me what you know about it!"

The message was from Brown in San Francisco, and it ran:

> Newman has confessed to taking money. Also claims that registered envelope bearing San Francisco postmark and containing five thousand is his. Has post-office receipt to prove it. Have suspended him pending receipt of your instructions.

"Now!" snapped the president. "No beating about the bush! Come up to my room and tell me every word you know about it!"

So Walter Bavin told him, omitting no single detail.

"And d'you mean to tell me that you actually borrowed money and sent it to the firm anonymously rather than expose your friend or see the firm robbed?"

"Yes, sir."

"And the lady you've since married did the same thing, eh? Sent the money straight back because she thought you'd stolen it?"

"Yes, sir."

"I'd like to meet her."

"I'm sure she'd be delighted, sir."

So Mrs. Bavin was produced, and blushed becomingly, and told her version of the story, while the president leaned back in his chair and wondered if the days of miracles had come again.

"So you want your job back again?" he asked, turning to Bavin. "Well, you can't support a wife properly on the salary you've been getting. If you'll catch the next train back I'll slate you for a thousand a year increase, and I'll send a wire on ahead confirming it. I like a man who can be loyal to the firm and his friends at the same time. That settles that."

"And about Newman, sir? I don't think he —"

"I'll deal with Newman when I get back!" snapped the president. "And now, Mrs. Bavin, would you mind telling me about that burglar all over again from the beginning?"

CHAPTER IX
Which Is Short, and Treats of Ikey

IKEY was out on bail; his wife had managed that. His address was quite well known to the police, and the president of the San Francisco, Los Angeles, and Sacramento Trust Company, being a very important person with a pull, had no difficulty whatever in obtaining it.

He refused to say why he wanted it, and he refused for the time being to commit himself with reference to the hundred-dollar bills that had been found on Ikey's person. He had grown rich by holding his tongue on suitable occasions, and like Ikey, it took more than a policeman to make him talk when he didn't want to.

Ikey was sitting one afternoon in the front parlor, looking very forlorn indeed, with his head between his hands and his elbows resting on his knees — not at all like the same Ikey of the race-course or the Ikey who had paid the money back.

He looked like a querulous and half-drowned Ikey, and Mrs. Ikey sat in the next chair and tried to comfort him.

"It's all very fine you talkin', missus," said Ikey; "but what you say's rot! There's nothin' to it! The minute a guy like me tries to act white he gets pinched, an' there y' are! Look at me! Have I been took once before since me an' you got spliced? No. An' have I been livin' on the square all that time? Not so's you'd notice it, I haven't! I've took what I wanted, an' kep' it, an' held my tongue. Any harm come of it? Not as I can remember! Then I goes an' listens you, an' tries to act white, an' gives back five thousand wads o' good gov'ment coin what I'd took, an' up comes a cop an' pinches me! There's a lesson for yer!"

"Never mind, Ikey dear!" said his better half. "You did it to please me, and because you couldn't be mean, and I know good will come of it."

"You bet it will!" said Ikey. "I'll get a nice long rest up the river! That's what'll come of it!"

A ring came at the bell, and Mrs. Ikey rose to answer the door.

"That'll be one o' them sheriff's deputys," said Ikey, hopefully. "He'll be come to tell me my bail's been raised an' I've got to go to jug till I can get a new bondsman. You see if it ain't!"

But it was not the sheriff's deputy. It was the president of the San Francisco, Los Angeles, and Sacramento Trust Company.

"And what can I do for you?" asked Ikey, with just a hint of venom in his voice.

"I've come to see what I can do for you!" said the president, laughing.

"Now you're talking!" said Ikey. "Fetch the gentleman a cigar, missus — no, not those, the good ones — that's right. Take a seat, mister, an' go ahead — I'm listenin'."

"Well," said the president, coughing a little awkwardly, "I understand that you're in trouble — under arrest — out on bail — that right?"

Ikey nodded.

"Well, I happen to know the lady whose money you — er — took, and to whom you returned it; she told me all about it. There's one thing I don't quite follow yet, though. Why didn't you give her back the same bills? Why bills of different denominations? Had you by any chance as much as ten thousand dollars in your possession?"

"Not at first I hadn't," said Ikey. "It come about this way. I gave the lady a sportin' chance. I played the five thousand all on one horse at Aqueduct races, an' the horse won at even money; I'd got ten then, hadn't I? Well, I gave the lady back her five, seein' as I'd had good luck myself, an' I kep' the hundred dollar bills partly because they'd brought me luck, an' partly because they was easier to get rid of. There y' are!"

"So that's it!" laughed the president. "Well, I've known worse crooks than you — a lot worse! Now my proposal to you is this. I've got a crook in my office who also stole money and who also paid it back, and I've decided to give him another chance; but it wouldn't be exactly ethical to do that and let you go to jail, would it? So I'm going to offer you another chance, too. There's a sum of five thousand dollars going begging at the present moment; the police have got it, but it doesn't actually belong to anybody; my firm has been repaid the money that was stolen, so I can't claim it, but I'm the only person who can dispose of it all the same. Now I'll sign an order releasing that money to you on one condition — that you give me your word of honor you'll go straight from now on. You won the money on the racecourse, and though the stake wasn't yours to begin with, still you have more claim on the proceeds of the bet than anybody else I can think of; and I'm assuming that you have a sense of honor simply because you wouldn't have paid the lady back her five thousand otherwise. At all events, I prefer to look at it in that light. Now, do you accept my terms? Yes or no?"

"Yes, sir!" burst in Mrs. Ikey, on her knees between Ikey and the president. "You leave him to me, sir, and I'll make him promise! Go away, sir, now, and leave him to me! I'll answer for it. The answer's yes! yes!! yes!!!"

DID Ikey promise? He did. And did he keep it? I can't tell you, for he's a secretive little cuss, is Ikey.

But he took the five thousand dollars sure enough and sold up the flat in Eighty-First Street, and shortly afterward disappeared along with Mrs. Ikey and little Ikey with the tooth, and nobody in New York has ever seen them since.

But there is a man over in Los Angeles who very much resembles Ikey. He says his name is Cole — Isaac Cole. He has a wife who is copper-haired and tailor-made, and one son; and he also has a nose that is pliable and restless and immense. But this Mr. Isaac Cole is a reputable merchant.

His ways of doing business are well known throughout the whole of California, and though they say you must get up very early in the morning if you want to catch him napping, they all admit that his methods are at least legal; and some say he is absolutely honest.

He smokes no cigarettes and never goes to a race meeting, and he may possibly be the same Ikey. But, on the other hand, he may not; and there is no possible means of finding out.

The End

Volume I, Number 1
April 1956

Editor & Publisher

George R. Heap
513 Glen Echo Rd.
Phila. 19, Penna.

HYBOREAN LEGION ORGANIZED

On a fatefull day, the 12th of November in the year 1955 of the Sixth Age, the Hyborean Legion was formed . Twelve stalwart admirers of Conan from New York and Philadelphia gathered in the latter city to give honor to Conan and his creator.

Officers elected were -
King of Aquilonia
   - Martin Greenberg
Count of Poitain
   - John D. Clark
Royal Chancellor
   - George R. Heap
Royal Sorceror
   - Oswald Train
Royal Chronicler
   L. Sprague de Camp
Commander of the Black Dragons
   - Manny Staub

Future meetings were planned in connection with the following fan conferences or conventions -
Fanvets (called off this year)
Midwescon - See below !
World Convention - New York
Fall Conference - Philadelphia

The Legion has attracted much attention in fandom since its formation . Any of you who are interested in joining the Hyborean Legion, drop me a card (my name and address are on the masthead) .

LEGION TO MEET AT MIDWESCON

This year's Midwescon is at the North Plaza Motel; 7911 Reading Rd. Cincinatti 37, O. May 26-27 . Write motel for reservations. Legion meeting will be Saturday nite. For more Midwescon info, write Don Ford; 129 Maple Ave.; Sharonville, Ohio .

CONAN AND THE HYBOREAN AGE
- EDITORIAL -

The imaginative tales that have had the greatest attraction to us are, in one sense, all composed of a combination of character and/or background . There are some whose appeal comes almost entirely from the scene the author has devised for the story . Pellucidar and Oz are such worlds of fantasy . Other tales are based almost entirely on the character and peculiar talents given to the hero . Good examples of this type are Conan Doyle's Sherlock Holmes stories and the Tarzan stories of Edgar Rice Burroughs .

Between the extremes are a host of tales with varying stress placed on the two factors, character and background . Where on the scale do we place the Conan stories ? Is Conan a strong enough character, in the literary sense, to exist without the Hyborean Age ? Would stories about the Hyborean Age be as readable without Conan ? The best answer to these questions lies in an examination of Howard's works .

The closest Howard came to an Hyborean Age without Conan is in "The Shadow Kingdom" and "The Mirrors of Tuzun Thune", the King Kull stories written before any of Conan . While these are highly readable, they lack something of the gripping spell of the author's Conan tales . Yet the Pre-Cataclysmic Age differs little from the Hyborean . Where lies the difference ?

For all their apparent similar -

(continued - page 2 , column 1)

(continued from page 1, column 2)

ity, Kull is not the figure Conan was . They were both Barbarians ruling civilized lanes, both def - ended their thrones in personal combat against foes, human and in - human . But Kull was in part a dreamer . He needed the hand of Brule the Pict to guide him through the treacheries of the serpent-men and a ain to wake him from the elder-wizard's spell of mirrors . No, Kull had neither Conan's instinct for self-preservation nor his abil- ity to use allies when they were available but yet to triumph with no aid at all when life or kingdom were at stake . The Kull stories then are good but none the less their hero is a man of a lesser breed .

To answer the second question requires more consideration , for Conan himself never appears outside the Hyborean Age . Still we can do this by examining the Hyborean Age itself . It was, basically, a world of fantasy, an age when sorcery was ever present , from the haunted swamps of the Pictish Wilderness to the green-stone ruins on the isles of Vilayet . In every adventure, Conan meets black magic, inhuman intelligence , or creatures from realms beyond our ken . Yet this almost alien world contained the normal, human institutions of sev - eral early civilizations and bar - barian cultures from our recorded history . With the supernatural el- ements removed, the Hyborean Age would be indistinguishable from the historical past . Although Conan would be an interesting character in any setting, stories laid in such an ordinary setting would not differ greatly from other histori - cal adventure tales .

Therefor , we must conclude that while both Conan and the Hyboria an Age are glowing examples of How- ard's creative imagination, it is only in combination that they are what we know them - - - - the fin - est works of a master weaver of literary spells .

NEW MEMBERS OF THE LEGION

Since the notice of the Legion's formation appeared in Fantasy-Times many of you have written to me ask- ing for more information . The num- ber has become so great that it is no longer possible to answer them all individually .

Therefore, this publication will have to do as an answer to all . As yet, there have been no formal req- uirements for membership set up. So until further notice all are wel - come . We hope to decide this and other questions at our meeting next month .

The group from New York & Phil - adelphia have decided to become the Aquilonian Lodge of the Legion . In the future, no doubt, other lodges will be formed in other parts of the country . To help this along we will try to get some lists made up so that members can get in touch with each other .

So, in the name of our King, a hearty welcome to the Legion !

- - - ROYAL CHANCELLOR OF AQUILONIA

TRADING - William H. Machette of 75 South St. ; Eatontown, N. J. would like to trade "Conan the Conqueror" "The Sword of Conan", or "King Con- an" for other Conan books or "The Fellowship of the Ring"

The Howard-de Camp story, "Hawks Over Shem", first published in the Oct. 1955 Fantastic Universe, was extensively rewritten before it ap- peared in Gnome's "Tales of Conan".

This is the first issue of a bul- letin and fanzine for members of the Hyborean Legion and other fans of Conan . AMRA will be published irregularly , which means whenever enough material is available . So any articles, poems, essays, or let- ters of general interest will be gratefully accepted . -- THE EDITOR

www.ingramcontent.com/pod-product-compliance
Lightning Source LLC
Chambersburg PA
CBHW080815250626
47159CB00010B/3395